DEATH IN THE LUNAR NIGHT

Yuri lifted his sun visor as the upper edge of the Sun disappeared behind the crater's rim. No, not enough. Still too dark. Yuri reached forward and flicked up the headlight switch.

Switch issued signal. Signal traveled to Power Switching Module, the new Module provided by the PRECISE technician. Enriched Software in Module's microprocessor activated three power-switching relays. One relay connected an electrical ground to a line from the cardiac-monitoring electrode built into Yuri's liquid-cooled undergarment, an electrode that pressed against his back directly behind his heart. The second and third relays connected another monitoring electrode on his chest to an Instrumentation Power Supply Bus. The electrical potential of the skin directly over Yuri's heart jumped to 2700 volts.

Mind monitored. Muscles contracted. Torso jerked.

Voltage remained steady. . . .

Head vibrated. Arms shook. Legs danced.

Current continued to flow. . . .

Eyes bulged. Jaws clenched. Teeth gnashed.

After 1 minute and 37.000 seconds, precisely, Enriched Software reversed the position of the three relays it had set, completely consumed itself, and ceased to exist without a trace.

And on into the lunar night, as in billions of previous lunar nights, dead silence reigned. . . .

Ask your bookseller for these Bantam Spectra titles you may have missed:

IN THE WRONG HANDS

edward gibson

SPECTRA™

BANTAM BOOKS
NEW YORK • TORONTO • LONDON • SYDNEY • AUCKLAND

IN THE WRONG HANDS

A Bantam Spectra Book / May 1992

ISBN 0-553-29567-5

Published simultaneously in the United States and Canada

PRINTED IN THE UNITED STATES OF AMERICA

OPM   0 9 8 7 6 5 4 3 2 1

To the memory of my parents to whom I will always be grateful for their guidance, patience, and love—as well as an adequate and unique DNA code.

ACKNOWLEDGEMENTS

I offer special thanks to Knut Butzinger for several stimulating and informative discussions on the promises and perils of genetic engineering. I also thank Janna Silverstein and Joe Vallely for many helpful editorial suggestions.

SPACE STATION EQUALITY

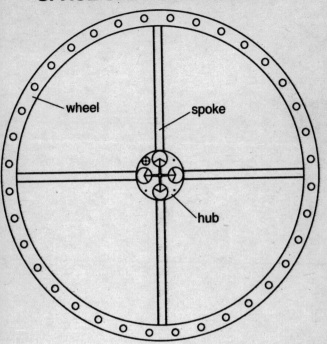

wheel

spoke

hub

HUB

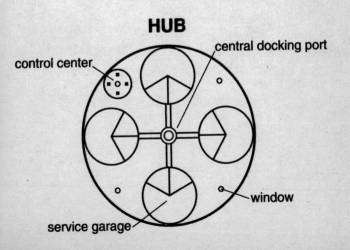

control center

central docking port

service garage

window

We've engineered only our environment,
so far—
now we turn to ourselves.

CONTENTS

IV CONTRIBUTE

V CHASE

VI FLEE

VII DIFFER

EPILOGUE

AUTHOR'S NOTE

Our understanding of human DNA, which we are just beginning to map and manipulate through research efforts like the multi-billion dollar Human Genome Initiative, is placing a power in our hands unlike any capability that previous technological advancements have bestowed—we are learning how to engineer the world *internal* to our cells, to alter at a fundamental level our very human essence.

As we should expect, all current applications planned for genetic engineering (of which I am aware) are intended to benefit mankind. In the future, many genetic birth defects, including cystic fibrosis, sickle-cell anemia and Down syndrome, will be detected and repaired long before birth. And given the DNA of a couple, the potential for defects can be accurately assessed even before conception. Certainly a good argument can be made to even the most prudent and moral among us that the current explosion of genetic engineering will improve our human condition.

But we only have to look to the past to feel concern for the future. Not every new-found engineering capability has been consistently employed with the highest of motivations. Eventually a few individuals with the engineering capability, incentive, and seclusion to do what moral men fear most have surfaced. Eventually a few individuals who believe that engineering might alone confers right have acted.

I have high confidence that researchers currently advancing the state of genetic engineering and those who apply it do assume the burden of balancing power with privilege and do anguish over where technical logic alone should leave off and moral deliberations begin.

Yet, I have equal confidence that at some point in the future . . .

Prologue

□□□

let me
help

friday—august 5

"Trouble?"

"Yeah."

"Let me help."

"Thanks, I could use it! Look here."

"Ahhh . . . I know exactly where the problem is."

"Oh, you do?" Yuri searched the eyes of the technician. Beneath bushy brows, black points flashed back from dark depths. Yep, quick eyes, quick mind. But why's he so sure of himself? Yuri's gut tightened a notch.

"It's in your Power Switching Module."

"You sure?"

"I'm sure. I've seen this symptom before, and I've got another Module in inventory that will work. I'll take this one out, get the good one, and be right back."

"Thanks!" Yuri watched Technician extract the book-sized Module in one smooth sure motion from the electronics assembly at the rear of the Rover, his two-seat vehicle. Maybe

I'm just too suspicious. He's just another good guy trying to do his job. But God, I hope he really does have a fix. I need to get home—and outta here!

Technician bounded away with what Moon inhabitants had come to call the Lunar Lope, that kangaroo hop first performed in the Moon's gentle gravity by Apollo astronauts back in 1969.

Yuri exhaled a deep breath and forced himself to relax. *If I get delayed another hour, damn rules say I have to wait here another two weeks till sunup. Can't drive solo across the crater in the dark no matter how much I want to get home. Yep, if he's got a fix, I'm gonna press.* He cinched his waist restraint tight. Its snugness brought a momentary surge to his sense of security. *May as well assume success and get buttoned up.* He withdrew the lifeline umbilical from the base of Rover's center console under his right elbow, scrutinized its electrical, communication, instrumentation and oxygen fittings for dust—none—then fumbled it twice before he could mate it with the connector on the chest of his astronaut pressure suit. He reached for his gloves in the vacant seat to his right, scrutinized their seals for dust—none—then slid them over his cold fingers and wet palms. Each wrist lock confirmed its integrity with a loud click as it snapped into place. Likewise, he inspected the seal in the neck ring of his clear plexan helmet, then lowered it over his face and pressed down.

—Click!—

Neck ring locked with a finality that echoed within the clear hollow globe around his head, a finality that seemed too permanent, too irrevocable, too . . . *nonsense—lighten up, Yuri. Get on with it.*

His gloved finger punched TEST 37 into the computer keyboard by his right knee. Oxygen hissed in and inflated his suit, oxygen that still smelled a bit like the lunar rock from which it had been extracted months before. He held his breath, watched the display panel above his glove, then nodded once to himself. *Good. Leak's small enough that it can't even be detected. Nothing's worse than being out there all alone at the bottom of a crater—miles from anywhere—in a leaky suit.*

Yuri leaned back, closed his eyes, loosened his hands, and forced all tension from his muscles. *There, I'm relaxed, in control.* A rapid pulse still fluttered at the back of his throat, and the rasp of quick, shallow inhalations still grated in his ears.

Technician returned. With a smooth, precise push to match the extraction, he slid the new Module into place. And again with the same precise push, he plugged into Rover's communication connector. "There, that should do it."

Yuri reached to the keyboard and entered TEST 3. Bright green letters popped onto the display:

SYSTEM TEST—GO

"Hey, Tech, you really have fixed it!" Yuri glanced at Technician's white jump suit, saw "*Kurt*" in black script letters right above "PRECISE," his company's name in bold red block letters, and extended his hand. "Kurt, thanks. Looks like I'm set to roll. Thanks a lot!"

Kurt slipped his hand into Yuri's, gave it three precise pumps, and expelled it. His hand then slid to the shoulder of Yuri's pressurized suit, paused to give it three even pats, glided in front of Yuri's visor where it pumped once with a thumbs-up, then slid down to smoothly extract the communications plug.

As his hand wavered to return the thumbs-up, Yuri yielded to an impulse. "Say, Kurt, do you know anything about 'Phase Five'?"

Kurt's face flickered with a scowl for but a fraction of a second before it snapped back and froze in its passive state. Only black points continued their quiver deep within their dark voids. "No, can't say that I do. . . . Enjoy your drive home." In one precise pivot, Kurt turned toward the airlock hatch, loped through it, and drew it closed behind him.

Through his helmet, Yuri felt the final firmness of the hatch slam and saw its handle snap downward to lock it tight. As he turned forward and watched the digital pressure readout mounted in the center of the eight- by eight-foot airlock door speed toward zero, he bit a tightened lower lip. Dumb thing to ask. Why would a technician know anything about that? And if he did, he wouldn't say. But whatever it is, it sure is important to 'em. And why on September first? A red light flashed above the blur of numbers. Dumb. I just let 'em know I'm suspicious. But so what? I'm almost outta here!

As the numbers raced down through 0.030 pounds per square inch, the door cracked open at its base. A residue of air and lunar dust shot forward over the floor, punctured the tranquillity of the lunar landscape, and disappeared out there somewhere in the vacuum of space. "Great way to clean a garage," Yuri mumbled to himself without moving his rigid jaw.

Door crept up. Sun flooded in. Yuri pulled his visor down and reduced the Sun's brilliance to a golden ball that hovered on the Moon's western horizon. As soon as the door reached the height of Rover's antenna behind his head, Yuri rammed the speed controller in his left hand forward. In pursuit of the dust, Man and Machine shot out of the airlock toward the lunar skyline.

Free! Worried for nothing . . .

The half mile to the edge of Karov Crater stretched flat and glossy before him, a gray carpet of lunar dust speckled with but a few rocks and secondary impact craters. Yuri jiggled the controller, then pushed it forward again. Yep, it's against the stop. This Rover's a hot one, a good partner to have today. Looks like it'll hit twenty-four miles per hour. Can make some time on the flats, make up for having to pick and poke my way down and back up the crater's walls. He smiled. Oughtta reach LB-13 and home turf in twenty minutes.

Yuri looked over Rover's nose and could see nothing but Golden Ball's brilliance in his path. He turned ten degrees left and the gray carpet with all its undulations and pockmarks emerged. He glanced to the side and the carpet revealed a tinge of brown. Funny how the ground here looks different depending on how you look at it. But no matter how you do, there's always this mat of dust and pulverized rock that hides the Moon's real face, always keeps its real secrets out of sight.

After a minute, Yuri turned to put Golden Ball ten degrees to the left of Rover's nose. About another minute to the crater. Better slow it down to twenty. Like Tech said, enjoy the drive home. Guess I really had no reason to be so nervous. And I'm finally relaxed . . . aren't I? Let's see. Numbers don't lie. He reached to the keyboard and isolated a single biomedical parameter. It filled his display:

$$HR = 107$$

107 beats per minute. Heart rate's too high. Relax, Yuri, it's in the bag. Show some self-control. See how far you can bring it down. His eyes lingered on the display as he tried to force his heart rate to slow.

The gray carpet offered a slight dip just before Yuri and Rover reached the drop-off at the edge of Karov Crater. As they accelerated into the dip, Golden Ball dove below the horizon. Brilliance switched to blackness, then burst on again as they hurtled up and over the edge. Moon's gravity, only one sixth that of Earth's, drew them gently back toward the crater's sloped wall. For almost three seconds, Rover floated, its nose dropped, and Yuri's stomach clenched. Thirty feet from its takeoff, Rover's nose dug into the dirt and exploded a fan of dust. Rover pushed down on its front wheels, bobbed its nose back up, then responded to the command from the controller in Yuri's hand. Man and Machine slid to a stop.

Yuri trembled as lunar dirt rained down around him and he glanced at the display:

$$HR = 137$$

Heart rate oughtta be high. You nearly flipped it—take it easy! He allowed Rover to start a gradual roll straight down the smooth, seventeen-degree slope of Karov's wall. After six minutes he reached the crater's floor and stopped. Yuri's eyes focused on pebbles next to Rover's wide metal-screen tires, then out ahead to black rocks and black boulders with their long, thin shadows that reached back toward him like lean black fingers. Yes, a definite challenge. Better go slow.

As partners, Man and Machine dodged rocks and snaked and swerved around boulders. Yuri grinned as he finessed the controller, cut around the last large rock—a small triumph but he savored it—then accelerated over the smooth crater floor toward the shadow from the opposite wall, a wall of open empty blackness that had crept upward and now loomed above. His frown reemerged. Sure wasn't worth staying behind. Should have left on time with the rest. No one would say anything about "Phase Five." Just like that technician, they all tightened up as soon as I asked—like I was their enemy. Maybe I can get a formal inquiry started when I get back to LB-13.

Yuri lifted his sun visor as the upper edge of Golden Ball

disappeared behind the crater's rim. No, not enough. Still too dark. Yuri reached forward and flicked up the headlight switch.

Switch issued signal. Signal traveled to Power Switching Module, the new Module provided by Kurt. Enriched Software in Module's microprocessor activated three power switching relays. One relay connected an electrical ground to a line from the cardiac monitoring electrode built into Yuri's liquid-cooled undergarment, an electrode that pressed against his back directly behind his heart. The second and third relays connected another monitoring electrode on his chest to an Instrumentation Power Supply Bus. The electrical potential of the skin directly over Yuri's heart jumped to twenty-seven hundred volts.

Mind monitored. Muscles contracted. Torso jerked.

Voltage remained steady. . . .

Head vibrated. Arms shook. Legs danced.

Current continued to flow. . . .

Eyes bulged. Jaws clenched. Teeth gnashed.

And trusty astronaut restraint held tight. . . .

After one minute and 37.000 seconds, precisely, Enriched Software reversed the position of the three relays it had set, completely consumed itself, and ceased to exist without a trace.

And on into the lunar night, as in billions of previous lunar nights, dead silence reigned . . . except on this one night, a steady green glow continued to broadcast its data into the dark:

$$HR = 0$$

I

□□□

REACT

A man will establish who he is within a second—but give him a minute . . . and he won't be sure.

1

□□□
react

"Uh-oh, it's gonna go out."

   "What?"

   "The Sun."

   "Won't go out, Joe."

   "Yeah, the gods are gonna pull its plug again. It's gonna go out!"

   "No, it'll just—"

   "It will! Just like last time."

   "No, that big rock there is just moving in the way."

   Joe laughed as he grabbed Dieter's arm. "Why do you geologists have to bring rocks into everything?"

   "Tough not to when the rock is the Moon and you're in lunar orbit."

   "Blasphemy! I'm keepin' the faith in my Plug Doctrine. You'll see, less than a minute now—"

   Just twelve short of thirty-seven hundred miles per hour, two specks of metal and plastic, each designed to shelter traces of bone and flesh, glided with security only thirty-seven miles over Big Rock. Cloaked in its gray film of dirt and dust, Big Rock had taken up residence in Earth orbit over four billion years before; Specks, the new guys boasting their bright white surfaces, had resided secure in their lunar orbits but seven.

Secure? Of course, everything remained secure.

Maybe Big Rock just felt a fondness for Specks, for it reached out and guided them along with all the precision required to keep them locked safe in stable orbits that just grazed its surface. Or, maybe Big Rock sensed the natural order of things and just passed on the security provided to it by the eighty-one times more massive Earth that reached out from afar and guided it. Then again, perhaps Big Rock only passed along the security provided by the far more distant and twenty-seven billion times more massive Sun that guided Earth, or maybe the security offered by the many distant and more massive Stars that maneuvered Sun, or maybe . . .

And the two traces of flesh and bone that floated outside the first Speck? Each one, snug in his own special suit to protect him from the hazards of space, also felt secure.

Of course. Why not?

"Hey, Joe. We're straight over the terminator. That means we must also be over Karov."

"Yeah, you're right, Dieter. Let me feast my eyeballs." Joe looked down through thirty-seven miles of nothing to the terminator, the Moon's surface where day terminated and night began. Lunar mountains and crater rims poked up and stretched out shafts of darkness that poured their blackness back into the lunar night. Black voids of crater centers, like open pits bored far into the lunar interior, gazed back up. Every hill, every pockmark, proclaimed its presence in the stark black and white. "There it is, straight down. Strange the way it just sits there all by itself."

"Yeah, rare for a crater on the far side, Joe. And there's Romanenko and Strekalov to the west and Markarov to the east."

"I really admire you geologists, Dieter. You have a name for every one of them suckers."

"Just look at it though. Karov's a beauty, a textbook impact crater! Perfectly round with a peak exactly in the center of its floor. And the Sun's at just the right angle to light up the peak's tip."

"You sure?" Joe, the kind who felt a friend worth having was a friend worth teasing, grabbed Dieter's arm a second time. "Maybe that's just a lighthouse down there in the center of one of them there lunar seas."

"You make me cry, Joe. Think of all that geology training we gave you Commanders, all of it, right down the drain."

The first of the two Specks, a lunar-orbiting space station called Unity, cradled an Earth–Moon Transfer Vehicle at its forward tip. Soon Joe and Dieter would burn EMTV's engines and trade Moon's secure pull for Earth's. The trailing Speck, a Lunar Ascent-Descent Shuttle, glided in an identical orbit but twenty-seven hundred feet behind the station. Just two hours before, Joe and Dieter had burned LADS's engine, lifted off from the Moon, and rendezvoused with Unity.

"Wish we were inside, Dieter. I'd have our telescope on Karov and be looking for Yuri."

"Might not be able to see him. He should have reached LB-13 by now or at least be in the shadows."

"Probably so."

"He sure got all fired up about PRECISE."

"Yeah, a real wild hair. I wonder if he found out what they're up to."

"I sure hope so, Joe. But I still don't see why he did it. He's supposed to be a Lunar Base Engineer, not a detective."

"Dieter, I always give smart guys like him, or you, a lot of rein. He felt PRECISE was trying to cover something up."

"You mean that Phase Five stuff he heard someone talking about?"

"Yeah, who knows? He might come up with something that'll help us out of the mess we're in."

"Joe, I'm worried. We didn't . . ."

"Zappo!" Blackness swallowed them. "There, they pulled the plug, just like I told you, Dieter."

"And there's those same two streamers in the Sun's corona that we saw last orbit. Oughtta be able to see 'em for at least another ten minutes."

"Dieter, you still clinging to all that wild-ass orbital-theory mysticism?"

"Joe, I'm worried. Logistics control will really be ticked that Yuri's not coming back with us."

"No sweat, Dieter. Yuri can make the next EMTV and be home only five days behind us."

"But we didn't follow the regs, Joe, or get a deviation approval."

"Screw all that horse hockey, Dieter. It wasn't required in

this case. I did what I thought was right, and I'll take the heat. Let's finish up this EVA and get back inside."

"Okay. But first I gotta go back to LADS one last time and get my rock samples."

"*More* rocks? Bit by bit you damn geologists are gonna move the whole Moon back to the Earth."

"But, Joe, I've got only a couple hundred pounds of Karov regolith for the oxygen extraction demos—and a few highly unique samples of dunite and anorthosite!"

"Bullshit. Seen one rock, seen 'em all. Unique as prairie pizzas."

"Joe?!"

Hidden in the darkness of his clear helmet, Joe's grin flashed. Dieter's always been too easy to tease. Better lighten up a bit on him. "Okay, but make it quick. I'll take my time. All I have left to do is drift up to our EMTV, terminate the LOX transfer, and then finish stowing the LB-13 repair equipment in our airlock. Bring your stones up there and we'll squeeze 'em in . . . somehow." But don't go too easy on him, he won't think you love him. "And if we can't fit 'em in there, I'll let you hold 'em on your lap for reentry."

Dieter laughed. "Thanks, Joe. I'll be back in less than ten minutes." Encased in his white pressure suit and silver Jet Pack, Dieter drifted away from Unity, flicked the controller in his right hand, pirouetted a half turn to face the LADS, then pushed the controller in his left hand forward to make a change to his flight path, just an ever-so-slight perturbation to his secure orbit.

Joe watched Dieter accelerate, silver and white darken and the flash of his Jet Pack's strobe light fade toward a twinkle. He's really movin' out. Conscientious. Good man. Always has been. Need more like him.

A ring of warm-red reference lights glowed on both ends of each of Unity's seven pressurized modules. Joe tweaked his hand controller and inched forward over the first of three modules between him and the open truss work that led to the staging platform and their EMTV. With the gloved index finger of his left hand, he punched the keyboard on his left thigh and the helmet-mounted spotlights aside each ear bloomed on at low power. He glanced ahead to the soft light that shafted from the last window on his side of the first Module, the Sleep Module. Got a little time to burn while I drift over to the EMTV and wait for Dieter. May as well not waste it.

Joe drifted with his helmet within inches of the Module's skin and, at each window, snapped his lights from off to high intensity as he peered in. At the third, a wide-eyed face, like that of a cat with a freshly crushed tail, recoiled from the window. "Gotcha!" Leo must've been trying to see the Moon by starlight. "Dieter, take a note. Now I'm only two behind Leo."

"No, Joe, you've gotta be at least two ahead."

Joe continued his drift past the next three empty windows until he reached the last. His spotlights overwhelmed the soft light that oozed from within. Within seconds, a flurry of clothes jammed against the plexan. "Oops, sorry, but don't worry, June, I didn't see a thing!" His wide smile flexed again. Man, they don't come more perfect than that.

As he crossed the fifteen-foot-diameter node that separated the Sleep Module from the Lunar Reconnaissance Module, Joe turned his spotlights out, slowed, then glided along a path far away from the lenses that protruded from the Module's surface. Out of consideration and respect for the equipment within the Module and its operators, he maneuvered with far greater caution than he had before. Not much to see by eye down there on the dark side, he thought, but a lot sure shows up in infrared, if you know how to interpret the data.

Once over the Logistics Module, Joe turned his spotlights up to full power, glanced forward toward his destination, then straight ahead into the Module's only window, into the face of its sole occupant. Occupant stared back with a fixed frown, looked out with unseen eyes, eyes hidden deep within dark voids beneath bushy brows. What's that tech doing in there? Module won't be restowed for at least another week. And the PIP in his hand is in the COMMAND TRANSIT mode. But so what? He's got nothing out here to command. Enough screwin' around. Get to work. On to the EMTV.

Joe's right. I'd better get moving.

Dieter pushed the controller in his left hand forward. Four jets of cold helium streamed backward from the Jet Pack on his back, the pack intended only for proximity operations. Not much of a system, as Jet Packs go, but enough to maneuver around Unity without contaminating its surfaces.

Dieter accelerated to a nominal closure speed of ten feet per second with the LADS, his destination, then glided. Just a straight shot back along our direction of motion, he thought. Be there in a few minutes. Orbital mechanics are negligible. Seems too easy.

"Gotcha! Dieter, take a note. Now I'm only two behind Leo."

Dieter smiled as he continued to glide. God love him, he never misses a chance. "No, Joe, you've gotta be at least two ahead."

Signal, one unknown to Joe or Dieter, left Unity. It impinged the antenna on Dieter's Jet Pack, traveled to its Command Processor, burrowed deep down into software, then nudged Enriched Software, a new module, a module of previously dormant software. Enriched Software awoke and muscled to the surface.

To Dieter, it still seemed that he only crept toward the LADS. Yep, I need just a couple more squirts. He pushed the controller forward again and released.

Now fully awake, Enriched Software cut power to all of Jet Pack's systems, all except for the jets that continued to control attitude—and those that thrust forward.

Dieter accelerated.

He pulled back the controller in his left hand. What the . . . ?

Dieter continued to accelerate.

He flipped a switch to CONTROL OVERRIDE, tugged, then yanked back on the controller in his left hand. Then he rotated and twisted the one in his right.

Dieter continued to accelerate.

He commanded EMERGENCY POWER, then continued to tug and yank, rotate and twist. Holy shit, what's going on here?!

Dieter continued to accelerate.

With rigid muscles and clenched teeth, he tugged and twisted, ripped and wrenched. . . .

"Ooops, sorry, but don't worry, June, I didn't see a thing!"

"Joe, help!" But no signal left Dieter's antenna, no plea reached Joe's ears—Dieter's screams only echoed within his helmet until his voice was exhausted and ran dry. And thrusters continued to thrust until, in time, their helium supply exhausted and they also ran dry.

Dieter drifted.

Enriched Software commanded all power to zero, completely consumed itself, and ceased to exist without a trace. Only Dieter's oxygen pressure regulator, controlled by mechanical logic, continued to function.

LADS's outline, illuminated by a single red light on Dieter's side, shot by three feet from his outstretched hand. As a reflex, his hoarse whispers continued to come one after another but no sound or signal left his suit.

And Dieter continued to drift.

Time to kill.

Joe floated over the last square of open truss work, tweaked the controller in his left hand, glided to a stop at the EMTV work station for LOX transfer control, and locked his feet into place. He verified full loading of the EMTV LOX tanks, terminated the transfer, and commanded auto disconnect of the supply umbilical.

Dieter continued to drift.

Joe's requested EMTV's primary instrumentation to measure the LOX loading and each of the transfer-line leak rates. Can't be too careful, he thought, as he requested its secondary instrumentation to again measure the same quantities. Satisfied, he closed, locked, then verified the integrity of the control panel cover. Yep, everything's safed.

Dieter continued to drift.

Joe unlocked his feet, tweaked his hand controllers, and started a slow drift toward the airlock hatch cut into the skin of EMTV. "Hey, Dieter. Get your hot buns and cool rocks back here . . . or do I have that backward?" He glanced at the red and green lights that almost merged into one, the only evidence of the LADS a half mile behind. "Dieter, how far out are you?" He turned off his spotlights and searched the open darkness. "Dieter, where'd you go, ole buddy? Hey, Adam. Can you see Dieter? He should be out in the direction of the LADS and headed this way."

EVA Monitor inside the station yawned and stretched. "Just a minute, Joe. Let me have a look. . . . No, don't see him."

"Check your radar!"

"Hang on."

"Hustle!"

"I've got a passive blip about three miles out and a little below LADS. It has no lights or telemetry. And it's receding at 51.3 feet per second . . . and holding."

"Moving away at 51.3? He's in trouble!"

The situation deserved further observation and examination, and certainly some consideration and deliberation, and then definitely some coordination and cooperation—most every other crewman in the astronaut corps of the World Space Federation would have paused for at least a measure of each.

Not Joseph Z. Rebello.

Joe turned and accelerated straight to Unity's airlock hatch. "Adam, I'm going after him. Be ready to support. Follow us both on radar and check my burn solutions."

"Will do, Joe! And I'm alerting Captain Lopez."

Joe impacted three feet to the side of CATS, the Contingency Attitude and Translation System, reached over to CATS's control panel, and hit the switch labeled MAIN POWER. Within thirty-five seconds, he had exchanged his own Jet Pack for the larger, more capable spacecraft now strapped to his back.

"Initialize my state vector, Adam."

"You got it."

"Thanks."

"Good luck!"

Joe faced the LADS and pushed his left hand forward. Propellants flooded into chambers, exploded, and fled through nozzles. CATS accelerated and pressed Joe against the back of his suit. 51.3 feet per second, all retrograde. He's headed down. How far? Delta V's about one percent of his velocity, times four for a Hohmann transfer, times Moon's radius of one thousand miles. That's forty miles. We're only up thirty-seven—he's gonna hit!

"Continue thrusting to one hundred feet per second, Joe, just to give you a good catch-up rate. We'll fine-tune it after you get radar tracking on him and we compare solutions. And you gotta hustle. His current trajectory, which appears not to be changing, puts him about 2.73 miles below the lunar surface at perigee, which is about 14 minutes after terminator."

"There, I've got an even one hundred feet per second. And I got tracking on him, Adam. I've set the rendezvous point for a minute before the terminator. Can't see him before that. How's our burn solutions compare?"

"Hold on. . . . They agree. But, Joe, if you don't get to him quickly, you'll never have time to deflect his velocity enough to clear the Moon's surface. You sure you want to do this?"

"Want? What's that got to do with it? I'm thrusting. . . . Residual delta V's going to zero."

"Joe, Captain Lopez advises that you are to break off the rescue and return. You don't have enough margin. He requests you to give it up."

Joe's frown lasted but a second. "Adam, did you read me? I've finished thrusting. How's my catch-up orbit look?"

"Exactly what you wanted. Captain Lopez orders that you—"

"Adam, do you read?"

"Affirmative, Joe. Captain Lopez commands you—"

"Unity, I'm transmitting in the blind. My receiver's gone dead." Joe's suited finger flicked the switch marked COMMUNICATION SYSTEM to OFF. He shook his head. Don't need that distraction. Next burn in twelve minutes.

Embraced by the security of gravity, the two human satellites drifted ever closer to Big Rock as they skimmed over its surface at one mile per second. If nothing changed, each satellite would impact, explode, and form one more crater; each would sacrifice its existence to make its mark just like the billions upon billions of preceding projectiles had made their marks; each would gouge out just one more pockmark in Big Rock's face to further confound and astound future astrogeologists.

Joe turned down the intensity of CATS's displays and looked at the sky. Isolated and faint, points of brightness appeared, points that leisurely intensified and bloomed to fill in his stellar audience. There's so many out there, always so many that all look the same. With a flick of his wrist, he rolled toward Big Rock. In blackness, his unseen enemy stared back. He let his body go limp. For the first time since he began, he forced deep breaths, heard their rasps, and smelled the odor of lunar rock, rock identical to that which crept toward him in silence below. He slowed his breathing and waited. His body shivered. He flexed every muscle until the strain in his back hurt again, the one he injured just before the mission as he swung his son in one last game of Tick-Tock. He shook his legs, arms, and head, felt the thin sheet of cold sweat slosh over his forehead, and then waited some more.

Soft shadows slid underneath and Joe looked up. A blue gem covered with white swirls inched above an invisible black edge. Funny how when you see only half an Earth, he thought, it looks like someone cleaved it in two and threw away a half. Maria and Ricky are out there in that missing half, about at sunrise. Wonder what they've got lined up for today? I oughtta be back there. Promised we'd go to Disneyrange. Always promise it every summer. And it's only right up the road in San Antonio. This fall we'll really do it. Little Guy would love it. So would Maria. And I'm happy just doin' anything with 'em. . . . If they knew what I'm doing now, would they think it's right? Hope I get the chance to ask. Two minutes to the next burn, another twenty-five to terminator.

Joe waited.

Light poured out from Sun, a little bounced off Earth, far less of that bounced off Moon, and only a trace of that entered the eyes of the human lunar satellite. Yet Joe perceived gray dust and crater outlines as they whisked underneath. They're moving right up here with me, almost over me. Don't watch. Won't help. Check the radar. He turned up the intensity of CATS's displays. They hovered at arm's length and seemed only a bit closer than the terrain under his feet. I got a lock on him. And he's exactly where he should be. Burn in one minute.

Joe waited.

Three . . . two . . . one . . . mark. For seven seconds Joe thrust away from the faint terrain that blurred as it drew closer. Thrusters cut off and the silence of his thoughts returned. What really are my options? Press ahead or break it off. Just say I got too close to the surface. And it'd be true. Everybody would buy it . . . except maybe for Dieter. No, no real options. None. Press.

Joe looked ahead and waited. He looked down and waited. And, for another eight minutes, he waited. Then he thrust, peered ahead, and waited again. At last it appeared—a spike—a faint diffuse coronal streamer that stood straight out from the black edge. Spike intensified. Sun's right around the corner.

Joe's breathing shallowed as he waited once more and studied his displays. Dieter's 1.03 miles away and I'm closing on him at 43 feet per second. Way too much. But I've got no choice. Gotta get to him and change his orbit—fast!

Joe looked ahead to where his displays told him Dieter should be. He saw nothing. He stared and strained. Still nothing. No, wait, there, I think. . . .

Blaze erupted on the horizon. Pain exploded on his retinas. Sun!

He looked away, then down to just past his feet where a gray blur scraped against his soles. He pulled his visor down, squinted ahead, then clenched his eyes closed and waited again for the pain to subside.

Might never see Dieter in the Sun, never get to him in time. . . . We're both gonna hit!

2

☐☐☐

rejoin

No choice. Joe rotated his back to the Sun. Have to back into him.

He turned his displays up to maximum intensity. Not enough. Sun's too bright. Displays are still almost all washed out. Only seventeen hundred feet out and closing at twenty-nine feet per second. Too fast—brake!

Joe pushed the controller forward. Burned propellants shot out the rear of CATS, sped toward Dieter, and, as individual molecules, rushed forward in their orbits. Some molecules had energy enough to break away from the security of lunar gravity, to flee, to escape. Some had only enough to remain in orbit. And a small fraction flew forward, hit Dieter, gave up much of their energy to him, and headed off to eventually impact indifferent dust below.

Dieter, the passive human satellite, started to tumble.

. . . 1400 feet out . . . 1050 . . . 800 . . . 650 . . . Cross range's too high. Get it out . . . there. Now a little down . . . kill all but a little relative velocity and move above him. He's 370 feet away and down. . . .

Joe turned around to face Dieter. Sun's ball sat a diameter above the horizon. Below and on either side, in a world without weather, without sound, jagged circles of crater rims gleamed and glistened. Crater shadows lengthened into the darkness, stretched backward, and tried to tug the craters back into the blackness from which he'd just emerged.

He squinted as he scrutinized the area in which his displays told him Dieter should be. For but a second, a silver object flashed with reflected light against the black void of a crater core. Dieter? And isn't that Crater Rhaeticus? Who cares? Concentrate.

The silver object reappeared as a flicker. It's him . . . and he's tumbling. Not going to make this any easier.

Joe glanced up and ahead. Nerves jolted. Mountains! Oh, Lord, why couldn't you have given me the plains. He glanced at CATS's readouts. I'm only 3.1 miles over the surface, and that's only on the average. Peaks are closer. And I'm still goin' down!

He thrust toward Dieter, down toward the gray blur. The flicker of the white and silver object enlarged as he drew closer, expanded to a whirl of arms and legs outstretched and a helmet with a gold coating, an opaque coating that hid the human within. Is he alive? Joe let his closure rate remain high right up to the last few seconds. Then he thrust and braked to a stop. His exhaust, close and directed straight at Dieter, further accelerated Dieter's tumble.

Legs and arms and helmet spun as a pinwheel, a blur. Joe put out a hand. Gotta stop him.

Whack.

Joe spun away. CATS stopped his tumble and he moved in again.

Whack.

Again, he spun away, stabilized, paused, then thrust full forward, rammed into Dieter, wrapped both arms around a leg—and held. They spun together until Joe pushed Dieter in front and away from his jets and commanded them to bring their rotation to a halt. Again CATS's displays demanded attention.

Only 2.9 miles up—outta time!

Joe looped a strap around Dieter's chest, rammed the CATS's displays to the side, ripped Dieter's back to him, and cinched the strap tight. Dieter's body snapped rigid for a second, then his arms flailed and legs kicked. He's alive all right.

As Joe thrust down and away from the blur beneath, he

looked to one side, then the other. The interfaces between rock and space smeared into precise gray swaths, swaths that continued to inch upward.

He glanced at CATS's displays again. Still goin' down.

Ahead, mountains and valleys and random lunar crinkles danced and flickered as they came over the horizon, drifted toward him, accelerated, then flashed under his feet. Joe stretched his head to the side and looked straight down past his boots. Lungs gasped. Legs jerked up. Sphincter clenched. And Dieter went limp.

Joe forced his eyes closed. Just keep thrusting!

Hand pushed. . . . Gonna tick a peak.

Arm shot pain. . . . Gonna hit any second.

Pain warned Brain. . . . Not a lingering death.

Brain ignored Pain. . . . Bye, Maria; bye, Ricky; sorry.

Thrust remained nominal. . . . Heart pounds, chest hurts.

Gravity remained nominal. . . . Gonna call it Rebello Crater?

Orbit continued to bend. . . . Lord, please get us out of this.

Joe looked ahead over Dieter's shoulder. A flat horizon— the Sea of Tranquillity—no more mountains!

CATS's jets continued to shoot hot gases straight down through the vacuum of space and, at over one mile per second, scribed a precision-straight line across the dust of the lunar plain.

Sun continued to rise.

Chest continued to pound.

Jets continued to scribe.

Joe watched the horizon, a sharp, flat surface whose bright gray cut hard against black sky. It seemed to nudge a bit lower, and the blur beneath seemed to edge a bit farther away. He glanced at his displays.

0.27 miles—and climbing!

Brain accepted warning, hand released, blood surged back into muscles, teeth unclenched, and lungs filled with air. Joe closed his eyes and also went limp—Thanks, Lord—then he snapped alert again. Made it so far, but we gotta get back to Unity. Don't blow it now. Joe stretched and tightened. Dieter's loose arms and legs dangled and flopped. Still alive? Maybe.

Joe configured CATS's guidance for rendezvous with Unity,

the lunar space station from which they had started, obtained a radar lock, computed the required burns, completed the first one, and continued on their climbing trajectory toward Unity and home. He loosened Dieter's restraint, turned him around, put his face to the Sun, and looked in. White eyes stared out, eyes locked wide open in a white face, a frozen face except for white lips that twitched and burbled. Joe opened the panel by his right hip, withdrew power and communications umbilicals, and plugged them into Dieter's suit.

"You okay in there, ole buddy?"

White head wavered. "Yeah. . . ."

"Like the ride?"

"I . . . I. . . ."

"What happened? Why'd you sneak off like that?"

"Je . . . jets. . . ."

"You sure know how to liven up an EVA. I bet you were just out after fame and glory."

"What? . . . No. . . ."

"Wanted your place in the annals of lunar geology. Probably sorry I stopped you."

"No . . . I. . . ."

"If it weren't for me, you'd now have the record for the longest trench ever dug by any lunar field geologist."

"Ohhh. . . ."

Seven seconds before Joe completed the terminal phase burn of the rendezvous, CATS's LOW PROPELLANT warning light popped on.

"No sweat, Dieter. We've got just about enough left for braking."

"I hope so. I don't want you to go by Unity like I did LADS."

"Dieter, the failures you had are just not a credible set."

"Yeah, I agree, Joe. A Jet Pack is a pretty simple thing. Not much can go wrong with it."

"Jets stuck on, attitude control still worked, and all else failed. Not possible, but it happened. We'll just have to wait till the folks back at Houston take a look at it."

"Joe, I'll settle for just getting back."

Joe pressed the communications switch on his left hip. "Hello, Unity, J. Rebello here."

"Joe, we gave you up for lost!"

"Hi, Adam. I'm two miles below and closing. I've got Dieter with me. And, oh, I think I've got my comm working again."

"Well done! I'll suit up and wait for you at the airlock."

"Thanks, Adam."

With slow, deliberate, propellant-saving maneuvers, Joe completed the rendezvous with Unity. At the airlock, he disconnected Dieter's restraint and umbilicals and floated him three feet to Adam who connected him into the ship's life support. "Don't close the hatch yet, Adam. I'll be right back."

"Where are you going, Joe?"

Joe coiled, sprang off the surface by Unity's airlock, and headed aft. "Just don't lock me out." Seven minutes later, he floated back to the same surface.

Adam helped pull him inside. "What did you do?"

Joe grinned as he handed a vacuum-tight suitcase to Dieter. "Here, ole buddy. You forgot your rocks."

3

□□□

rethink

"What is it with you, Rebello? Are you one of those misfits who thinks you're above it all?"

Joe, an observant man, a thoughtful man, studied the veins on the neck of Captain Lopez as they bulged and surged with every word. Ahh yes, fury level's right up there. Guess I punctured another bubble of authority. Needle him again? No, better just let him vent. If he doesn't take too long, we can get into EMTV and make our burn on time. But my God this guy's tempting. . . . No, don't, don't do it!

"Maybe you can't read." Captain Lopez banged his index finger on the open page of a three-inch-thick computer printout. A Velcro strap popped loose and the printout floated upward. The Captain slammed it back down onto the ward-room table, the best surface in the station to serve as "Thee Official Desk." "It's all here in WSF Mission Regulations, Section 17.3.11. 'When a rescue attempt places additional personnel in jeopardy without concurrent creation of a high probability of success, the attempt shall *not* be conducted.'"

Using fingertips and toes, Joe pulsed up and down two feet as he floated between ceiling and floor and presented himself front and center before Thee Official Desk. "Success? Tell me, Lopie, is there a new crater down there, or is that Dieter in the head right now still cleaning out his suit?"

Captain Lopez scrutinized the figure that oscillated up and down before him, a neat figure of crisp composure, a squared-away figure of military bearing, a sharp figure of lean muscle that always appeared coiled and ready to strike. Yes, a figure with all the ingredients of a fine officer, yet a figure with one irritating trait, that one trait Captain Lopez found most maddening—that face with eyes that sparkled every time his tan skin flexed with all those smile creases, a face that flexed far too easily and far too often, like now. "Mister, you've got an *attitude* problem!"

Again, eyes sparkled and smile creases flexed. And like a cat, Joe reversed ends and floated upside-down before Unity's Captain. "Better?" Damn, I shouldn't have, but I just can't help myself.

"It is abundantly clear that you have no respect for authority. When operations are conducted in or out of *my* station, *I'm* in command. And that failed comm trick's older than smoke signals. You ignored *my* direct order to *abort!*"

Joe drifted through a pirouette of one and a half turns, then let his calves accept the full heat of the Captain's glare. "The lawyers wouldn't see it that way, Lopie. Dieter is part of my crew, and we hadn't become a part of your station yet when I started the rescue. As Commander of Lunar Expedition 336, the responsibility for my crew was still mine."

Captain Lopez wrenched himself out from behind Thee Official Desk to find a suitable section of Joe to address and glared down at Joe's upside-down head. "Responsibility? Crew? First you leave Yuri down there by himself and don't formally coordinate his schedule with Personnel Logistics Control. Then you—"

"Yuri's a big boy. He knows Karov inside and out. And he stayed behind to better understand a very real problem we have to fix." Joe started to rotate about his long axis and brought his arms into his body to accelerate. "Besides, he's scheduled for leave when he gets back. In effect, he did it on his own time."

"Then you perform that peeping-Tom stunt with June?"

Joe stopped his spin, did a forward half flip, came face-to-face with Captain Lopez, and flexed his irritating grin again. "C'mon, Lopie. June was laughing harder than I was." He shrugged as his smile creases flexed even wider yet. "The female form in zero gravity—wondrous to behold. Just classify it as, ahhh . . . space exploration of the finest kind."

Captain Lopez tried to ignore Joe's retorts, but they slipped through and stoked his boiler to a full head of steam. "And as if that isn't enough, you let Dieter take off by himself on the dark side to another vehicle over a half mile away!"

"That's a common procedure. We require two crewpersons out on every EVA in zero gravity, but not that they hold hands."

Captain Lopez brought his nose to within an inch of Joe's. "Now I see why you have the reputation you do. You violate a regulation with every breath. Rebello, why can't you do things like everybody else?!"

Joe's body remained relaxed, his breathing slow and deep as his smile creases flexed and eyes sparkled at Captain Lopez. His chest puffed with pride. He actually seemed to take the Captain's accusations as a compliment! After a long ten seconds, the Captain backed away, shook his head, wrenched himself back behind Thee Official Desk, and started to scour his regulations for one last zinger. With one eyebrow raised, Joe sized up the situation, turned his back, and reached for a handhold. "Lopie, thanks for the pleasant conversation. I really do understand your position and don't mean any offense. I just do what's right at the time. And right now it's time to get back to work." With a flick of his wrists, he accelerated toward the hatch. "The next EMTV launch window is less than three hours away, and it's time to get into the cockpit and start the checkout. It's time to go home."

Was the old man a genius? Hard to know through conversation, for Thaddaios Alexandru Wojciechowski let few thoughts escape into words. But results spoke for themselves.

Hunched over in thought, the fingers of his right hand, long and slender and supple, manipulated his clear plexan BioProbe. The four fingers flipped and twirled the probe, only slightly larger than a pencil, down and around one finger after another: . . . first . . . middle . . . ring . . . baby . . . then back up again in the opposite direction: . . . ring . . . middle . . . first . . . and straight into the next lap. Twirl after twirl, lap after lap, BioProbe replicated its path without deviation.

The fingers of his left hand spread out and raked spikelike tips through the precise triangle of fur that covered his face. Over and over again they raked through the thick layer of fine gray hair that suggested the features of a well-trimmed wolf, a thick mantle that hid the yellow pitted skin, sunken cheeks, and pointed chin, a smooth cloak that concealed all but the tips of his jumbo-sized ears and spike nose, the lower half of his pallid forehead, and the dark circles split by yellow slits from which black pebbles now peered into empty space.

No doubt about it, even when his hair was jet-black, Thaddaios Alexandru Wojciechowski bore more than a little resemblance to a wolf, a fact that, along with the difficulty of his real name, earned him the obvious alias "Wolf," by the end of his first term of graduate studies fifty-four years previous in 1985. Although his nickname had rapidly received near universal usage by his fellow students, and what few other acquaintances he had, he initially resisted it. In fact, he hated it. "Wolf," a weird name for anyone. People aren't animals, especially him. He couldn't help how he looked, why pick on him? But eventually he sensed that "Wolf" was never uttered in jest or mockery of his physical deformities, but spoken more with a sense of awe and respect, even a bit of fear for his intellectual capability and the fearless way he employed it. With the instincts of his namesake, he never hesitated in his ruthless attack on any intellectual problem, but aggressively slashed his way through to its real meat and didn't cease until it was fully ravaged and consumed. No, Wolf was not one to be ridiculed. And as he established his clear intellectual superiority, he began to take pride in the comparison with the savage predatory animal, a pride that had strengthened with years.

The black pebbles in the yellow slits shifted focus to the muscular body of the young man who approached, to the fluid motions of his long limbs, to the strength that rippled beneath his fair skin, to the intelligence that flashed in eyes beneath a thick mat of blond hair. Wolf prolonged his gaze for a full five seconds before he spoke. "Yes, Otto?"

"It's for you, sir."

"Who's calling?"

"Kurt, sir."

"Good." Wolf unfolded from his slouch and gawked left, then right. "Where's my PIP?"

"It's there under your calculations."

In a single sweep of a muscular arm, Otto's hand passed under the loose pile of papers and plots, retrieved a book-sized screen and keyboard, and placed it in Wolf's lap.

"Thank you, Otto. This should be good news." In small green numbers, "17, 18" winked at the top left corner of the screen on Wolf's Portable Information Processor, his PIP. His fingers, though knurled early in life with arthritis but since biochemically repaired, sped over PIP's keys. COMMUNICATION, ACTIVATE, 17, ENTER. PIP's screen flashed awake and presented a man's face.

"Hello, sir."

"Hello, Kurt."

"I'm at Karov. Yuri Strekalov has been excised just as you planned."

"I was successful? Excellent!"

The scowl on the screen's face remained fixed as did the murk and gloom that radiated from the face's dark voids. Wolf typed in "18, ENTER" and faced changed, yet it remained the same. The name above its pocket also remained unchanged. Only the word below that, "PRECISE," melted away as "WSF" firmed up in its place. "Hello, sir."

"Hello, Kurt."

"I'm on Unity. The excision of Dieter Dietrich has not been successful."

Wolf's fists tightened. "I failed?!"

Face's scowl deepened. "Dietrich was deorbited just as you planned. He would have impacted, but Joe Rebello interfered. He sensed Dietrich had a problem and used CATS to retrieve him much faster than we calculated anyone would respond."

Wolf jerked up straight. His shoulders ascended and swallowed the narrow neck below the cone of fur. "I failed!" Pallid skin turned red. From feet to fur, his body tightened, quivered and vibrated, entered a tight tremble that seemed to burn up the last of its energy, then sank back down into the black leather folds of his couch. Wolf's yellow slits blinked twice, then fluttered, then blinked and fluttered again. "I will not permit them to interfere with the start of Phase Five." He glared into the small glass eye below the screen. "Kurt—for sure—I am going to excise this threat, especially Rebello!"

"Yes, sir."

"When do they plan to return?"

"They'll make their first engine burn in about another hour

and dock with Station Von Braun in low Earth orbit in two days, four and one-half hours from now."

"That does not give me much time." Again yellow slits blinked, fluttered, closed tight, then finally opened to let black pebbles stare straight ahead. By reflex, Wolf shifted one more time in his couch in another vain attempt to relieve the pain from his sharp bones that cut into the meager flesh of his backside. Both Otto and screen's face waited a long minute until the fur below the nose spike hinted a smile. "Yes, I have it, a fix for both of them. I will need access to their onboard computer before they reach Earth's atmosphere. Kurt, can you provide me that access?"

"Yes, sir."

"I will be back to you in thirty minutes with the Enhanced Software for their computer. Stand by."

"Yes, s—"

Wolf terminated screen's face, struggled vertical, and turned. "Otto, our schedule is too tight, too exact to let any of these WSF misfits blunder in and slow us down."

"Yes, sir."

Wolf couldn't resist. He stepped forward, reached up, gripped Otto's forearm, and massaged it as he stared upward. "Otto, for our future, for all that I will make you, I'm going to succeed." Wolf's fists dropped to his sides and tightened as his body quivered one more time. "I will!"

Otto stiffened to full height and looked two heads down to Wolf with disciplined respect. "Sir. You always do. Thank you."

Resources, so many available for service.

Energy, so much ready for release.

At LB-13—Joe's point of departure and Yuri's intended destination—and also the thirteenth lunar base and processing plant that the World Space Federation (WSF) planned to place in operation after its purchase from PRECISE—energy flowed and put resources to work. Just three days previous, a radioisotope nuclear energy source released electrical energy and sent it to batteries in a front-end loader, a loader that now scooped up the top two feet of lunar soil at the edge of crater Karov and dropped it on a conveyer. More electrical energy flowed from a fusion reactor and powered the conveyer as it carried the soil into the mouth of LB-13. In fact, the reactor released enough electrical energy to bring life to all of LB-13, enough energy to power all of the functions of this new living lunar organism.

Within, LB-13 first converted electrical energy to microwaves that heated the lunar soil and drove off trace amounts of hydrogen, nitrogen, and helium-3, which over the past four billion years Sun had spewed out and deposited on each grain of exposed lunar soil. LB-13 collected and hoarded the hydrogen and nitrogen, rare elements on the Moon, for its own internal needs. But it sent all of its helium-3, an isotope of helium and rare throughout the Solar System, back to Earth where it was fused with deuterium to power "clean" nuclear reactors and provide ever-increasing amounts of electricity.

Next, LB-13 converted electrical energy to magnetic forces that separated ilmenite, an oxide of iron and titanium, $FeTiO_3$, from the lunar soil. Using more electrical energy and recycling some of its hydrogen, LB-13 produced and liquefied its main product—oxygen, life-giving, thrust-giving oxygen.

But LB-13 didn't stop there. It used additional electrical energy to heat and process the spent reacted solids to distill out silicon, the Moon's most abundant metal. Then it further processed the reacted solids with fresh soil to produce building blocks and cements for the construction of LB-13's expanding facilities.

One last step, one of immediate importance to Joe. LB-13 pulverized the distilled silicon, mixed it with liquid oxygen, and dispersed the resultant slurry to storage tanks. Ultimately, the slurry exploded in combustion chambers of rocket engines. Some engines energized vehicles to escape Moon's surface; others, Moon's gravity. Silicon, when burned with oxygen, didn't provide the most energetic fuel possible, nothing like what hydrogen could do, but it did the job and came at the right price—cheap, a cost negligible compared to the use of the Moon's rare hydrogen or hydrogen transported from Earth.

All in all, not a bad trade if you're a species that utilizes God-given resources for outward growth. Add nuclear energy to lunar soil and harvest oxygen, silicon, building materials, and valuable traces of hydrogen, nitrogen, and helium-3. Like the water, land, and lumber that had supported the migration of the more adventurous of the human species across a continent on the adjacent world only three centuries before, these lunar resources had supported explorers, and now early settlers, who spread outward into the Moon's open territory.

Incentive? Plenty.

Easily recognized by the exploring mind, the different mind, but something that had to be demonstrated time and time again to the stagnant mind, the conforming mind, the Moon served as a gateway to the Solar System and its resources provided the key. Night after night, Moon, as humanity's stepping stone to worlds beyond, hung before any human eye that wished to see, any human mind that wished to understand. Its presence proclaimed its role; its substance screamed its utility.

And in time, the Different did see, the Different did listen.

Yet, it took time. For many generations kept their eyes to their feet, even though they had necks that could swivel, and kept their touch to their sides, even though they had technology that could reach.

But in time, the Different did look up, the Different did reach.

Yet in a grander scheme, humanity's current hesitation was but another hitch in its history of general outward progress, a hitch that didn't really matter. For billions of years stretched before humanity that would host millions of generations, each of which, once motivated, could easily surge ahead and gain ground on what might've been. But most important at this point in time, the move outward through the Moon had started. The Different at the edge had continued to nudge the mass in the middle, had tweaked the direction of the herd ever so slightly, had changed the path of its push.

In time, as they usually did, the Different made a difference.

"Ready?"

"Yeah, burn in two minutes."

Joe remained poised in his EMTV, ready to release the energy in the silicon and liquid oxygen slurry from LB-13 that he'd packed into his propellant tanks. He turned again to Rakesh Shivakumar, his copilot to the right who looked a bit anxious. "Shiva, how's your side look?"

"Good, Joe, real good. Systems are perfect and our propellant tanks are completely full."

"That's the way I like it—propellant comin' out our ears."

"Me too, but weren't you supposed to fill the tanks only to
the mission requirement plus nominal reserve?"

"That's what's in the regs, but the folks who wrote 'em
aren't up here with their fannies on the line. I always take all
the margin I can get. Besides, in this case it's almost free."

"Sounds good . . . as long as it's not me that takes the
rap."

"Shiva, is the targeting still converged?"

"Yep. And it's settled down. Had a slight transient as we
made a pass through the last two solutions, but now it's
converged again and both guidance systems agree to within
0.02 feet per second."

"Transient?"

"Yeah, Joe. The targeted delta V jumped up 0.83 on one
calculation, then right back down the same amount on the next
pass."

"I've never seen that kind of hiccup before."

"Me neither. But now all systems are lookin' real good."

"It's time. Engine goin' to ENABLE . . . four . . . three . . .
two . . . one . . . ignition."

EMTV pushed. Joe relaxed. He, Shiva, Dieter, and three
WSF crewmen who'd just completed their tours of duty on
Unity sank into their couches at 0.67 G, a force two-thirds
Earth's pull where they now headed, but four times that of the
Moon's pull they had just left. For two minutes and forty-
seven seconds, they felt the engine's push, heard its purr.
Then push and purr faded to zero.

"Shutdown on time with negligible velocity residuals."

"Yep, perfect burn, Joe."

"Let's start this big hummer rotating for passive thermal
control, then get these systems cleaned up. We've only got
forty-nine hours till we hit Earth interface, and I plan to get in
a lot of huggy-pillow time before then."

"You know, Joe, you've got only two configurations—full
afterburner or engine at idle with speed brakes full out."

Joe beamed his ear-to-ear grin, a contagious grin that
triggered one from Shiva. "Now you're catching on. Anything
worth doing is worth doing to excess; everything else, sleep
through it."

"Ahh yes, words to live by."

As Joe started the EMTV in a slow rotation to evenly distribute Sun's heat load over its structure like meat on a barbecue, he glanced out the overhead window. Terminator again. And those two craters, Romanenko and Strekalov Dieter called them, with Karov to the east. Wonder what Yuri found out. He was right. Something did seem strange down there, something poised and ready. But for what? He frowned as a coolness settled on his skin. Glad it's not me that's going back.

Alarm sounded.

After four hours of sleep, Joe popped awake. He could sleep through any dream, except for one, and any sounds, except for three: an Emergency Klaxon, the two-tone beep of a Caution and Warning Alarm, and the high-pitched squeal of a Priority One Interrupt like the one that now invaded his ears. "Houston, this is EMTV-3. What's up?"

"Hello, Joe. Sorry to wake you, but we've got a concern. Yuri has not shown up at LB-13. And he didn't return to PRECISE's Observatory. In about another three hours the oxygen in his backpack and his Rover will run out. Help us. Retrace his steps for us."

Joe paused as he sensed his frigid skin tighten over cooling flesh. Yuri? Him too? No! "Okay, Houston. After our five-day inspection of LB-13, we crossed Karov, reached PRECISE's Observatory, and gave our findings to Sturdza, PRECISE's foreman on the LB-13 construction, and to his engineering team. They disagreed with a number of the items Yuri identified as being in noncompliance with WSF Standardization Requirements, and try as we might, we resolved only a few of them by the time we had to leave. We had a hard deadline to meet if we were to get back to Unity and return this EMTV on schedule. That's when Yuri volunteered to stay behind and continue to work with Sturdza. He said he'd make it back to LB-13 before official sunset. And he, of all people, would make sure he was on time. Since he's traversed that crater many times alone before, we had no concern about leaving him behind. In summary, we last saw him at the Observatory and expected him to be at LB-13 long before now."

"Thanks for the rundown, Joe. It's just as we thought."

"Houston, check with Unity. They should be able to pick up his locator beacon whenever they're over Karov."

"We did, Joe. And they said that on every pass they get nothing but dead silence."

"Did you send out searches from both LB-13 and the Observatory?"

"We have, but in the dark they really can't do much. Karov's too big. Right now none of us can do much but wait it out."

"You're probably right, Houston. Wish you weren't."

"Joe, we've got a second request."

"Go."

"Change your GROUND COMMAND switch from BLOCK to ACCEPT. We have an update to Von Braun's state vector for you. They've changed their orbit slightly since you left."

"Okay, you've got it."

At the speed of light, digital data flowed into EMTV's computer software from a WSF ground computer—and Enriched Software, from a second source.

"Joe, you can go back to BLOCK . . . and to sleep."

"Thanks, Houston. Good night, troops." Joe closed his eyes and tried to close his mind. Yet the sentry in his gut stepped forward and refused to be ignored. His mind continued its sprint.

As Moon released EMTV, Earth reached out, took hold, and pulled it in.

Senors measured. Computer calculated. EMTV determined its attitude, position, velocity, and acceleration with great precision, superb precision, in fact, unmatched precision.

And, for the time being, Enriched Software slept.

4

□□□

reenter

The fuzz on the peach waited.

At Mach 31, and with great precision, EMTV glided toward the fuzz—the air above Earth. Air hung motionless, ready to perform its function without a flinch.

EMTV planned ahead, far ahead. If it hit the atmosphere at just the right angle and thereafter maneuvered in just the right way, it would skim through the top layer of Earth's coating, lose half its energy of motion, and emerge with just the right speed and be traveling in just the right direction to rendezvous with Space Station Von Braun in low Earth orbit—aerobraking. Clever. EMTV would use Earth's atmosphere rather than propellant to achieve just the right reduction in velocity to complete its mission.

Risk? Just a little. If EMTV entered at too steep an angle, high forces would break it apart; too shallow, it would skip out and not return to Earth. And if it slowed down too little, it would never make it to Von Braun; too much, it would continue to reenter and impact land or water, neither of which it or its crew would likely survive.

And today? No problem. For EMTV headed toward the fuzz at just the right angle. And its heat shield, shaped like a saucer, pointed in just the right direction. Even if not everything started out just quite right, EMTV had the intelligence to pull it off. With its weight concentrated at a point a little away from exactly behind the center of its heat shield, it would tilt a little to one side when it hit the air and slide in that direction. Because EMTV could rotate about its line of motion, its direction of slide could be controlled. Engineers disguised this ability to maneuver with the term "lift vector control." Nonetheless, it worked. If initial errors were small, EMTV could maneuver to exit the atmosphere at just the right speed and just the right angle.

And today?

"Noooo problem." Joe returned Shiva's stare with his perceptive smile, as he sometimes did, for he understood Shiva just like he did the many others who stared at him in the same way.

"You're right." Shiva nodded back in agreement. "Guidance and nav look right on. We're set up just as well as we can be. Everything looks by the book." Yet Shiva still squirmed, about as much as anyone could in zero gravity, for he felt anxious, even a little suspicious. Like so many others, he always felt on edge when he flew with this Rebello character. Some Commanders did everything by the book, the predictable kind. Some deviated from procedure only after significant coordination and deliberation, the prudent kind. But this Rebello guy, as competent as he was, just seemed to shoot off in random directions at random times; he was the kind who made you feel like you were standing on a perfectly firm platform—but one that, in reality, served as a trapdoor to the alligator tank. Yet each time the smoke had cleared, he also commanded your respect because he was invariably right. Ahhh yes, Rebello—thank God—one of a kind.

"Stowage rechecked, Shiva?"

"Yep, but really not much to do. You had everything nailed down pretty tight already."

Joe smiled his perceptive smile once again. "Yep, keep a tidy spacecraft and you never have to clean up."

"Fifteen seconds to sunset." Shiva squirmed.

"And about the fastest one we'll ever see. Not every day we can slip into Earth's shadow at thirty-five thousand feet per second."

". . . three . . . two . . . one . . . mark. Perfect. Right

on. Hey, this is dark, Joe, dark dark. We'll never be able to see the horizon for an attitude check at Earth interface."

"Yep, from here on we've got to put total faith in the computer and follow the instruments." Joe pushed his face against the window. In silence, the blackness of the real world absorbed his vision. His eyes tried to adjust. Still solid black. No . . . call it just dark. Well . . . maybe dark with just a little background glow . . . a soft violet glow.

Glow intensified.

"Mark! It's started, Shiva. What's the altitude?"

"Comin' down through 421,000 feet."

"Earliest I've seen it."

EMTV rammed into atoms of air like they were bowling pins and knocked them to the side. As they scattered, they smashed into their still-lethargic friends at over twenty times the speed that, at more relaxed and playful times, they would've just bounced from one another. But now each smash ripped away electrons that at once fled back to naked atoms, cascaded down through energy levels to where they liked to rest, and, as they did, squibbed out photons of light. Stingy samples of light entered the eyes of the observers at the core of the glow.

EMTV descended.

Air thickened.

Light intensified.

Joe's vision returned to EMTV's displays. His eye swept across numbers and diagrams created by the computer on the single display panel that stretched across the space before them. A single green dot illuminated on a plot of acceleration versus height, the traditional ".05 G how-goes-it light" that indicated a drag of one twentieth of normal gravity on the spacecraft, an indication that helped keep astronauts busy since the beginning of manned reentries almost eighty-years before. "There's .05 G at a minute and 37 after 400 K, Shiva. Again, right on the money."

Not only astronauts noticed .05 G. Enriched Software promptly awoke, divided the measured deceleration by 1.7 everywhere it appeared within the computer, reset its alarm for another twenty minutes, and dozed off again.

Joe noticed the .05 G light go out, then come on again. Strange, he thought, it's never done that before—and it shouldn't. His firm, stable couch reached up, absorbed, and gripped his body as he looked over at Shiva's face pressed against the window, a face sheathed in a violet glow. "Did you see the .05 G light go out, then come on again, Shiva?"

"No. Didn't. We're about to lose the Moon, Joe."

Joe's attention shifted outside again. His eyes followed a long, thin, violent flame as it swept out behind EMTV, out to the half Moon that now crept below the horizon.

In silence, flame intensified as it formed a white-hot sheath. Sheath glared as it swept around EMTV's heat shield, a glare filled with electrons that blocked the flow of all communication and navigation signals, a glare that continued to fly back and away from Joe without sound or vibration.

Glare intensified as it flowed out to a point, out to a distant apex where it ended in a gold-white fireball that burned like the Sun through a layer of haze.

Burn intensified as it filled in the sheath with shades of green and blue and violet and displayed a core that turned orange-white as it blazed and lengthened.

Blaze intensified as it . . .

Joe's mind snapped back inside his spacecraft. "Shiva, have you seen any roll jets fire?"

"No, I haven't. But that's because the computer still wants lift vector down."

"It shouldn't. . . . No—it shouldn't!" Acceleration riveted Joe's body to his rock-solid couch. His eyes jerked inside and jumped from one display to the next. "We can't still be going that fast, can't still be that high. Shiva, it feels like we're pullin' five G, but it shows less than three. Something's wrong!"

"I feel that way too, Joe, but we have to follow the computer. We've got no other reliable reference. We're in communications blackout. We can't get any readings from either the ground or a nav satellite."

"But we've got ourselves. I've never been through one like this. We started out right on the money and now . . ." Joe sneered. "Shiva, screw the computer. I'm goin' lift vector up!" He pushed the rotation controller to the left. EMTV started a crisp roll.

"Joe, are you trying to kill us?!"

EMTV completed its roll over onto its belly, lift vector up. Joe released the controller.

Computer took command again and, with crisp precision,

flipped EMTV over onto its back. EMTV dug into the atmosphere harder than before.

"Joe, do what the computer says!"

Joe snarled. "No way!" He grabbed the controller and rolled EMTV back onto its belly. "Damn computer's trying to kill us!" He slapped the FLIGHT CONTROL switch from AUTO to MANUAL and EMTV remained on its belly. Joe then seized Shiva's wrist with both hands as he reached for the controller. "Trust me."

"Joe, if we've learned one rule it's trust the computer, not your gut."

"Every rule's gotta be broken at least once."

"But, Joe . . . ?!"

"Trust me!"

In time, EMTV started its slide back out of the atmosphere. Descent slowed, then reversed. Couch loosened its grip. Blaze faded back to burn. . . . Glare. . . . Flame. . . . Glow. . . . Sun lifted above the horizon. Glow vanished.

Shiva's eyes bulged as he gawked at the panel. "Joe, we really *are* in trouble. Computer says we're still going 28,800 feet per second. Way too fast like I said. We'll never make it to Von Braun—we're headed out again!"

"Hold on, let's see what Houston says."

"EMTV-3, Houston."

"Go, Houston."

"Joe, our tracking shows your inertial velocity at 23,607 feet per second. You're too slow. You're going to drop in. Burn posigrade!"

Shiva's eyes and mouth gaped farther open.

Joe flipped the engine control switch to MANUAL, pointed EMTV along its direction of flight, and punched the MAIN ENGINE—ON button.

Engine lit.

"Shiva, get a fix from Navsat."

Shiva, shaken and confused, changed EMTV's navigation sensors. EMTV accepted signals from the network of navigation satellites in orbit around Earth and recalculated its velocity.

"Got it, Joe." Shiva's eyes narrowed. His voice squeaked. "Says we're down at twenty-four thousand feet per second and increasing. How could . . ."

Joe continued EMTV's engine burn until Navsat indicated

that they'd reached 25,600 feet per second, enough speed to
remain in orbit.

"EMTV-3, Houston."

"Go ahead."

"Joe, we don't know where you got all the extra gas, but it's
good you had it. We show you with just enough propellant left
to rendezvous with Von Braun."

Joe winked at Shiva. "Right, Houston. We had it all
carefully planned since we started."

"Then how'd you blow the aerobraking?"

"We have to blame that one on the computer. That digital
devil really tried to stick it to us. When we get back, every bit
and byte's gotta be checked, along with Dieter's Jet Pack.
Houston, I may be paranoid—but I also know that someone's
out to get us!"

Within computer's logic, a silent alarm sounded. Enriched
Software awoke a second time, returned the logic it had
modified to its initial state, completely consumed itself, and
ceased to exist without a trace.

II

SUBMERGE

Sharp edges can be lethal—especially those hidden by smooth surfaces.

5

□□□

return

"One World, One People—for sure—I'm going to make it happen!"

Otto glanced at the frail body that spit out its words, at the flimsy flesh slumped in the black leather couch contoured to its slouch. An emotion, akin to a son's love for his father, erupted again, mellowed and mingled with other feelings of respect and appreciation, feelings that had dominated Otto's earliest memories, feelings that had strengthened and matured over the years with his mind and body.

Otto respected and appreciated Wolf for his intelligence, his leadership, and, most of all, his ability to focus and direct his energy and aggression like that of a laser to accomplish whatever the situation demanded, yes—whatever the situation demanded. Otto also appreciated that he, unlike any other creature alive, would never become a victim of that directed laser energy.

At this instant, the laser's intensity focused on The Plan depicted in a multicolored, three-dimensional hologram that hung in the center of the Program Control Room. Black pebbles in yellow slits darted over three-dimensional lines, dates, and logic. In a few scans, data flooded to brain. Able to give just superficial justice to data, lips only muttered. "Conception . . . Evolution . . . Verification. . . ." Brain reviewed, comprehended, and reanalyzed The Plan's integrated scope and all its details. ". . . Recognition . . . Reproduction . . . Domination . . . Elimination. . . ." Brain scrutinized each milestone, each time-phased logic network, each interconnection of events, then one dense red line that twisted and turned through colored space, that one critical path that snaked its way to the end result. ". . . Perfection!"

Wolf's facial fur parted to let a smile escape. "No, I have no single point failures. And only twenty-three days left to the start of the Reproduction Phase." His smile broadened as he traced over the lines with the laser pointer in his left hand; BioProbe twirled around the fingers of his right at an accelerated pace. "At 1830 on the thirteenth, I will leave for my Prime Laboratory. Then finally, on September first, I will initiate Phase Five!" His gaze snapped to Otto, sauntered its way down his body, then labored its way back up to his face. His fur flexed again. "Otto, I promise you, on that day and from that day forward, you, especially you, will be fulfilled."

"Yes, sir. I appreciate all that I will become, all that—"

The Display Controller in Wolf's hand buzzed, and in small green numbers, "20" winked at the top left of the empty wall screen. He punched COMMUNICATION, ACTIVATE, 20, ENTER into the Controller and a familiar face of gloom diffused onto the screen. Wolf stiffened, dragged himself erect, and glared at the face.

"Hello, sir. This is Kurt in Houston. The excisions of Dietrich and Rebello have not been successful."

For the second time in three days, Wolf's shoulders reached up and swallowed his narrow neck up to the apex of his inverted fur cone face. Shoulders and arms shook as fingers dug into the black leather arms of his chair. Patches of pallid skin on his forehead and that surrounding the dark circles split by yellow slits turned a shade of crimson that Otto had rarely seen before. "I failed again?!"

"Yes, sir. And again the problem was Rebello."

Wolf quivered tightly, then vaulted from his couch and half slinked, half hobbled toward the screen. "Rebello?!"

"Yes, sir. He ignored the computer's directions, flew by the seat of his pants, and did not reenter like you planned. He also had a full load of propellant on EMTV, something else we did not anticipate. He is about to complete the rendezvous with Von Braun and will return with Dieter Dietrich on the next shuttle in seven hours."

With feet apart and hands clenched, Wolf's rigid body vibrated and shook as it tried to rid itself of its rage. As he glared at the floor-to-ceiling head on the screen but one step away, his lips fluttered but issued no sound. Head and Otto froze and waited as Wolf clenched his yellow slits, stretched his neck out of its shell, then slunk back to his couch where he gasped in a few shallow breaths and slumped into a loose pile of flesh and fur. Yellow slits fluttered and blinked for ten seconds before Wolf could speak. "Once they're back on Earth, it will be much more difficult to excise them without creating additional suspicion. And yet, I cannot allow them to spread their suspicions to others. All this could begin to snowball." Wolf nibbled on the mat of gray fur on the back of his hand. "I have two courses of action. First, Kurt, you are to remain ready as we monitor Dieter Dietrich, and if he knows anything about Phase Five, you will be called upon to excise him in a manner that arouses no suspicion when the first opportunity presents itself."

Wall screen spoke. "Yes, sir. But down here we will have to be more direct."

Wolf shook his head. "We cannot afford to do anything that inflames additional suspicion. If excision is required, we shall discuss the operation."

"Yes, sir."

"Second, Otto, you will return to WSF as our LB-13 Coordinator in Houston, a position I created and have used before. There you are to monitor Joe Rebello and Dieter Dietrich closely, determine how much they really know, who, if anyone, they have influenced, and how this influence can be negated. Also, notify me if excision is required."

Otto braced at attention and squinted down at Wolf. "Yes, sir, but will I not lead the delivery as promised?"

"Yes, those are the current plans. Although, if required, another could be . . . ahhh . . . inserted into your slot." As if projected by an isolated frame of film, a cringe flicked on and off Otto's face that Wolf appeared not to notice. "But it is still best not to change my plans this late in the game. Otto, you will lead the delivery as promised."

"Good. But sir, will we not have an immediate problem as

soon as Rebello returns and passes his suspicions on to others in WSF?"

"Only if he is believed. And I am confident that until he has further evidence, no one will take him seriously enough to cause us a problem. Our informants tell us that Rebello, even though he is a Commander, has little influence. That is, he is largely ignored because he appears to be the exact opposite of you."

"Oh? In what way, sir?"

"They say that he's a real nonconformist, a maverick who just can't accept existing rules nor seek his reward within the system. He has to be noticed by being different rather than, like you, Otto, achieving perfection. As Kurt mentioned, he flies by the seat of his pants, relies on his instinct rather than the real strengths developed by the system. He is the exact opposite of you, Otto, emotional and unpredictable."

"It sounds like he's lucky to have survived as long as he has. But he must have enough self-discipline to perform his job."

Wolf scoffed. "Discipline? It's got to be all luck." He looked to the screen. "Kurt, I will be waiting for your call." Wolf finessed his Controller and face faded as he turned to Otto. "Likewise. Keep me informed."

Otto nodded. "Yes, sir."

"Are you about to leave?"

"Yes, except that I plan to visit Anna first, sir."

Facial fur flexed upward and held position as Wolf's eyes widened. "Yes, Otto, go see Anna." He beamed and his voice softened. "Yes . . . please do." Wolf blinked several times again as if to clear his thoughts. "I shall see you at my laboratory on the twenty-sixth."

"Yes, sir." In one smooth motion, Otto swiveled, accelerated, and glided toward the exit. "I'll see you then."

Wolf, his yellow slits wide again with anticipation, his mind consumed with vicarious pleasure, followed the fluid flesh of his surrogate as it disappeared through the door.

Like froth, questions bubbled up toward the top, toward the light. Answers sank.

In silence, Dieter unbuckled his restraints, pushed out of his couch, and floated forward toward the dim light of the instrument panel. His head stopped at the midpoint between the two crewmen at EMTV's controls. He turned to the Commander. "Hey, Joe. I've been thinking."

Joe jerked his head around toward the voice and found himself nose to nose with Dieter. "Damn! Don't scare me like that. I've got a weak heart."

"Since our reentry problem was caused by a computer malfunction, maybe my Jet Pack problem was also due to a computer failure. We oughtta look for that type of commonality in the two incidents."

"You're right, Dieter. As soon as we get to Von Braun, we'll have the computer memories in our EMTV as well as your Jet Pack dumped onto a light disk, then down to ground. Back in Houston, they can compare every shred of logic and data with the original programs in their Operations CT 7000. Discompares will pop out in milliseconds."

Shiva's voice came around Dieter's head. "But if the computers caused the problems, how could they have failed?"

"The answer I have to that one, Shiva, is the same that I have to what happened to Yuri—zippo. Don't have a clue." An image, unseen eyes buried in the depths of dark voids, surged up, bounced off the bottom of Joe's awareness, then sank back down . . . yet enough seeped through. "But one thing off nominal I did notice was a tech in the Logistics Module about the time you had your problem, Dieter. There was no reason for him to be there, and he had his PIP in the Command Mode. Probably just a coincidence, but I'll check him out when we get to Houston."

"I wonder if anybody will take us seriously when we get back," said Dieter.

"Might be hard," said Joe. "If the world is sure of one thing, it's that computers are reliable—it's the Rebellos that screw things up."

Neither Dieter nor Shiva chose to argue.

Above the lights of the instrument panel, out the single-piece window and out ahead of EMTV to the east, Glow, a soft blue, intensified and competed for their attention. Glow marshaled red flanks and dispersed them across the horizon. Then Glow strengthened, pushed bands of yellow and white above it, and strengthened again. Layers of blue and violet spread over the others and they all strengthened together, all drawing their life from Glow. On schedule, Glow exploded into the white light of Sun.

"Sunrise, troops. Let's dock with Von Braun and get back on the ground."

"I'm ready for that, Joe." Dieter's head withdrew into the rear cabin.

Joe pressed his external communications control. "Hello, Von Braun. This is EMTV-3 callin' from fourteen out for terminal phase and dock."

"Roger, EMTV-3," Von Braun's controller spit out in precise staccato. "We have you loud and clear. How do you read? Over."

Joe winced and shook his head. Of all the controllers in the whole WSF inventory, why do I always end up with this guy? Regulations *über alles*. Sounds like a machine gun. And he always loves to fire in that final "over" bullet just for good measure. "Roger, Von Braun, I have you loud and clear also."

"Good. Now let us not have the same communications problem you had with Unity. Over."

"Rog."

"We show you 13.3 miles out and 0.07 miles left of centerline, 0.09 miles high and 4.1 feet per second fast. Please switch control to auto immediately and remain on the standard approach. Over."

Joe's eyes glazed over as he flipped the CONTROL MODE switch from MANUAL to AUTO. "You got it, Von Braun." His body loosened and turned inert as he sighed, "Yep, Shiva, I think we're back home."

Gratitude, he often felt it, and now it drove him on the one last task he'd assigned himself before he left for the airfield.

As he entered the Project Control Room, he inspected the frail figure of Wolf exhausted and in a deep sleep in his contoured couch. He smiled. Yes, almost invisible, but there it is—Wolf's clear BioProbe about to slip from his fingers. If he wakes up and can't find it, he'd only go into another rage. Why not spare him that? He removed the BioProbe and placed it in the exact center of Wolf's desk, unfolded a blanket and tucked it around the flimsy flesh.

He turned. Gratitude dissolved and duty returned. Otto's face hardened as he charged the door.

6

□□□

relive

A goose among eagles, American Airlines's flight 1370 lumbered down toward the ancient Houston airfield.

Compared to American's ram-turbo airliners, this antiquated Boeing 977 howled and whistled, bumped and buffeted its way toward the ground. It didn't cut and slice, or slip and streak through the air; it strained, it struggled against the invisible wall even as the hand of gravity pulled it along.

Built before the turn of the century and adequate in its day, the 977 took abuse only because it couldn't conform to the standards of the modern crop of Mach three airliners from Boeing, Fokker, and International Aircraft. Its bulky body restricted it to speeds below Mach one and to altitudes below forty thousand feet. Moreover, today its low performance won it a conspicuous and final indignity—denial of landing at the Houston-Galveston Air Complex, the facility at Alvin reserved for medium- and high-performance aircraft. Instead, as if it were only just another local, low-performance leper, regulations segregated it to Hobby Field, a facility threatened with closure year after year, decade after decade, but which clung on to life through a continuous string of minimum upgrades.

The 977 deviated three degrees east of course to wedge

between two thunderstorms. Although not yet ten A.M., the two isolated cells surged above thirty-seven thousand feet. As 977's central computer activated its passenger restraint system, Joe's belt cinched tighter and stirred him from a light sleep. He squinted out his window into the sunlight reflected from the two ivory columns of clouds. Like doormen, they glided forward to welcome him home, then slipped by. Just your standard Gulf thunderstorms, he thought. Not much different than all the other cells on all the other days—slow learners—a little like all of us. Just like its parents, each one boils up, deluges cool water down, then fades as it watches its life's harvest steam back up, form cells just like itself, and try again.

Through the window, Joe sensed the humid heaviness of the Gulf air, sensed that invisible fluid that sniffed out and water-coated every human haven of refrigeration, smothered the city with lethargic tranquillity, enveloped it with a mood that never flinched though poked and prodded by thunder and lightning or even hurricane's threat.

Joe could feel it, his mind could taste it, even through the window, and he relished it—Mood—Houston's Mood, the Mood of Gracious Old South who preserved her identity, her individuality even while she remained a tolerant hostess to the bluster of every upstart generation, even while she indulged every new kid on the block as he boasted and bragged about his own unique triumphs, technologies, and toys.

To Joe, Mood seemed to have a unique instinct to seize the best of the new, yet cling ever tighter to the best of the old—cling to the hearts, hands, and lips that still created Dixieland a wall away from computers that conducted electronic horns and strings; cling to the worn wood and cracked plaster of ancient taverns that still vibrated with country and western though buried amid the city's hardness of steel and plexan; cling to the walls of rich red brick, soft and crumbling, that still furnished shelter though shadowed by sturdy graphite composites and dwarfed by invincible domes of transparent plexan; cling to open fields where polished silver rods still nodded down and lifted oil only twenty miles from the bright spinning shafts of nuclear power.

His eye scanned the streets of the inner city that had taught him early lessons in survival, structures that had provided the orphan shelter throughout his teenage years. He knew that Houston's unique Mood came not from metal and plexan and pavement—but from its people; from strangers who, in the time it took an elevator to drop a few floors, joked and laughed together as friends; from Lieutenants in three-piece pin-striped suits and their bosses, the Generals in open western shirts and boots, the guys with the bucks; from leaders and laborers of industry who, decade after decade, hammered on failure with guts and tenacity until it surrendered success.

Joe stretched and flexed his muscles. Energy and excitement seemed to flow from Mood—that same energy and excitement that had driven the three prongs of Houston's growth: world's largest complex for cancer diagnostics, treatment, and research; a world focus for petroleum and nuclear energy development; and World Space Federation's Center for Mission Operations.

Oh, God, he loved it, this town, and he hated it.

As the 977 continued on its gradual descent and shallow turn, Joe's eye crossed homes and harbors, canals and creeks . . . creeks. His pulse quickened. No, he wouldn't look at it this time. It wouldn't do any good. Never did. But it was there, somewhere along that creek, somewhere upstream. His eye raced ahead, his mind pulled back. Eye won. That's it—the Spot.

Joe slumped back, closed his eyes, and tried to close his mind.

Doesn't look much like it did then. Now all concrete and superstructure, not wood and rod like it was . . . like it was when . . . Joe forced his mind to something else, anything else. A sunrise, yeah, a space sunrise, all those layered colors, those . . . *No!* Yet it came back, that memory, that dream, it came back right in the middle of the damned day. Don't need it, don't want it, don't . . .

Seven is a great age for a boy—old enough to explore all the world he could know yet young enough to be fascinated by it all. And today, July 3, 2009, on Joey's seventh birthday, the technology of his exploration had taken a quantum leap—a bike! Joey turned and looked again at his present snuggled in the backseat of their car, at those narrow tires that promised speed, at that bright blue and white plexan paint as hard as the carbon frame underneath, at the stripes of red trim that made it look like it was going a hundred miles an hour just sitting there.

Joey looked back up at his dad. "Thanks again, Dad. I love it!"

Dad turned toward Joey but said nothing. He didn't have to. His eyes said it all. They always did. Pride, happiness, of course love, but also like, for they just plain liked one another, father and son, no matter what they did together. Dad leaned over, looked down, squeezed Joey's knee, and smiled. His eyes spoke and Joey warmed. Then Dad looked back at the road as the traffic accelerated. "Where do you want to go with it first?"

"I wanta show Boone and Pete and Tucker, and then go riding with 'em."

"Where to?"

"Wherever they wanta go."

"But where do *you* want to go?"

"Ahhh . . . to Clover Field to look at the planes. But the other guys said it was too far and they don't care about planes and they—"

"Then do it yourself."

"Myself?"

Traffic stopped.

Dad looked at Joey again as he did when he wanted to make a point. "Yourself, little guy, don't be afraid to be different. Especially if you got a good reason. And wanting to go see airplanes is about as good a reason as I know of."

Think of it. His dad was not only going to let him pedal to the ends of the earth just to explore, but he was actually telling him to do it. "Okay. I'll go!"

"But I'll make you a deal."

"What?"

"Wait till next Saturday and I'll go with you."

"Together? Neat! We can pack a lunch and . . . hey, Dad, why not go today?"

"No, still too much water. Many of the roads are still too wet."

"Oh, yeah." Joey looked out the window at the water that shimmered in the grass and the residue that still steamed off the road. Just another one of those hot, muggy, sweaty summer days, a day when their air-conditioned car provided only temporary relief. It had rained for three days, and with all that new building upstream, they said, there was way more runoff than in the past, runoff that now all came together and flooded the creek far above normal. It always flooded every few years, but not like this, though Joey was too young to remember the last time it did happen in order to compare. He looked ahead and to the right at the creek as it edged closer to the road. Murky brown water swirled and lapped at its banks. Never seen it like this. It's just like a real river!

"But next Saturday we can . . ."

Joey sensed urgency in words not said, in the screech of tires. He looked forward just as the back end of a car popped up in the air, then disappeared two cars ahead . . .

. . . then the one in front screeched to a stop—almost . . . before it too flipped its tail up in the air and disappeared.

. . . and their car? Yeah . . . they stopped—right at the edge!

For two long seconds Joey stared at the surface of the brown water only twenty feet from his face, at the swift surface that rolled and roiled under the bright noon Sun, at that surface that churned and boiled as it rushed by with the strength of some special urgency. Then the motion of the bridge caught his eye as it pulled farther away from the bank and started to roll. It looked like it too would drift downstream.

"Joey, they need help! One followed the next, right off the edge, just like lemmings. Let's get—"

Just a nudge, not much of a bump, not even much of a screech, but the car behind didn't quite stop—until it hit them.

Front dropped. They dropped. Water smashed into their windshield. Seat restraints jerked. Light faded. Brown water and bubbles slid by windows. They drifted with the stream. Joey felt strong hands rip at his restraint . . . push him up . . . up? . . . up into the rear seat with his bike.

—Whomp!—

Hit something. They stopped. Coldness seeped over his ankles. Wet cloth and rigid muscle wrestled beside him. Dim light provided only the outline of Dad.

"Door's stuck. Gotta get out the window, but it's stuck too." Dad's voice sounded strong, confident. Joey knew everything would be okay. "Ughhh. . . ." Dad broke off the mirror and its support from his bike's handlebars, jammed it between metal and glass, twisted and pried, and opened up just a slit.

As a sheet, water poured in. Wet cold sloshed upward around his waist.

"Ughhh. . . . Won't budge!"

Dad's hands grabbed Joey's fingers and pushed them into slit.

"Help me. Pull hard!"

Joey pulled. Slit opened. Water rushed.

Coldness lapped against his chest.

"Joey." Dad's firm hands gripped his shoulders. "Don't be scared. Take a deep breath and pull harder. We'll have you outta here in no time."

Joey took a deep breath.

"Now!"

Joey pulled and strained and bit his tongue and . . .

Window moved.

Coldness splashed over his shoulders and chin.

He held his breath and pulled and pulled and . . .

Window continued to slide.

A layer of wetness slid over his mouth and nose and eyes. Joey pulled and pulled and . . . *No space, no air, Dad— we're gonna drown!*

Rigid hands, determined hands, grabbed his waist and pushed him through the opening . . . pushed out his head . . . shoulders . . . waist . . . feet. . . .

Joey kicked and rose with the bubbles.

Air! Sunlight!

He gulped in water and coughed.

"Dad?"

Nothing but water, water so strong and swift, water so brown and muddy, water that rushed and swirled, water that . . .

"Dad!"

Joe felt water surge in his eyes, his hands wring the arms of his airline seat. For me—he did it for me. I never should've left him. Never should've gone first. Relax. Can't go back and do it over. Damn dream. Wish it were only that.

Mom seemed to take the funeral all right, but after that she just never seemed to stop crying. And there was only so much I could do, or say, or . . . Hell, what's a seven-year-old kid know or understand anyway. Like that damn water, her sorrow kept flowing, just kept covering and smothering until it snuffed ut her will to live. Took less than a year for the pneumonia to inish off what grief had started.

Damnit! That was *my dad* and *my mom* and they had no ight to kill them . . . the damn lemmings. Lemmings, that's vhat they were all right. Joey hadn't known what Dad meant vhen he said it, but he looked it up right after the funeral: emming—a small rodent that, when his identical brothers and sisters become large in number, can engage in a mass march and feel compelled to follow those in front, compelled even as hey crowd off the coast, surge into the sea—and drown.

Joe glanced out the window again. A string of identical glass buildings that paralleled a freeway with its monorail system running down its spine had replaced the Spot. Then came endless apartments and blacktop as the 977 rolled out level on final approach. Joe squeezed the moisture from his eyes. The streets—hell of a place for a kid to grow up. But I can't hold it against Aunt Anita. Lucky she did anything at all.

In fact, Joey knew it from the first day, Aunt Anita never really wanted him. Putting meals on her own table was hard enough. She certainly didn't need the little food furnace around to enhance her quality of life. Marriage, children, and money had all eluded her and fifty-three years of age was too old to change any of her ways. But after her younger sister died, she felt a short spurt of duty, mixed with just a twinge of pity, when the court laid it in her lap. "Mam, we ain't got but two options. You take 'em or he goes to the orphanage." She hesitated, gave in, then wished she hadn't. He demanded food, clothes, space, time, and attention. As he soon learned, she could scare up neither money, energy, nor patience for any of it.

—Click—

Just a single key turning in a single lock, but the sound resounded in his mind day after day, month after month, for it set the tone of his life for years to come.

At the end of the fourth evening with Aunt Anita, he lay on his bed and stared up into blackness. No blanket, too hot for even sheets, he in only his skivies lay flat on the mattress immersed in the rank foulness of its odors, the mattress she had him haul over from the house two doors down after she screamed enough to make the man, the one embedded in the fort of empty bottles, give it up. He felt strangely detached, like he was an external observer of himself. His emotions had been wrung and squeezed and extruded over the past thirteen months and there seemed to be no residue remaining. Nothing left to do but coolly observe what the world had in store for him and try to react. Maybe he'd taken his cue from Aunt Anita herself for she treated him the same—cold and aloof—as if he were just another obstacle in her life to be circumvented like a salesman or electric bill. But Joey sensed that her emotions toward everything had died and withered many years before; his, he knew, he could put into deep freeze temporarily. He listened to her footsteps approach the door, a pause, a long pause that seemed to scream with the intensity of her thought, then the key turn in the lock. His body stiffened with the click, the sound resonated in his skull, its meaning clear in his mind.

She'd made her decision on how to best deal with her new problem.

From there on all he could count on from Aunt Anita was minimal: a bed, four walls, a roof, a door to the outside, a school district, and an occasional leftover, although Aunt Anita ate like a bird and the scraps rarely added up to a full bite, when he could get to them. Everything else would be up to him. Strange, he didn't panic. In a sense, he welcomed it. Freedom. If he couldn't have his own dad and his own mom, he didn't want anyone else telling him what to do. Yet the streets were no place for an eight-year-old to grow up, but grow up he had to. Fast.

Survival necked down to one essential. Money. Whatever the necessity—jeans, a pizza, tires for the bike they'd pulled from the car (along with Dad), pretzels, sneakers, donuts, a bike lock, an enchilada—they all required money. To an industrious kid with his back to the wall, it seemed not all that complicated. He just looked at what was in front of him in Southeast Houston: cars, boats, airplanes, shoes, doorknobs, and, oh, God, let me at it, just any other man-made object. No matter. If it was dirty, clean it. If it was clean, polish it. Initially, his hit rate was low, but he made up for it with hustle. In time he built up regulars who appreciated eagerness, effort, and honesty, virtues he took pride in, virtues that came from Dad. And as he reflected back on it, Houston, all in all, was not a bad place with all its people, all its friendly people. Lucky. A kid doing what he was doing in other cities could've gotten killed.

Swipe a radio? Pocket some loose change? Pop some

drugs? Sure, all easy to do. But he didn't, for his mind still felt the hands that'd pushed him out the car window. No, Dad didn't give his life up for any of that. There had to be something better, something more important, something higher, something. . . .

Months turned to years, street hustling turned to permanent jobs, and challenge turned to boredom. Hell, he'd proven to himself many times over that there was but one thing on Earth he needed to survive—himself. For the kid who forced himself to mature years before his time, school seemed infantile, its social life inane. Other than football and track, life bored him out of his always-hustling-for-a-buck mind. No, nothing left to do, and in the middle of his junior year of high school, he did it.

Joe quit and joined the Marines.

Inferior, but he studied it.

Otto watched the scenery glide underneath as Lufthansa's Fokker RT-37 turned back on course and sliced down toward Alvin's white ribbon of concrete. He felt in harmony with RT-37's precision, an identification with this rigid lance that pierced forward without sound or vibration. RT-37 banked, not a big bank, yet the pilots in the cockpit up front noticed it on their instruments—Otto felt it, a two-degree left bank; the pilots up front read their location—Otto glanced outside and sensed it, 120 miles out on a straight-in approach to runway 17 and a descent through 60,000 feet. No, not a single thing left to do, he thought, nothing but stab RT-37 right down into Houston's soft belly like a spear.

He continued to gaze at the world below as he again sensed glimpses from his left. Glimpses? Well no, actually stares came once again from the dark-haired woman who'd tried to make conversation with him throughout the flight. Her rich brown eyes probed him, seemed to devour him, and demanded he give her recognition. For an instant, he did. No, hasn't changed. Young with vigor, yet aged with experience. Elegant and sophisticated, yet sensuous and sexy. She turned her face toward him and smiled. The tip of her tongue traced over full lips. Yes, there's that same flaw. Her nose. Turned just a little to the left. An imperfection on a scale much greater than Wolf would ever tolerate, and certainly far greater than any of Anna's.

Yes, Anna. Perfection.

Otto sat back and closed his eyes as a murmur, The MurMur, came again like a muted scream at the back of his mind. It rose up, hovered, cried out to him in its near silence, then faded again like it always had.

But no matter, for his memory of Anna returned. He'd left her but seven hours before, and her perfume, her scent, still lingered, still triggered her image that now flooded back sharp and clear. His mind's eye studied it, savored it.

Yes, Anna, a beautiful woman, a desirable woman—perfect.

As always, she'd drawn him in with those sultry blue eyes, that sharp, hard, ice-blue that pierced out from half-closed lids, those eyes that screamed with her own special needs and hunger, yet pleaded with her own intense desire to please. As always, her smile welcomed him, warmed him, and it animated her face, her delicate and precisely symmetrical face, her superior face, her perfect face. And, as always, her slender and supple body moved toward him with that familiar effortless flow, that flow in perfect harmony with her vibrant animal sensations and strength.

Yes, Anna displayed not a single defect—perfect.

Blond hair folded forward around the graceful lines of her neck and shoulders, urged his eyes down to the sensual swell of full breasts . . . sleek surfaces of a satiny midriff . . . flair of smooth hips . . . fluid lines of long, slender legs.

Yes, Anna's every line, every curve, every surface, excited him—perfect.

On time, it all unfolded with precision, as it always did. Attraction swelled to desire. Soft whispers strengthened to gutteral purrs. Soft pecks and nibbles intensified to hot kisses and gnarls.

On time, caresses and fondling escalated to passion and lust; hugs and presses, to thrusts and strokes. Every sight and sound, every aroma and movement, as if choreographed, detonated psychic stimulations that flowed from mental images, exploded physical sensations that flooded from nerve endings.

And, on time, they met each other's every thrust and flexed and writhed with a strength and skill dedicated to heightening the explosions of fire in their loins, explosions they called forth with exactly the right movements at exactly the right times.

No, it couldn't have been better. The optimum could never be surpassed—perfect!

Otto sought to retrace his memory of Anna even as it faded, to relive those perfect moments a second time, but something rung hollow, something hung empty at the back of his mind—MurMur. It came again, without warning, without invitation, without reason. Suspended for but a few pulses of time, MurMur stayed its distance and screamed, yet resisted recognition. Then, just as quickly as it had come, it drifted back below Otto's threshold before he could really hear it or see it or feel it or grab it—MurMur—now a part of him, a part he'd come to accept without question.

The woman to his left sensed him stir and touched his arm. He looked at her once more. No, that nose, that imperfection. He wrenched his body around to the right and focused again on the outside world, looked down at modern buildings that spiked up through ruins of yesteryear to blanket them with their midmorning shadows, peered down through domes of plexan at graphite composites that stood sturdy amid the crumblings of brick and plaster. He tried to make sense of it. Yes, the weak need their security blankets, their physical ties with the past. He felt the sudden onset of RT-37's flare, just a slight nod up in pitch, and its touchdown, one wheel just before the other. The pilot must have been egotistical enough to land it manually. It showed. A twinge of sympathy forced a frown—all these imperfect people and their imperfect world.

Soon, very soon, thanks to Wolf, all this will start to change.

Little legs pumped. Arms flailed. Body sprung. "Daddy!"

Joe's face exploded into a smile as he bent down and caught the tiny torso in midair. "Hi, Ricky. How's my little guy?!"

Ricky beat Joe's chest with his palms and laughed with his happiness. "Ma-daddy, ma-daddy!"

Joe hugged his son—his own little human packet of pride and potential, of love and joy. "Sure did miss you, little man."

Maria, only a few steps behind, slid an arm around Joe's waist and smiled, laughed. "C'mon, Ricky, let me get in there too."

Joe's eyes and mind locked with Maria's as Ricky wriggled to the ground. It took but an instant, it rarely took more. Her kiss, though not that long, not that warm by their standards, left little doubt—we've a lot to make up, a lot to share—I'm ready. Ricky charged back in to hug a leg.

Joe chuckled. "C'mon, I wasn't gone all that long."

Maria hugged him again. "Seemed almost as long as a station tour."

"But a little more exciting. I've got a lot to tell you. Hey, Ricky, leave go for a minute. We've got to walk down and pick up my luggage."

Ricky squealed and ran out ahead. Maria took a few steps after him. "Ricky, stay with us and act like a gentleman!" She turned back to Joe. "He just loves to watch the bags come down the chute."

Joe shook his head. "Glad he loves it. I hate lines. I'll never get used to this archaic operation."

"Why'd you come in here again rather than Alvin? You could've been home seven hours ago."

Joe leaned down and scooped Ricky up in one arm. "Same reason as always. The bean counters in the travel office have just one criteria for every trip—lowest price. Tends to stream-line the decision process."

"I bet when they travel they don't drive all the way over here. They probably take the tube to Alvin like everybody else."

Joe reached for his wife's hand as they started the trek toward baggage claim. "For me, that's the only good thing about this airport. You know how I feel about the tube."

Maria giggled. "Do I ever. What would your buddies say if they found out you had a phobia about traveling through a simple little hole in the ground?"

He glared at his wife and laughed. "They'd better not!"

"Joe, there's a rumor that something's happened to Yuri. Is he okay?"

"He's still up there. And there's a good chance he may not be okay. . . .He may not come back." He felt her hand tighten.

"What's wrong?"

"He was in a Rover by himself and disappeared. I'll give you the full story at home."

Maria brooded for a moment, then relaxed. "Anything else

happen? Not even your Space Week CompuMag had anything
about your mission."

"A few things out of the ordinary." Her hand tightened
again. He knew she sensed anything left unsaid almost before
his mind censored it. "Ahhh . . . might take a while to
explain. I will when we're alone."

Maria stopped cold. Tension shot from her eyes. "What?!"

Joe let Ricky wriggle free and slide to the ground again.
"Just a few things out of the ordinary."

"Well, you're alive. That's a good starting point. Do you
still have a job?"

"Yeah. I didn't screw up that much."

"Too bad. At least if you got fired you wouldn't have to go
on any more missions. Is that what you're trying to tell me?
You're going on another flight? When?"

Ricky huffed once, set his face with as much grim determination as a five-year-old could muster, and jerked forward
on his father's hand.

Maria reached out for him. "Ricky!"

"Little guy's okay. Just wants to follow his own mind. And no
need to worry about another mission. Buck told me that I
probably won't pop up in the queue for some time. First they'll
fly that whole gaggle of new folks they hired back in '36. I'll be a
ground pounder for at least another year."

Maria's eyes softened. "Good. We need a real husband and
father, not a holovision image."

They started forward again and Joe laughed as he watched
Ricky skip ahead and heard his wife's reflex scream. "Ricky!
For the last time. Stay with us . . ."

Yep, good to be home.

With no visible support or push, it accelerated.

Once clear of the cabin's bay doors that split open RT-37's
belly, the passenger pod had hovered for an instant on
magnetic forces from the superconductors underneath, then
accelerated in smooth silence toward the terminal. The pod,
which contained RT-37's seats, floor, and individual luggage
compartments below, remained 27.3 seconds in the tunnel
before it emerged and glided to a stop. Nominal. Side rails slid
down and passengers stepped out. Once the seat struts and
floor panels sensed all passenger weight had been removed,

the rails rose again and the pod lifted to bring the luggage compartments to chest height. As most passengers stretched, adjusted their clothing, or fumbled with their luggage, one man reached over up-turned faces, grabbed his thirty-eight-pound suitcase in one hand, and lifted it over the humanity below. He turned, glanced across the sea of expectant faces and past its edge, then strode toward the cavern-eyed face fixed in the shadows. Otto's face remained frozen and registered not a flicker of recognition as the man stepped forward and spoke.

"Hello, Otto. You're over two minutes late."

"Yes, I know, Kurt. A plane going into Hobby interfered with our descent."

They knifed through the crowd that jammed the exit, then glided toward the tube entrance at a brisk pace over the moving sidewalk that stretched as it accelerated.

"Wolf sent me a message after you left, Otto."

"Yes?"

"If I am required here, I am to finish up by next Monday. I am needed elsewhere."

"Where?"

"He didn't say."

The sidewalk split. They remained on the right fork and continued to stride as they descended through the opening marked CLEAR LAKE. Seventeen feet below the main level, they stepped off the sidewalk and into a bullet-shaped pod just before its doors sliced closed.

"Kurt, if that's what Wolf wants, then I must make my determinations on Dietrich and Rebello and you must take any necessary actions all within the next two days."

Magnetic forces from the outside, strong, silent, and invisible, acted on the magnetic coils under the pod. The vehicle accelerated.

"Yes, that's clear, as is something else. Even Wolf now agrees."

"What?"

Kurt's jaw tightened. "This time, if I am required, I must be a little more aggressive."

7

□□□

review

The complex—WSF Mission Operations—glistened white against the surrounding green and black under the early-morning Sun.

White rocks in a matrix of white cement, a conglomerate geologists might call it, formed the skin of building after building. Offices? Sure, always plenty of those. Laboratories? Only plenty if most of the current crop of hardware had completed final tests and graduated to space. And simulators? No, never, never could there be enough simulators to keep those astronauts satisfied.

Green grass separated the buildings, a thick mat of bright, coarse Houston grass, tough enough to persuade even the strongest newcomer to discard his push mower after but a few feet into his first swath.

Black asphalt streets and parking lots, lots and lots of lots, hogged all the remaining space. To perfection, the current epoch of planners had embedded white stripes in the seas of black to promote precise placement of each and every vehicle and arrows to assure orderly flow of each and every traffic stream.

One car whipped into the lot adjacent to the building that

housed the astronauts, accelerated upstream against the arrows, wedged between a tree and the former end car of the row, and rolled to rest directly over a stripe with its two left tires buried in the grass. Its two occupants squeezed out and started to walk in different directions, one toward the walkways, one over the grass.

"Hey, Dieter, this way. We don't have time for a hike."

"Helluva fine park job there, Joe."

"Thanks."

"But maybe just a little close?"

"Naw, not this time, Hell, we didn't even have to squeeze out the sun roof."

As they approached the building's front door, they intersected the path of Norm Steerman, WSF Director of Standardization, who had proceeded at a normal pace along all the correct lines, arrows, slots, and walkways. Norm had the appearance of carrying all of WSF's problems alone on his shoulders and, as Joe once noted, "Just standing there, the poor guy looks like he's pulling four G's." Joe understood Norm, and although on the other end of the spectrum than himself, he liked and respected him.

Norm frowned as he spoke. "You guys parked a lot closer than I did. And I've got a reserved space, one I waited eighteen years to get!"

Joe grinned. "Gosh, Norm, that wasn't really necessary. All you had to do was buy a thinner car."

Norm's frown faded as they entered the building's packed elevator, then returned when Joe placed his back against the closed elevator door and flashed his wide grin into the faces of the other forward-facing riders. From his nose-to-nose position with Norm, Joe asked, "Have you seen our mission debriefing yet?"

"Yes, I've read it several times. And I've set up a meeting with Buck and yourselves in another fifty minutes." Norm's frown dropped into its bottom notch. "We're in a bind. A lot of new work's required . . . and a follow-up mission."

Joe's face also dropped. Follow-up mission? Return to Karov? "Okay, Norm. We'll be glad to tell you all we know."

The elevator glided to a stop at the third floor, opened, and disgorged half its occupants. Norm slid out. "Good. We have a lot to understand. See you soon."

Joe and Dieter remained silent until they reached the

seventh and top floor. As they stepped out, Dieter grabbed Joe's arm. "Follow-up mission? Not for me. I'm using up some leave, and Karov's not one of my favorite vacation spots."

Joe looked at Dieter in horror. "What? You'd disappoint all those lunar rocks that have been waiting billions of years for just one tiny tap of your rock hammer? Actually, Dieter, I don't care to see that place again either. Besides, Maria would have me sanded and dipped in alcohol if I volunteered."

They reached the end of the hall and the corner office. Joe glanced at the old-fashioned, government standard, central-computer-controlled, liquid-crystal name plate by the door, the kind where the occupant's name could be changed before his chair had cooled. It announced the current owner: BUCK C. BAILEY, MANAGER, ASTRONAUT OPERATIONS. As they entered the reception area, Joe again felt his sentiments split, his drives diverge. Buck, a few years Joe's junior, had been selected for the head slot, vacated by Jake Ryder, over a number of older, more experienced astronauts, as well as a few of his peers, many of whom some claimed could run Mach two over water. Yep, no doubt about it, good ole Buck baby somehow pulls off the optimum balance—pushes his profile up just enough to be noticed but not enough to be offensive, conforms just enough to be within the system but not enough to be totally confined by it. Joe grimaced. If I learned that, this could be my office: eight windows, jumbo armchairs and couch, conference table, holographic wallpaper, executive desk and chair, and, hell, even an executive wastebasket! What's wrong with me? Why don't I care about any of this crap?

"Hello, Joe, Dieter!" Buck charged out of his office past Ms. Selbemacher, his secretary, who waited to perform her official duties of introduction, and wrung their hands. "Glad you guys made it. You shaved it pretty close—twice."

Joe laughed. "No sweat, Buck. Just your standard Sunday afternoon stroll along the creek."

"Oh, yeah?" said Dieter. "Let me tell you, Buck, if it hadn't been for Joe, I wouldn't be here—twice."

"Joe would never let anything happen to you," said Buck as he winked at Dieter. "He likes you too much. . . . You're one of the few who really tries to keep him out of trouble." Buck put his arm around Joe's shoulder and beamed. "Yep, guess we put the right man on this mission." Then, as he looked Joe in the eye, his mood collapsed inward toward a tougher, more serious core. "Joe, now that we're done with all this bullshit, let's find out what really happened." He released Joe, turned, again swept past Ms. Selbemacher, as if a pass in the opposite direction would nullify the travesty of the first, and disappeared into the open spaces of his office.

Ms. Selbemacher sighed. Someday Mr. Buck C. Bailey would learn the correct way for an executive to greet guests. It shouldn't be all that hard. In fact, it's all laid out in the WSF Regulations for Office Administration, a book she kept inserting into his electronic in-file to read. It took almost two years to train one of her previous bosses—that all-time slow learner—but it looked like Mr. Buck C. Bailey, even with concentrated spoon-feeding, would soon capture the record. Who ever said astronauts were trainable?

"I've read your report and have a few questions for both of you," said Buck. "Also, Norm Steerman is coming up in another forty-five minutes. He has a lot of questions for you primarily, Joe. And I just got an Instacom from Dr. Daro's office that PRECISE has sent us another 'coordinator' to help resolve the LB-13 controversies. Could check in here at any time." Buck walked behind his desk, rustled through its top layer of loose paper skin, and extracted a single flake. "Here it is: one Otto Stark. Never heard of him. New to the flight program. Says we'll see a lot more of him. We're to extend him every possible courtesy."

"Uh-oh," said Joe. "Sounds like another baby-sitting job."

"Yeah, that last one they sent was a bit of a wimp." Buck glanced at his watch. "And, of course, Dr. Daro's gonna call in another thirteen minutes."

Joe's mind kicked into high gear at the prospect of facing Dr. Daro. He dropped into one of the eight jumbo chairs around Buck's circular conference table and let its immensity engulf him. Yes, Dr. Daro. Guy's always fair—but no less decisive than a guillotine. Every conversation's like a game of sudden death. And kickoff's only minutes away. But first things first. "Before we unload, Buck, what can you tell us about Yuri?"

"Unfortunately, not much, except that it doesn't look good. What searches could be performed in the dark haven't located him. And with the limited oxygen supply he carried, most feel there's no way he could still be alive."

Joe slumped. Yuri was a part of *my* crew, a part that might still be alive if I'd been more protective, if I'd not let him stay behind to play his hunches. Why didn't I request clearance from Personnel Logistics Control and let procedures rule? Would've made the decision simple. They've accumulated enough regulations to say no to anything. But no, there's a helluva lot more to it than that.

"I understand most of what happened," said Buck. "But I still don't understand why PRECISE's noncompliance with the WSF Standardization Requirements became such a big, unworkable issue."

"Buck, the problem was the intense motivation on both sides," said Joe. "Yuri was the man on the spot to ensure that this lunar base would come into full compliance with WSF Standards. To me, the noncompliances seemed small, things that we could've easily ignored. But they also seemed like they could've been easily brought into compliance. However, PRECISE's foreman, Nikolaos Sturdza, and his construction crew, right down to the very last one, stubbornly refused. They said their design and construction techniques were superior, actually, the best, and that we would have to yield. They plan to keep LB-13 exactly as they've built it and to build any others in the future the exact same way. They said that we would have to change our twelve other bases if we wanted standardization. So there we were, both sides pushing to make our points and not getting any closer."

"Then why did Yuri stay behind if he knew he couldn't change Sturdza's mind?"

Joe leaned forward, paused, and looked square at Buck. "We felt it, we knew it. Just as we speculated in our report, they really don't want us to accept their facility and take full occupancy quite yet because of some other activity they have going at Karov. Yuri thought that if he could find out what this other activity is, we might know how to get the standardization issues settled."

"Do you have anything concrete to justify your suspicions?"

"No. Nothing except our gut feel and offhand references to 'Phase Five' as well as the first of September that Yuri heard."

"Weak suspicions are going to be a tough sell to Dr. Daro."

Joe nodded. "Yeah, maybe even career limiting."

"No sweat there, Joe. Even though you seem to keep falling in the pot, you never fail to come up shining." Buck turned his grin away from Joe and faced Dieter. "My second question is about your Jet Pack. We've had it checked out, and every last valve, circuit, and microcomputer came out exactly as advertised. Dieter, did you notice even the slightest anomaly before you lost control?"

"No, Buck. It worked perfectly up to the time the thrusters couldn't be turned off. Full control to no control in a flash. But then, what a ride! Thought it was all over when I got to the day side and saw the mountains."

"I would've too," said Buck. "Damn near spun outta my chair watching the TV from your helmet camera." He looked squarely at Joe with a warm intensity that carried his major message. "What you did was extraordinarily brave." Then he looked down, shook his head, and laughed. "But now we have Lopez to deal with. He sent in a thirteen-page report on how you busted every reg known to mankind and then, on top of it all, you disobeyed his local authority. I can probably keep him contained this time, Joe, but I know I won't be able to the next time you give him another one of your friendly little tweaks."

"No worry there, Buck. I'm not going anywhere near Lopez for the rest of my career. But before we get off Dieter's Jet Pack, I did notice one thing a little strange during that EVA."

"Oh?"

"I spotted one of Unity's technicians alone in the dark of the Logistics Module just before Dieter lost control. And the PIP in his hand was in the COMMAND TRANSMIT mode."

"Are you sure?"

"Yep, even though he was about seven feet away, I'm positive."

"Would you recognize him again?"

"Definitely."

Buck swiveled around to his work station. After a few stabs at his keyboard, his office turned dark and a nine- by twelve-foot Matched-to-Eye Resolution Televison display illuminated on an inside wall. Like a college yearbook, the faces of Unity's crew crowded together in a computer-generated montage that filled the flat screen. Thirty-nine faces in all, but Joe didn't need to scan each one, for one stood out, one jumped out from the wall like it was an eye test for three-dimensional vision.

"Row three, column seven," said Joe.

Within three seconds, only that one face covered the wall. MERT reproduced the image exactly as the eye would see it;

its microcomputer automatically enhanced the resolution of the display to show all detail at and above the visual acuity of the human eye at their viewing distance. But unlike holovision that reproduced an object in three dimensions, MERT reproduced only a flat, two-dimensional image of the face. Yet to Joe, its eyes, or the dark halos around darker cores where they belonged, seemed to tunnel into the wall, but also to reach out, to . . . "That's him!"

Buck jabbed his keyboard again. As data diffused onto the wall, Joe started to read. "Name is Kurt Grimm. Worked for PRECISE before he joined the program three and a half years ago. This is his fourth station tour of duty. Strengths are electronics and computers. That might explain why he was in the Logistics Module."

"Right, Joe," said Buck. "He could've been there checking out some of the resupplied electronics including a PIP."

Joe frowned. "Maybe. Just the same, Buck, could you send up a query and ask him if he knows anything about Dieter's problem?"

"Sure, but don't expect much back."

"Yeah, even if he does know anything, he probably wouldn't say."

Buck continued to scan the data on the screen. "There's nothing out of the ordinary in his background, Joe, except for the one thing I noted when PRECISE submitted him for candidacy. See the last line? He has a twin that used to also be in the program who, for some strange reason, also has the same name—Kurt Grimm. Of all things, we had two identical Kurt Grimms in the program at the same time. Could only keep them straight by their USINs."

USIN. Joe hated the concept but had to accept the fact, and he even had to accept one of *them*. Since 2031, every living soul on or off the Earth had to be identified and branded by a Universal Serialized Identification Number (USIN). Thanks to the wonders of computers and the United Nations's task force for Standardized Human Reference, the system applied to all people in all countries. Joe estimated that to date, only a handful of humanity's members could've escaped its own insatiable drive to inventory and catalog itself, quite possibly just a hermit or two still cowering deep within an abandoned mine in Kentucky, or an igloo in the Arctic, or a mountain cave of Tibet, or a . . . "That's strange all right, Buck. Where's the second Kurt Grimm?"

Buck jabbed the keyboard once more. The last digit of the USIN, 313-125-28-5237, changed to an eight. All of the other data remained identical except for the bottom three lines of the display. "Look at that—an identical background except for their different tours once they joined WSF. And this Kurt Grimm went back to PRECISE three years ago just at the time we noticed them turning up the heat on their own space effort. Unfortunately, they've not forwarded any data on this activity since he left."

"Well, no doubt they're a strange pair, Buck. But so what?"

"Right, Joe. So what?" Buck checked his watch again. "Let's get to my last question before Dr. Daro calls. What actually happened with the EMTV? You said that the .05 G light came on, went off, then came back on again?"

"It did."

"Are you sure? Shiva doesn't recall it."

"Yes, I'm sure. And the whole system behaved as though it didn't properly measure our G level during reentry, as though it measured only a fraction of what we actually encountered."

"We've had that whole system checked out as well, Joe. The computer, the accelerometers, the signal processing, all of it, and just like the Jet Pack, everything functioned well within their specifications."

"I was afraid you'd say that. Buck, I know something went wrong. And we'd better find out what before we really do lose an EMTV crew."

"I'm on your side, Joe, but I can't ask for fixes to things that aren't broken."

Joe's eyes studied the table as his mind sought a second option, a more acceptable alternative.

"Guess we just have to accept it, Joe," said Dieter. "There's not much else we can do."

Joe's eyes followed the swirls of the polished wood grain on the table surface before him, the sweeping swirls of uniform luster that seemed to isolate the different, darker and uglier wood of a knothole, to segregate it, to insulate it, to protect the rest of the normal wood from its influence. "You're right, not much else we can do."

An electrical current tingled Buck's WSF Alert Ring as his

PIP squeaked a high-C pulse. He reached out to his PIP and pressed TRANSMIT. "Yes?"

Ms. Selbemacher's voice screeched back. Her shrill tones sliced into Joe's ears as she articulated each and every word. "Dr. Daro, Director of Mission Operations, is calling from WSF Headquarters in Oceanside, California. He requests that Mr. Rebello *immediately* make himself available for a holovision conference. He stressed *immediately!*"

Joe knew that the stress came more from Buck's status-minded secretary than from Dr. Daro. But as Buck set the controls, Joe stared into the blank space between the holovision cameras in front of the MERT display, clenched and unclenched his fists several times, then took a deep breath and waited.

8

□□□

encounter

Like a ramrod, even his head stood at attention.

Projected at its normal size in Buck's three-dimensional holovision, Dr. Daro's head quivered, then stabilized at eye level eleven feet in front of Joe. From square chin to thin black hair combed straight back, his face projected discipline, his own and that which he demanded of everyone he managed, everyone in WSF Mission Operations.

"Hello, Joe."

"Hello, sir."

"I have studied your Mission Report and have two comments and two requests."

"Yes, sir?"

"You demonstrated again why we have high confidence in your ability to perform under pressure. You have done well."

"Thank you, sir."

"You have also demonstrated an attitude of contempt for working within the system—an attitude that you no longer have!"

Joe studied the narrowed eyes focused on him. No, not a question, not a request, but a fact that Dr. Daro just willed into existence. "Yes, sir!"

"Now my requests. First, something covert is operating

within or around the WSF. Evidence, such as you recently encountered at Karov, indicates that PRECISE may be involved, and that the pace of this activity is accelerating. Whatever it is could be harmless, but we cannot take that chance. We must uncover it, then pass judgment. I request that by next Tuesday at 0900 CST you, Buck, and Dieter review all that you know and provide to me a recommendation on how we can obtain concrete information on this activity. As soon as I have hard data, I am prepared to initiate a formal inquiry and quite possibly more."

Joe glanced left, then right. Buck and Dieter each nodded. "Yes, sir. We will certainly do that."

"Second, you are to give your complete cooperation to Otto Stark, PRECISE's coordinator for LB-13. And, of course, stay close to him and see if he has any knowledge of the activities at Karov."

"Yes, sir. We will."

"Thank you, Joe. Good day."

Dr. Daro's head snapped to a point, then faded.

Finally, Joe exhaled. Muscles in his neck and shoulders twitched twice, then relaxed. "Not your standard pussyfoot administrator."

"Don't take it personal, Joe."

"Yeah, I know. That's just the way the guy is—one after another, he just bores through everybody like a human drill press."

"Keen insight there, Joe." Buck laughed. "But it's good that he also suspects something's up. At least we don't have to sell him on that."

"True, but now we really do have to learn what's going on, something we haven't done too well on so far. Buck, what I need is a little time to let things jell. Let's see what Norm has to say, talk to this Otto Stark character, then think it over this weekend. We'll still have lots of time to make additional inquiries and work up our specific recommendations on Monday."

"Okay, Joe. Considering how little we know and how limited our data sources are, that's probably as good a plan as any. But remember that we need to be well prepared for Dr. Daro on Tuesday. Let's hit it again first thing Monday morning. Seven-thirty?"

Joe and Dieter nodded.

Buck grinned at Joe, then Dieter. "Sounds like you guys have something hot going this weekend."

"I do," said Dieter. "I'm going to take the family on a SportSub ride. Been promising them for several years now. Wife's got it all set up with a friend of mine. We leave for the Keys first thing Sunday morning."

"Good for you, Dieter," said Joe. "You've put that off more than once. Glad you're finally doing it. Have a good time."

"Thanks. We will. And you?"

Joe chuckled as his eyes flashed. "Ohhhh. . . . Maria, the little guy, and I will probably just lay around the house all weekend and suck our thumbs."

"Joe, Buck, if you want to bring your families down for a sub ride, I can work it out. My friend is half owner of Superior SportSubs in Key West. He'll give us the ride at cost. And I'm sure we can reserve another sub, or even two, if I call him today."

Joe turned red. "Thanks, Dieter, but I really wasn't fishing for an astro-freebee."

"I know, but the invitation stands."

"Sounds tempting." Joe looked past Dieter as visions of two excited and happy faces flashed through his mind. "Okay, if Maria and Ricky are free, we'll do it. Thanks, Dieter. Maria won't like me puttin' the honey-do list off for another weekend, but I know she'll enjoy this a lot more."

"Great!" Dieter turned to Buck.

"Thanks, wish I could. But this weekend I'll be in here with Ms. Selbemacher trying to standardize our personnel data base." Buck's eyeballs took a couple of laps in their sockets before they drifted back to a vacant gaze.

Joe laughed. "Yep, always said you managers have all the fun."

Buck blanched and shook his head. "Dieter, haven't I read that those subs can dive to almost 170 feet with no special—" His alert ring tingled. "Yes?"

Ms. Selbemacher's voice stabbed into Joe's ears once again. "Dr. Bailey, Mr. Norman Steerman, Director, WSF Standardization, is here for your eight-fifteen meeting." Woman must drive Buck unstable. Guess she comes with the job.

"Send him in, please."

The door opened and Ms. Selbemacher marched forward. Behind her, Norm paused, then, after the standard officious nod from Ms. Selbemacher, he bustled in. Ms. Selbemacher uncoiled her elbow, wrist, hand, and fingers toward an open seat, issued another standard nod to Buck, then bustled out and closed the door softly behind her, but not too softly . . . firmly, but not too firmly. Joe smiled to himself. An electrifying performance. Wonder if Norm's any more here than he would be if she just zonked off at her desk.

They stood to greet Norm, then, after the standard nods, smiles, and handshakes, they sat again.

"Buck, I want to thank you for the opportunity to discuss PRECISE's noncompliances with these gentlemen so soon after they've returned. I've read their report and have a few questions and recommendations."

Joe leaned forward. "Hope we can help you, Norm. What have you got?"

"They all center on the nature of the infractions themselves. I have documented my position here." Norm handed out hard copies of an electronic memo and Joe started to read:

WSF PROPRIETARY

Date:	August 11, 2039
To:	Lawrence W. Chang, Director, WSF Lunar Base Engineering
From:	Norman W. Steerman, Director, WSF Standardization
Subject:	Noncompliance with WSF Construction Standards at LB-13

Discussions on the failure of PRECISE to comply with WSF Standardization Requirements in their construction of LB-13 were held at the construction site between 28 Jul and 3 Aug '39. The following were in attendance:

Tudor A. Cuza	- PRECISE, Director, Uniform Excellence
Dieter L. Dietrich	- WSF, Astrogeologist
Joseph Z. Rebello	- WSF, Commander, Lunar Expedition 336

Nikolaos S. Sturdza - PRECISE, LB-13 Construction Foreman
Yuri M. Strekalov   - WSF, Lunar Base Engineer

All open Items of Noncompliance (IONs) with WSF Construction Standardization Regulations LB–37–1313 (Rev. N) were reviewed at the subject discussions. These IONs, defined in detail in enclosure one, fall into the following areas:

Area	ION
Oxygen Plant	Emissions Reduction Higher Efficiency of Soil Microwave Heating Dust Filtration System Improvements
Building Materials	Enhancement of Ceramic Furnace Solar Heating Optimum Fiber Alignment in Composite Beams Total Water Elimination in Glass Manufacture An Improved Epoxy to Reduce Cement Porosity
Habitation	Exit Labyrinth Changes to Lower Radiation Regolith Cover Contouring to Lower Radiation Smaller but More Efficient Personal Space
Surface Operations	Stability Enhancement of Three-Legged Walker Increases in Mobile Miner Speed Higher Utilization of Launch/Landing Pads

Although PRECISE justifies each ION with a different technical argument, a single conflict appears to underlie them all: Do we allow PRECISE to continue to make improvements to each system that provide only slight improvements in their performance, or do we hold the design fixed and gain the full advantages of standardization across all of our lunar bases, especially in the areas of training, logistics, and crew performance? Or, more simply, has "better" now become the enemy of "good"?

T. A. Cuza stated that we should allow inclusion of all of their improvements in LB-13 and modify our other twelve bases to bring them up to the same standards, an obviously expensive and unacceptable alternative. In his written statement, displayed in enclosure two, he sums up their hard-line position. "Once a design or system is identified as inferior, it *MUST* be either upgraded or eliminated to ensure uniform perfection. We will tolerate nothing less."

It is clear that the urgent demand for a resource base on the lunar far side can only be satisfied in the near future by use of products from LB-13. Thus, we have three options:

1. Let PRECISE finish the base and purchase their products. At present, PRECISE does not favor this option and has accordingly set their pricing at exorbitant and unacceptable levels.
2. Purchase LB-13 from PRECISE, as is, and undo the modifications. The transport of equipment, materials, and personnel to the far side for these modifications creates an excessive and unacceptable cost.
3. Purchase LB-13 from PRECISE once they bring it into compliance as they originally agreed to do. Because of the unacceptable expense of the first two options, and because we should not set the precedent of allowing PRECISE to renege on their commitments, we should continue to pursue this option with our full efforts.

In pursuit of option three, Yuri Strekalov remained at LB-13 after the subject discussions in an attempt to define compromise solutions to each ION with the PRECISE engineers. In each case, he was able to define tentative but relatively simple and inexpensive modifications that seemed to meet the objectives of PRECISE's improvements and, at the same time, are acceptable to us because they could be implemented at our other bases without significant impact. However, in each case, PRECISE refused to agree to any modifications to their construction plans, which they are currently implementing at an exceptionally slow pace.

I recommend that we thoroughly debrief Yuri Strekalov upon his return, further define compromise solutions along with their justifications in much greater engineering and fiscal detail, then return to LB-13 with our proposals. To further this course of action, I request the full support of your Lunar Base Engineering Division as well as your support for the immediate formation of Lunar Expedition Mission 337.

cc: B. C. Bailey
     M. P. Daro
     D. L. Dietrich
     J. Z. Rebello

WSF PROPRIETARY

Norm's eyes probed Joe and Buck as they sped through the memo and thumbed through the enclosures. "Since this memo was written, gentlemen, I have learned that the prospects for Yuri do not look good. I am sorry and hope we are wrong."

"We all do, Norm," said Joe. "Thanks for your concern. What are your questions?"

"Before we discuss each ION, let me ask if you think it is realistic to expect that we can work out compromises with PRECISE."

"It's possible," said Joe, "but it'll sure be difficult. Without asking first, they've just gone ahead and built in their improvements. Although several of them are ingenious, they offer only small enhancements in performance. And, to me, it seemed that their obsession with uniform excellence has replaced their logic. It's like a religion to 'em."

"Then what do you think we ought to do, Joe?" asked Norm.

"Press them as hard as possible to get what changes we can, then accept the base, even if it's not too different than it is now."

Norm's head wagged back and forth. "Can't do that. WSF has placed far too much emphasis on the cost savings of standardization."

"He's right," said Buck. "We can't back off now. If the standardization program is perceived as violated, the contributions of many of our member nations will be in jeopardy."

Norm continued: "Besides, we have to set the right precedent for Mars colonization when it comes."

"Standardization seems to have become our own religion," said Joe.

Norm shrugged. "Whatever it's become, Joe, it's real and we're committed to it."

"How'd we ever let a damn contractor work us into this box anyway?" asked Buck.

"If you remember back in 2033," said Joe, "they recognized

our need for a base on the far side and started to build LB-13 on speculation long before we could get the WSF bureaucratic machinery to take any action of its own."

Norm nodded and smiled, happy to finally be in agreement with Joe. "That's right. They already had their Karov Astronomical Observatory in operation there, the one they built and now operate under a long-term contract to the East European Astronomical Consortium. It made sense that because of their local presence, they could construct LB-13 at a much lower cost than we could. That's why our member states approved the commitment."

"Just a case of being in the right place at the right time?" asked Buck.

Dieter, now with the conversation in his area, jumped in. "No, there's much more to it than that. They must've had this plan in mind way back when they chose Karov as the site for an Observatory. The Karov region has by far the highest concentration of ilmenite from which to extract oxygen on the far side. It's the optimum place for a resource base, exactly the location we finally picked once our Development Subcommittee could sell the Executive Council on the need to build."

Buck's jaw pushed outward. "Sounds like they've got us by the short hair and are now twisting to extract maximum profit. What few options we have are—" Buck's alert ring tingled again. "Yes?"

"M . . . Ma . . . Buck, Mr. . . . Mr. Stark is here," a faint voice trickled out of the intercom.

Joe's quizzical look matched the others. Sounds like Selbemacher finally shorted out. Must have uncovered a procedure to disregard all previous procedures.

The office door glided open. Ms. Selbemacher, still seated at her desk with eyes glazed and mouth open, gazed up at the flesh that filled, no, actually seemed to stretch the frame of the door.

Silence reigned. Awe demanded it.

Joe gawked. Gotta be seven feet tall. Massive shoulders, no waist. All lean muscle, no fat. Square chin. Strong face, perfect symmetry. Smooth features. Not even a pimple. Adonis squared! Yet also rugged . . . and threatening? Quick eyes. Warm . . . yet cold.

Door frame relaxed as the young man stepped toward Joe and held out his hand. "Hello, I'm Otto Stark." Low precise tones tumbled out and enveloped Joe, then rumbled away as the room struggled to digest them.

Not since childhood had Joe felt a hand encircle his own. As he offered up the little stub on the end of his arm, it seemed far too inadequate. "Hello, Otto, I'm Joe Rebello. I look forward to working with you." His eyes fused with the blue orbs that rolled downward to bite into him. He tried to read their message. Strength, lots of inner strength. But what's it directed at? Joe stepped back and watched Otto's hand swallow the other inadequate stubs in the room. Then, as rubes plucked from the outreaches of the boonies and tossed into the center of the city, they continued to ogle upward at the massive skyscraper. Joe snapped to first. "Otto, please sit down. You're right on time. We were just considering how to best resolve the discrepancies we have at LB-13."

With the precision of a foot sliding into a tight shoe, Otto inserted his frame into the jumbo chair opposite Joe's. For a moment, the lenses of his eyes locked on the paper in front of him and soundless apertures clicked. Then he reached over the table and handed the WSF proprietary memo to Joe. Norm collected the other copies.

In silence, they each tried to deal with Otto. Finally, Joe laughed. "Actually, Otto, what we were working on the hardest is what we should do this weekend."

Dieter picked up on Joe's lead. "I was just trying to talk Joe and Buck into coming on a SportSub ride."

"Buck's declined with a lame excuse about some work to do," said Joe, "but I think I'm going to take my wife and boy."

Dieter glanced back and forth at Norm and Otto. "I haven't had a chance to ask yet, Norm, but you're both welcome. It's one of those small transparent plexan subs. We're going down off the Florida Keys. They say the water's been exceptionally clear and there's a lot to see."

A wide smile consumed the lower half of Otto's face. "Thanks for the invitation." He paused.

Looks like a big happy puppy dog, thought Joe, except for his eyes.

"Yes, I'd like that very much," said Otto. "Thank you."

All eyes shifted to Norm whose face seemed to be pulling more than his standard four G's. "No thank you, Dieter. I'd like to do it, but I've got orders from my wife to seek and destroy the computer glitch in our air conditioner. It keeps flipping us between the arctic and the tropics at random."

"Sorry, Norm. Good luck." Dieter started to rise. "But I'm glad you can make it, Otto. Right now I'd really better get on it and make the arrangements before all the subs are reserved. Also, I need to spend most of today at the Lunar Mapping Display."

"I thought you were getting set to go on vacation," said Buck.

"I am, but there are some high-resolution IR scans of the Karov region at the terminator that I really should correlate with my fieldwork before I forget what I saw. It's part of our resource definition effort."

Otto's eyes flicked over to Dieter and darkened as Joe asked, "Should we take the Sunday 0800 shuttle out of Alvin to Key West?"

"Yep, that'll do it." Dieter glanced at Joe and then Otto as he stepped toward the door. "See you there about 0745?" They both nodded.

As Dieter exited, Otto started to uncoil like a large cat. "I don't want to take up any more of your time." Cat stretched upward. "I really just needed to let you know I was here." A smooth swivel swung its fluid form to a position precisely behind its chair. "Joe, Buck, Norm, I'm happy to be working with you and hope I can help solve some of the LB-13 issues." Cat glided toward the door. "I have some check-in procedures I must complete in the administrative offices before noon." Door flowed open. "Joe, I look forward to seeing you Sunday, and you, Buck and Norm, next Monday." Cat coasted by the frozen figure of Ms. Selbemacher as door frame relaxed again.

After a long pause, Buck turned to Joe. "What mold did they pull that guy from?"

Joe's unfocused eyes still gazed in the direction of the door. "Beats hell outta me." Then he turned a pensive face toward Buck. "Sure left in a helluva hurry."

9

□□□

communicate

"Oh, shit, look at the time. . . . Wife'll kill me!"

Dieter grimaced, then yawned, stretched, and leaned forward again. His fingertips pushed the joystick hard over as he studied the three-dimensional black and white satellite images of the Moon's surface that sped over the wall screen fifteen feet from his control station. Across the top of the screen, two digital readouts of the lunar latitude and longitude, each to six significant figures, displayed only a blur. He released the stick. Movement froze. Readouts froze. Dieter glanced at the numbers, then studied the screen and finessed the joystick as he mumbled to himself. "There, just north of Romanenko. . . . Numbers are nice sometimes . . . northwest of Strekalov . . . now they're just unnecessary middlemen . . . and directly east of Karov . . . guess I've come to know this area all too well . . . that puts it almost right on the Observatory. The fracture zones probably don't extend that far over there, but for completeness I should do this area too. Glad it's almost the last one. Good, I'm there. Now get the IR up. Go manual. Easier to blend. How'd it get so late? Gotta hustle. Be hit with the divorce papers before I reach the door."

In fact, Dieter had taken far longer than he intended for it was now twelve past ten, over four hours later than he had planned to finish his geologic analysis of the Karov data they'd just brought back. Three hours before he'd called his wife and said he wouldn't be much longer. Lucky for him she'd come to accept what "not much longer" could mean. Many husbands would get bolted out of the bedroom, then the house, if they kept up the "on-time performance" of Dieter Dietrich. But she understood that when his mind got locked into his work, the clock got locked out. Given some of the alternatives, this vice seemed just about acceptable.

Fingertips caressed levers. The black-and-white image faded almost to zero as a soft red image blossomed and warmed the screen with a nearly uniform pink, uniform except for a large circular spot with a single thin but intense line running straight down away from it. Dieter blinked several times as his back popped vertical.

"Holy shit, look at that!"

Pink swelled to a deep red. What's that line? Where is it? Levers moved and the original black-and-white display blended with the red and pink that now faded a notch. It's right at their Observatory and at that rille that runs south. That's gotta be a lava tube under there like the seismic data implies . . . and it's got a strong source of heat—they must've built something in it. He rubbed his eyes with both hands as if the image would change when he stopped. It didn't. "No wonder they wanted to keep us away. Observatory's literally a cover for something, something they've never disclosed. Have to document it . . . but then what? Who do I take it to?!"

Fingertips fluttered again. Black and white sharpened, red spot and red line strengthened and the scene compressed into the top two thirds of the screen. The bottom third turned blank, then started to fill with words as Dieter typed:

Location—Karov
Black and white sun angle—17.3 degrees east
Red overlay—emitted thermal IR 2.7 days before sunrise

Note the linear red feature at the center of the image. It is
    located directly under Karov rille south of the PRECISE
    Observatory and runs for 7.3 miles.

Seismic studies of the area suggest that the rille overlies a
hollow and exceptionally straight lava tube that extends at

least 13.3 miles south from the Observatory. Since the Moon is volcanically inactive, the source of the heat that gives rise to the IR emission must result from something manmade. But what?

I recommend that we confront PRECISE with this finding and, under the WSF Open Disclosure Policy permitting complete inspections of any extraterrestrial facility upon approval of a formal request, immediately initiate such a request for inspection of the Observatory and the region to the south on the upcoming return mission to Karov.

He glanced at the display once again, pushed a button marked HARD COPY, and waited for the Holographic Image Display to generate a reproduction of the screen. The machine ticked several times, its innards whirred and gurgled, then it settled down to a steady businesslike hum. Dieter leaned back and waited. Now what? Who do I show it to? Most wouldn't understand what it is, and the others wouldn't take any action.

Embers blazed—orbs of fire seared into his memory, eyes that burned with determination—flared again in Dieter's mind. Yeah, get it to Joe. He'll get results.

For Dieter, Joe had become not just a close friend over the years, but he'd also become one of the few people that he really respected, one of the few he could count on in sticky situations to step forward with the grit and guts necessary to make the right things happen. Although he'd seen the twinkle in Joe's eyes detonate and blaze many times, blazes Joe always followed up with ferocious and incessant determination, Dieter never forgot his first glimpse. This original "searing into memory ceremony" was held back in the lazy summer of 2022 while they vacationed together as foot soldiers in the UN Peace-Keeping Force along the south bank of the Guapore River, just north of Puerto Alegre, Bolivia, Joe with the US Marines, Dieter with the German Army. It started just as casual conversation during one of their midday frolics in the 108-degree warmth and humidity of the jungle. Side by side, they slogged and slipped up the slope of the riverbank enjoying the view of the right rear tread of a Bolivian tank. Along with their machine guns, grenade belts, and sweat-soaked fatigues, their thirty-seven-pound backpacks helped ram them into the mud up to their shins and thereby supply an extra measure of stability. Each time they mustered up the strength to rip a foot free, the foot hole slurped and sucked and gulped in fresh air and diesel fumes. Again the tank roared as it gunned its engine, again its treads spun, and again a wall of country-fresh muck, mire, and leeches coated their frontal surfaces.

Dieter spit out his fresh wad of mother earth first. "Joe, are you gonna re-up?"

"Reenlist? Are you shittin' me, Dieter?"

"Just thought I'd ask."

"Are you?"

"Don't know. I got another ten months to make up my mind."

"Crazy if you do."

"Why?"

"Sloggin' around in mud for another four years isn't gonna turn you into a geologist. If that's what you really want to be, get your ass out of the army and back into school. Something I finally figured out for sure—if you want to do anything, you gotta get an education first. And another thing I'm sure of now that I know you: If you really want to be a geologist, you can be the world's best."

"Maybe. . . ."

Joe grabbed Dieter's arm and yanked him around nose to nose. "Maybe nothing! If that's what you really want outta life, go make it happen. Do your own thing. The only person stopping you is you!"

Dieter stared into Joe's eyes, eyes that blazed his message even more fiercely than his words. "Thanks for the confidence, Joe. You're about the only one who's ever really given me any encouragement. You really are. Thanks."

Looking back, if Dieter were to point to a turning point in his life, it had to be that moment. In an instant he just *knew* Joe was right. Joe's encouragement, driven home by his visual and verbal kick in the butt, finally ignited the drive that, until then, had only smoldered beneath layers of fear and self-doubt. At that moment Dieter made the required emotional commitment. A year later he walked into his first day of freshman geology, seven years later he walked onto a stage at the Max Planck Institute to be awarded a Ph.D., and twelve years later he walked into a one-on-one holovision conference with a WSF representative where he was informed of his selection as one of Germany's candidates for the WSF Astronaut Corps. The representative was one Joseph Z. Rebello.

But at that instant, Dieter's mind hadn't really been seared . . . not yet, not until he pushed back on Joe.

They'd slogged along in silence for another two minutes before Dieter spoke again. "If you're not going to re-up, Joe, what are you going to do?"

"What do you think a dumb jarhead like me could do?"

Anger froze Dieter in his tracks. "C'mon, Rebello, what's good for me is good for you. Like I keep telling you, inside that thick skull of yours is a hell of a sharp mind—use it!"

Joe heard, heeded, and appreciated every word, although he continued to slog forward and study the tank tread, almost as if trying to anticipate its next burst. "I don't know about this sharp mind crap you keep fantasizing about, Dieter, but I have decided what I'm going to do." Then he too stopped, looked up, and pointed to an F-27 barely visible overhead, its howl now faintly audible even with the tank's engine at idle. His eyes flashed. "I'm going to fly one of those, a single-seat fighter."

"Why do you want to do that?"

"It looks like inside that cockpit is the only place in the world where I'd be fully in control of something . . . something that moves . . . something that can make things happen."

"Maybe a little naive, Joe, but noble. But you gotta have a degree to even fill out the application. And you said you never even finished high school."

"Didn't."

"Then . . . ?"

"Next month I get a high-school diploma courtesy of Uncle Sam."

"Think you can get into college?"

"I've applied to fifteen of 'em."

"Hear anything back . . . ?"

"They all turned me down, real cold and final like. And it didn't take 'em long either. My applications just bounced right off 'em." Joe's body seemed to sink a few inches lower in the mud. "Guess they don't highly value the intellectual prowess of good old Jarhead High."

"Sorry, Joe, it looks like you hit a wall. Do you think you can—"

As Joe glanced up, the tank's engine gunned again. Then, even while he was spitting out his fresh ration of muck and mire, he erupted. His face wrenched into a sneer as he exploded up and out of the mud. His eyes, as flares, ignited and blazed—then seared. They screamed determination even before he opened his mouth. "Like hell! Those bastards aren't gettin' rid of me that easy. I *will* get into one of those fuckin' schools and I *will* max their damn program!"

Joe relaxed, his gun, grenades, pack, and fresh suit of muck seemed to weigh on him more heavily than ever as he sank back into the soup. Blaze faded from his eyes, sucked back in, reduced to just a pilot light waiting for the right time to reignite the inferno within.

Joe had later written to Dieter and told him of his modest success, but it wasn't until Dieter joined the Astronaut Corps that he learned the real story from Buck about the "finesse" Joe had employed to initiate his college career. "When Joe left the service, he went to what he judged to be the best small school for engineering and liberal arts in the East, the University of Rochester. He showed up a week before the freshmen were due to arrive, waited in the office of the Dean of Admissions until the Dean finally agreed to see him, and then announced, 'Dean, I know that you turned me down because you think I can't hack it. But let me make you a deal. There's bound to be a few freshmen who don't show up. Let me sleep in one of their open beds, take up a few of the open slots in some classes, and pay you the tuition I've saved up in the service. If at the end of the first term, I don't get at least a B average, you can toss my butt right outta here.' The Dean didn't wait. He looked up Joe's application and tossed him out immediately. The next day Joe showed up in the Dean's office again . . . and got tossed out again. This went on for another five days until the Dean realized that this Rebello kid might just be determined enough not to flunk out. He gave him a chance. At the end of the first term, Joe didn't make his B average—it came out close to an A."

The hum stopped, the innards of the Holographic Image Display ticked a few more times and an eleven- by seventeen-inch paper fluttered into the output tray. Dieter grabbed it with both hands. Perfect repro. Colors are even sharper than the display. This picture tells it all—dynamite! His hands trembled and fumbled as he folded the hardcopy in half three times and crammed it into his pocket. Too late to show it to Joe tonight. I'll get it to him first thing in the morning.

With his right index finger, he stabbed at the POWER OFF push-button, missed it twice, but then got its edge on the third try. Display faded, room lights returned to normal, and Dieter headed for the exit.

In an adjacent room, Otto's left index finger stabbed once and hit the precise center of the POWER OFF push-button at a work station that could and had functioned as a slave to the one used by Dieter. The television display of the Karov area and the accompanying message faded to zero.

Otto waited for three minutes, then also exited. Outside in the dark, he extracted his Portable Information Processor, set its CODE to SCRAMBLE, typed in his message and defined its destination. Then, with a few microtweaks of his wrist, he dithered PIP's pointing until he maximized the readout of the signal that emanated from one point of light in the night sky.

Otto spoke into his PIP. "Send."

As a single packet, an electromagnetic signal left Otto's PIP, traveled to the twenty-seven-acre antenna of the Central Atlantic-3 Geosynchronous Satellite, returned to a point on Earth 6237 miles from its source, and activated an alert.

Wolf reached for his PIP.

10

□□□

submerge

sunday—august 14

With full awareness, they thought, they started down.

The brightness of high noon contracted toward a small overhead patch. Ocean water swirled in, slapped together, and replaced blue sky with diffuse light, transformed Sun's painful glow into a tame, intriguing yellow ball that danced and shimmered behind a pale blue-green luminescence. Turbulent water's roar faded beneath the soft, steady hum of electric motors as the floor under their feet ceased to bob and pitch and stabilized into a firm, steady platform. Every movement, damped by the water's resistance, relaxed to a slow, deliberate pace.

They continued down.

"Joe . . . I'm hypnotized," said Maria as she slid her hand along the waist-high handrail, found Joe's and squeezed it. "It's so clear and colorful, so peaceful."

"Sure is. Looks like we lucked out today. It's as clear as I've ever seen Gulf water."

"Visibility's seventy meters," a voice whispered that, nonetheless, echoed throughout the plexan hull.

Joe looked up and to his right at the whisper's source, toward Otto who peered outside and scrutinized the clear, empty water. What's he looking for? Joe looked to his left at Maria and past her to Ricky. They stood spellbound, their noses a hand away from the clear wall. An inner warmth surged. Great, they like it! Not often we share adventures together. Happy stuff for future memories. His eyes swept forward, then aft as he admired SportSub's shell, a hull the size of a bus yet with qualities he valued—streamlined, powerful, and open. SportSub's teardrop body let light pass undistorted and undiminished, immersed its passengers in the beauty of a watery world without any of its discomforts.

Moto, the sub's operator, sat at his control station in the aft end above the engine compartment. His streamlined and powerful vee-shaped torso and head seemed to mimic the sub he guided. A mat of close-cut black hair covered the flat top of the head's upper vee; a precision-trimmed black goatee, the point at its bottom. Moto's black, wide-set eyes penetrated Joe yet also opened up his inner substance for inspection. His dark skin resembled the leather of a well-worn shoe, leather that could come to life and communicate in a flash when he smiled, like now. "Hope you folks enjoy the ride today."

"Thanks, Moto," said Joe. "We will. Hey, this is one fine-looking machine. How long can it stay down?"

"At a depth of 160 feet and 5 people on board, we could stay down for 7 hours and 3 minutes. The time increases if we go with less people or to a shallower depth."

Maria's eyes questioned. "Ahh . . . but how safe is it?"

Moto's leather face flashed another smile as he welcomed her probing stare. "No problem. Its safety is fully automated. For example, if we lose power, we also automatically lose ballast and slowly return to the surface. The only problems we've had so far are with people who want to plunge immediately to maximum depth, stay there, then pop back up. With this system, that type of carelessness could give you the bends. As a minimum, you must wait at the surface for thirteen minutes to sweep the nitrogen out of the atmosphere after hatch closure, just like we're doing now. To prevent this problem entirely, we've installed a CompuThink 1700 safety computer that monitors our air composition and pressure and gives fair warning if a bends potential exists."

Joe put his arm around Maria and gave her a comforting hug. "But also, Moto, haven't you built up a lot of experience with this sub's operation, enough to really perfect it?"

Moto beamed his smile toward Joe, then again Maria. "Exactly right. We have 256 in operation now, and that number's about to double again. They're all identical. Our sub is exactly like the one that Dieter and his family are in as well as all the others. Automated manufacturing has done it." Moto's eyes sparkled as he winked. "Our manufacturing engineers have applied the fundamental rule of automation to it: Everything up to but not including their job can be automated. And since they've perfected it just about as much as they could, their only task now is to just keep on replicating it over and over again."

Otto shifted his scrutiny from the water outside down to Joe. He paused as if to speak, but only smiled.

Joe sniffed the air. "Smells like we've traded the odor of salt and fish for sterile air. Like being back in a spacecraft."

"Is it really like a spacecraft, Daddy?" cried Ricky as he scurried over his mother's feet and turned wide eyes up to his father.

Joe brought his face down to Ricky's level. "Smells just like one, little guy. And we're going exploring too. But down here we're going to explore different things."

Ricky jumped up and down on his mother's feet. "We're goin' 'splorin', Mom, we're goin' 'splorin'!"

Maria grabbed Ricky's arm. "Ricky, I know, but please behave like a gentleman."

Joe nudged up next to Maria as he peered at the bubbles that danced and dodged upward past his eyes, bubbles like he'd seen wiggle their way toward the surface many times before. His mind felt the water's coldness shock sun-baked skin as the boy of over twenty years before awoke, seized the adult and sped south into the waters off Yucatán's coast, raced him back to a more innocent time when only impulse governed action, only the joy of exploration provided the reward. Scuba diving. Joe loved it. Always fresh and exciting. Natural. Oughtta be a kid forever. Salt water creeps in around mouthpiece, bites tongue and throat. Inhale and skull echoes. Exhale and bubbles mush around face. Up or down or sideways, just water, all open water. Happiness is freedom, large fins and a friend to share it. Turn and explore . . . show your friend. Grab gun and hunt . . . stay with your buddy. Accelerate forward . . . check behind. Hunted? . . . Yeah, always protect your friend.

"Enough talking about it," said Moto. "It's time to go see

some sites. I'll stay back here at the control station. Why don't you folks move up to the bow for the best show."

Ricky scrambled forward over his dad's feet to a position just port of the bow's center. Then Joe and Maria followed.

As Otto sauntered forward, his eyes never left an object that hovered just at the limit of his vision.

They slipped below the ocean's flat glasslike cover that, like matching guillotine blades, sliced together above.

Their sub made a quarter turn away from the shore, then began a slow cruise seven feet above the white sand, a cruise that followed the sand's gentle slope toward open water. Dieter forced his mind outside, let himself be hypnotized by sand grains that sparkled as shafts of sunlight fluttered over the rippled ocean bottom, by cobwebs of light that danced and undulated, by fish that meandered through random zigzag courses.

He reached inside his pocket and again felt the worn folds of the hardcopy he'd made the night before. Damnit! Why had Otto always been there between he and Joe ever since they met this morning? Not a minute alone. Have to show it to Joe after the ride. Dieter glanced at his wife and three boys, followed their stares outside, and forced himself to be absorbed by vivid colors that flickered and glimmered and . . .

Two miles away a third sub left a private enclosure, sliced downward, and left but an ephemeral slit on the ocean's smooth skin. The sub, identical to the 255 others, except for a single enhancement, proceeded forward on a precise course toward its destination.

The sub's sole occupant stared straight ahead, stared out from deep sockets with eyes that sent human vision's full complement of data to a brain with the capacity for the full richness of human thought, but a brain now disciplined to sort out and discard all color and shape, all presence and movement, all interpretation and meaning of every object—except one.

Moto's low monotone slithered into Joe's awareness. "Let's move out toward the reef. We'll find more sea life out there.

Hey, there's a hogfish over on our port side. See him? He's the red fella with the black stripe under his eye. And there's one we don't see often. That little fella over there with the green scales and pink trim. That's a queen parrot fish. Let's sneak up on him. Must be nearly two feet. Look at that color! Great, found us some playmates. Look ahead just off starboard. A school of spotted sea trout. We'll tail 'em. Some of the big guys get nearly three feet long."

Moto slipped the sub in behind the school and followed. Sunlight flashed off sleek silver bodies that slid through the water as one. At random times, it appeared they all responded to a drum major's command and, as a single unit, made a sharp break in a new direction.

"Otto, look at those guys," said Joe. "They all turn together. The herd instinct underwater. As soon as each one senses the break, he just can't seem to fall in line fast enough."

"They each sense the best direction to go at the same time," said Otto. "They're all equally matched and do the right thing together."

"No, they're all just following that guy up front," said Joe.

"Not him," Otto growled. "He's running scared, just a loner afraid of the strength in the numbers behind him."

"Scared maybe," said Joe, "but still a leader."

Maria laughed. "No guts, no glory. Right, Joe?"

"Right. Given a choice, why would any of those fish want to be just another speck of flesh buried in the school?"

Otto opened his mouth, paused but said nothing.

"That's something you'd never understand," said Maria.

"You're right. Now there's my hero. See him? Mr. Frisky Fish off to the side there doin' wifferdills."

Maria laughed. "Yep, there you are, the reincarnation of Joe Rebello."

"That fish is in for trouble," said Otto.

"Why's that?"

"He's inferior to the others. He can't stay with them."

"Nope, he doesn't want to. Enjoys doing his own thing. And he's probably smarter."

Maria laughed as she looked over at Joe, then up at Otto. "What're you two arguing about? They're all just dumb fish."

"They are," said Joe. "But they're still a little like us in a way—controlled by instinct. They just don't have the intelligence to keep trying to justify their every action, or the greater intelligence to actually understand them."

Joe watched Otto's smirk fade and his eyes defocus as his thoughts turn inward.

Moto's voice boomed out. "Here comes our good buddies! Over on the port side at ten o'clock. Bottle-nosed dolphins. Gotta be at least six of 'em."

"Now those folks are having fun," said Joe. "If you're gonna be in charge of reincarnation, Maria, let me come back as one of them."

Ricky pressed his face against the plexan. "Daddy, are they really smiling?"

Maria shook her head. "No, Ricky, they can't think. That's just the way they look."

"They're just one more lower form of life," Otto's voice resonated.

With a flick of its body, a dolphin moved to the edge of the sub, peered in, and came eye to eye with Ricky, then Joe.

"No, there's real intelligence behind that eye," said Joe as Moto cut the sub's power. "It's just a different kind than ours. There's not only some animal in the human, but a little human in the animal. Listen." The sub's plexan hull acted like an antenna as dolphin squeaks and squeals echoed inside. Joe stepped back as the dolphin moved on to Otto. "Wish we understood their language. Looks like he's got something to say." In silence, Otto examined the eyeball less than two feet from his own. "He's probably wishing he understood our primitive language," Joe continued. "Probably thinks we'd live in the water too if we were only smart enough." Otto's pensive gaze never left the dolphin's eye.

"It's getting a lot darker," said Maria as she snuggled up to Joe. "Kind of sneaked up on us. Everything's hidden in shadows."

Joe looked toward the surface. "Yeah. We must be down over a hundred feet now. Colder also. Feel the wall."

Moto's voice slipped in like that of a tour guide. "Look carefully at the top of the large brown rock down there at two o'clock. You'll see a medium-sized octopus. Blends in well. Must be about two feet from head to toe, or toes. He can change his color to match the rock. He's also not dumb, something most people don't realize."

"Interesting," said Joe.

"Interesting, but still inferior," said Otto. "And in the end, his life really makes no difference."

"Makes no difference?" asked Joe. "In the end, how can you ever determine if a life has made a difference?" Otto froze as Joe's question wormed its way inward. Joe decided to give it an extra push. "Just what qualities must a life have to give it any permanence or meaning?"

After a reflective lull, Otto spoke in an unusually soft and hesitant voice. "Just one—perfection."

Almost more of a question than an answer, thought Joe. What's going on inside this guy?

"Hey, look below his tentacle in that crevice," said Maria as she leaned forward and looked down. "Faint, but see his eyes?"

"See his mouth?!" cried Ricky.

Moto spied the creature, trained a searchlight on the bottom of the crevice, then let the sub drop until they came face-to-face with the head of a large snake. Two feet of its brown-and-black mottled body floated outside its cave. Its wide mouth extended far back into its head, a mouth that seemed to have acquired far more than its fair ration of teeth. It hovered motionless and stared back from eyes hidden within dark voids.

Maria backed away. "He looks just plain evil."

"In his own way he is," said Joe. "That's a moray eel. I learned to fear them as soon as I started to skin dive. They'll leave you alone, as long as you don't go near their turf. But as soon as you put a hand in their cave, like you would if going after a lobster, they'll strike. They not only have a vicious bite, but they just won't let go. Venture into their world, and you may not come back."

Maria frowned as she watched Ricky press his nose against the plexan. "No thanks, I'll just stay out."

Moto turned off the searchlight and only faint shafts of emerald light that lanced downward from the murky layers above remained. "Let's let our eyes adjust before we start upward. We'll see more that way."

Maria put both arms around Joe's waist. "What a place to live. You'd never see what's after you."

"Not all that different above the water, my dear." Through the darkness, Joe sensed cold tension stream from Maria's body as she pressed against him. Guess that wasn't the smartest thing to say. Hey, is Otto smiling?

"We'll ascend slowly and see what we can find," said Moto. "Keep your eyes up."

For over a minute Joe peered into a diffuse green and yellow brightness that outlined isolated plant and animal life. Finally he spoke. "There, see 'em? Nearly straight up."

"Yes, I've been watching them," said Otto, "another school of fish."

"Sea trout again?" asked Maria.

Joe strained his eyes. "No, they look bigger and different. And there's a lot more of 'em."

"We've come up under a school of snook," said Moto. "See the long front snout? They can get much bigger than sea trout, up to almost five feet. And these don't seem to be in much of a hurry." He continued his gradual ascent and maneuvered the sub twenty feet under and slightly to the side of the school. A stray glided less than twelve feet away.

"He's kind of pretty except for his face," said Maria.

"Yeah, and that's plain ugly," said Joe. "Jaws's too big. And he's always lookin' out the corner of that eye."

"But the rest of him is pretty," said Maria. "That full-length, black stripe really highlights his silver body, his gold fins and tail and his—"

Without sound, without warning, the slow organized motion above them burst. A silent bomb sent every fish on a sprint in a different direction. From the side where the stray had wandered, a dark form darted toward a silver flash, then disappeared. From the point of intersection, the forward half of a snook began a lazy drift toward the sub. Blood streamed from one ragged red surface, streamed out of its silver half body with its neat black stripe still intact, streamed from its eyes and brain that had failed to warn. Before the half snook reached the sub, another dark form darted forward and the remains vanished. More dark forms crisscrossed from different directions and churned the water with blood and mutilated fish. A soundless horror, a cold horror rained down, imprisoned the sub, penetrated its walls, and pressed into its occupants.

Otto nodded slowly as he followed the carnage. "Dumb stray deserved it!"

Otto's words speared into Joe's brain. His flesh stiffened as a colder, more urgent terror exploded from an inner primordial sense, displaced the external horror, and screamed of the threat right at his side. Does Otto also think . . . I deserve it?

"Hold still, gang," said Moto. "No problem for us, only for the snook. They've been jumped by some tiger shark. And they're gettin' fired up into a frenzy. Don't worry though. Our sub can take far more than they can dish out."

Surprised by his own anxiety, Joe pulled his eyes away from Otto and took quick, shallow breaths to exhale his fear in lung-sized chunks. His heart pummeled the back of his throat as he looked over at Ricky who stood fixed and fascinated, then down at Maria's one eye not buried in his chest. He struggled to give her a comforting look but felt his attention yanked away by the flash of an open jaw only a body length away, the flash of a weapon studded with rows of sharp white points beneath a hollow black eye. The jaw clamped around a silver body, thrashed left and right, ripped loose its supply of protein, then disappeared. Another tooth-packed jaw loomed up, hurtled straight at Joe, and rammed into their invisible shield. A dull thump echoed in Joe's ears as a stunned shark meandered away. Dull thumps increased in frequency, leveled off, then faded as their sub ascended through nature's butchery.

Ricky leaned forward to follow the action as it drifted below them. "Daddy, why did they all leave? Where'd they all go?" His mother pulled him back.

"I don't know, Ricky. They must be attracted to something else."

"We'll continue up," said Moto. "Most of the remains will drift down and what sharks are left should follow them." He stepped forward. "Sorry, Maria. Hope it didn't scare you too much."

She managed a weak smile. "No, just enough."

Ricky landed on Joe's toes. "Daddy, let's go back down and do it again!"

Maria seized the exhilarated little body. "Ricky!"

Joe put both arms around Maria and gave her a long hug. "But you have to admit that it was fascinating—and exciting."

"Just savage."

Otto turned to Moto. "When that shark clamped onto the snook right in front of us, a white lid covered its eye. What was that?"

"Bet his conscience got the best of him," said Maria. "He didn't want to look at what he was doing."

Otto gazed at Maria and remained fixed in thought until Moto laughed. "No, it's just for its own protection. Pure instinct. Its brain is only a small extension of its nervous system. And most of that's devoted to their sense of smell."

"Even though they can't understand pain or terror," said Joe, "they're sure masters at inflicting it."

"It's hard to fault them for it though," said Moto. "Like with every living thing, their own survival's the name of the game. And if you keep score, they're way ahead. Without much help, they've evolved into a most efficient killing machine."

"And one that's always on the prowl," said Joe as he watched Otto's eyes turn passive again and look outward as if still in search of something. What drives this guy? What side of the teeth is he on?

Maria pushed herself face-to-face with Joe. "Just a relaxing little ride to see the sights you said. A quiet family day together you said. Now Ricky's turned into a little ghoul. And look at me. I'm shaking inside, soaked with sweat, and my skin's a freezing mass of goose bumps!"

Joe's tan turned red, his smile broadened, and his eyes sparkled as he laughed. "Yep, dear, it's just like I promised . . . something we'll always remember."

The squeaks and squeals of his sons overpowered those from the dolphins. Dieter shouted directly into his wife's ear. "They look almost as happy as the kids."

One son, just big enough to perform a two-handed overhead press with his toy, pushed the face of his stuffed dolphin against the plexan. Outside, the gray-and-white creature of flesh flicked his body once to place his eye next to the smile of the creature of cloth and cotton. For a moment it appeared uncertain who mimicked who before the dolphin of flesh frolicked through a few rolls and swam away.

"There has to be real intelligence there," said Dieter.

His wife smiled and nodded.

"Make them come back, Daddy!"

"Sorry, they'll have to do that on their own," Dieter said as he watched the gray bodies shrink to dark specks in the emerald-green background. In silence, all eyes searched for the return of their newfound playmates.

"There's one, Daddy. He's coming back!"

Like his wife and children, Dieter pressed his face against the plexan and watched the dark speck grow in size. Funny how this one swims straight toward us, he thought. Not a single bob. Not a single weave.

Dark speck fattened into a black spot. At 25.000 meters from the plexan, precisely as black spot measured it, a single bit in its CT 130 computer changed state—transitioned from a one to a zero. In turn, CT 130's operating module changed state and issued a signal. Signal triggered igniters. Igniters lit propellant. Propellant burned. Black spot accelerated.

Spot's tip contacted hard plexan and detonated.

To Dieter, black spot never deviated left or right or up or down. But surrounded by a halo of light that flashed, then bloomed, it exploded in size.

Exact!

Precise!

Dead center!

Black spot's body continued to accelerate as it passed through and out the second plexan wall. For but an instant, Dieter had sensed its precision and, upon reflection, would've appreciated its engineering perfection, admired the efficiency of its targeting, marveled at its operational performance, if it were not for his own change in state.

Dieter also transitioned from a one to a zero—and ceased to exist.

11

□□□

surface

This time, no twirls, no cycles—BioProbe performed its real function.

Wolf sat in darkness at his state-of-the-art MicroBioManipulator, his MBM updated with, of course, his own enhancements, and scrutinized the soccer ball-sized hologram that hung three feet before him. Thin fingers finessed BioProbe over an electronic pad, surgeon's fingers that could wield a scalpel with equal ease.

Wolf—the calling of a surgeon? No, not in the classic sense, although he certainly had the requisite intensity and training. Something else motivated this man to hone his inherent skills. Something else boiled within and ate at him daily to provide constant drive. Something else propelled him toward the Gift for humanity he planned to bestow.

Something else . . .

Out of his yellow eyes, Wolf glanced down at his frail limbs and torso seen in the room's background glow, then up at his reflection from the flat face of the blackened television to his right. Yes, hasn't changed—still the same yellow, pallid and pitted skin, that damn pointed chin and nose and those laughable pointed jumbo ears. He sneered another one of the hundred

sneers that reflexed across his face each day, not so much from
the revulsion that brushed his mind, but from a caldron of anger
on a constant boil within.

Something else . . .

Wolf had come to understand that nature, in the form of
rubella, had engineered his jaundice and deformities a whole
seven months before his birth. Rubella had invaded his
embryo at only seven weeks after conception and deflected his
body from its path of normal development. Specifically, the
virus had inhibited the rate of cell division within his liver and
forever retarded its normal growth and function. Okay, if that's
the way it is to be—fight fire with fire. If nature could engineer
his cells and leave him with this joke for a body, he'd do his
own engineering and make up for it, far more than make up for
his own deformities with the gifts he'd soon bestow—for the
virus had left the brilliance of his mind intact.

Damnit! He just didn't deserve it, this atrocity that God's
natural order inflicted on his body. How could a helpless
embryo that lay unprotected in his mother's womb be guilty of
anything? Didn't he have a right to normal development too?

But still, something else . . .

Revulsion? Of course. It flared and fueled internal fires
with every glance.

Rage? Certainly. It seethed and built like molten magma
forever ready to erupt.

But mostly—*revenge*—revenge he'd worked for, revenge
he'd now pulled just about within his grasp.

The fingers of Wolf's right hand flexed. BioProbe stroked.
The electronic pad sensed the change in location of the
magnetic fleck of superconducting metal at BioProbe's tip and
the added pressure on the pad's surface. It sent this three-
dimensional signal to MBM's computer that processed the
signal and altered the electrical currents sent to coils, coils
which in turn changed the deflection of the supports of a
microscalpel.

Microscalpel sliced.

Wolf studied the eight-inch incision in the hologram before
him, the magnified replication of the clean slice through the
membrane that surrounded the human embryo buried at
MBM's core.

Judgment.

Yes, only a little judgment required here for he still operated at a crude level. MBM's system of light and electron microscopes detected the outlines of most of Embryo's structures and replicated them in the hologram in shades of green. Structures too small or too transparent to be observed directly were inferred by the computer and presented in red. But so far, his yellow microscalpel had touched only green. No real judgment required yet. Red would come later.

With a second BioProbe in his left hand, Wolf maneuvered a micropipette through the incision in the membrane around Embryo, held the incision open with the BioProbe in his right, and, with a slight push from his left foot, injected fluid through the pipette into the membrane around Embryo. Embryo paused as it squeezed through the incision, then accelerated and whisked out of the hologram's field of view. Damn! Pushed too hard.

With his right foot, Wolf pressed the view controls and moved the holographic scene in pursuit. And with the Bio-Probe in his left hand, he chased Embryo with a second pipette. As he caught it, he nuzzled the pipette's open tip up to it and held it steady with the pipette's light suction.

Wolf stretched his neck out of his shell, relaxed, then examined Embryo details as he rotated his view with the controls under his right foot. He smiled. Good. Only split into four cells so far. This'll go quick. But still should've had a tech do it.

"Hold pipette." Wolf's lips and tongue expelled each syllable with sharp precision. "Change solution to D-CMF. Freeze old solution, designate Zona Pellucida 3037, and save." MBM received its voice command, declared the frequency distribution of the sound legal, matched the words with those in its vocabulary, and responded. Embryo swayed on the end of the pipette as saline water flushed out the old solution, then again as the new solution washed in. The old solution that contained the empty membrane or zona pellucida swelled to the size of a dewdrop as the saline water flooded into it. Then MBM froze it, cataloged it, and saved it. An assistant would later store the membrane with other enucleated membranes to host the growth of other cells at other times, to receive more products of Wolf's genius.

A female voice slipped from MBM and caressed Wolf's ears. "Sequence complete."

Wolf grimaced as the idle BioProbe in his right fingers took off on a few quick laps. Sounds like she's in heat. Has to be changed. Need a male voice, one with authority.

The new solution, an enzyme in a calcium-free, magnesium-free salt solution, performed its function. The four cells dissociated from one another, and with a jiggle of the pipette, three cells drifted away from the one retained by the pipette's suction.

"Hold pipette." Again, with his distinct staccato, Wolf spit out his words. "Change solution to culture saline. Freeze old solution, designate as Backup G 737-3, and save." And again, with its standard precision, MBM marched through its response. Wolf could only wait. He glanced at his watch. Yes, should of had a tech set all this up. Crude labor. Time consuming. He shook his head. Exciting maybe fifty years ago when I started, but not now.

In truth, up to the present point, Wolf had worked only with crude and ancient technologies, but nonetheless useful technologies. They all contributed, the old and the new, and Wolf, a versatile man, appreciated them both: operations, which applied and exploited old technologies, and research, which invented and developed the new. Operations and research, like old and young friends on either side, continuously yanked on his sleeves for sole attention.

He switched his vision from Embryo to the yellow depiction of the thin titanium needle that now served as his scalpel. Talk about crude? As a microblip, an image of his early career escaped and spurted upward into his awareness. He cringed. It had all sounded so logical back in 1986 when, at the age of only twenty-one, he started his doctoral dissertation at the University of Leipzig in East Germany, then still the German Democratic Republic. Although from Rumania and a student in East Germany for only five years at the time, his intense commitment, his unmatched capabilities, and their shared ideals quickly moved Wolf to a central position of trust and leadership as he helped the State pursue its goals.

The productivity of the GDR Olympic Training Program depended not only upon the efficiency of the training but also upon the biological quality of those who entered the system. Of course screening and trials helped, and steroids and drugs enhanced performance. In fact, the GDR with an area no larger than the state of Virginia dominated an ever-increasing number of events at each successive Olympiad and hauled away an ever-increasing and disproportionate share of Olympic metal. "Your personal best is insufficient—only uniform superiority counts." Although Wolf's deformed body could not support the State's philosophy, his mind could.

Oh, yes, Wolf's mind certainly could.

Wolf and the State's megaminds reasoned together that sustained uniform superiority could only come through the effective breeding of optimized flesh to feed into the front end of the State's athletic machine. And, of course, Wolf's mind constructed the most feasible mechanization. His head swiveled back and forth as he watched the four cells sway in the fresh fluid that circulated around them. He waited. Not a bad idea at the time, and actually the seed of The Plan being followed today, but still crude—crude, crude, crude.

In his dissertation, "On the Selection, Optimization, Verification, and Replication of Biological Extremum," Wolf laid out the architecture of a plan to meet the State's objective to dominate world-class athletics. But with equal ease, his mind expanded the architecture out to include "leadership" in all of humanity's endeavors. Confrontations with the State's megaminds over his methods usually narrowed down to the opposition of natural intelligence versus acquired habits. Or, as Wolf put it, "We must forever maintain a tight focus on excellence achieved through precision, an inherent capability of the human mind, and eradicate the mindless application of brute force, a knee-jerk reaction so prevalent throughout our Eastern Bloc cultures. If something doesn't quite fit, we must learn to finesse it with a fine file, not just to beat it into place with a bigger hammer."

With the State persuaded to throw its full support behind his Plan and Wolf at the reins, unheard of within the Party for a man of only twenty-four, especially one from outside the GDR, it happened. Who would have ever guessed it?

The wall came down!

The damn wall toppled and left nothing but the chaotic residue of reunification.

At first, Wolf saw only the end to his dream, his drive. No tolerance remained for his Plan or its objectives, even for its sentiments. With unprecedented vigor, Germany purged all remnants of Wolf's epic cause right down to its core. Mankind's moral principles they called it, just all part of the appalling larger picture. First in the Soviet Union, then throughout all Eastern Bloc nations, the iron-fisted and the disciplined ("the hard-liners" in Western vernacular) oscillated in and out of control, then lost it altogether. Though a heroic struggle for many years, eventually the people slipped their hands around the reins—then just casually flipped them right into the laps of politicians— politicians! It didn't take these flabby-fisted, sponge-bellied orators long to let humanity's harlots grab hold, those that touted free enterprise, or, as Wolf clearly understood, those that acted only out of their selfish and insatiable drive to maximize profits at every turn. In time, they grounded every lofty cause and smothered every budding achievement at all levels within the once-proud Eastern Bloc—except at the very deepest.

Yes, fortunately, as some doors closed, others opened.

If today one viewed Poland, Czechoslovakia, Hungary, Yugoslavia, Rumania, and Bulgaria, all once rocked and churned by the shock waves of *glasnost* and *perestroika*, now not even surface ripples remained, just a placid, smooth sickening film greeted the eye. But far below, isolated currents still flowed, strong currents that at first had only eddied and nullified, but currents that finally coalesced and now moved together along several well-defined directions, one defined by Wolf.

As Wolf continued to wait, he smiled to himself at his own lack of faith in those early years. True, the Germans had to be finally written off for good. But it had come as a surprise that many others, though isolated at first, felt the same as he throughout the remaining corpse of the Warsaw Pact nations. For regardless of whether the surface paraded under the banner of the Warsaw Pact, or now that odious Berlin Pact, enough people in the depths cared, people with strength and discipline. Still, if they wanted to make things happen, even they, to a degree, had to join in. For no longer was it possible for the State to dictate the noble actions of its citizens. Rather, each and every movement now had to be greased by that one universal lubricant—money.

So. . . .

From the depths, the courageous currents that had converged and now moved as one in Wolf's epic cause rose to the surface as required, skimmed off excess lubricant, and descended again to progress according to The Plan. Of course, when they surfaced, they had to wear the disguise of the weak, the costume of just another harlot of the World Stock Exchange, the cloak of the People's Research, Exploration, and Commercialization In-Space Enterprise—PRECISE, Incorporated.

Wolf raked his fingernails through his fur as the scene before him showed signs of stabilizing a single cell. Perhaps he'd come along at just the right time. For no one else appeared with mind and vision focused on such a noble cause, no one else stepped forward with such a ready plan to regain dominance for the disciplined—no one else but Wolf. Responsibility? Destiny? Must be. For under Wolf's leadership, humanity would soon kick out on the first of its several epic strides forward.

Cell locked in place. Wolf shifted in his seat and hunched his shoulders. Enough menial labor. Time to do some real work.

"Mode change." He gripped BioProbe. "Scalpel to laser." MBM received its voice command and again responded. Titanium needle withdrew. In its place, MBM focused a low-power, ultra-thin needle of X-ray laser light down to a point on the cell's surface and represented its direction and location in the hologram with a needle of violet laser light.

Wolf danced over the view controls under his right foot, the cell in front of him tumbled like he was inspecting a melon, and violet laser light traced a path over the cell's surface. He stopped its tumble, started to manipulate BioProbe, and whispered to himself. "There . . . right there . . . that'll do it." Then he propelled his commands straight into MBM's receiver. "Power to three."

BioProbe scribed.

X-ray laser cut.

PIP rang.

"Damn," he whispered, "never fails. But maybe it's what I've been waiting for." Again he called out. "Power to zero. System to hold." He turned, reached for his PIP, checked the message source, and allowed it to proceed.

"Go."

Kurt's placid face illuminated the TV screen to his right. "Hello, sir. This is Kurt in Key West. The excision of Dieter Dietrich has been successful."

For the first time in thirteen days, the clouds of failure over Wolf parted and he basked in the warm rays of triumph and victory. "Excellent!" But by nature, the clouds quickly swirled together again. "Kurt, I have another assignment for you."

Kurt's face seemed to sharpen, to take on extra clarity of focus.

"I have received information from Lothar in Los Angeles. Acting without hard data, Dr. Daro, WSF's Director of Operations, may be about to initiate a formal inquiry into our facility at Karov. He is pushing too hard. We need to hold off any such inquiry until we can have our people in control of it. As a preventive measure, Daro is to be excised. And again, do it in a manner that throws no suspicion in our direction. Contact me from Oceanside as soon as you anticipate an opportunity."

"Yes, sir. I am forty-eight minutes away from my aircraft. I will land in Oceanside in another three hours and twenty-one minutes."

"That is all."

Kurt's face collapsed toward his eyes, then faded back into the blackness of the screen.

Wolf, a careful man, reviewed his contingency plans as he did several times each day. Only the slight nod of his head indicated his positive thoughts. At last, I've cut away almost every obstacle. Only low-level threats remain. Kurt will excise Daro. Can't ask for a more efficient scalpel. And Otto will call in Kurt if Rebello also proves worthy.

Wolf's attention shifted to the cell that hovered at arm's length. His research, so interesting, so pivotal to the distant future, would have to be put on hold. But he could take it with him, and he would. Now and for the month ahead, operations would become his prime passion. For the real fruits of his labor, the end product of his dreams, would soon bud and blossom in Phase Five. Now's the time to join in, to move into the center of the action—to lead!

"Freeze specimen, designate it as Enhancement Research Specimen 0-14, and configure it for external transport." Wolf waited as MBM performed. Wolf's BioProbe, its status once more diminished, took off on more twirls and laps.

MBM finished, and as its hologram blazed just before it died, Wolf's image flared and reflected off the television's blacked face and back into his yellow orbs. Tears welled for but a blink before his fists reflexed closed, his sneer radiated into darkness, and his body released another quiver of rage.

Wolf bolted from his MBM and hobbled out of his private laboratory, through a corridor, also part of a ninety-six-year-old bomb shelter, and into a storage basement. There he boarded the elevator up to the surface, the ground floor of a satellite office of PRECISE in Sovata, Rumania.

As the elevator door cracked open, Wolf bolted again. Karov waited.

Nothing but empty, flat, smooth water.

Nothing but ever greater fatigue and strain in his legs as he danced and slipped on the boat's sloped hull to maintain his balance. He could sit down, but then he couldn't see as large an area.

Nothing but ever greater pain in his eyes as the brightness of the Sun, now at a low angle on the western horizon, glanced off the watery mirror and continued its assault on his retinas.

Nothing but nausea, an incessant nausea that continued its steady upward creep.

Nothing but . . .

"There." Joe pointed. "What's that over there? Light-colored, right below the surface."

Moto finessed the lever and the hum from the motor boat's right electric turbine strengthened. They turned.

The boat drifted alongside a small, formless white mass. Joe reached down, and as the boat rocked to his side, his arm plunged into the water up to his elbow and his hand grabbed. He pulled the white mass up in front of his face.

Frigid water ran down his arm as it drained from the innards of the mass, from the white, cold, soggy softness that beamed its friendly smile back into his face, an endless incessant smile that only a stuffed animal could maintain.

Nausea surged above threshold. Joe choked it back, retched several times, then scanned the surface of the surrounding water. He saw nothing . . . heard nothing . . . felt nothing. He glanced back at the drained, cold, stuffed toy dolphin in his hand. His eyes filled. His hand opened. Mass fell.

Smack! . . . Lifeless.

Joe dropped down beside the cold remains and wept.

In time, sorrow drained from the human as water did from the toy. Only an open emptiness remained. Again, his hand reached down, clenched the soggy mass, and turned its smile upward. As a single endless wave, rage swelled and erupted from deep within his bowels.

"Why?"

Moto shook his head. He had no answer.

"Why?!"

Water rippled and smoothed, rippled and smoothed. It had no answer.

His muscles tightened and shook as rage continued to explode outward, a rage that built with time and ordered thought, yet a rage drawn back inward for lack of an external target, a rage that—so far—could find no release.

He looked toward land. "Who?!"

VOLUNTEER

Nothing confines and suffocates—like constraints from within.

12

□□□

mindlock

Precise. It could not have been more precise.

Throttle slid back, engine howl dwindled, and the RT7 aircraft slowed as its nose wheel came to rest on the precise center of the runway centerline.

Status check. Perfect.

Throttle slid forward, howl erupted, and RT7 accelerated as its nose wheel rolled down the centerline—down the precise center of the white stripe . . . until it lifted off the ground.

Relaxed hands on the controls dithered within narrow limits. The precision they finessed from the aircraft, indeed from every one of life's assignments, required focused intensity, yet a precision not inconsistent with relaxation, a precision that had, in fact, dominated every effort learned since birth.

RT7 continued to accelerate.

Side arm controller flexed. The black carbon aircraft banked. From the hollows of his eyes, Kurt glanced back. Runway, now a dot on the landscape, moved off his left wing and started its slide back toward obscurity behind RT7's tail. Likewise, Kurt's recent assignment shrunk to a single point of memory and slid into mental shadows at the rear of his mind to be cataloged and saved with all the others. And just as the scene before him, his next assignment bloomed and filled his awareness. Kurt mentally prepared to command the totality of his concentration for he felt the human desire to please, to make himself acceptable to his peers, and to be recognized and appreciated by Wolf and Otto, his only superiors. Again, energy started its slow ramp upward as he looked ahead and focused.

RT7 continued to climb.

Kurt's challenge, unlike those around him, never came from the attainment of perfection as most people understood it. That came as a given. Instead, it came from the attainment of ever-greater accuracy of measurement that allowed extension of his perfection to ever-greater levels of performance. In fact, he performed at levels of perfection inferior to no one, except, of course, for Wolf who penetrated levels of perfection far greater than those at which anyone else performed—biological levels fundamental to them all.

RT7 leveled at 91,000.0 feet.

Three navigation satellites updated his inertial position and reduced its error to 0.0073 feet. As the Sun, now on the horizon to the left of center, inched upward in the western sky, Kurt pointed RT7 on its course, the precise course to Oceanside, California, the location of WSF Headquarters and Dr. Daro. He saw no need to ever point anywhere else except to the precise center of his target.

RT7 accelerated to 3.381 Mach.

"Hello. This is the Office of the Manager of Astronaut Operations."

"Hello, Mrs. Selbemacher. This is Joe. Is Buck there please?"

"With whom do you wish to speak?"

Joe pressed the antiquated receiver to his ear. More than the hunger in his stomach, the ache in his muscles, or the wet cold in his skin, seas of grief and rage continued to boil within his body. Only a slick of patience floated over the surface.

"Buck Bailey, please."

"Do you refer to Dr. Bailey?"

Joe's eyes bulged. Buck must cringe every time he hears

this. Not the type to hide behind a degree, especially if it's honorary. "That's the guy. Let me talk to him, please."

"Who is this? Does he know you?"

The slick of patience stretched. Sunday evening, 8:37, my best friend and his family have been killed, left my PIP home, have to huddle in the wind in this open-air Commercial Light-Link Booth, and she can't even get her nose out of her damned Administrative Procedures Manual. "Ms. Selbemacher, this is Joe Rebello. Please tell Buck I'm on the line."

"Is he expecting your call?"

"No."

"What is the subject?"

"Personal."

"I must know what this call is all about before I can supply you access to Dr. Bailey."

Slick split. "All about, Ms. Selbemacher? All about? Right now it's about my cold coarse fingers that're comin' through this light link to wrap around your throat if you don't get Buck on line."

". . . I . . . I . . . I never. . . ."

"We all have our personal problems. Buck—*Now!*"

Silence sounded rational. Slick closed.

"Hi, Joe?"

"Hello, Buck."

"Sorry for the delay. I've worked myself into a foul mood. Standardizing our personnel data base is a lot bigger job than I thought."

"Buck, Dieter and his family are missing and most likely dead."

"Explain, Joe."

Joe welcomed the open conduit to another human who shared his empathy, attitudes, and rationality. As he talked, his thoughts lined up in logical order, flowed into the receiver, and brought the comfort of release—until the tail of the line approached where it loomed up, clear and crisp and alone with no other option.

Muscles shivered. Chest pounded.

He paused and retraced. Yes, there it is again—obvious, inevitable. No, don't mention it. Don't even think it!

"Joe, I'm sorry, very sorry. I know how close you were to him. Thanks for the rundown. Are you coming back tonight?"

"Yeah, we are. I'll see you first thing in the morning at seven-thirty."

"Yeah, I'll see you then. I've gotta hustle now, Joe. Lots of notifications to make. Take care of your family . . . and yourself."

"Buck, one last thing. I think Dr. Daro's right. Something's going on around us. No matter what they find, I think Dieter was murdered."

"Unlikely as hell, Joe, but tomorrow you and I'll explore it first, then try it on Dr. Daro if warranted."

It loomed up again. "And . . . ahhh . . . Buck?"

"Yeah?"

". . . nothing. See you tomorrow."

"Till then, Joe."

. . . observe error—eliminate error . . .

. . . observe error—eliminate error . . .

Just your standard feedback loop, and Kurt, no different than any other human, kept many of them in operation at any one time. But he did differ in two respects: He eliminated error at a rate that exceeded normal human standards by at least an order of magnitude, and he always applied his full efforts until the measured error read precisely 0.00 or 0.0000 or whatever the level of accuracy that the error could be detected and displayed.

The flight control switch in RT7's cockpit rested at MANUAL where it had remained since takeoff. Kurt checked his heading, 277.37 degrees true; his altitude, 91,000.0 feet; and his Mach number, 3.381. Then he rechecked them all once again. RT7's automated feedback loop, used by almost all pilots once they reached altitude, could also have flown the aircraft. But that loop tolerated an error that sometimes even wandered—the last digit in the error measurement sometimes remained at "1" and on rare occasions even drifted all the way up to "3"!

. . . observe—eliminate . . . observe—eliminate . . .

. . . Mark—250.00 miles out of Oceanside . . .

. . . observe—eliminate . . . observe—eliminate . . .

In a single well-timed glance, Kurt's eyes swept the horizon. The light sands of Baja cut sharp against Pacific's electric blue. Sunlight reflected from ocean textures and detailed the edge of the California current and the eddies that it shed. At cold water upwellings, plankton exploded in vivid green and twisted and contorted over the surface. Like searchlights, shafts of sunlight pierced high-level clouds along the shore and mottled the blackened surface beneath with patches of blue and green. The solid gray band of humanity's metropolis consumed the coastline as it expanded, contracted, and snaked its way from Tijuana to San Luis Obispo. Colors, varied and rich and vibrant, ate into the edges of the gray and buffered the barren desert and mountains from the relentless human invasion from the west.

Kurt's mind never appreciated, never marveled, for his eyes also never stopped their sweep for an instant until they re-entered the cockpit.

. . . observe—eliminate . . . observe—eliminate . . .

Eyes darted to and from the clearance on the TV display:

AT 220 NM FROM OCEANSIDE, CALIF. (OSCA):
— CLEARED TO EXIT SONIC CORRIDOR 7,
  THEN DIRECT TO WSF AIRFIELD
— DESCEND AT 400 FEET PER NM

AT 3700 FEET OVER OSCA:
— ENTER LANDING PATTERN ALPHA

. . . observe—eliminate . . . observe—eliminate . . .

Sloppy instructions, he thought. Should start the descent at 218.25 nautical miles from the field. He set up the flight parameter display for OSCA and the 400.0 feet per nautical mile angle of descent.

. . . observe—eliminate . . . observe—eliminate . . .

Distance from the field dropped through 217 nm. Descent angle almost came to rest at 399.9 before it froze at 400.00.

. . . observe—eliminate . . . observe—eliminate . . .

The corridor of green vegetation, with its patches of gray split by the Colorado Reservoir, swept underneath. Wide swaths of white water cascaded over the seven stages of the Yuma dam to Kurt's left.

. . . observe—eliminate . . . observe—eliminate . . .

To Kurt's right, sediments rolled and swirled upward, then burst onto Salton Sea's palette from microshifts in the San Andreas fault beneath its floor.

. . . observe—eliminate . . . observe—eliminate . . .

The thunderstorm cell, just an isolated cell, drew life from the heated mountainside and boiled skyward. RT7 pierced cell's skin at an altitude of 21,737 feet. Turbulence punched and slammed the aircraft. Kurt jolted and jerked and shook. Hailstones, as if sprayed from hundreds of machine guns, smashed and pulverized on RT7's surfaces. One of many stray current filaments from the lightning bolt arced into RT7's nose and out its tail, passed up Kurt's left arm and out his flight boots. For but an instant, Kurt's body jumped and jiggled.

. . . observe error—eliminate error . . .
. . . observe error—eliminate error . . .

Another stray filament, just a microamp or two, had slithered through one of RT7's three CT 210 computers. Problem? No, not really. One of the computer's channels that fed a display driver had shorted out. The other two CT 210s periodically corrected the display and the error remained insignificant; the displayed rate of descent bounced between only 400.3 and 399.7.

. . . observe + 0.3 error—eliminate error . . .
. . . observe - 0.3 error—eliminate error . . .

Kurt accelerated his cross-check and, eager to rid himself of the error with speed as well as precision, amplified his control inputs.

. . . observe + 0.4 error—eliminate error . . .
. . . observe - 0.4 error—eliminate error . . .

Kurt remained loose and relaxed as he accelerated his cross-check once again.

. . . observe + 0.5 error—eliminate error . . .
. . . observe - 0.5 error—eliminate error . . .

As RT7 passed over the field, its descent angle equaled four hundred feet per nm, plus or minus an insignificant amount.

. . . observe + 0.6 error—eliminate error . . .
. . . observe - 0.6 error—eliminate error . . .

When RT7 again exceeded 2.00 nm from the field boundary, the CT 7000 that hosted the Air Traffic Monitoring and Warning System annunciated an unsafe condition. Sharp intense yellow light from the Air Traffic alert indicator, adjacent to the readout of the angle of descent error, penetrated Kurt's eyes and pierced inward toward his brain.

. . . observe + 0.7 error—eliminate error . . .
. . . observe - 0.7 error—eliminate error . . .

At 7.3 nm from the field, the light from the alert indicator changed to red, brightened, pulsed, and jangled Kurt's optic nerve and again lanced inward toward his brain.

. . . observe + 0.8 error—eliminate error . . .

. . . observe - 0.8 error—eliminate error . . .

At 730 feet below, the tip of the instructor's pointer smacked the screen of the MERT display at the center of the third word in the seventh regulation . . . "shall be accomplished precisely without deviation from procedure as mandated by" . . . In unison, as RT7's howl cuffed their ears, the instructor and students jerked their heads up and mouths open, then froze as Kurt, bearing a lesson of greater significance, soared straight over their heads.

Below RT7's cockpit, ground continued its upward rush. Within RT7's cockpit, acoustical energy detonated from the WARNING Klaxon, jarred and rattled the bones of Kurt's middle ears, and stabbed inward toward his brain.

. . . observe + 0.9 error—eliminate error . . .

. . . observe - 0.9 error—elimi

13

▢▢▢

question

monday—august 15

"And what'd Otto do?"

Joe yawned. "Nothing, Buck." No smile creases flexed in his pale skin, no glitter scintillated in his eyes. He stretched in an effort to evict an emptiness that devoured him from within. Awful feeling, like I'm hollow. Maybe it's just lack of sleep. Two hours seems worse than none at all. "As soon as we got back to land, Otto headed for the airport. He said he couldn't wait for Dieter to surface because he had to catch the 1700 flight back here. Didn't say what for." No, probably more than anything, it's Dieter, it's the loss of Dieter.

"Then, so far as you know, no one has talked to him about Dieter."

"No, but I'm sure he knows about it—all about it . . ." Joe drew a fuzzy bead on Buck. ". . . because he's part of it."

"It?"

"The same activity Dr. Daro sensed, something that PRE-CISE is up to. I felt it all the time we were at Karov, once more when Dieter and I nearly bought it on that EVA, then in the EMTV and now again. As soon as we got below the surface, Otto seemed distracted, always looking out in search of something . . . and I don't think it was fish." For a moment

oe's eyes sharpened. "Buck, I know it—PRECISE killed
Dieter."

"That's a pretty strong accusation, Joe." Buck didn't look all
hat rested either. Only his lips twitched. "We'd better not go
public with that one till we have a lot more than just feelings
or suspicions."

Neither Joe nor Buck had budged since they started their
recap of Dieter's loss twenty-five minutes before. Slouched in
their chairs at Buck's conference table, the shallow breaths
required for their conversation appeared to be just about all
either could muster.

Joe summoned the extra energy required for a frown and
another sentence. "Dieter's sub just couldn't have disintegrated all on its own."

"One report quoted an old fisherman as saying it must have
been sharks. There were a lot of them in the area and probably
the reason no bodies have been recovered. The old guy said a
shark could barrel right through a sub's hull."

Joe struggled upward to a semislouch. "No, he's wrong.
Dieter and I checked that out before we ever climbed in with our
families. That plexan could take far more than any fish or any
sledgehammer or, for that matter, any rifle could inflict. Besides,
we know it's shark-proof from firsthand experience. Ask Maria.
She and Ricky will be talking about it for months."

Buck paused as he studied his loose fists that slowly
drummed the table. "Joe, there's another thing that happened
yesterday that could be related. Along with the story on
Dieter, it's probably been on World HoloNews for at least six
hours."

"Didn't even glance at it before I came in."

"Kurt Grimm, one of the twins, was killed late yesterday
when he crashed at Oceanside."

Joe's eyes popped open. "Grimm? That's too bad. What
happened?"

"Simple, yet incomprehensible. After he descended to the
entry point over the field, he never honked it around for
landing. He just kept plowin' straight ahead—right into the
ground."

"Was he in the soup?"

"No, VFR. Not a cloud in the sky. Clear and twenty."

"Strange. But how's it related?"

"His flight was from Key West and he took off about two hours after Dieter's sub disappeared."

Energy swelled outward from a fresh source. "Damn . . . that's the same as on our EVA, Buck. Grimm, or his brother manages to show up just when something goes wrong. Why the hell would he, or they, have anything against Dieter? What was Grimm's reason for being in Key West?"

"Don't know. PRECISE has ignored our request for data. They said that as a matter of general procedure, they will not respond since this Kurt Grimm had been pulled back into their internal program and therefore was not under our jurisdiction."

"What did he actually do there?"

"So far, Joe, no one remembers seeing him after he landed. He just melted into the countryside. WSF Security is all fired up and they have a full team down there this morning. Maybe they'll turn up something today."

"Hope so. I'm scheduled to talk to them at 1300. Now I know why. What do they think's going on?"

"They don't think the sub's hull could've failed in its normal working environment either, but they don't share our suspicions of Kurt or Otto."

"Any clues on why Grimm crashed?"

"None. No weather, no traffic, and his tissue analysis showed no body chemistry outside nominal limits. And check pilots who've flown with him say he was one of the best, if not the best instrument pilot they've ever seen in the program. His only equal was—" Two raps on the office door interrupted Buck's train of thought. And like Joe, this morning Buck could process just one input or one output at any one time. ". . . was his brother, and now they say Otto also."

After the proper seven-second delay, the door swung open and Ms. Selbemacher bustled toward them. "For your review and signature, Dr. Bailey." Squarely, with both hands, she bestowed her creation upon Buck like a chef who delivered her prize dish—The Memo. "Remember, since they are the originators of the request, the Training Directorate is required for final approval. You are now required to review, sign, and return it to them by noon so that distribution can be made over LightNet at 1300." She nodded at Buck as he blanched, then discharged a corrosive glare down her nose at Joe, a procedure not yet found in the Manual, swiveled, and exited in the prescribed manner.

Weariness weighed on Buck as he grasped The Memo, assessed its bulk, and started to flip through its pages, each jammed with information he'd helped develop over the weekend. "Thought we'd get this blivit out the door on Saturday. But it turns out that training had to be more fully addressed. The system has latched on to this standardized personnel data base concept and is pushing it far beyond just the reformating of data."

Since The Memo had all the markings of just another wad of dreary administrivia, Joe only nodded out of politeness, then continued. "Buck, whatever PRECISE is up to, the stakes must be high if they're willing to kill for it."

Buck's attention remained with The Memo for another few seconds before he let it drop between them. "What?"

"I said they must have something big goin' if they're willing to kill for it."

"Joe, don't get obsessed with that idea yet. We have no proof. Even the hint of an accusation like that could cause the politicians to come unglued. Since PRECISE has become the model entrepreneurial corporation for all new businesses rooted in the old Eastern Bloc, they can never do any wrong."

"Entrepreneurial? I never understood that, Buck. Take the first and last words of their name, People's Enterprise, a real oxymoron if I ever heard one. I've always felt there's something phony about them."

"Maybe so, Joe. But there again we have no proof."

Joe sighed, "Afraid you're right," then glanced at The Memo by his fingertips:

. . . *analyses of background, skills, proficiencies, and resulting performance of the total WSF astronaut population reveal large spreads in several areas of major importance to . . .*

"Let's focus on what we're going to tell Dr. Daro in another twenty-four hours."

"Right, we'd better. Can't sit in front of the boss with just our bare faces hangin' out." Joe glanced down again:

. . . *only the creation and rigorous enforcement of comprehensive standardization requirements can ensure the well-defined and predictable baseline of astronaut performance required by the engineering design and procedures development communities. Therefore . . .*

An extra gloom invaded Joe's mood. "Buck, as I see it, the only place to really find out what's going on is at Karov, at their Observatory, just like we felt when we first came back."

"That's a good place to start. We could piggyback our objectives onto those Norm has specified for Mission 337."

"Yeah, we could. As the new evaluation team demonstrates our proposals and tries to negotiate a handover of LB-13, they could also do some serious looking around."

Buck's head made a micronod, then rested again. "If we do end up recommending this approach to Dr. Daro, we'll also have to define mission objectives and a timeline."

"As well as specific requirements for crew selection and training."

. . . mandatory that every astronaut receive intense continuous training and testing in order to ensure predictable, uniform performance and . . .

Joe's gloom continued to mount and marshal fresh energy reserves.

"Yes, we can do that, Joe, but we're going to receive a lot of pressure to treat this mission just like any other—grab whoever's at the front of the line and fly 'em. The wave of the future."

Joe tightened, surprised by his own energy rush. "But this mission has some unique requirements."

. . . need for predictable and uniform interfaces dictates mandatory leveling of astronaut performance without exception across the total population of . . .

Something inside Joe torqued and twisted. He popped vertical, leaned forward with fists clenched on either side of The Memo, and glared into Buck's eyes. "We need at least one crewperson familiar with Karov and the players in this thing, someone who can come up to speed fast on what's been going on." Reserve energy exploded. "And most of all, someone who flat ass cares!"

Buck yawned as he rubbed his neck. "Spoken like a true volunteer."

Volunteer?! A shock jolted Joe's spinal cord that rippled out to his fingers and toes. Energy fled. He drooped back in his chair. Only gloom continued its climb. "I just got home. Like you said, it's not my turn. No thanks, Buck. No way."

Buck shrugged. "Okay, just a thought."

"Not a good one."

"C'mon, let's get our proposal for Dr. Daro pulled together. We don't have much time."

Joe yawned. "You're right, but not only with Dr. Daro, but with Phase Five and this whole thing. Buck, September first is coming fast. I feel the pace is pickin' up."

Buck's yawn echoed Joe's. "Maybe, but to what?"

At the instant Wolf glanced out the window, Earth, his ultimate target, receded at 17,373 mph.

He studied the blue sphere with its patches of brown skin, leered back at Mother Earth as she tried to cloak herself in wisps of white. No, she just can't cover her total self, can't hide her fertility. She's just offering up all that raw material, craving for someone to lead it away from its aimless evolution, begging for someone to give it optimum form.

Wolf smiled and nodded. Yes—*someone*.

"Sir, a message for you."

"Who is it?"

"Otto, sir."

"Put him through."

"High bit rate?"

"Yes, I want holography."

Wolf pushed off the window and floated back into the Command Center toward the camera array. He liked zero gravity. It acted as an equalizer, for it not only fleshed out his face, made him look healthier and younger, and reduced the pain in his body, but better yet, it allowed all motions, all actions to be controlled by his fingertips. Life as it should be—finesse in place of force.

Otto's head snapped into existence at arm's length as his voice reverberated within the confinement of the Command Center's six walls. "Hello, sir."

"Hello, Otto. Good image. You look like you're right here with me. How's mine?"

"Excellent, sir, and you also look good." Otto paused as his features clouded. "There's been an accident."

"Oh?"

"It's Kurt who took off from Key West. He crashed at Oceanside and was killed." Hurt registered on Otto's face before he looked down.

"Kurt? No!" Wolf's tones slashed through the air where Otto's head hung. "How did it happen?"

"After his descent, he never entered the landing pattern but flew straight into the ground. It looks like he went into Mindlock."

"*Mindlock!* Again? No, damnit, I thought we had that fixed!"

"The training on the new Secondary Demand has helped, sir, but apparently not enough."

"Doesn't everybody know it thoroughly by now, Otto?"

"Yes, and we all repeat it to ourselves many times daily, just as you instructed." Otto paused, then, as if controlled by some inner command, recited, "Judgment Demand: When I focus on my task, I will leave part of my concentration outside to monitor and redirect myself as required."

"Then what could have been the problem?"

"There still is some confusion, sir. Every now and then some of us find that this Secondary Demand conflicts with our Primary Demand, the Perfection Demand: Achieve perfection through excision of all errors."

"Conflicts?"

"Yes, sir. We always focus on all errors until they are completely excised. Only then can we meet the demands of lower priority, like the Judgment Demand. The problem is how should we know when the Judgment Demand must interrupt and take priority?"

Wolf fingered facial fur. "That takes judgment."

"What should we do different, sir?"

"Nothing. Don't change. Perfection comes first. I must give this more thought."

"But what about Kurt's loss?"

"It makes no difference." Wolf didn't acknowledge Otto's wince.

"But Daro presents a potential flaw in The Plan, and therefore, isn't it a firm requirement that he be excised?"

"No, in my judgment it's now not worth the extra suspicion it would create under the enhanced scrutiny we must surely be under. And even if Daro sends another team to meddle in our plans at Karov, they'll be too late to find anything."

"But Kurt's assignment is not complete."

"Otto, trust me! It makes no difference. And I can always slip another into his slot for the next assignment."

Otto winced again, more intensely this time, just before his head snapped to a point.

Wolf frowned but a second before he pushed off his control station and floated back to the window.

Wolf shrunk.

Otto watched Wolf's head contract to a point. But not until the point faded to black did he dare mutter to himself. "Trust? Just slip another into his slot? Makes no difference? Kurt made a difference . . . didn't he?!"

House ignored Joe.

"Close the drapes." Nothing. Joe turned and spoke straight into the voice receptor. "Close the drapes, now!" No motion. "Maria, House isn't listening to me again."

"Honey, you're not asking it in the right way," said Maria as she bounced into the bedroom and over toward Joe. The spring in her step matched the cadence of her voice. "I've made a few changes." She took both his hands in hers, tilted her head to the side, and spoke through her smile with a happy lilt. "You have to address it properly, my dear husband."

"Properly? Why do I sometimes feel like Ricky's younger brother? I gave it my good old instructions, just like always, and it ignores me. I'm away for only two months and House forgets who I am!"

"Joe, relax." She patted the back of his hand. "You're making too much of it. Let me try. Bedroom drapes, close."

The drapes whisked closed.

"There now, that wasn't so hard." More pats.

"But why do I have to say it that way, 'drapes, close'? . . . What that's noise?"

"Joe, you just closed every drape in the house. You also have to say which ones or House closes them all."

"All drapes are closed," said House.

"Hey, that's your voice."

Maria beamed. "Like it? It's a new option." Her tongue peeked through her lips as she smiled. "I recorded all of House's responses in my voice and House calls them up as needed."

Joe chuckled. "That I like, but why can't it listen to me like it always did?"

"They said this new system must have more rigid standards to enable it to perform more functions."

"Damn, even in my own home."

"It'll work just fine, dear, once you learn what House expects of you."

"House expects of me?!"

"House's rules are pretty clear, honey." She gave him a light kiss in an attempt to calm him down. It helped. Then she giggled. "They even tell you how to keep the floodlights and burglar alarm from coming on at two-thirty in the morning."

Joe turned and headed for the bathroom. "Zippady-do-damn! I step outside for just an instant with Charlie in the middle of the night, then have to sweet-talk House just to get back in."

"House's protection system recognized your voice okay, but you didn't use the proper words."

"Zippady-do-double-damn! Do I need a checklist just to live here?" Joe shook his finger at Maria and smiled. "One thing's for sure though. If that cat wants out in the middle of the night, it goes out. I'm not going to let it have another crack at my briefcase."

Maria giggled again. "Joe, why don't you just keep your briefcase closed? How's poor Charlie supposed to know it's not a litter box?"

Joe shook his head. "Got every shred of paper. Didn't miss a one. Must've saved up for the whole day. Everything I put in there for years will come out smellin' like cat urine." He looked down as something brushed his knee, then watched a solid, shiny black body lunge up onto the counter, a cat large enough, Joe speculated, to be accepted as a small panther. He scratched its neck as it stretched its chin up toward him. "Charlie, that was my briefcase. Be reasonable." Joe glanced in the mirror to the side of the counter where his image reflected off mirrors on opposite walls of the bathroom and formed a string of uncountable Joes that converged and disappeared into a vanishing point far behind the glass. God, what a thought.

"Joe, are you going to putter around all night in there complaining about House and the cat, or are you coming to bed?"

He glanced at Maria as her bathrobe slid down over her skin and disappeared. Clothed in only a glow of vitality, she pulled back the covers on her side of the bed and smiled.

"I'll be right there," Joe called back as he reached down and lifted the toilet seat. My God she's beautiful . . . my friend and lover. Why'd I ever leave her for two months, even two days? Really do love her. Always so inviting . . . so warm against me . . . smooth skin brushing over me . . . so quick to . . .

"Joe, you left the seat up," said House.

"Maria, that's not funny!"

"Then why are you laughing?"

"What other goodies does House have in store for me?"

"Get in here and find out."

"Best idea of the day. But do I have to say just the right words?"

"You don't have to say anything."

"That I can manage."

"Sure you're not too tired."

Joe snuggled in next to his wife. "Tired, yes—dead, no."

"Relax, honey. Slow down. I'm not going anywhere."

"Good. That would really slow me down."

"You're not going anywhere either, are you? . . . Another mission?"

"No, I'm back at the tail end of the line again."

"I like you there. Maybe you'll have time to find a real job, one that lets you stay home like everybody else."

"Don't think I'll do anything that drastic, but don't worry. My number won't come up again for at least another year."

"Good." Maria pressed the full length of her body against Joe. "This is where you belong—right here!"

"How could I ever argue with that?"

14

□□□

commit

tuesday—august 16

Rested. Relaxed. Rational.

Joe's body felt alive and loose; his mind, quick and clear. He sat serene and cool at a composed attention; his hand lay lax on his communications controller as his torso pushed straight up and stretched for more. Nothing like a good night's sleep.

He looked forward and studied a distant point of holographic light. It budded and bloomed into a three-dimensional image of a human head, magnified and intensified into a replica of their leader, stabilized and clarified into a duplicate of Dr. Daro.

"Good morning, gentlemen."

"Good morning, sir," said Joe.

"Morning, sir," echoed Buck.

"Before you give me your recommendation, I have two comments and some information for you."

Two necks flexed forward, two voices blended into one. "Yes, sir?"

"First, let me express my sorrow to both of you on the loss of Dieter and his family. He was a valuable member of our team who I held in high regard."

Two voices blended again. "Thank you, sir."

"Second, Joe, I have read your preliminary report."

"Yes, sir?"

"Although what you do with your own time is your own concern, you are to remember that you have been developed into an asset to the program—by the program. You are expected to exercise good judgment by not putting yourself at risk more than is necessary in the performance of your normal activities."

"I understand and appreciate that, sir. But neither Dieter nor I felt any risk was involved, especially since we had taken our families."

"Clearly there was some risk as events have demonstrated."

"Yes, sir, I agree. But I also believe that Dieter's death was not an accident. Sir, I suspect that Kurt Grimm, and maybe Otto Stark, had something to do with it."

"Do you have any proof?"

Joe stared at Dr. Daro, at the face that nudged just a bit closer, the eyes that, as he thought of Kurt Grimm, shrunk into fathomless voids in his mind, then reappeared as he fought to focus. "No, sir."

"Then public accusations such as that, especially of an individual who died while in the service of an established and reputable firm's flight activities, cannot now be made. Is that clear?"

"Yes, sir."

"Now my information. Yuri's body has been recovered. He was located on the floor of Karov Crater adjacent to the west wall. He was seated in his Rover with his restraint system tight. The Rover's system configuration was in the traverse mode. That is, everything was configured as if he just took his hand off the forward speed controller and sat still. Ninety-three percent of his oxygen supply was left and the integrity of his suit was not compromised. The initial autopsy, accomplished on station Unity, did not reveal any heart or brain damage." Dr. Daro paused.

Joe watched Dr. Daro's head as it crept forward again, then looked above and to either side at the lenses of the holovision cameras that simultaneously also creep forward, cold clear glass that nudged forward to refocus the light that defined his own person to Dr. Daro, light that was turned into a data stream, then reconstructed over thirteen hundred miles away. Dr. Daro's controlling the viewing distance to us, and for some reason, the comm tech must have our cameras slaved to his. Joe pictured the replication of his own head that hung suspended in Dr. Daro's office in Oceanside, California, of his own face that also crept toward Dr. Daro for higher levels of scrutiny. Dr. Daro had paused, Joe realized, not because he didn't have more information, but because he wanted to examine the effect on its recipients.

"Poison and electrical shock are two candidates still under investigation, although sources for either are not apparent. His remains, because of the low temperature of lunar night, were well preserved and . . ."

As Dr. Daro's head continued its forward creep, an image poked upward into Joe's awareness and, for a moment, shoved all signals from optic nerves aside, an image of Yuri as he sat erect, torso stretched up to straight vertical, hand lax on his controller—just like Joe now—but frozen solid.

Again, sharp eyes nudged a bit nearer, pierced a bit deeper, lenses crept a bit closer. ". . . are being returned to Houston for further tissue and neurological analysis. Questions?"

"None here, sir," said Buck.

"Sir, could there be any relation between Yuri's death, Dieter's death, the problems we experienced on our last mission, and PRECISE?"

"We cannot rule out such a connection. Also, although nothing has ever been brought to light to validate them, claims exist that PRECISE is guilty of infractions of UN Human Biological Engineering Restrictions. And like you and others, I am also suspicious and would like to initiate a formal inquiry into PRECISE's activities at Karov. However, without clues or solid understanding of what is taking place beneath the surface—and proof—we cannot go on the offensive. That brings us to your recommendation. Proceed."

Buck glanced at his notes, then at the cameras. "Sir, we admit that the understanding to support our recommendation is soft. That is, all we have are observations and suspicions but no hard data. What we believe we have is the following:

"First, whatever the activity of PRECISE, its focal point appears to be at their Observatory by Karov Crater. They have carefully controlled every visit we've ever made there."

"That's right, sir." Joe watched Head and Lenses, acting as a team, nudge toward him again. "Some of the old-timers who have been there say the same thing. It feels much like the old days, the times when the hard-liners were in control, the days before the

Eastern Bloc completely opened up to the West with their 'One World, One People' policy."

Buck nodded, then continued. "Second, their construction on the lunar base appears to have slowed down. It's clear they don't intend to finish LB-13 and turn it over to us until we give in to demands they must know are unreasonable. They're stalling. In truth, sir, Yuri stayed behind to find out what was really going on. He felt an undercurrent there, heard some reference to 'Phase Five' and a deadline of September first. Thus, there may be a time element that we also have to recognize."

Buck's glance at Joe offered him a turn. He took it. "Lastly, sir, we suspect that Otto Stark as well as Kurt Grimm, or his, ahhh, twin, are involved in whatever they are doing."

Head loomed and Lenses lurched!

"Sir, our recommendation is simple," concluded Buck. "Proceed as Norm Steerman has proposed with Lunar Expedition Mission 337. That is, return to Karov with compromise proposals on their items of noncompliance and, at the same time, do whatever is required to find out what's really going on at their Observatory."

Now but a few paces away, Head asked, "Since the Observatory is far removed from the construction site, how do you propose our crew will gain access to it?"

"If they could not gain access to the Observatory on official business like Yuri did," said Joe, "they would have to fake a systems problem with their Rover while they were on a traverse adjacent to it. PRECISE would have to take them in. From there on they would have to play it by ear. We admit that it's an old trick, but old tricks often work."

Head nudged. "Continue, Buck."

"We propose that Mission 337 be launched as soon as possible, which we've determined is the twenty-sixth of this month, if we commit to it today. They would land at Karov on the twenty-ninth, only three days before September first. That's not much time, but it's the best we can do. Our launch constraint comes from the availability of an EMTV at Station Von Braun. An Agile booster for launch to Von Braun could be ready at Kourou within two days from a go-ahead."

Head, with its thin black hair lying straight back like it aligned itself with a stiff wind, nudged forward to prod again. "Please continue."

"Our last general consideration is the composition of the crew," said Buck.

Joe's toes curled under.

"We believe that it should functionally be the same as Mission 336. That is, it would require an Astrogeologist, a Lunar Base Engineer, and a Pilot who functions as the Commander. We would assume that PRECISE would want Otto Stark also on the mission to function as their 'coordinator,' whatever that may be. We would like to discourage that because his presence will make it harder for the crew to do what might be required to gain access to the Observatory.

"In summary, sir, if we are to be as proactive as possible, and based on the limited information we have, we recommend that we accelerate Mission 337 and augment its objectives."

Head held fixed. "So far your proposed actions are logical. In fact, they coincide with what I have asked Mission Planning and Implementation to initiate this morning. Please continue."

"Continue?"

"Yes, finish your definition of the mission, Buck. Who specifically do you propose be assigned to the crew?"

"We have only given that cursory thought, sir, since our current procedure is to take whoever comes up next in the rotation for each slot. We also assumed that because of the renewed emphasis on uniformity of crew capabilities, that we would continue to operate in this way."

Joe's toes clawed at his shoes as his legs tightened.

"And what does that tell you?"

Buck turned to the side and punched his keyboard, then glanced at his screen. "The Lunar Base Engineer would be Hunter Middleton; the Astrogeologist, Roxanne Jama; and the Commander, Anthony Apathenio."

"Are they the best ones for this mission?"

"We're no longer used to thinking in those terms, sir, but let me review their individual situations. Hunter has three previous tours of duty on lunar bases and has worked with Norm Steerman on Mission 337 since he assumed that would be his next flight. Yes, because of that, he's the Lunar Base Engineer best suited for this mission. And Rox, the Geologist—"

Head frowned, wagged, side to side, and exhaled.

". . . ahh, Roxanne, sir, has worked with Hunter and Norm getting ready for this mission. She knows the geology of the region and its engineering implications and is therefore likewise best suited. And Tony, the Commander, is a competent Pilot, a real level head who has a meticulous sense of detail. If we can define and detail the specifics of the mission, he'll make sure it happens without fail."

The tightness in Joe's legs rippled up his back and invaded his neck.

Head crept closer.

"Obviously he is current in lunar approaches and landings," Buck continued. "Yes, he should perform the job very well."

"Very well or the best?"

"Ahhh . . . sir, since we now strive for uniformity, have we not said they would be one and the same?"

Head jumped toward Joe. "Mr. Rebello, what do you think?"

"The same?" Rigid fingers dug into rock-hard thighs. "If someone is competent and does a uniformly adequate job, is that the same as someone who's highly motivated and does an outstanding job when it's really required, the very best possible? No, sir, despite our push for uniformity, I don't believe that is the same . . . No, not the same." Joe paused as he tried to understand it one more time. Uniformity equals diversity? Conformity produces excellence, not mediocrity? Double talk, it's all . . . "Hell no they're not the same!" My God, remember who you're talking to, Rebello. "Excuse me, sir. But the Commander is the one who can really make the difference, especially on this mission where experience with PRECISE is required. No, it's not just experience, it's the strong drive to find out what they're up to, what they're willing to kill for, and the commitment to stop it. Damnit, he has to have commitment!" Though loud, Joe never heard the table resound with the thud of his fists.

Head hurdled forward. Joe's mind felt its hot breath on his face. Black pupils framed in ice-green pierced into his eyes as a staccato of words sliced into his ears—together, they cut into his brain. "And tell me, Mr. Rebello, who is corps is so committed?"

"Right now? Only one, sir . . . myself. *Me!*"

Joe watched Head glide away as pulses in his ears echoed the explosions in his chest. He unclenched his teeth, sucked in a deep breath, and tried to relax the rock in his chair back into flesh. Rebello, are you out of your mind? What have you done? It's not your turn . . . no . . . but if not me, who?

Buck nodded at Joe and smiled.

Head nodded at Joe and smiled—actually smiled!—something Joe had never seen before. "Joe, I agree. You are the best one for the mission and that is what is required here. As Commander of Lunar Expedition Mission 337, pull together the training plan for Hunter, Roxanne, and yourself and obtain Buck's written concurrence by 1600 tomorrow. We expect a lot of you and of this one, Joe. Don't disappoint us."

A few beads of sweat joined together into a single drop and ran down the back of his neck. "Yes, sir. I . . ."

Buck leaned over and extended his hand. "Congratulations, ole buddy. Make it a good one."

"I . . ."

"Joe and Buck, for your information I also do not believe that forcing uniform behavior comes close to optimizing achievement. Unfortunately, large systems that must predict or control performance rarely can be flexible or creative enough to find any other way to proceed. And right now, it's become bigger than all of us."

One part of Joe's mind, the emotional part, tried to backpedal, to turn, to run. The other half, the logical and trained half, moved forward to chew on its new task. "Who will notify Rox . . . Roxanne and Hunter?"

"I will," said Buck. "I'll have them both here by 0800 tomorrow."

"And what about Otto?"

"He will not be available for this mission," said Dr. Daro. "PRECISE has requested that he return home by the end of this week."

"Did they say why, sir?" asked Joe.

"Yes. They have another mission for him."

"Did they say what it is?"

"No. But we have determined that it is a mission classified with their highest priority."

Joe tensed again as thoughts of Yuri and Dieter surfaced. The other side kills for what they want . . . whatever *that* is. Sharp lines are being drawn, and now, Rebello you turkey, you're about to step in their way. I've gone far beyond being just professional. Now I'm totally committed—me, my *life*—committed up to the hilt!

Big Rock looked distant, dark, and dead.

At the instant Wolf glanced out the window, Moon, his

temporary target, approached at 4374 mph. The half-lit ball of dirt and rock, the human outpost now under attack by the first wave of human settlers, looked lifeless, but not useless, Wolf reflected, no, far from useless.

With his fingertips, he pushed off the wall, then floated to the opposite window. With glassy eyes, he looked back at Earth and familiar thought patterns once again coalesced to shape his daydreams. Sometimes you have to work at the fringe of civilization, beyond eyes that pry and inspect, beyond minds that poke and question. In the old days, the good old days of strength and discipline, it would've been all too easy. With no risk, unnamed facilities behind locked doors down there would've been sufficient. But not now.

Damn Soviets were the first with their glasnost—simply threw up their skirts and let the West see all their privates, let the West convince them that the discipline and secrecy of their central control was an anachronism. Stupid. Weak. Then their sickness seeped into all of us like cancer. Although we forced it into remission many times for many years, once it first got a foothold, it just couldn't be killed, couldn't be excised. Eventually, we replicated their system on our turf and now look the same . . . on the surface. A smile inverted Wolf's frown. Maybe it's worked out for the best. They've forced us to operate on two levels, made our covert level burrow down deeper, take more liberties, seize more power. No longer have to bring everybody into every decision. Yes, let the soft bellies play around up there and look good to get reelected. We'll stay down here and create our real strength, our real future.

With his toes and ankles, Wolf pushed off and shot back to the opposite side of the spacecraft. He grabbed the handhold and wrenched his face to the window where only lunar gray and black returned his stare. Yes, a little inconvenient at first, but the autonomy's been well worth it. Just had to learn how to hide it, disguise it, hold it under wraps until we got it fully developed, until it can't be stopped—and at last we're there, ready to take those epic strides that'll return us to unquestioned leadership. Wolf broke into a rare grin. And it's all fit in so well with what I want, what I have to give.

Wolf looked at the center of Moon's face, at the surface illuminated by harsh radiation, then mentally burrowed straight through Big Rock to his destination, to the darkness of Karov, the region on the backside always farthest from Earth's vision.

Our future, it's all right there only seventy three feet below the surface.

Sounded like a harebrained idea at first, but it's worked out well. Mother Nature made it easy, like she always will if you know how to use her. Everything worked so well in that lava tube. Just lay the sealex membrane along inside the tube, inflate it up against the wall, and now we've got it, instant laboratory and production facilities. And now I don't have to worry about the loyalties of the technicians being torn in two directions. Isolation's fixed that. Better yet, once had to depend on Earth for all supplies. Not now. Need Earth for just one thing—organic raw material.

In fact, now Earth needs us, although they don't know it yet. They'll resist with a lot of sentimental rhetoric at first, but we'll soon counter that. In the end, uniform superiority will dominate just like it always does. Wolf nodded as his grin widened. Yes, just like it always does and—for sure—always will.

This one's the biggest.

Ricky put his ear on his shoulder and leaned over just enough for his eyes to peek around the corner. He flinched. Mommy and Daddy had had them before, but this one's the biggest in a long time. "Discussions" they call them. Kinda sounds like screaming.

Ricky pulled his head back and screwed his index fingers into his ears. There. Oughtta work. No, still hear it. Mad Sound. He peeked around the corner again. Yep, Mommy's jaw's still moving. Why doesn't she stop? This time Daddy's hardly saying anything. Just backs up. Says he's sorry and . . . and something. Can't understand it. Guess Mommy can't either.

Ricky moved his hands to his eyes to wipe tears that seeped onto his cheeks and started to roll. Mad Sound flooded back in, stronger than before, and he jammed his fingers back into his ears. Can I stop 'em? Should I go between 'em? No, only would have to go to my room. Mommy'd just tell me to act like somebody or something.

Good. She stopped. But if she's mad, why's she crying? Daddy's hugging her. Good. It's over. Must be over.

Ricky removed his fingers, stepped around the corner,

started toward his mother and father and . . . Mad Sound pummeled his ears again! He scurried back, replaced his fingers, and felt tears flow again. He hadn't cried like this in a long time. No, not since last spring when he laid down to watch those birds with the big orange stomachs build a nest. How ya 'posed to tell which bumps on the ground are just bumps and which are homes for all those big red ants that bite? But that felt different. Hurt outside, not like now.

Why's she so mad? Just 'cause Daddy has to go away again?

IV

◻◻◻

CONTRIBUTE

If both are the best—must both be the same?

15

◻◻◻

duplicate

Cell carried Life . . . along with Wolf's ambitions.

Within Cell, a single human cell, Life, with its relentless vitality, pressed forward.

At the heart of Cell, Wolf's specimen O-M313 located seventy-three feet below the dust that separated the nothingness of space from the rigid substance of lunar rock, the physical essence of Life took the first step toward the most violent and cataclysmic event of Cell's existence.

Within the central nucleus of Cell, lengths of DNA, those storehouses of information that defined Life, relaxed to new configurations. Forty-six human chromosomes made of DNA, deoxyribonucleic acid in formal scientific terms, Life's genetic blueprints in more informal descriptive terms, unraveled as they hovered within Cell's protective nucleus. Forty-six human chromosomes, each slender like a human hair an inch or so in length but less than one-thousandth times as thick, unfolded from their tight wraps. Forty-six human chromosomes, blueprints for protein that linked together hundreds to thousands of shorter segments called genes, uncoiled to expose their entire lengths.

Long and lean.

Uncoiled and exposed.

And most certainly, clever and elegant.

Yes, Chromosome's DNA broadcast cleverness and elegance in the uniform simplicity of its structure, a simplicity that aided its faithful replication and enhanced Life's survival. It resembled a helical staircase, stairs supported by a double helix frame that spiraled upward around an invisible column, one with hundreds of millions of steps, one that would stretch thousands of miles into the sky.

Chromosome's DNA—blueprints for Life!—the essence of Wolf's tools.

For, if one were to slice every stair in half, each frame with its half steps would appear identical to the other . . . almost. Each step was in reality a chemical bond that formed only one of two possible connections, joined together only one of two possible pairs of molecules. Thus, each side, though not exactly identical, complemented the other, looked to be the mirror image of the other, formed a mold for the other.

Yes, no doubt about it—clever and elegant.

But, by design? By evolution? Or both?

DNA first, then Intelligence? Or Intelligence first, then DNA?

A Grand Choreographer? Or just chaotic chance?

Many logical questions. Few logical answers.

Was logic even relevant?

To Wolf, yes. But now, as always, only his own.

Ahhhh yes. . . . Wolf. He used the logic of his intelligence to "complement" the Choreography that thrived around him, Choreography of Life that he took for granted, Choreography like that soon to be in evidence again within Cell's nucleus where Chromosomes had uncoiled and unraveled, turned open and accessible, and now lay tranquil in wait.

In time, it started.

Workers, on cue, flowed into action.

Workers, themselves long molecules of protein called enzymes, flowed in to perform their assigned functions. First, they split each Chromosome into more manageable lengths and unwound each helix in a fraction of a second. Then they severed one chemical bond after the next, sliced in half step after step, and opened up the staircase like a zipper. They marched along one side liberated by the successive slices and, from an ambient soup of raw material, used the template provided by the half steps to replicate the side just split away. And along section after section of the other side, they marched in the opposite direction and also replicated its missing half.

Thus, each Chromosome of Wolf's specimen split into two daughters, each daughter being identical to the mother, and, therefore, identical to each other. That sounds logical. Things equal to the same thing are equal to each other. Copies, the same as the original, therefore the same as each other.

The same. The same.

Exactly the same? Errors not possible? Well, occasionally a few. But more workers, much like building inspectors, prowled along behind the moving fork of replication, detected pairs that didn't match, and made corrections.

But c'mon now, exactly the same? Corrections to all mismatches? Could not a few sneak by? Well . . . occasionally a few. But only about one in a hundred million matches remained in error to form mutations in the genes to assist evolution, to originate improvements from one generation to the next . . . or the reverse.

So now, seven hours from the start, ninety-two Chromosomes waited within Cell's nucleus where before there had been only forty-six, two identical sets waited where before there had been only one.

Self-duplication of Chromosomes.

Big deal. So what?

To what purpose could Wolf ever put this innate ability of Cell? Surely, if the purpose was just and good, wouldn't the Grand Choreographer already have done it? To a limited degree, He had—but only to a degree far less than Wolf.

"No doubt about it," said Joe. "They'll realize we're suspicious."

"Ahhh. . . . Perhaps that might pose a bit of a sticky wicket." Hunter's fingertips, like they searched for unseen cracks, meandered over the smooth skin of his cheeks and chin as his head tilted to one side, brow wrinkled and eyes focused at bare wall.

"Sticky wicket my ass!" protested Rox as she jumped in front of Hunter and banged her fists on the table under his nose just to make sure her words didn't go unnoticed. Hunter's fingertips hesitated for but a few seconds, then, as Rox continued to bestow her wisdom, they continued their search. "Them suckers would not only realize we're investigating them, but they wouldn't let us anywhere near their damned Observatory, no matter how serious we tell 'em our problem is. I'll bet those hypocrites would even turn hostile, show their true colors, and cancel the handover of LB-13. Then we'd lose access to the facilities and the richest source of oxygen on the far side. WSF would be in a hell of a fix—and so would we!"

Buck nodded. "All true. And since we've been assuming we'd have that access, our development of the far side would be delayed at least six years until we could build our own plant. We'd have Dr. Daro, the Director General, and every member nation screaming for our heads."

Hunter's fingertips paused over his quizzical frown—"Yes, that's what I said, a bit of a sticky wicket"—then took off again to roam, stroke, and search.

Joe glanced across Buck's conference table at Hunter and smiled. A raised eyebrow from this guy must be the code for stark terror. "All of you are right. Faking a systems problem might be too obvious, but how else can we get into their Observatory?"

Rox paced.

Buck pondered.

Hunter stroked.

Rox reached the end of her invisible chain, spun and accelerated in the reverse direction. "And that's not the worst of it. From what you said, Joe, it sounds like we should feel lucky if that's all that happens to us."

"Oh, yes," said Hunter, "I do believe that if Yuri or Dieter had been given a choice, they would've preferred to have only been fired."

"Regardless of what we think," said Joe, "we must be careful not to make accusations against PRECISE in public. As yet, we don't have proof that they're responsible for either death."

Rox stopped, swiveled, and erupted. "Proof?! Like you said, Joe, all that can't be just coincidence. How many more of us do they have to wipe out before we're allowed to act suspicious? Face it, they'll turn this into a massacre just to hide whatever they're up to!" Rox clenched and pumped her fists once for emphasis, then shot off again toward the end of her chain.

Hunter coughed into the back of his hand. "Ah-hem. . . . I do suspect that conclusion might be a tad hasty."

Rox jolted to a stop, swiveled, and . . .

Joe stood. He stepped between Rox and Hunter as he grinned back and forth at both. "Troops, this won't get us anywhere. Let's move on to the overview of our mission timeline." He searched their faces for concurrence . . . maybe even some cooperation? "We can work this problem for at least another week. I'm confident that if we continue to think about it, we can come up with some acceptable and sure way to get into their Observatory. So let's not force it now." One face pouted, the other remained frozen. Both heads nodded.

Buck punched two keys at his work station to modulate the litran coatings on the inside of his plexan windows, and the room dimmed. After a few more punches, a blend of letters, lines, and numbers jelled on the wall in front of them. Rox and Joe sat as Buck stood. "On Friday, September twenty-sixth, a little over a week from today, you will lift off at 0937 from our Southern Test Range at Kourou. Rendezvous with Von Braun will nominally occur at . . ."

Joe's body sunk into his chair. The surface of his mind listened to Buck while his mind's core assessed his challenge. His eyes shifted to Roxanne Jama. Bright, dedicated, and one of our most experienced Astrogeologists—but headstrong! Once the "right path," the ideal path, seems obvious to her, usually through her intuition supported with "just enough" rationale, she throws her full trust behind it. And why shouldn't everyone else also not barrel down that same path with her at full speed? Sure makes life simple. Use the intuitive forks in the road to separate the good guys from the bad. But don't sell her short. Underneath she's just impatient to get the job done and done right. Yeah, that's the one thing she really respects—quality performance—regardless of its source. Maybe that's just her way of dealing with her own diversity. Born in the French Territory of Afars and Issas, educated in France, China, and the United States, she's a combination of cultures, a combination, like her body . . . petite, wiry, wrapped in light brown skin with fine features, an attractive blend of French, Japanese, and Ethiopian, itself a combination of Negro and Semitic. Truly a random dip of the ladle into a well-mixed gene pool. More than most of us, she must think of the world as just one people, and one people with just one way to proceed, the ideal way—her way. But she does respect those who deliver quality performance. That's the route to making her part of the team.

". . . and dock. Then you'll transfer your gear from Agile to EMTV-7 and prepare for the translunar injection burn that Joe and Shiva will perform at 1517. After the burn, your time is your own until . . ."

Joe's eyes and his mind's core shifted to Hunter Middleton whose stocky, sandy-haired body sat at casual attention with one hand in his lap, the other stroking his face. Same as Rox, yet different. He also sees just one way to proceed, but the logical way, the way thought out in detail by the system and documented in standards, regulations, and procedures. That's good. If you're building lunar bases, that's the kind of engineer you want. But he's a Brit from just from one stock, one culture, one ethnic origin. Yet he seems to show no bias, just logic. Has a gut that processes only food, no decisions. A reservoir of quiet, stable, dependable thought—backbone of our system, but unfortunately, also the kind our system finds so easy to ignore. They say he's got a lot of humor buried inside. Hope so, but so far he's dispensed it with an eyedropper. And he's also bright and dedicated. I know that in time I can get us operating as a team . . . but do I have enough?

". . . extra thirty-seven minutes added to the nominal descent prep time to execute a thorough checkout of your Jet Packs that use the new TACS, or ATACS we're calling it now for Advanced Test and Checkout System. No one wants to repeat Dieter's problem."

"Buck, how do they know that thirty-seven minutes is long enough for the checkout?" asked Hunter.

"It's an estimate based on the unit's acceptance test run last Tuesday."

Rox glared at Buck, then Hunter. "What? That simple system? I'm willing to bet our butts that thirty-seven minutes is way too long!"

"You are?!" Hunter's wide eyes turned toward Rox as he grabbed his buttocks. "Please, not till we've tried it ourselves."

16

□□□

stress

". . . Three . . . two . . . one . . . zero. . . ."
". . . ahhh. . . . Didn't go!"
With the precision and speed of a robotic octopus, Otto's left hand jumped from one location to the next over spacecraft panels while its fingers flicked switches and circuit breakers; during the same three seconds, his right hand hovered over the computer's keyboard while its fingers fluttered over keys.

Left Hand Performed:	Right Hand Performed:
FUEL PUMP 1 & 2 - OFF	PROPAGATE STATE VECTORS, ENTER
OXIDIZER PUMP 1 & 2 - off	HALT PROGRAM, ENTER
ENGINE VALVE 1 & 2 cb - OPEN	EXECUTE
ENGINE VALVE 1 & 2 cb - CLOSE	RESET IGNITION + 2 SEC, ENTER
OXIDIZER PUMP 1 & 2 - ON	START COUNT, ENTER
FUEL PUMP 1 & 2 - ON	EXECUTE

Joe watched, his mouth open, his breath frozen. What's he. . . ?
"Two . . . one . . . zero . . . ignition." Otto's voice, strong and intense, rang through the cockpit. "Ignition slip of 6.73 seconds. Altitude of catch-up orbit will be 0.743 miles lower."

Joe hitched in a deep breath as their simulated Lunar Ascent-Descent Shuttle (LADS) accelerated straight up for nine seconds, then pitched over to start its acceleration along a rendezvous trajectory to their simulated Unity Space Station that sped overhead. He glanced out the window at Karov Crater and the WSF launch pad, both precise visual replications, as they shrank in size. He looked to his left at Otto, the real one, then over his shoulder. Hunter and Rox, just spectators in the simulator today, occupied the first row behind Otto and himself; the other four passenger seats behind them remained empty. Hunter's narrowed eyes sped through the launch malfunction procedures presented on the book-size screen of his checklist computer; Rox's wide eyes remained fixed on Otto.

"Where did that procedure come from, Otto?" asked Joe.

"Prop Malfunctions Checklist, July 17 Rev. It's in the software procedures, but we had no time to call it up."

"They gave you the old valve lockup problem."

"Right, Joe. They're still a few valves in the system that because of manufacturing imperfections occasionally lock up under full line pressure. The lockup usually clears itself once the pressure and power are cycled off and then back on."

"But how did you know that was the problem?"

"Logically, it all seemed to fit." The intensity in Otto's voice remained level. "But also, I instinctively did the right thing."

Rox smiled and nodded. Hunter ran his finger down his computerized checklist, then smiled and nodded.

Joe studied Otto. Intuition and logic, the guy not only covers the middle of the spectrum, but he also hits both ends. Decisive. Smart. Most of us would have aborted lift-off and waited until Unity's next rev.

With Otto, Joe monitored the thirty-seven- by seventeen-inch flat screen before them. It presented dynamic, multicolored displays that gave the crew only hints of what motives and deeds really lurked in the bowels of their simulated LADS spacecraft. In the center of the screen, computer health readouts from their CompuThink (CT) 8000 remained nominal. In the upper left, their inertial velocity, flight path angle, and six other dynamic parameters marched with precision up recalculated curves. In the upper center, propulsion system parameters marched with precision up their recalculated curves. In the upper right, electrical power parameters marched with precision up . . . no, currents to the engine gimbal drive motors ran a bit high, spiked up, then dropped to zero.

Alarms flashed!

The computer health monitor indicated three of the five redundant computer modules disagreed with the other two, and in the vote, the three won. The flight path started to deviate. The use of attitude control propellant shot up. The temperature climbed. . . .

Again, with the speed and precision of a robotic octopus, Otto reconfigured the cockpit. And again, each parameter marched back toward nominal as Joe hitched in another breath and looked back to another wide-eyed smile, another pensive checklist search, and more nods. Now I understand what happened, but only now. He understood it and fixed it—even as it happened! "Looks like they gave you one of the few single point failures left in the system, Otto."

"Yeah, single point failures—the worst kind! One engine drive shorted, burned and shorted the two drives positioned right next to it, and the current overloads caused power surges in three computer modules. That distorted each of their computations in the same manner. They voted out the two modules that were correct and then took control. I reconfigured the computer architecture and used the attitude control system to gimbal the thrust vector."

Joe found himself also nodding.

"Once you find an error, eliminate it before it grows and causes more problems." Otto's eyes flared, his voice boomed, and his hand crushed the backup checklist. "Eliminate all errors—immediately!" The scowl froze on his face.

Joe shivered. All of a sudden the cockpit had cooled.

Outside at the instructor's console, Sim Sup, the simulation supervisor, knew he'd met the challenge of his career as he prepared his grand finale of problems, another flurry of system failures, a flurry sufficient to devastate any Commander . . . almost any.

Joe watched and waited. He sensed it would happen soon, would appear at the most critical time, would occur in those few critical seconds before engine cutoff. . . .

It did.

Warnings and alarms flashed and rippled across the displays. Robotic tentacles pounced over panels and keyboard in hot pursuit.

Tentacles won.

"Engine cutoff on time," said Otto. "Nominal catch-up rate. All systems back to one hundred percent. All problems eliminated!"

Otto's rumble once again richocheted from spacecraft walls and sliced into Joe's mind—all problems eliminated! Cockpit's coolness dropped another notch and wormed through his skin into his interior. Joe tried to shake, to move, but he couldn't seem to budge his frigid flesh.

Hunter sat erect at stunned attention as his head twitched in micronods of agreement. And Rox, through eyes that refused to blink, continued to scrutinize Otto. She managed to close her mouth just enough to speak. "My God, Otto, that was fast, decisive—I've never seen anything like it!" Her eyes warmed as she continued to explore the specimen before her.

"Configuring for rendezvous," said Otto. With the same precision but at a lower speed, Otto reconfigured the cockpit's controls and displays for rendezvous with the simulated Unity Space Station. "Complete."

Joe eyes narrowed, then he smiled. At last, a mistake. "Looks good except for one thing, Otto. The primary comm for Unity's Control Zone is 252.1, not 237.3."

"Right, Joe." Otto's fists tightened. "That's the default number the computer presented. I shouldn't have changed it."

"Don't sweat it. It's only a frequency. Wouldn't kill us."

Though now directed inward, anger again gnarled Otto's face. "But it was an error!"

Sim Sup's voice invaded the cockpit. "You guys want to continue with the rendezvous or reset?"

"Otto, things are going to get slow if we continue. And if they couldn't kill you in the ascent, they sure can't do it now unless they fire a meteor right through the cockpit. Let's reset and get in a few more lift-offs."

"Good idea, Joe, but let's trade places. The next one's yours like the first one should have been."

"Okay, I'll take it, but all's fair. I lost the flip." Joe pressed the control button on his hip that connected his mike to the instructor's console outside. "Sim Sup, we'll take the reset. Thanks."

"Comin' right up."

Joe turned to Otto. "Buck said PRECISE requested that you get in some simulator time while you're over here. Does it help much? I mean, how close is the spacecraft you folks fly to our LADS?"

"Except for a few of our enhancements, it's the same. At any one time, we have over half of our pilots flying with the WSF. Makes sense to use the same spacecraft to reduce logistics requirements and crew training as well as save money on additional spacecraft and procedures development."

"Yep, that's what most other WSF participants have done," said Joe.

"Once something's developed that's the best, the only thing that makes sense is to duplicate it."

Hunter looked up from his checklist and nodded. "Sounds reasonable."

Rox also nodded as she continued to gaze and grin at Otto.

Joe's shivers reappeared, cracked his flesh, and brought some life back to his body. Eliminate all error? . . . the best? . . . and duplicate it?

Life pressed forward as Wolf knew it would.

Within Cell, Chromosomes coiled for the task ahead. Double their number again?

No.

For as if the Grand Choreographer had once more assumed direction, Cell's troupe positioned itself for the next number, one orchestrated with fresh animation to move the action forward.

Within Cell's nucleus, each of the ninety-two Chromosomes coiled and supercoiled, folded and refolded, condensed their lengths back down to microscopic dimensions. But in the process, each Chromosome remained attached to its twin at one point along its length, remained linked to its equal like a Siamese twin, remained hooked at a junction that itself would soon become the center of action.

Outside the nucleus, two "anchors," which had hovered together until Chromosomes started to coil, slid toward opposite sides of Cell. Anchors, sometimes called centrioles by Wolf and others who cataloged the dance, also grew as they moved. Spindle Fibers, much like the microtubes that formed a transportation network throughout Cell, sprouted from Anchors and grew out in all directions. And the thin film, which had contained the nucleus and defined its turf, dis-

solved. Many Fibers now had an open shot at Chromosomes.
They took it.

As each Fiber reached out and contacted a Chromosome
pair at their Junction, Junction grabbed it, pulled, and turned
its opposite side to grab a Fiber from the opposite Anchor.
Once Junction had gripped Fibers from opposite Anchors,
each side of Junction strained to pull its Chromosome away
from its twin, to pull itself along its own Fiber like a mountain
climber thrown a lifeline.

Junction pulled.
Fibers straightened.
Junction strained.
Fibers stretched.
Junction tensed and tugged and . . .

". . . Three . . . two . . . one . . . zero. . . ."
". . . didn't go—again!" Joe's fingers flew over switches,
circuit breakers, and keys. "Two . . . one . . . zero . . .
ignition." Their simulated LADS spacecraft once again lifted off
the lunar surface. "Ignition slip of 5.37 seconds. Altitude of
catch-up orbit will be 0.582 miles lower." He frowned. Same
failure they gave Otto. And I just performed the same recovery
only faster because I was ready for it. No accomplishment there.
Joe's smile returned as he flipped the YAW CONTROL switch from
AUTO to MANUAL. This'll probably tick off Sim Sup, but what the
hell, I gotta find some way to make this interesting. Joe torqued
the right-hand controller and LADS started a rotation about its
vertical axis as it ascended straight up. Lunar horizon slid by their
windows from left to right.

Otto blinked several times, then with a face contorted by
curiosity . . . then disdain, he glared down at Joe. "What're
you doing?"

"The closest thing I can to a victory roll." Joe stopped after
one complete rotation. "Put my signature on the lift-off just for
sport."

"Signature? Sport?"

Joe returned YAW CONTROL to AUTO. "Yep, there's no challenge unless you do something a little different every time."
He continued to study the displays as LADS pitched forward
and started its acceleration over the simulated craters. All
systems continued to function without error.

"Challenge?" asked Otto. "The challenge is to always do it the *best* way—*every* time."

"C'mon, Otto, loosen up. That's boring. If you never do anything different, you're just the same as everyone else."

"So?"

As Joe's fingertips danced over the keyboard, each display magnified the difference between the actual and planned performances tenfold. All systems appeared to function without error. His eyes darted from the panel to Otto and back again. "You really want to be redundant? Don't you value difference?"

Otto studied Joe and snickered. "Redundant? No, you'd be the best, not flawed." Then he shook his head as he turned away and mumbled, "Value difference?"

Joe called up the first set of backup systems displays and focused on the electrical power system where a slight error appeared, a slight increase in the currents to the engine gimbal drive motors. Again, alarms flashed from all areas of the display. "This one again! They gave me the same single point failure they gave you. These guys have no imagination." Joe called up the computer architecture display, reconfigured it, then called up the guidance display and commanded the system to freeze the engine drive motors and to gimbal the engine's thrust using the spacecraft's attitude control system . . . just like Otto had done.

"Fast, Joe," said Otto. "Faster than I did it."

"Again, I was spring loaded to respond to this one failure." Joe called up the main display to watch each parameter march back toward nominal. And, indeed, each parameter marched back . . . marched. . . . No, this time they accelerated away from nominal!

Cockpit lurched. Out the window, black lunar sky traded places with gray lunar surface.

"What the . . . ?!" Joe flipped the control switch to MANUAL and torqued the hand controller. Nothing. LADS, now inverted with engine at full thrust, accelerated straight back toward the cratered surface. He recalled the computer display. "Reconfiguration, I must've done it wrong!"

Joe froze engine drives a second time.

LADS's velocity continued to build.

Joe wrenched hand controllers.

LADS remained inverted.

Joe punched keys.
Went faster.
Closer.
Plink!
Light exploded. Horn blared. Sim Sup spoke. "Ladies and gentlemen, welcome to Rebello Crater."

Joe let the noise dull, lights dim, voices fade, and eventually the embarrassment subside. "Sim Sup, why didn't the simulator respond to my commands?"

"Simple, Joe. We gave you the same single point failure we gave Otto, but this time when the one engine drive short spread to the other two, the power surges distorted the computations of only two of the computer modules, not three. You assumed everything was the same and took control away from the three computer modules left—the three good ones."

"I should have looked closer. Guess I got too cocky, too impulsive."

"That's right, Joe. Take time to look. Things that look identical on the surface are not always the same underneath."

"Yeah, you're right. That's a good lesson." Joe glanced over at Otto. Hey, I'm the one that screwed up, not him. Why's he all tense again?

17

□□□

split

—Split!—

Junction severed in two, as The Plan, Wolf's plan, mandated it should.

One of the half Junctions, with its Chromosome in tow, started outward along its fiber lifeline toward its Anchor; the other half, toward the opposite Anchor. Which went to which? Wolf knew that it made no difference. Both were identical.

Within about a quarter of an hour, each Chromosome hovered with forty-five companions at one end of Cell or the other. Time to relax. Chromosomes began to uncoil. Thin films formed around each, then fused together like soap bubbles until only two remained, only two films survived to define the turf of two new nuclei on opposite ends of Cell.

But Cell itself could not relax, for it had one very last act to perform—suicide.

Cell's torso, now with a head on either end, tightened the belt it wore around its waist, a ring of musclelike filaments that girded the membrane. Filaments contracted . . . belt cinched tighter . . . membranes pinched in like an hourglass. . . .

—Split!—

Cell severed in two just like each Chromosome had done

before it. Two replaced one. Wolf's specimen O-M313 ceased to exist, but his specimens O-N626 and O-N627 came into existence. Suicide and survival. Two daughters now carried Life's spark forward, two daughters identical to their mother, therefore identical to each other.

The same. The same.

Human cell division and growth—Life!

Yet common. No big deal. For, of the hundred trillion or so cells that made up Wolf's body, or any adult human, millions divided every second.

And by this time, also mechanistic. For Man had probed and found "Understanding," a mechanistic picture of biological events that pushed his wonder and mysticism further down to ever lower layers of ignorance and discovery.

But also useful, extremely useful. For, when in the minds of men with moral motivations, Understanding alleviated a multitude of human miseries from cancer to genetic birth defects. Immediately after conception, defects including cystic fibrosis, sickle-cell anemia, and Down's syndrome could be detected and repaired long before birth. And given the DNA of a couple, the potential for defects could be accurately assessed even before conception. Yes, Understanding added undeniable value to the human experience—when in the minds of men with moral motivations.

But what of each Cell's future?

Both would be frozen. Then, once thawed again, one Cell's offspring would continue to be separated after each division by Wolf's technicians; the O–O series would be replaced by the O–P series, then the O–Q and so on. The other Cell would be allowed to continue as the Grand Choreographer had intended. That is, of the 8192 cells in Wolf's O–O series, cells from the "O"th (fourteenth) division of the original "O" cell, half their number would continue division and separation by Wolf's technicians, the other 4096 would be implanted and allowed to grow unrestricted.

Grow unrestricted!

At last. With only minor further interference from Wolf, each Cell could become two, four, eight, then a ball of sixteen cells. At that point, by geometry alone, cells at edge would see a different environment than those at its center and, as their DNA directed, start to specialize, to differentiate, to develop along different paths. And once one of Wolf's technicians implanted the ball into the membrane of a human embryo from which its former occupant had been evicted, then implanted this freshly brewed embryo into a uterine wall, all cells of the ball would plug into sustained nourishment, would grow unrestricted in both size and complexity. DNA would send ball's many cells down many different paths that together led to the creation of a single, independent, complex, living organism—a human!

But hold on here, Wolf's numbers don't work out. If the O–O series is the fourteenth division, that's two times itself fourteen times . . . that should yield 16,384 cells, not half that or 8192. What happened?

Thirty-one years before, back in 2008, Wolf divided the sixteen cells in the O–E series in half. Eight he froze and saved for the replications he just recently continued. Each of the other eight he immediately implanted in uterine walls and allowed to continue their replications unrestricted, to grow from embryo to fetus to infant to adult. Eight complements of forty-six strings of DNA each matured to eight individual organisms—eight identical humans!

And now, satisfied with the result, Wolf headed for his lunar laboratory, his research and production facilities, to retrieve and return with the first wave of his life's labor—THE GIFT!

4096 cells.

Each one superior.

Each one the best of the best.

And, of course, each one the same . . .

18

□□□

SOW

A ripple, just a tiny ripple, nibbled at the shore.

Ocean's surface, flawless and flat, cloaked what lay below. Along its edge, a ripple swelled, just a stingy slice from that uniform bulk that lay in wait. Ripple peaked, just a harmless precursor of that to come. And finally, ripple spilled and washed up and over land, just a miniature sample from that endless mass that, with the irrevocable might and right of nature's tidal forces, would soon surge up and onto shore, soon rise up and wash over plant and creature, soon cover and smother all natural diversity with cold uniform bulk.

Yes, a ripple, just a tiny ripple nibbled at the shore.

Tension rose.

Moonlight poured into the seventeen-foot clear plexan sphere suspended three stories above the ripples that nibbled at the land called Galveston. Moonlight also glazed up from the mirror that veiled ocean's bulk and it shimmered upward from the foam at bulk's edge before it too penetrated the sphere and mixed with the soft glow within.

At the center of the glow, a single slender support sprouted up from the clear floor, flowed upward, and disappeared under the overhang of white tablecloth. Above the cloth, a center-piece of red and white carnations continued up to discharge its fragrance into the enclosure. Fragrance, heavy and electric, spread upward and outward and permeated the senses of three couples seated around the table.

Candlelight appeared to intensify as it glittered up from the silverware, crystal and plates and glistened from the rich brown eyes of the woman facing the ocean, although her eyes appeared to have enough internal fire building to sparkle all on their own. She glanced at the attractive tan-skinned woman seated next to her husband on the other side of the table, then glared back at her husband. The fine features of her own fair-skin face, the outline of her trim figure, and her rigid pointed finger, all pulsed with each and every word she projected across the table, words that she'd amplified to carry well above the background electronic orchestrations. "If Rox here comes back wearing just one little tiny paw print, Joseph Z. Rebello, you'll never see your family *or* your fanny again!"

Joe's wide eyes shifted to the man seated to the right of Maria, then widened farther as they shifted back to her. He gripped the edge of the table and straightened his arms as he leaned back. "But . . . but . . . but what if they're Hunter's paw prints?"

Hunter lifted his chin, massaged his neck, and studied Rox who seemed to tremble with extra verve and vitality. "Don't worry, Joe, there is a distinct possibility the prints will be smudged."

Maria and Lori, Hunter's wife, only chuckled while the others broke up in laughter and guffaws, a chorus that floated above Otto's low uniform rumble.

Maria shook her head as she returned Lori's frown. "Maybe you and I ought to review the Mission Objectives."

"Right, then we're going to write a few Mission Rules of our own!"

Joe winked at Maria, then rubbed his forehead as he continued to chuckle. "Ooooh, boy, let's order drinks." He entered a single stroke into the keyboard on his right armrest. Six flat-screen, colored-video drink menus descended to face level and broke eye contact between husbands and wives, between Rox and Otto. They each dithered their individual cursor controls as they scrolled through the selections.

Otto and Rox hit their ENTER keys before the others and their menus ascended out of view. Their eyes locked and primordial messages resumed their flow.

Joe and Hunter continued to scroll through their menus long after their wives had made their selections. Finally, Maria peeked around Joe's menu, returned his wink, entered a keystroke that raised the two remaining menus, smiled at Rox, then jabbed her finger at Joe again. "Nice try, Rebello. Now, back to our Mission Rules."

Joe grinned at Maria—Okay, we'll play some more—then rubbed his forehead again. "Ooooh, boy." He punched another key and dinner menus descended. "Their steak and lobster combo drowned in butter is excellent."

"With those tastes, Joe, it's a good thing you're not like my grandfather," said Hunter.

"Oh?"

"Wait a minute, Hunter," said Lori. "You're not diverting this inquisition by sneaking your grandfather into it!"

"Aw go ahead," said Joe, "sneak him in."

Hunter inspected the backside of his spoon. "Yes, he was one of the few left who had to worry about cholesterol. He died of a coronary when he was only ninety two."

"How come?" asked Rox.

"He didn't believe in preventive measures like vitamin or mineral supplements with arteriosclerosis inhibitors. If he had, starting even as late as eighty, they'd have flushed his arteries out clean as a whistle. He'd be about 107 now and still goin' strong."

"Sounds stubborn," said Rox. "What about laser routing of arteries? It's been around a long time, although now it's rarely used outside underdeveloped countries where they haven't accepted chemical prevention. Why didn't he do that?"

"Like you guessed, Rox, he was stubborn, a real individualist. Believed that diet and exercise would take care of everything. Did only what was intuitive or he could understand in detail. He just couldn't conform to any accepted norms or practices."

Maria pointed at Joe, nodded, and smiled.

"That type of mental promiscuity will not be tolerated in the future." Otto's growl reflected off plexan walls and reverberated within the spherical enclosure.

Joe, caught off guard like the others, let the growl fade

without comment as he stared at his menu. Mental promiscuity? Tolerated? Steak and lobster sounded good before, but now I've lost my appetite. What's churning around inside this guy?

They each entered their orders in silence. Joe keyed in his last. As his menu ascended, a green light and soft tone pulsed from the cabinet beside his left elbow. Robo Waiter had arrived. He glanced at the cabinet, then back along the seventy-foot tunnel that Robo Waiter had traveled, back to the central hub that supported twenty other tunnels and spheres, back to their connection to the outside world where soon . . .

Joe forced his eyes inside to the illuminated SERVE button on the cabinet. He pressed it and a tray supported by Robo Waiter's mechanical hand glided forward. He distributed the drinks and held up his glass. "Here's to happy homecomings after each of our missions."

Otto's eyes focused on Joe as he held up his glass, then slid back to Rox.

Maria touched glasses with Joe, then Hunter. "Hunter, I really like your suit, especially your vest. You look very prestigious."

"Well, thank you, Maria." Hunter stretched his earlobe with a pained look. "Actually, I wore this suit only because of the problem I encountered getting dressed. I ran out of dirty clothes." He leaned back, hooked his thumbs in his vest, and glanced side to side. "You're right though, it does make me feel rather extinguished."

Joe peered at Otto. "What's your mission going to be like?"

"Just your standard logistics flight." Otto gazed over Joe's shoulder. "A routine mission to a lunar station and return."

"What kind of resupplies will you be carrying?"

Otto's gaze shifted to his hands. "The standard resupplies for an Observatory. Just a routine mission to Karov."

Karov! Joe's eyes dropped from Otto to the multiple reflections of the candle's flame that burned on the surface of his ice water glass, then to the reflections that flickered off crystal glasses to his left and danced off the flat faces of silver to his right. Furrows deepened in his forehead. At last something Otto can't do to perfection—lie.

"Otto, what kind of propellant is that you're pouring into yourself?" asked Rox.

Otto snapped back into a jovial mood. "A VodKorn Blitz Original. It's made with equal parts vodka and korn. Try it." Otto reached his hand across the table to Rox who cupped it in both of hers like an open book as she sipped from his glass.

"Ughhh . . . This really *is* propellant!"

"Try this, Rox," said Joe. "It's a VodKorn Blitz Classic, just the same as Otto's Original but with a touch of vermouth."

"Mmmm, smooth. Much better. Where'd a VodKorn Blitz ever come from?"

"Back in the old East Germany," said Otto. "It's been a favorite in a few places there for almost a century. When some of the Soviets first visited the GDR, they thought their vodka was stronger than the German korn. The Germans thought the reverse. So when they tried to spike each other's drinks, they created the VodKorn Blitz. The Original, the pure drink, the best drink, is made only with vodka and korn. Over here you add vermouth and call it a Classic. Some claim it's smoother." Otto stared at Joe. "Actually, it could only dilute it and make it weaker."

"Ever tried it?" asked Joe.

"No."

Maria turned to Otto. "Here, try mine. Joe got me hooked on it several years ago."

Otto slipped. "It's okay, but I know the Original is the best."

Maria laughed. "You're almost as stubborn as Joe."

Otto took a second sip.

Lori raised her glass. "Here's to next week's launch and a successful mission." She took a sip with the others and turned to Joe. "They sure didn't give you much time between missions did they?"

"No, only a little over two weeks."

Otto licked his lips as he studied Maria's drink.

"Yeah, next time I'll probably just find a 'Hi-Bye' note on my pillow," said Maria as she watched Otto reach over and take a third and larger sip. "And after that it'll be zip in the door, bounce off the first wall, and out again. Yep, Thee old Rebello Bounce 'n' Out."

"Why so soon, Joe?" asked Lori.

"Right, why?" asked Otto.

Joe pushed his gaze down to the table. "Sometimes that's

just what's required." He looked up to meet Otto's stare. "When's your next mission go?"

"I have to return home Saturday, tomorrow. We lift off Monday."

Monday! Electric and sharp, it lanced into Joe. A whole week before September first—we're days behind before we even start!

The Gift, only a ripple, but so all important to Wolf, so central to The Plan.

Even with the cool breeze in his face, a warm glow enveloped Wolf as his vehicle sped toward his lunar laboratory. Soon he would add 4096 more perfect specimens (perfect and therefore identical) to the 8 already in existence. And The Plan, a highly reliable plan devoid of single point failures, called for more, many more. In fact, it aimed for the pinnacle of the human condition—uniform human perfection—the condition that, by definition, could only promote uniform human happiness that lasted—of course—forever!

Wolf's hands, momentarily without a BioProbe, resumed their love affair as they dry washed one another. Yes, so much better than the Inferiors do it. With their antiquated method of sexual reproduction, rather than the asexual method of cloning, they take a gamble every time. Wolfe smiled. Sexual union—best they can ever do is nothing more than just a crap shoot, nothing more than just a lucky stab in the dark. All risk and surprise. Wolf's smile overflowed into an audible snicker. "Haven't ever seen hair that red on anyone but the holovision repairman!" Mother Nature they call it. Only Inferiors could let a random set of twenty-three male chromosomes fumble their way to a random set of twenty-three female chromosomes—then be forced to raise the forty-six chromosome disaster. No selectivity. No intelligence. All libido. Wolf let his mental images loose again as he cackled.

"Look, dear, she has *your* father's hook nose."

"But that's *your* sister's double chin."

"Well, look at those ears! Is Dumbo back there somewhere in *your* family tree?"

Wolf's cackle stopped as he shook his head. Oh, my God, yes, there's such a better way. Go with the sure thing. Why tolerate one genetic road apple after another? His frail chest puffed with pride. Soon he would be appreciated worldwide for his distillation and purification, for his perfection. A step forward light-years in evolution.

And all of it—soon.

Ronny's fingers pinched the fabric of his pants into another microcrease just below his right pocket. He stopped, wiped the moisture in his palm over the crease he'd just made, and started a fresh one. If he'd counted, he'd be up to twenty-three microcreases and going on twenty-four. He looked at Brett who'd dropped his rumpled half sheet of paper again, then giggled when Brett dropped his pencil as he scurried to retrieve his paper. Fingers of his left hand ached as they squeezed harder on his own paper that he'd clutched into a moist wad. Uh-oh, Brett dropped it again, but this time it floated down right between the feet of the man in the black suit. Black Suit must own the restaurant because he talks to everyone who comes in and tells them which tunnel to go down. Black Suit bent over and picked up the paper. He's got one of those heads that doesn't have any hair on it, kinda like a shiny melon. Hope Brett gets his paper back or I'll have to rip mine in half again.

"You boys need something better than this," Black Suit said as he reached under the funny narrow computer work station he stood behind. As he stood up again, he handed Brett two sheets of paper—fresh, clean, stiff, white paper!

Brett reached up with both hands. "Thank you, sir."

"You're welcome. It's not every day you can get autographs of astronauts, especially those who are about to go on a mission."

Ronny pushed his moist paper wad into his pocket and nodded. Yep, autographs of famous people. When I get to camp next week, I'll have something really good to show too, just like all the other kids did last year. He skipped over to Brett who handed him his sheet, then looked up at Black Suit who still smiled downward. "Thank you, sir. Do you know if they're gonna come out soon?"

Black Suit studied his work station. "They've just reviewed their bill and entered their acceptance. They should be here any minute."

Ronny tried to hold just the corner of the paper by his

fingertips so he wouldn't wrinkle it while Brett searched for his pencil again.

"Boys, they're coming."

Ronny looked down the tunnel at the people who approached. Gee, they look just like anybody else except for that guy at the end. His head sticks way up over the others. What do I say?

Black Suit stepped forward. "Good evening, Mr. Rebello, I trust you and your party enjoyed your dinner?"

"Did we ever! Thanks very much, Raymond. I can never pass up your steak and lobster. Excellent!"

"Thank you. It is always our pleasure to have you with us. Mr. Rebello, these young gentlemen have been waiting with much patience for your autographs. Would you be so kind?"

Mr. Rebello glanced at Ronny and Brett, then broke into a wide smile. "Sure, be glad to."

Ronny looked straight into Mr. Rebello's face when he bent down. Friendly face. And happy eyes that kinda twinkle, blue with little gray flecks—but sharp blue that kinda cut right into me like he knows what I'm thinking. Rebello? Never heard of him.

"What's your name, little man?"

"Ronny, sir."

Mr. Rebello took the paper to Black Suit's work station and scribbled on it. Then he did the same for Brett. The next man did the same. Hunter Middleton, Mr. Rebello said his name was. Never heard of him either. The woman with the tan skin signed them also. She must be one too. Then the next . . . Hoppin' Holy Holo-Man, is he huge! Ronny backed up and watched Huge Man take a single step to the work station and dwarf it . . . huge but still moves like a cat.

Huge Man reached down and picked up a pencil in each hand. Fingers of his right hand pulsed through short precise movements, movements that seemed identical to the precise movements made by the fingers of his left. One side of him copied the other. But which side took the lead? They both looked to be the same, both operated in identical fashion.

Ronny glanced back at Mr. Rebello who also watched Huge Man, watched with his body locked in place and his mouth wide open, its smile gone; his eyes wide open, their twinkle gone. When Huge Man straightened up, Mr. Rebello snapped back to his happy self and said something to Black Suit.

"You're welcome. And thank you for coming. We shall look forward to the pleasure of serving you again."

Mr. Rebello turned and, with the light-haired woman holding on to his arm, glanced back as he headed for the door. "So long, guys."

Black Suit then stepped back to his work station and handed down the two pieces of paper. "Here you are, gentlemen."

"Thank you, sir." Ronny looked at his paper. He could just make out the words scrawled at an angle across the top. "Be yourself! Best wishes, Joe Reb . . ." or something. Must be Rebello. Funny thing to say. Then, in neat letters came "Hunter Middleton" and in not-so-neat writing "Roxanne Jama." At the bottom, in writing that looked too perfect to be done by hand, letters braced with rigid precision as they marched straight across the paper, perfect script letters that leaned neither left or right. "Otto Stark—Equality for All." That seemed to have a familiar ring to it, like something they kept telling him in school.

Ronny looked out the door just in time to see Huge Man slip down into a black car with the tan skinned woman seated on the other side and drive away. Wow, he's perfect! When I get big, I wanta be just like him!

In her half sleep, Rox nuzzled against his shoulder and hummed a sigh.

Otto tried to slow it, but panic quickened. He tried to simplify it, but thoughts conflicted. His body tightened as MurMur, ever present at the back of his mind, rose and fell, rose and fell. Rox nuzzled in once more, then returned to slumber.

Have to restore order, select a single goal, achieve perfection—always perfection. Have to!

In the soft light of the silent holovision, he studied her face, shoulders, and breasts, then pulled her closer. Beautiful, exciting—yet different. And not Anna. But I did it. Shouldn't have. No, she's not Anna. So she can't be the best. But it felt so natural. Shouldn't. Wolf didn't select her. Competition didn't select her. She can't be the best.

He looked at her again. Skin's smooth, but she's dark, a mixture. Not light and creamy, not single and pure. Impulsive and moves in different ways at different rhythms. Not predictable. No, not at all like Anna. Can't be the best.

What am I doing here?!

She drew me, pulled me, but I went after her too, first Wednesday night, then last night, and now here I am again. And I don't want to stop. But it'll never work. Wolf wouldn't let it. So far we seem to match, but what if this time when she wakes up, we don't? There's no choice. But with Anna there's always at least one who will agree with me, one I can find to share my mood, one to match my desires, at least one of the eight. I always have the option of Anna or Anna or Anna . . . Anna . . . AnnaAnnannannna. . . . MurMur spiked and faded. But with Rox, there's only one of her—only *one*. Makes for conflict, all that conflict. Strange way to live. Far from perfect. No, not the best.

But does it really make a difference? Rox isn't worse and she isn't better. Or could she be better because . . . because she's different? What am I thinking?!

Otto yawned, stretched out flat on the gel-flex surface that generated its own internal warmth, then closed his eyes and again tried to relax.

Rox shifted slightly. "Otto, are you still awake?"

"Yeah, can't sleep."

Rox snuggled in and nibbled his ear. "Otto Stark, that's about the only thing you can't do. You are gooooood! But are you really good at everything?"

"The best."

"Really? How can you be so confident?"

"It's been proven by selection."

"You make it sound so formal, so rigorous."

"It was."

"Much more than the WSF?"

"Much more."

"How so?"

"They lined up a few candidates, the best of the best, and put us through every type of competition possible. I won."

"I believe it. Otto, I admire you, everything about you. I only wish we could have more time together. I want to really know you, everything about you, to understand you. . . ." Rox yawned, then stilled and softened in preparation for further sleep. "I want to know why you sometimes look so sinister, and yet can be so gentle . . . why you always appear so relaxed with everything completely under control, and yet seem to have a fistful of energy balled up inside you like you're ready to explode." Otto tightened but said nothing. Rox nuzzled in again as her voice trailed off into a sleepy whisper. "Tell me about the competition, was it close?"

"Only in spots, especially at the end." Otto paused. He'd left out only a few details so far. The "they" was one person—Wolf. The competition actually had started one generation before him and included 512 candidates, along with cells split off from their embryos, candidates each bred by Wolf from parents with specific outstanding characteristics. Early in their lives Wolf had narrowed the number to sixteen and then cloned eight more of each for the real competition, competition that started before Otto could remember and lasted up till just three years ago when he reached twenty-seven, competition that determined not only who was the best in an astronaut race, but which of the sixteen sets of superior genes would become the future of the human race.

Rox mumbled something too soft to understand.

Otto opened his eyes but they never focused as words slipped from his mind and out through his lips. He'd never felt this close to another human—one who would listen to *him*, try to understand *his* thoughts, overlook the heresy of *his* inner drives—even if only in her half sleep. "Toki Nakamura had an intellect almost equal to mine. We had tests in the lab and spacecraft, at the computer and composer and Toki hung with me right to the end. They couldn't decide. Finally they made us go one on one." Otto gauged Rox's breathing. It had turned slow and even, steady and deep. "I devised some ingenious questions all right. Worked harder than I ever had—until I had to answer his. The engineering questions were almost routine. But it took me two whole months just to derive the time variations of the second order perturbation of the contour of a black hole event horizon due to its angular momentum. Sensed it was zero before I began, but I couldn't prove it without setting up and grinding through a whole unified treatment of general relativity and graviton hyperstrings. No, I didn't come out best until I got him hung up on the computer-generated holographic simulation of the brain's parallel superset field processing.

"And Vito Dipola ran a good thousand meters. Beat me by over a second every year. But he tossed the shot like it was hooked to his shorts. Couldn't come close to me. Only Pepin Lipinski could. He edged me out by an average of eight centimeters in the last three tosses. Usually got me in wrestling too. But good old Pepi ran and jumped like a hippo. All dense muscle driven by fierce determination. Never laughed so hard since I watched him speed through the hundred-meter butterfly—running on the bottom of the pool. In the end, skiing probably gave me the best competition. Three of us all about the same in the downhill. Finally they figured that if we couldn't eliminate each other, they'd keep us racing and let the oaks or the boulders or the cliffs do it. They wouldn't let up, wouldn't let us stop until only one remained— *me*.

"It all took so much discipline. Wonder if I'd win again. I should. It all comes down to inherent superiority. Everyone started the same, received the exact same training and motivation. And in the end, the best genes won. Yes, I deserve it, deserve to be One."

Otto stiffened as MurMur again started at the center of his brain but this time spread outward until it resonated throughout the entire cavity of its human host. And it sounded a bit louder, a bit shriller, and lasted a bit longer. Does it really come only from my own mind? Why's it there at all? Otto blinked several times and MurMur faded. A shiver ran through his body, a rare event, and aroused the warm flesh pressed against his side.

Rox hugged him as she whispered, "Otto, you've been through so much. How's it feel to know you're the best?"

"Satisfying . . . a real strong sense of accomplishment . . . and also responsibility for the future. But then, there's other times, Rox, when I feel so . . . insignificant, like I'm lost in the noise and I just don't know who or what I am."

"We all feel that way at times, Otto."

"You do?"

"I certainly do. But it's hard for me to see how you could. You're one in a million!" Rox felt Otto shiver again. "Well, there's one thing I know you are for certain, and that's cold. That I can fix." Replenished energy surged within her body as she moved over him again.

What's Rox doing this time? Hmmmmm . . . that's different . . . really different!

V

CHASE

Be noble and true, run the righteous race—unless you're behind.

19

□□□

ignite

Only a warm breeze, yet birds dropped.

Grass swayed, then bent as the warm breeze swept by. Birds, those that could still fly, fled the furor, fled the sound that came not as a whisper, not as a roar, but as an acoustical carnage that'd burst into being and now exploded outward to escape its source.

Closer in, hot wind lifted grains of earth from concrete, sucked them into hotter air above, and heated them to incandescence. Like high-performance fireflies, grains shot outward for a fraction of a second before they smashed into cooler air and slowed and faded. Yet hot wind continued to come, continued to flee outward and away from that distant violence—away from Source.

Closer in, a steady torrent of flame blazed as it tore over flame bucket's surface. Flame poured heat into bucket's skin and forced its metal body to swell and buckle. Skin softened and turned cherry-red as it tried in vain to radiate the heat back into the hotter flame, flame that continued to spew downward and away from that reservoir of rage above—away from Source.

Closer in yet, white-hot gas pushed on rocket nozzle walls as it surrendered some of its heat and pressure to accelerate, to propel itself down and out through nozzle's throat, to flee out and away from that butchery above—away from Source.

Within the birth chamber's core, Source resided, a fixed and stable holocaust at peace with itself. By undeniable laws of nature, trillions upon trillions of oxygen atoms and twice their number of hydrogen atoms mated with one another each and every second, annihilated themselves, gave birth to molecules of water, and, in the process, unleashed the energy that fed it all. Upon precise inspection, every molecule born was identical in form to the others and to their brothers outside except that they now radiated and vibrated and spun with excess energy as they rammed into the walls of the caldron of their creation, pushed it upward, and escaped out its throat.

Above Source, a bulk of raw material resided in frigid tanks, a bulk of hydrogen and oxygen that, in time, would also annihilate itself, also feed Source's holocaust, and also propel its offspring with their superior performance into an oblivious world in wait.

Farther above Source resided the one in control, that one who now vibrated and shook with waves of energy from below, that one who'd already burst from the caldron of his own creation with his own superior performance.

"Evolution One, you've got tower clear and five good engines."

"Roger that, Control. All lookin' good here."

"Bring it back to us, Evolution One."

"You can count on it. See you in ten days."

"We'll be waiting, Otto."

Deep down, it consumed and burned.

Yet, after dinner, Joe relaxed. He had no choice. Another four days to lift-off, and he could only wait. Otto had a head start, at something, and he could do nothing to change it. Logic told him that, and experience and discipline, the edge of the veteran, clamped a lid tight on his impatience. Yet deep down, something consumed and burned . . . and just a little leaked.

Joe reclined flat in his favorite couch in front of their holovision, his cherished niche in the world that nourished him with rest, closeness to this family, and a full-scale, full-color, full-dimensional view of the physical wonders and intellectual richness of the world outside. He studied the two holovision images that hung before him.

Bluto's iron fist smashed into a soft stomach. Spinach spurted. Popeye wheezed.

Joe's right thumb pressed the up-arrow button on his controller. Images dissolved, others appeared.

Ricky thumped on his father's chest, "Daddeeeee!" Then he spun around toward the new images.

"Live, from Cosmos Creations' own Lunar Studios, it's . . . The Gaps!" Three men held hands as they bounced in unison on the edge of the thirteen-foot platform. They each wore identical canary-yellow rope shirts and pink silk leotards that ended in purple slippers with toes that curled up toward their lighted tips. Holovision cameras isolated the face of the center figure. Long knots of chartreuse hair straggled from the right side of his head and face in sharp contrast to the clean-shaven, powder-white skin on the left. Sweat beaded on the extra pair of eyes tattooed on his forehead and dripped from the baby coral snake skin looped through his nose.

"One . . . two . . . three. . . ." Together they leapt from the platform with hands still clasped, performed a single back flip, and fell through the bank of 256 multicolored horizontal laser beams that extended up to ten feet above the floor. On the first bounce they released hands and belched a single grunt. Then they continued to bound as they barked and howled and flapped their arms and flailed their legs in and out of the beams. A cacophony of noise produced by the disruption of the beams, a noise that reminded Joe of hundreds of fingernails scraped across slate, tore at his eardrums. He pushed the up-arrow button again.

"Daddeeeee!" Again Ricky's fists pommeled his father's chest.

Joe laughed as he grabbed his son around the waist and lifted him high, high enough to be just out of reach of the jabs from his little fists. "C'mon, Ricky. Those guys are just another second-rate imitation of the Voids. Must be hundreds of groups just like 'em."

Ricky flailed and giggled as Joe jiggled him in the air, then turned again to study the new image as his father lowered him to the floor.

A robot, the same structure but three times the size of an

adult human, shuddered and shook off foul dirt and debris, refuse and rubbish, crap and crud as it stalked away from an unending wall of garbage and into a rolling field of high green grass and fresh clean air. "And closer to home today, there is concern over labor unrest at the waste conversion plant east of Tijuana where a Tele-Operated Robot refused to obey all external commands as it strode from the plant humming a tune that one old-timer identified as 'Take This Job and Shove It.'"

"Can it do that, Daddy?"

Joe chuckled as he hit the up-arrow button one more time. "I think someone's pulling our chain. . . . maybe."

". . . a representative of the moral scientific community, I argue that the limit, if it must be changed at all, be raised from the current two to no more than four, the largest number of identical humans ever created in nature, a number that more than permits the psychological, sociological, and developmental studies proposed here today. More than this number would be inappropriate on practical, economic, and ethical grounds and would . . ."

Joe glanced at the life-size image of the man that hovered three inches off the floor just seven feet from his couch. The image stood erect in a brown tweed sport coat whose earth tones matched his tan face, whose crisp lines complemented his eyes that flashed and signaled an agile mind. "Hey, that's Jeff!"

"What's he doing there?" asked Maria who sat on one end of the couch with Joe's sock-covered feet against her side.

"Don't know yet."

"He looks good."

"He does. I don't think we've seen him since Ricky was born."

The image reached down and advanced its computerized text on the podium, a clear plexan stand that displayed the title DR. JEFFREY SITTLICH. "We should carefully weigh the known resources that must be expended and the nascent human beings that must be sacrificed against these highly dubious gains claimed for mankind's quality of life. That is—"

"Daddy, I want Popeye—pleeeease!"

"Hold on, little guy. Your mom and I want to watch this Special Report because we know that man who's talking. At eight o'clock, you can watch anything you want till bedtime . . . almost anything."

With concentration, Ricky contorted his face into an impressive expression of "pain extraordinaire," then relaxed it back to normal when his father returned only a "nice-try" smile.

Jeff's voice continued. ". . . exorbitant cost $237,000 for the specialized procedures required for the safe replication of each individual is, in reality, negligible compared to the callous taking of a human life each time a fertilized human egg is enucleated to obtain its membrane and the indifferent destruction of yet another human's right to individuality, or for that matter, the rights of the whole new identical set of humans so produced. A human's right to individuality dictates protection from conception forward now that . . ."

Dr. Sittlich's figure shrunk to thumb-size as the walls of the chamber around him materialized, walls covered with vertical wood strips that grew upward and inward and dwarfed him as the cameras backed away from the podium.

"Looks like the UN General Assembly," said Joe. "That hall always reminds me of being trapped inside the forward end of an inverted hull of an old sailing ship."

"Trapped?" queried Maria. "Joe, every nightmare you have involves being trapped inside something." She laughed and tweaked his big toe. "I've told you, I'm going to tell Daro and all your astro-buddies."

"They wouldn't believe you. Besides, you're exaggerating." Joe tickled his wife's ribs with his toes. "It's only every other nightmare."

"I didn't realize they were back in session. Must be one of the first ones for this year."

"And they have a full house. Probably a hot topic." Joe tuned in again to Jeff's voice.

". . . and only alter the DNA of the embryo after conception in those cases where we can clearly improve the quality of one's life by correcting or preventing genetic-related diseases such as cystic fibrosis, Tay-Sachs Syndrome, retinoblastoma, thalassemia, and the three thousand others or so that we're now able to address. It's clear, however, that mass duplication of human embryos would be just one more form of depraved manipulation for it degrades the life of the unborn by creating a world in which he has lost all possibility of uniqueness. Even more heinous is the fact that it influences the evolution of our species forever more. That type of manipulation of human genetics is simply not within our right. Instead, what we should again learn to value is the God-given uniqueness of each human being, the human diversity that develops naturally and can enrich all of our lives, if we can only again learn how to appreciate it and to—"

"Dr. Sittlich. I must object to this childish emotionalism and gross distortion of facts." The holovision cameras zoomed in on the figure of a second man ten feet to Dr. Sittlich's left at an identical podium but labeled DR. GHEORGHE VOITEC, BIOENGINEERING CONSULTANT. He stood pigeon-toed as he waggled his raised index finger toward Dr. Sittlich. "Surely the delegates deserve better than these absurdities." His rumpled gray jacket, with its left pocket flap half in, half out, hung open to display brown suspenders that lassoed in a baggy red shirt and a loose one-foot length of black belt that twitched in time with his finger. Above the crooked yellow bow tie but below the chaos of gray hair that straggled outward, his blue orbs, magnified by thick lenses parked askew on a pointed peg, darted back and forth between his notes and his target. Sharp gaunt features postured again for attack. "Face it, your views are naive and archaic."

"Marie, this is one of those times when holovision's just too real, too sudden," said Joe.

"I know. Just popped right in here with us. Worse than the Gaps."

"Looks like he just logged a couple of minutes on a paint shaker."

"In particular, Dr. Sittlich, your whole concept of the individual is outmoded. For example, it is—"

"Outmoded? In no way!" Dr. Voitec's body dissolved as Jeff's form materialized as before except with a crimson face. "Make no mistake about it! It is at conception that two strings of DNA join to define the essence of a new living being, a unique human that from that time forward is entitled to the same respect and rights as any of us, and most certainly the right not to have its DNA replicated and manipulated for another's misguided purposes. Our resources and energies should be spent enhancing the quality of life for each individual conceived, not in immoral manipulations of his genetics."

"Dr. Sittlich, your intrusions have progressed from the childish to the bizarre. Clearly, they're just another strong indicator of your weak arguments. Your infantile concept of the individual is outmoded, and like past irrational dogma used to shore up courage in weak minds, its time has also come to be relegated to mythology." Dr. Voitec pulled back his coat, put his hands on his hips, looked at Jeff, shook his head, and exhaled a long hiss. "It is alleged you have at least a basic medical education, but I see that I must tutor you. About a week after fertilization, but before any cell differentiation has taken place in an embryo, nature—all on its own—can cause the division of the inner cell mass into two halves. Twins result. Did one individual somehow magically turn into two? Or this division could be incomplete and Siamese twins result that share common parts of their combined anatomy, even a common head. Did one individual mystically turn into one and a half individuals, or how about 1.5373 individuals? And the reverse can be made to happen. Before cell differentiation, two individual embryos can be fused together into one and a single individual produced, one with four parents. What voodoo do you suppose caused two individuals to become one? Or did one die? And we can . . ."

"And you can produce more contorted and gruesome flesh that imprisons God-given souls in your man-made hells, produce more grotesque human forms with coalesced genitalia like we uncovered from the Sovata experiments in 2017, produce more malformed flesh just like—"

"Once again, Dr. Sittlich, I shall show restraint in ignoring your inane interruptions and return to the truth. It is possible to create human forms with 6, 8, 10, 12, or, for that matter, 512 parents, just as we can create the reverse, create thousands of humans, identical humans, all with the same parents—and all *after* conception! Clearly, the concept of the individual is meaningless. Only humanity as a whole is a viable concept. We are all of the same and one body, a common body that we should seek to improve to its ultimate."

"Bullllllshit!"

"Joe!" Maria wrenched his big toe. "Don't swear in front of Ricky. You want your son to grow up like a gentleman don't you?"

"Sorry."

"Daddy, what's a b . . . b . . . bullllllshit?"

"Never mind, little guy. Forget it."

"Dr. Voitec, what is inane and naive to expect is that the quality of life will in any way be improved, either of our lives or of those who are fused or replicated, by any of your manipulations. All the genetic engineers and researchers I know would never engage in such practices—for any reason.

What we *all* must learn again is to fully respect human life, life that begins at conception!"

"Dr. Sittlich, again you are totally wrong. It's been reliably observed that life really begins *not* at conception, *not* at birth, but when the kids have left home and the dog dies."

Jeff waited for the snickers to die before he tried to continue. "In summary, my plea is simple—respect the rights of each and every individual, born and unborn, and stop thinking only of ourselves!"

Dr. Voitec looked down, shuffled, sneered up at Jeff, rubbed his neck, then frowned at his watch. "I'm hungry. I'm going to lunch."

Evolution One accelerated.

A cloud, a cool tissue of condensed water molecules, just a soft and static wisp of nature, rested as a layer at thirty-seven thousand feet. With Otto at its tip, Evolution One tore through the wisp, spun it, shredded it, and heated its remnants into nonexistence.

Otto grinned.

As Booster climbed through thinner air at the top of Earth's tenuous cloak, it leaned to the east and accelerated over the bulk of ocean water below.

Propellants poured. Thrust pushed.

Mass dropped. Acceleration multiplied.

Otto, with a holocaust at his back and Evolution One as his mission, savored the thrust that rammed him forward.

Natural and simple, dynamic and strong, dominant and unchecked—just an extension of himself.

Otto's grin broadened.

Joe yawned.

The narrator's image faded, but his voice continued. "After a short introductory discussion of the proposal to equilibrate member nation's tax structures such that all citizens of the world receive identical disposable incomes, the UN General Assembly continued discussion of the proposed change to the Individual Rights Amendment to raise the current limit on the number of human clones permitted from one per individual to three. As the discussion resumed, Ms. Canace Bulloss, a

lawyer representing UN Legislative Affairs, made her conclud-
ing remarks."

Joe stretched, rubbed his face, and sat up straight as a new
figure hovered in his living room. Her immaculate business
suit, well-groomed features, and look of composed intelligence
provided a welcome change. "At last, a fresh approach, maybe
even a perceptive one."

"That we could use," said Maria.

"I will make my summary brief and to the point." Ms. Bulloss
stood rigid until quiet blanketed the hall. "Mankind now stands
on the threshold of explosive growth in human biological engineering capabilities and of a desperate quest for fundamental
principles to undergird the existent corpus of human biological
reproductive law and thereby replace moribund norms and
practices." As she inhaled, like a diver seeking an underwater
record, she again commanded total silence. "And, indeed, the
aforementioned undertaking ostensibly posits attendant aptness
of continued facilitation, congruous with judicious inceptions, of
course, of feasible administrative systems and peaceful manage-
ment environments inculcated so as to evince manifest implications and binding obligatory force!"

Joe shook his head and muttered, "Some of these people
should never be let loose in public."

"Certainly, in this regard, polemical discourse has engen-
dered notions containing more latent than apparent actual
value and posing only inferential relevance to arbitration
implementations of contemporary practices, *consueturdo pro
lege servatur*, versus emergent principles of genetic engineering law, consensus *facit legem.*"

"Daddy, turn back to an English channel!"

"Additionally, moreover, as we have so vigorously pondered
throughout deliberations of this esteemed corps diplomatique,
arbitration under the stipulated auspices of . . ."

Joe's eyes glazed. "Like whales, you have to be one to
understand one."

"I think she's almost done," said Maria.

"Right, and none too soon. Here it comes, The Big Finish."

"*Summa summarium*, humanity, *uno animo*, posits, therefore, our future lies before us!"

The announcer faded in. "So . . . there you have it."

"Have what?"

"Mommy, what did she say?"

"I don't know."

Joe nodded. "Maria, I think you're right."

Computer sensed velocity and slowed propellant flow. Holocaust weakened and thrust dropped. Computer continued to sense, continued to wait for just the right . . .

—Crack!—

Computer snapped valves shut, propellant in pipes slammed to a stop, and acceleration ceased. Otto's hands floated off his thighs and toward the spacecraft's display panel that swept at arm's length from his side of the cockpit to that of his copilot to his right. Fingertips of his left hand grazed the complex of colored lines, graphs, and figures that danced and flickered onto the section of the display labeled ONE ORBIT RENDEZVOUS, then glided down to the computer keyboard that appeared and brightened on the panel below. Fingertips punched. A line of new data, crisp clear data, flashed onto the display:

$$\text{MANEUVER 1 DELTA V} = 000.000$$

Perfect. Otto's velocity required zero change; Evolution One's booster had injected him on a trajectory that required no correction. Otto now only had to coast up to precisely the correct point in his trajectory that he'd now reach at precisely the correct time and perform a single engine burn to rendezvous in a single orbit with Excellence, PRECISE's Earth-orbiting space station.

Otto's features remained placid and cool as his mind absorbed the number and its implied perfection with the same ease as the image of the yellow-green plankton streak at the edge of the equatorial current below—something natural, something to be expected of the real world.

"Commander Stark, sir," Copilot said, "may I please have permission to initiate automatic system reconfiguration for rendezvous?"

"Yes, you have my permission."

"Thank you, sir."

Otto watched his displays fill with data. "Systems appear nominal over here. What's your side show?"

"Also nominal, sir. Commander, sir, we have just picked up

line-of-sight tracking on Excellence and our new relative state vector is exactly the same, that is, to within three picodeltas as that calculated by NavSatNet."

Otto nodded at Copilot. "Satisfactory." He scrutinized the horizon, studied his displays, then peered outside again. Soon he'd see it, just a flash at first, but then with a few more pulses of time and spurts of propellant, he'd dock with Excellence, transfer to his EMTV, and, with his fresh supply of propellant, thrust toward Wolf and the product of his genius.

Yes, soon.

Horror, a rare look, flashed over his features.

He jiggled his fingers, ripped them up before his eyes once more, and stared. Orange Ooze remained! He shook and snapped his hands over and over again. Yet Orange Ooze clung, even spread up his wrists and onto his wet blue sleeves. He scrubbed his hands against his wet blue leotards. No change. In a blur, he buffed them with his red cape, but Orange Ooze slithered up and over his elbows.

"At last I've found the answer," Lex Luthor cackled. "So simple, yet so effective." He slipped from his soft cackle into an all-out, gut-busting laugh. "Heavy water—the only substance known that rusts the Man of Steel!"

"Be with us tomorrow when . . ."

"Okay, little guy, that's it for tonight." Joe glanced at Ricky, detected another wince of pain extraordinaire, brought him eye to eye, and said, "*Good night*, little guy." Then he gave his son a bear hug and received a baby bear hug in return.

Ricky laughed, "Night, Daddy," then hopped off his father's lap and bounded from the room behind his mother.

Joe's thumb mashed the controller.

". . . nor do we agree with Dr. Voitec's unfair characterization of his remarks. Please let me attempt to put Dr. Sittlich's arguments, most valid and timely arguments, into different words," said the image of the man that now lectured from the podium in Joe's living room. The man glanced at his prompter, then beamed a smile around the hall, a warm, expansive, confident smile to touch all of the delegates. On the face of his podium, the high-resolution electronic nameplate declared MR. LOTHAR LOPESCU, DIRECTOR OF PUBLIC RELATIONS, PRECISE, INC. "Each and every team member of our firm holds sacred certain fundamental truths that are in agreement with those of the moral scientific community so ably represented here today by Dr. Sittlich. Equality for the individual is the underlying tenet of . . ."

Joe stood, took a few steps around the hologram, and studied the man from the side. Standard dark blue power suit, white shirt, and red silk tie. He conforms. But neatly tailored and well groomed. Trim, looks in good shape. Not nervous, almost affable. Commands both empathy and respect. Must have done this many times before, and he's probably very good at it. Maybe too good?

". . . human threshold of opportunity. Genetic engineering—the ability to altar our very essence—is the most powerful tool ever to be placed in the hands of mankind. Our ability to split the human cell is far more powerful, and far more consequential, than our ability to split the atom. As Dr. Sittlich has said, the ability to act does not always mandate action. As in all human activity, and especially in biological engineering, our wisdom and ethics must channel our needs and desires. We must seek only to improve the quality of human life, to move us toward the mankind of extraordinary quality that we all know now lies within our grasp. Yes, it is the quality of life that we all must . . ."

Joe stepped around to the front of the image again and studied its eyes. Sharp, intent, full of purpose. But "mankind of extraordinary quality"? What's he really mean?

". . . rather than selfish motivations. Indeed, we strongly agree with Dr. Sittlich's demand that we carefully weigh the resources expended for genetic engineering against the potential to assure that no individual suffers an unfair disadvantage at birth. In our firm, I am proud to say, resources are expended on individual genetic engineering efforts only if it's clear that the result enhances the human parity that we all seek. And now, as citizens of the world, we expand our principle of fairness to 'One World, One People!'"

Human parity? Citizens of the world? He's smooth, a few cuts above your standard holovision preacher.

". . . without discrimination or bias. Thirdly, we furthermore agree with Dr. Sittlich's comments on the protection of the human from conception onward, for each unborn human must receive equal respect, equal treatment, and equal opportunity for a quality life through equal exposure to mankind's excellence. Each unborn human is entitled to equal entry into a world where quality of life is cherished, where it is nurtured through equality of excellence. In short, and in conclusion—quality through equality!"

Joe waved a hand through the image. Is this guy for real, or is he all boast and bullshit? Then, as he flopped back down on the couch, the entire image evaporated in a snap and was immediately replaced by that of a woman with her arm coiled across her chest and her hand quivering by her shoulder. She screamed downward into the whimpers that seeped from a small face frantic with fear, one that rested atop a frail and fragile body only one-third her size. ". . . oughtta put a rubber band on it, let it wither off. Then maybe you'd learn not to pee in your pants, you dumb little runt. Why, you don't have the brains of even your father!" The face of lovable old mom exploded with an extra burst of crimson as her arm uncoiled and the calloused back of her hand made contact once again. *Whack!* The scene of domestic bliss faded as a man in a white coat seated behind a massive desk (and therefore authoritative) materialized.

Yep, here he comes again, Doc Savior to the rescue. Joe reached for the control. Damn, when are they gonna ever get a new commercial? The more it insults the intellect, the longer it lasts. He turned down the sound but enough still leaked through to be understood, or maybe he just knew it by heart. Joe couldn't tell which.

Doc Savior's face filled with compassion as its large brown eyes bored into Joe. "Didn't your parents make just a mistake or two in raising you, mistakes that you still suffer from today? And aren't you the one best qualified to specify how you *should* have been raised? But mostly, wouldn't you like the opportunity to go back and raise yourself—*all over again*?!" Doc Savior nodded. "Of course you would. Anybody would . . . even *your own* children, regardless of how perfect a parent you try to be." Doc Savior leaned forward and beamed his most earnest look into Joe. "Now it is possible for you to give them that gift! Before the conception of your next child, come to us at Quality Cloning. Let us describe our Embryo Duplication, that's ED for short (Doc Savior winked). Let us show you just how safe and how reliable the procedures have become. And lastly, let us also present the many options that ED opens up to you. For example, after ED, you may elect not to freeze the duplicate but rather give birth to twins immediately. Or, you may pass the frozen embryo on to your single sibling so that it can raise itself all over again at its own discretion. You may even elect to place it in your will to be passed down and brought to life at some future date. Maybe as your sibling exits this world, it may wish to have another one of itself reenter? Whatever your desires, call us today for our free brochure, request a free holovision interview with one of our friendly counselors, or, if you like, immediately visit one of our nearly four thousand conveniently located, personalized institutes." Doc Savior's face clouded with a stern look. "However, if you are still among those few who feel you would rather not have ED for your next child, please ask yourself, 'Can I in all good conscience deny the right for a second self to my own son or daughter, that second chance to raise themselves all over again?' Can you?"

Joe turned away with an extra effort to tune out the remainder of the commercial. Just gotta find a way to keep these things out of my home. Oughtta be a way to rig the holovision so that all commercials are automatically replaced with scenes from the great outdoors, or last week's football highlights, or even short bursts from a symphony orchestra, or . . .

Quality Cloning. Obnoxious bastards. Get your meddling mitts off my embryos! Try to make you feel guilty if you don't put seven thousand dollars in their pockets every time you decide to bring another life into the world. And it's only really just beginning. Did the sages of the last century know what they were starting with the Human Genome Initiative? Sure they're right. . . . Genetic diseases, cancer, AIDS, and almost all other plagues of our biological existence are fading fast, thanks to the applications of gene mapping. But everything's a trade. Always a little bad with the good.

They always make it all sound so logical, so ethical. Of course everybody's just got to have a Genetic Employee Map—a damned GEM. How could anyone ever live without one? Try to make you feel it's going to be a privilege to have your every gene—right down to your last base pair—coded and stored in some sterile computer. The ultimate response to Know Thyself. But once they do it, who really owns *me*? Suppose they wanted to make another me (unlikely as hell, Rebello) or even a million or two more (no one's that crazy), they'd just plug my code into a DNA synthesizer and let it grind out another string of that highly valued, womb-ready Rebello DNA. Or maybe they could play with the code a bit.

Yeah, why not be a bit taller next time, a bit stronger, maybe straighten the nose a little, or even be a bit smarter? Ahhhh, smarter you say? What's that number of that institute again?

And how soon till we fully replace nature's diseases with our own set, those we invent? "Woman never should have been allowed . . . Look at that short frail body, those close-set eyes, those stubby fingers, that flat chest. . . . Her parents must've evaded screening—how sinful, how despicable!"

Even now, if you don't let every official with a "need to know" run his grubby little incompetent mitts all through your genes, you're branded socially irresponsible, even immoral. After all, how else can insurance companies spot and eliminate those high risks with the genetic land mines, or law enforcement have a computer identify anybody and everybody who was close to the scene of a crime, or airlines passengers know for sure that there's no incipient physical or mental time bomb in their Captain, or the State know for sure that your proposed offspring won't become one of their wards? Whose rights do you protect? Answer's coming in fast—and it sure as hell isn't the rights of the individual.

Basic problem is that once something's accepted as socially desirable, it's not long till it's institutionally enforced. Hey, why not get it over with right up front? Let the social, insurance, police, and State planners define the optimum human, then eliminate everybody else. This whole thing is headed for a real nightmare. Yep, once you let 'em in your genes, you never get 'em out.

Joe fell back on the couch, yawned, and closed his eyes. Energy, you really deserted me early tonight. Pretty soon I'll be going to bed before Ricky. I must be losing it, or gettin' old, or both. . . .

—Crack!—

Again, computer snapped valves shut and acceleration ceased. Copious quantities of water molecules, now escapees from the holocaust in EMTV's engines, fell back into Earth's atmosphere and inertial and gravitational forces once again balanced, exactly, to produce zero gravity.

Charged with energy, EMTV coasted as it sped away from Earth—as Otto sped away from Joe at over thirty-seven thousand feet per second.

20

☐☐☐

initiate

friday—august 26

Gotta relax whenever you can.

Joe's eyes drifted half-closed. He pushed his arms straight over his head and stretched every muscle as he filled his lungs through a wide-mouthed yawn. Then he relaxed and let his couch reabsorb his full weight. *Maybe I'll just close my eyes for a second here.* Funny how after a yawn you don't need to take a breath for five or ten seconds. *Back hurts. Why don't I ever learn? Ricky's getting too big to play tick-tock with anymore. Or am I just getting weaker? Humid. Chest is wet. Shorts are hot and clammy. Air flow feels good. August is always the worst. Coffee taste sure stayed with me. Rich flavor. Still get aftertaste when I exhale, but only when I exhale through my nose. Must be just the location of the olfactory nerves. Just on the edge of sleep . . . don't drop off . . . need another yawn. . . .*

"Rebello! Are you awake up there?!"

"Noooo sweat, Launch Control. Just buildin' my reserves."

"We're coming out of launch hold on my mark . . . three . . . two . . . one . . . mark! Fifteen minutes and counting."

Joe sat alone in the forward crew station of the Agile

spacecraft; Rox and Hunter, in the station behind. Joe rubbed his eyes and squirmed in his couch. Time to get serious. He sent a SYSTEM STATUS request to Agile's brain from its computer keyboard. Brain snapped from slumber to full awake and filled the solid wall of display panel below Agile's windows with data on spacecraft systems. Wall flickered, numbers flashed, and lines fluttered as Joe skipped from one system to the next. DC Bus-B volts are still a little high. Avionics Bay P-4's running a bit hot. And YAW-3 reaction control jet driver's still a little slow on the open command. But all's still within nominal range. And nothing else has changed, nothing except Otto's lead—*gotta catch up!* . . . but can't go till it's time to go.

"Hey, Joe, would you like to leave a wake-up call for launch minus ten minutes?" asked Rox over the intercom.

"I do not believe that would be sufficient," said Hunter. "Better make it five."

"Hate ridin' with these veterans," said Rox.

"Yes, I too prefer a rookie—at least they pretend to get excited."

Joe drew in a breath in preparation for his verbal defense as Launch Control came at him again.

"At twelve minutes and counting, all systems are fully activated and lookin' good, Joe. And we see you finally got your heart rate worked all the way up to sixty-three. Don't slip back into another doze."

"Doze? Me? You got it all wrong. That was just an essential, time-honored medical maneuver—passive body energy replenishment."

"Yeah, right, Joe. The weather here remains gringy. Our overcast is solid moisture from the deck up to thirty-five thousand feet. But Agile will punch you through it just like always. That makes you folks the lucky ones—you'll be the only ones to see the Sun today."

"Gringy's right, Launch Control. All we can see now is solid fog."

"Also, on the way up you'll also see a little ice goin' through twenty-five thousand."

"Rog. Thanks for the report."

"We're ten minutes and counting. Cabin holovision cameras are activated. We've got good images of each of you. And the best odds goin' around down here, Joe, are that you'll slip into another doze somewhere between three to five minutes before launch."

Over two hundred feet below, swivel tests slammed Agile's rocket engine nozzles into stops. Muffled thumps rippled up the booster.

"Nope. Time to fire up. I think you guys are gettin' serious."

Otto, as a foot-forward spear, hurtled ahead in LADS's lunar orbit.

"Ignition's on time, sir. Engine's at forty percent."

"Right," said Otto.

"Altitude's 47,300, sir, and starting to come down again."

"I see that."

"Landing radar's locked on and we're right on laser center-line, sir."

Otto turned to Copilot. "I've got all that data displayed on my side, I'm in command and I'll make all the calls required by Karov Approach. Understood?"

Color gone, Copilot shrank against the switches in his corner of the spacecraft. "Yes, sir. Just trying to help, sir."

Otto turned back to his panel. Why'd I snap at him? Must've sounded egotistical, and that's a fault not to be tolerated. But something's gnawing at me . . . something. Otto tried to lock out all internal thought, all signals from his viscera, and let his rational mind wrap itself around the mechanistic world he had to control. He studied the display at the center of his panel entitled POWERED APPROACH TRAJECTORY—KAROV LANDING PAD A. A red dot, labeled LADS, marched down a blue line labeled PLAN. It pulled behind it a red line labeled ACTUAL. Red line crept down and consumed blue line—exactly.

Inside LADS, Otto's Lunar Ascent-Descent Shuttle, one of thirteen such vehicles PRECISE purchased from WSF, Otto rested with his feet brushing the floor, his back toward Moon's surface, and his vision directed out through LADS's windows into black lunar sky. His feet pointed in the same direction as LADS's engine that now throttled up to maximum thrust, according to schedule—exactly.

LADS slowed. And as it did, the centrifugal force of its orbital motion decreased below the pull of gravity and LADS started to fall. But with slow precision, LADS rotated forward so that its engine's thrust supported most of its newfound weight and forced its rate of descent to equal plan—exactly.

With abrupt precision, engine thrust dropped to eighty-three percent and LADS pitched forward. Otto squeezed his mike control. "Karov Approach, we've had pitch-over at High Gate. We're on centerline and altitude and coming down through seventy-three hundred feet."

"Roger, Evolution One. Pad Alpha is clear."

Otto looked ahead through his window at PRECISE's Landing Pad A on the east rim of Karov Crater, then to the left and the gray dust that cloaked the terrain, the exact strip of lunar soil under which Wolf operated. With no atmosphere to diffuse it, nature's sunlight sliced sharp against black shadows. Something continued to gnaw at Otto's gut. Everything's black or white. Everything. No shades of gray permitted, anywhere, anytime.

"Karov Approach, we're 4.3 miles out and have Pad Alpha in sight." Otto glanced at the computer-generated cross pointers on the display above his right-hand controller. "We're on approach centerline and altitude profile with all deviations zero."

Otto monitored LADS's automation as he continued to descend, glide forward, and rotate toward vertical. "Karov Approach, we're at Low Gate coming down through five hundred feet." He switched to MANUAL and LADS performance continued without flaw.

"Set 'er down, Evolution One. We're ready . . . all of us."

Below, LADS's exhaust dug into lunar dust and flung it outward in a uniform fan. Through the fan, Otto peered at pebbles, rocks, and boulders as he glided forward.

LADS lowered. Dust thickened.

The horizon and all but the largest craters disappeared. Below, boulders waited, boulders large enough to tip LADS over if a footpad should land on or even graze one, a peril proved possible back in '34 by the late Commander Tony Luzzaro.

LADS eased down to thirty-seven feet and hovered. Dust thickened. Otto nudged LADS forward. Dust disappeared and harsh sunlight reflected off Landing Pad Alpha's hard surface, a smooth white surface of lunar concrete marked with a landing target of black concentric circles. Otto halted his descent at three feet over the center of the bull's-eye and pushed ENGINE—OFF.

LADS dropped.

As he hit, Otto spied the sign fused to the concrete precisely in front of his window:

OTTO—OUR FUTURE, WELCOME!

He nodded once in recognition of the fact, then turned to Copilot. "Move it!"

"Yes, sir!"

Fog, thick and milky white, detonated with light.

Joe's eyes slammed shut.

". . . ignition . . . two . . . one . . . lift-off. . . ."

Agile leapt. As a giant high-intensity bulb lit by Holocaust's flame, Agile's halo of light accelerated upward. Light from the flame reflected many times from Fog's droplets before it entered the cabin, found fresh cracks in Joe's eyes, and attacked again. And again his lids slammed shut. But as Agile's exhaust cleared the tower and without a flame bucket to bend it back, its plume lengthened. Bulb dimmed. Joe's eyes, with points for pupils, reopened.

At the base of Agile's stack of metal and propellant, Holocaust thrust. Rigid stack quivered as it relayed Holocaust's message of raw power upward. As Agile thrust into Fog, its mass continued to drop and its acceleration continued to mount. But Fog fought back with turbulence that buffeted and battered the cabin, that jarred and jolted Joe.

Agile rammed. Fog resisted.

Violence peaked. Joe smiled.

At last we're movin' out . . . we're on the hunt! Joe's face fluttered as he scanned the blur of his panel, then looked ahead through his window. In a flash, Fog unloaded a layer of ice, but it could reach no higher. Agile burst into sunlight.

Ice vanished. Violence faded.

Agile won. Fog lost.

Joe's smile dissolved. Could all conflict be this quick, this decisive, and this favorable?

Four spaces—all empty.

Otto pulled the lunar rover that had been left for him at

Pad A into the first space and parked. He unstrapped, bound out, and entered the Observatory's airlock. In the absolute silence of vacuum, the outer door slid down and sealed tight. As Otto stepped into one of the airlock's shoulder-high shower stalls, his weight actuated air jets that tore into his pressure suit, ripped off particles of lunar dust that clung to its fabric, and carried them away to a collector. Jets continued, pressure rose, and suit softened. Otto removed his helmet and gloves, then peered through the hand-sized window of the inner door. Eyes, intense black pits embedded in a yellow matrix, peered back.

Door lifted. A frail body, one that stood with a hunch even in one-sixth gravity, half hopped, half hobbled forward.

Otto extended his hands. "Wolf!"

Black-yellow orbs that glistened with moisture rotated up. Long slender fingers, smooth and callus-free, trembled as they reached up and gripped fingers on each of Otto's hands. "Otto, today I start!"

Otto beamed down at Wolf. Excitement, long suppressed, broke loose, welled up, and gorged muscles with stored energy. For the first time since he'd left Rox, Otto's ear-to-ear puppy-dog grin surged. "Right, today."

Wolf blinked several times and turned. "Let's go downstairs. Before we start the transfer, I want to show you the Production Tube I'll use in the Domination Phase."

With flicks from his ankles, Otto glided after Wolf whose normal hobble, magnified by the light lunar gravity, reminded Otto of a wounded kangaroo. As they crossed the Observatory, he washed the irreverent thought from his mind. They passed through the door at the base of the support for the eighty-seven-inch telescope, the central instrument in the Observatory that could open Man's mind to the universe far beyond his incubator, the instrument that had not changed position since a technician tinkered with it during his time off three days before. Inside, they each wrapped a hand around a drop pole and plunged two flights to another airlock. Otto again donned his helmet and gloves as Wolf hopped into a quick-entry, low-mobility pressure suit, a task easy for even Wolf in one-sixth gravity. Airlock depressed and its hatch opened.

An electric car waited.

As they accelerated through the lava tube toward their destination three hundred feet south, Otto plugged a comm cable into Wolf's suit and leaned down to study the face inside the helmet. "How're we doing on The Plan?"

Despite the lack of air in the tunnel, their car's rigid frame carried both the hiss of its oversize soft rubber tires and the hum of its electric motor into Otto's suit and up to his helmet where they mixed and resonated. By habit, Otto bent over farther to pick up Wolf's soft reply.

"We're ahead by three hours and seventeen minutes."

Otto relaxed, pulled in a deep breath of rock-scented air, and looked ahead. He let himself be mesmerized by the reflected glare of their headlights, a glare mirrored from wavy walls of black glassy lava, a moving cylinder of glare suspended forty feet before them that undulated and shimmied as they sped through the tube. Otto looked to his left and down again. "As we landed, I saw a LADS on Pad D. How come?"

Wolf's yellow and gray features seemed to take on an added glow in the light reflected from the black lava. "Just as we've planned, The Gift will be taken up to Equality in the LADSs on Pads A, B, and C. But, for redundancy, I've also ordered another one to be ready for launch from Pad D. In fact, since you were last here, I've established redundancy for all of our transfer operations." They slowed to a stop as Wolf glared up at Otto. His yellow orbs bulged. "I've made sure that there are no single point failures left anywhere in The Plan—anywhere!"

Otto nodded, smiled as he watched Wolf bound out and enter the laboratory's airlock, then followed. Within two minutes, he again removed his helmet and gloves as the airlock's inner hatch lifted. And once again, but at a faster pace, he followed Wolf's hobble-hops thirty feet down an entry tube to Wolf's laboratory, a tube lined with a triple layer of sealex pressed flat against the lava walls by breathable air.

Once through the door to the laboratory, Otto examined the room for changes. Eight DNA synthesizers each rested adjacent to and ready to feed its own MicroBioManipulator. Each set of equipment stood at precise angles to one another unchanged from their initial placement seventeen years earlier. But unlike all of Otto's previous visits, dust covers had replaced technicians' hands at all of the work stations. Wolf weaved his way through the equipment to the other end of the laboratory and, with a kid's new-toy grin, looked back at Otto before his hand brushed a light control and he disappeared through a door that Otto had not seen before. One more time, he followed.

Otto's eyes could not fix on the exact end to the new pressurized section of the straight lava tube, for it only seemed to taper to a vanishing point at some undefined distance. He glanced at a waist-high, two-foot-long enclosure to his right. Simple and straight, the lines of its stark-white envelope gave no indication of what lay inside as it snuggled against the wall. With only a three-inch clearance, another enclosure stood in precise alignment with the first. More identical stark-white enclosures followed, each with their precise alignments and separations. Otto's eyes flicked over to an identical row of enclosures to his left, down to a monorail at his feet that ran along the exact centerline between the enclosures, then ahead and down the tube toward the far end where rows and rail merged into a soft uniform glow. He had to close his mouth before he spoke. "This is it?"

"This is it—the Production Tube—and it's almost operational, almost ready for the Domination Phase."

"How far's it go?"

"37,073 feet, or about 7 miles. There are 16,384 units on each side."

Otto's eyes and mouth opened wide again. "Seven miles?"

"That's right, almost as far as this lava tube is structurally sound."

"Almost? What's at the other end?"

Wolf paused as he forced his features into their passive state. "Just my private laboratory."

"Laboratory? I thought we were no longer in need of research and development support."

"Ahhh . . . almost."

Otto studied Wolf—*almost?*—then looked down the tube to the far end. "How do you get there?"

Wolf pointed at the monorail, then behind him to where the rail split in two. Each of the two rails supported a one-man vehicle. "I take one of these." Wolf's enthusiasm seemed to wane. "But the trip takes nearly a quarter hour each way, and we do not have the time for it now."

Confusion flashed over Otto's features before he pointed down at the enclosure to his right. "Wolf, what exactly's in each of these?"

Wolf's enthusiasm returned. "Each one of these units has

three sections: a Cell Division and Separation Section, an Embryo Development Section, and a DNA Synthesizer Section that feeds the other two. And every unit is fed organic raw material by the Supply Chord that runs behind them against the wall."

Otto smiled. "And the product is—"

"Yes!" Wolf glowed. "A fetus—a full-term fetus! Mostly from lunar material, I have at last mass produced these units that I've perfected in the laboratory, units that reproduce, no, actually improve upon the biochemical, thermal, and mechanical conditions of the womb. It's unfortunate that I could not have perfected this capability earlier. I could use it now in the Reproduction Phase rather than having to depend upon the more antiquated and unreliable technique I must continue to employ back on Earth."

"How much of this have you been able to automate?"

"All of it. The Domination Phase is fully automated!"

"But, sir, can you handle the production rate from over thirty-two thousand units? Is the logistics of all this feasible?"

"Yes. I will be pressed, but I can do it. I'll operate in a continuous flow rather than the batch mode. That is, the Tube will produce a fetus once every twelve minutes. That's almost forty-four thousand per year. With my enhanced fleet of LADSs and EMTVs, I can just about support the resulting requirement for eleven thousand pounds of payload return once every week."

"Just about?"

Wolf shrugged. "On occasion, if logistics suffers a slight drop in performance, there may be a little, ahhh . . . product spoilage."

Otto's features sagged. "Sir. . . . Everything here looks ready. When will you start?"

"The Domination Phase will begin in this facility exactly thirteen months from now. And it will continue to be operated here for as long as it takes me, working through you, Lothar, and Kurt, to secure the required level of acceptance, a process we have discussed with you many times. Then I will replicate this capability back home and expand it. Right now, that date is the only uncertainty in The Plan—the transition of the Domination Phase back to Mother Earth."

"We will try to make that as early as possible, sir."

"Yes, you will." Wolf glanced at his watch. "It's time. Let's start the transfer. Let's get on with the Reproduction Phase. At last, we've hit the knee in the curve!" With fresh energy, Wolf turned, accelerated, and bound through the exit.

Otto studied the tube one more time, its simplicity, its enormity—its existence!—then followed. Outside, as Wolf returned the Production Tube to darkness and secured the door, Otto's eyes fell on a single line of small discreet letters on a thin plaque over the frame. Even for one at the heart of The Plan, Otto flinched as he read:

ALL MEN ARE CREATED EQUAL

21

□□□

accelerate

Three more residents arrived in New Earth.

European man voyaged over three thousand miles to reach New England, yet not till four centuries later did Man make the relatively short trek of one hundred miles to reach New Earth—straight up. But, as always, whether he settled in New England or New Earth, Man took the culmination of his evolution with him: his wisdom and principles, his folly and vices, and his itches and urges and all.

One of the new residents, a man at the controls of his Agile 37 spacecraft, watched as a point reflection on the horizon continued to grow toward a recognizable object, Space Station Von Braun, one of Man's first settlements in New Earth. That man, the kind always motivated to perform his best, yet impulsive enough to sometimes achieve far less, the kind who'd spent most of his youth growing new skin, depressed his mike button. "Hello, Von Braun, Agile 37 is eight miles out for automatic rendezvous and dock."

"Agile 37, how'd you get here so soon? You're a rev early. Over."

"I performed a one-rev rendezvous." The man clenched his eyes and gritted his teeth.

"Rebello! You were not authorized to do that! Why didn't you fly a standard rendezvous?! Over."

"We need to hustle."

"Why? Over."

"We're behind."

"Behind what? Over."

"Where we should be right now."

"Where's that? Over."

"We'll talk about it after we dock, Von Braun."

"Yes, we will! Over and out."

Joe paused, smiled, and an extra sparkle came to his eyes as he flipped the FLIGHT MODE switch from AUTO to MANUAL. He gave a slight forward nudge to the translation controller in his left hand and waited . . . thousand one . . . thousand two . . . thousand th—

"Agile 37, you're comin' at us too fast. Go back to AUTO! Over."

"Hey, that's quick. You guys are really awake today." Joe returned control to AUTO and peered ahead. With the Sun at Joe's back, Von Braun blossomed from a single point to multiple reflections that highlighted the station that he now viewed on edge. Joe could just resolve four long modules that hung vertical above the horizon, one pair side by side and in line with the second pair below. His mind filled in the eight modules behind the four he saw, like one six-pack stacked atop another, and the six spherical nodes that, like the wheels of Tinkertoys, interconnected them all.

"Von Braun, please ask Shiva to get on the loop."

"Roger. Over and out."

Faint reflections from carbon trusswork emerged. A horizontal truss divided the two pairs of modules, and at its distant left and right extremities, Joe could just perceive reflections off the radiators of redundant nuclear electrical power sources. Another truss, one crossed with the first, ran vertical along the centerline and also extended far beyond the modules to an assembly and servicing bay above and a spacecraft refueling and propellant storage bay below. Joe focused on a dot reflection that hung on the edge of the refueling bay, an Earth–Moon Transfer Vehicle (EMTV) that, with men from Earth, replacement parts from Von Braun, and oxygen from the Moon, functioned year after year at minimal expense.

Respect, awe, and maybe even reverence, Joe always felt a

touch of each as he approached Von Braun. The station, like the man after which it was named, had grown into a legend, one Joe had come to revere about the time the focus of his youthful passions had ascended from a Schwinn racer (Dad's gift) up to an Aeronca tail dragger. But, by now, as with hundreds of space pilots before him, Von Braun took on the warmth of an old friend, a functional home, a sanctuary in New Earth.

"Hello, Joe. Shiva here. I'm over in our EMTV doing the post-refueling checkout."

"Hi, Shiva. It's a bit sooner than expected, but I'm glad we're working together again."

"Me too. Think it'll be as exciting as last time?"

"Hope not. Shiva, think we could do the separation and burn a rev early?"

"It's possible. But why?"

"Ahhh. . . . We'll talk after we dock."

"Okay, Joe. I'll speed things up and redock at Port One."

"Thanks. See you there."

Joe's attention returned to Von Braun as his friend loomed larger. Last of the old-timers—and ungainly, nothing like the new guys. Yet he's got character, even his own kind of elegance. Not in appearance, but in function. Just keeps on provin' his worth day after day. Granddaddy of 'em all. Down there, he'd be in a museum. But up here, he's just too useful. Besides, not much of the original's left to show, just some trusswork. Time and technology keep advancing, and we keep refurbishing and replacing. A basic advantage of you guys— continuous evolution. Joe smiled, then surprised himself with a chuckle. Yep, old man, you keep on gettin' older, but also better.

Reaction control jets fired forward; mechanical shocks pulsed back. Agile slowed a tick as Joe scanned his displays: 421 feet out and range rate nominal. He looked forward to the modules again. Sunlight from the fireball behind his back screamed off the modules' white surfaces that cut sharp against the merged blackness of ocean and sky.

"Agile 37, dock at the plus Y port of node eight. Cleared manual. Over."

"Roger, Von Braun. Plus Y, node eight. Goin' manual." Joe bumped his translation controller right. Von Braun slid to his left. He twisted his rotation controller left and the station again hovered straight off his nose. Eight more modules emerged from behind the four he'd just observed. The immensity of all twelve overflowed his window. He moved his face forward.

"Love that Tourist Module," said Rox over the intercom. "Look at 'em. Gotta be at least one flat nose for every square foot of window."

"To maximize viewing," said Hunter, "I believe they select the passengers based on how well their heads interlock."

"Yep, the big double feature," said Joe. "Really packs 'em in. A beautiful sunset and a homely spacecraft."

Joe held Agile 37 at about one hundred feet from the lower module closest to the Sun as he drifted down its length. Sharp and precise, a terminator cleaved the module in two as if to mark his course. The half to his left blazed in reflected Sun, a red Sun that flattened as it settled on the horizon. The half to his right hid in shadows, exposed only by light that spilled from windows of the next module over. At the lower end of the module, he glided over a belt of the flags of the eighty-seven nations of the WSF; straight off his nose, the flags of England, France, Spain, Germany, and Italy blazed their presence; across the terminator, the flags of Czechoslovakia, Hungary, Yugoslavia, Bulgaria, and Rumania faded into the shadows.

Joe maneuvered toward the port on the node at the base of the center module. Seven standoff rings on the port's docking target stabilized into the concentric formation of a bull's-eye as he glided onto the docking centerline. Behind, a radiant rainbow wedge drove into the crevice between black earth and black sky, a thin delicate wedge that expanded and brightened as it arced to his far left over a violet-caped thunderstorm toward the setting Sun.

Thunderstorm flashed.

Joe blinked, then flipped on his external searchlight array. Nothing left to do but dock, a simple task, one with well-defined requirements. He accelerated. Agile 37 hit the docking port exactly on centerline, a touch fast according to the book, but right on according to Joe.

Computer signals pulsed, steel fingers tensed, and Agile 37 snugged down tight. The two satellites now drifted as one. And as a single unit, the muscles of Joe's body tensed. For a time, until he could undock in his EMTV, he'd be limited by the pace of something larger, the pace of the system over which he had little control. But, as always, he'd take what he could get.

"Hunter, Rox, let's move. As soon as you check in, hustle on over to the EMTV and help Shiva. Let's hold on to the gain we've made on our timeline. I'll be over as soon as I finish the post-dock checklist and also check in with the Captain."

Rox grabbed the handholds overhead—"Will do, Joe"—then jerked her arms to her sides and shot through the docking tunnel.

Hunter's whisper emanated from just behind Joe's ear. "Joe, how much are we behind Otto, and what event are we trying to intercept?"

Tense muscles tightened a bit more. "Don't know . . . just don't know."

"Oooops."

Otto fired a glare down into Technician's face. "Kurt, be careful!"

Black points flinched as they peeked back up from their dark depths. "Yes, sir!"

"We've already had to wait while you replaced that connector once. Let's not have to do it again."

"Sorry, sir." Kurt examined the electrical connector, reached for its mate on the Rover, and slid the two halves together. This time, under Otto's scrutiny, they mated without error.

"We're right on schedule and have dry run this many times before," said Wolf from behind them. "There's no need to either rush or panic."

They both turned, looked down, and nodded as their softened voices joined together, "Yes, sir."

"I understand why you are both nervous. This time we are doing it for real. But what is required now, more than ever, is care and precision." Wolf bound forward and bent his neck back to look up into their faces. "We were ahead of schedule, the connector problem has moved us back even with it, and if we make another error here, we would fall behind. Then, while the problem here is fixed, our recovery plan would be to accelerate the installation of Gift Case Two into LADS Two so that it could lead."

Otto's chin set as the corners of his mouth turned down.

His glare intensified. "Wolf—as I always have and always will—I'll be first!" He turned, ignored the quizzical look that crossed Wolf's face and motioned Kurt to continue.

Kurt's movements flowed smooth and precise as he continued installation of Gift Case One into its magnetic stowage between the two front seats of the Rover vehicle. Then he straightened up. "There, that's the last connector. I'm done."

Otto plugged the umbilical of his thigh-mounted computer into Gift Case One. "I'll run the validation checks." He unfolded the computer's display and typed in a command. Data diffused onto display's blank stare. "Electrical power, instrumentation, vibration dampers, shock attenuators, and all internal temperatures display nominal performance. Wolf, we're ready."

As Yuri had done twenty-one days before, Otto and Wolf slid into their Rover seats, cinched their restraints tight, donned their helmets and gloves, pressure tested their suits, and gave Kurt a thumbs-up. Kurt disappeared. Within thirty seconds, the airlock door again cracked open and dust fired outward. The door rose and Otto crept forward.

"We can go a little faster than this, Otto. The Gift is well isolated from vibrations within its Case and the Case is well isolated from Rover's structure."

"Yes, sir."

Gift Case One, the size of a basketball and covered with Thermaplex, a white cloth of woven plexan filament, hovered just above and between their heads. Supported by magnetic suspension from currents that flowed in superconducting wires, it wavered and appeared to balance on its flexible power and instrumentation cables in the bright lunar sun. Wolf's eyes darted back and forth between Gift Case One and Otto several times as his smile broadened. But Otto's eyes remained intent and locked on LADS One as it glowed ahead on the horizon. He used his peripheral vision to make only those small deviations from a straight course that were required to snake around pockmarks in the irradiated dusty gray carpet.

At LADS One, Otto locked Gift Case One into its magnetic suspension in stowage compartment CDR-A1, the prime stowage area between the Commander's and the Pilot's stations. With precision, he mated the male and female halves of the power connector. The instrumentation connector hung up just a bit before its two halves also slid together.

Otto paused. Didn't feel right. This is the same connector Kurt replaced. He pulled the halves apart again. Pins look all right. . . . No, lead pin's bent—bent all the way over! Have to fix it. Take time. But then I won't lead—won't be first! Otto's viscera tightened. How'd this happen? His hand shook as rigid muscles rotated the face of the female side of the connector toward him. It's clocked opposite from the male. Lead pin receptacle's on the bottom, not the top. It's not the same as the others!

Otto jerked away from Gift Case One. Power's hooked up. Okay to leave it. Only one thing left to do. . . . He hurled himself out the LADS's hatch, sailed over the ladder, dropped onto the lunar dust, and threw his body into Rover's seat. Wolf bounced, bounded, and rebounded from the impact.

"Otto, what are you . . . ?"

"Instrumentation connector's broken. Kurt used one that was different!"

"Then we have to—"

"No!" Otto rammed the speed controller forward. "I have another solution."

C'mon, Rebello, hustle.

Joe put his fingertips on the handrail, flicked his wrists, and floated through the docking tunnel. The space around him burst open as he entered the node's cavernous volume. A blue flight suit sprang from the wall to Joe's left and propelled a handlebar mustache, a grin, and an extended hand toward him. "Hi, Sami!" He reached for the hand.

The two humans collided, fused, spun, and drifted. Friendship flowed between eyes and hands for two seconds before they mashed into a water tank on the wall twenty-five feet away and almost opposite from the opening Joe had just entered.

"Joe, what're you doing up here so soon again? I thought you hot-shot Commanders got at least six months off between missions."

"Sami, that's a story for another day. Hey, it's good to see you again."

"Same here."

"Where's the Captain? I need to check in and be movin' on."

"Captain Gibenivich is over in the Exercise Facility. He planned to be here to welcome you aboard, Joe, but you showed up ninety minutes early. He's still pedaling his way through his weekly cardiovascular checkup."

"Yeah, we did kind of sneak up on him. Thanks, Sami. I'll check in with him over there."

"I'll come along. I've got twenty minutes before I'm on duty in Satellite Repair."

"Great." Joe pressed a handrail on the water tank and soared through the adjacent hatch into the Experiments Module, a seventy-five-foot-long, thirty-seven-foot-diameter cylinder. Although larger than the volume he'd just left, the Experiments Module felt more confined, more crowded. With a precision specified by a long-since-retired WSF design team, equipment racks and stowage lockers covered the outer walls as well as an inner seven-foot-diameter central shaft that extended almost the full length of the module. Gridwork extended into the open annular space to support smaller pieces of laboratory gear, gear that in turn supported what Joe could only identify as miscellaneous paraphernalia held in place by gray tape, the space technician's universal tool. Although some gray-taped sections of each experiment often extended beyond its regimented metallic turf, each experiment appeared to have its own unique function and identity.

Sami grabbed Joe's foot just before they reached the end of the module. "Joe, over there on the hub. That's Braumbach's gear. A week ago last Thursday they finally achieved separation of therapeutic-grade Gamma T-Lymphocyte."

"Yeah, *World Press* carried several stories on it. Sounded good. Looks like their days of meager financing are over."

"Sure are!"

They drifted through a second node into the Health and Life Sciences Module. The first half resembled the Experiments Module they'd just left; the second half, a medical monitoring and exercise laboratory. Close to the end, Captain Gibenivich, monitored by a Medtech, exercised on a bicycle ergometer. Mounted on vibration isolators against the outer wall, the bike contacted only his feet and fingertips as he pedaled; without gravity, he had no use for a seat. Wires extended from each of thirteen electrodes on his chest and back, joined, then flowed along a hose that stretched from his mouthpiece to a metabolic analyzer mounted immediately below the window in front of his face. Over the years, the window through which Captain Gibenivich now studied Earth had provided the crews an extra enticement to exercise.

Two-inch numbers on a timer at the top of the analyzer marched upward through 1800. At the prompting of the Medtech, the Captain returned his thumbs-up.

"Hello, Cappy," said Joe as he glided to a stop.

The Captain turned and, with effort, shook Joe's hand. The Captain's eyes widened as he nodded but his lips, stretched into an "O" around the mouthpiece, flexed but could issue no sound.

"Just checking in, Cappy," said Joe.

Sweat, like thin slabs of Jell-O, oscillated side to side on the Captain's chest and back as he pedaled and huffed. "Looks like you're just getting warmed up, Cappy. On the twenty-one-minute protocol today?"

"That's right, gents," said Medtech. "He's almost up to the max load level, and twenty-one minutes is about all he'll be able to take. His heart rate's at 167 and climbing."

"Cappy, we need to hustle. We docked an orbit early, and"—Joe paused as he watched the timer march forward—"and we'd like permission to move our EMTV undock time up a rev."

Timer marched upward through 1900, the bike's load increased again, and the Captain struggled and huffed with ever-greater intensity.

"Is that okay?" asked Joe with eyebrows raised, as he, along with Medtech, extended a thumbs-up to the Captain.

The Captain returned Medtech's thumbs-up.

"Thanks," said Joe. "We'll be getting a move on." He turned, reached for a handrail, yanked, and shot toward the hatch behind the exercise facility followed only by unintelligible noises that gurgled from the Captain. Within a few finger flicks, Joe glided into the EMTV.

Shiva reached up, grabbed Joe's hand, and pulled him toward the Commander's couch. "Hi, Joe. How's our reentry wizard?"

"Great! Thanks for picking up the pace, Shiva. How're we doing here?"

"Perfect timing. Hunter, Rox, and I are about ready to go. Just the undock checks to run. Do we have clearance for early undocking?"

"Ahhh . . . kinda. I'm sure we'll have a slight review of the situation with Cappy in a few minutes."

"Slight review, Joe? Oh-oh. I don't think I want to know."

Joe buckled in, finished the undocking checklist with Shiva, then flashed a thumbs-up and wide grin at Captain Gibenivich who wrenched to a stop at EMTV's entrance. The Captain stared at Joe, opened his mouth as if to speak, sighed, shook his head a full five seconds . . . then flashed his own grin, returned Joe's thumbs-up, and disappeared.

"We just got our clearance, Shiva."

"I still won't ask, Joe. Hatch comin' closed."

As the event timer counted down through zero, muffled clunks reached Joe through his couch, and EMTV started its creep away from Von Braun. Once the separation passed two hundred feet, Joe snapped EMTV around to the burn attitude with its usual crisp precision. He grinned. Von Braun's like a stable house on the ground and leaving in an EMTV feels like pulling out of the garage in a sports car—we're flying again!

Timer counted down to zero. Engines lit. EMTV accelerated.

Joe scrutinized his displays. Good engines, good systems. He glanced out the side window. And good station. Thanks, Von Braun, thanks for the trade-in. You've always been one to rely on.

"Joe, did you know that Unity's reported PRECISE has four LADSs waiting at Karov?"

"No! Four? More than two at any one facility is abnormal, even on the front side. Something's cookin'."

"What do you think they took there?"

"Wish I knew. Shiva, maybe it's what they plan to bring back."

"To where?"

"First to Equality."

"Then Earth?"

"Could be. Do we know what they have at Equality now? Any more LADSs? How many EMTVs?"

Computer continued to measure the velocity change and issued a signal. Propellant flow terminated and thrust dropped to zero.

"We don't know, Joe. We have no way to know what's at Equality."

Joe frowned as he glanced out his window toward the

Moon. "Shiva, our propellant's far above redline. And there's no need to make this coast any longer than it has to be." He stroked the keyboard and the UNITY REVOLUTION NUMBER on the RENDEZVOUS TARGETING display decreased by two.

"Three whole revs early, Joe? We're already going to get to Unity one rev early if we just fly the standard trajectory. Lopez is gonna rupture!"

Joe smiled and shrugged.

Again, timer counted. Engines lit. Computer measured. Thrust terminated.

"Joe, if you don't know what you're after, how do you know if three revs is good enough?"

"I don't. But we also don't have a choice. Unfortunately, we can't give up any more propellant margin, can't go any faster." Joe's hands contracted into fists. "This is just about the best we can do."

22

□□□

incite

"How well did I do on my tests, Doctor?"

"We'll have the results in just a moment."

"Did I make it?"

"I'll be out with the results in a moment, Miss Stoica!"

Despite the size and strength of her hands, Gretta Stoica could compress her wet handkerchief no farther. She let it fall into her lap as the ache in her fingers finally surfaced in her mind. Must relax. Can't look too eager, too emotional. No, I have to look eager or they won't want me.

Gretta sat back in the tight chair and looked at the hologram that hovered four feet before her. It'd grown old. A little, thin woman in a little, thin dress. Pretty, but not for me, and way too much money. Darn it, how do I turn the page? Again, she tried to understand the controls at her fingertips. Maybe that red button. She pushed it. Hologram faded. She pushed it again. Hologram returned. I just can't ask the nurse again. But there's no one else here. Sunday. I'm the only patient. Gretta smiled. That makes me special! She returned to a study of the buttons that swarmed at her fingertips. Didn't she say something about one with an arrow on it? Good, that did it. Oops, back to the cover. Maybe it's the one with the other arrow. Yep, back to the dress. Next page? Oh, darn. Just another advertisement. Makeup. Just for hussies, not for me. How do I get to another magazine? Maybe the one with the sideways arrow. Maybe they have *Agricultural Digest*. That'd be more interesting. Maybe—

"So!" The Doctor swept into the waiting room at his normal pace—white coat trailing. He had to make this visit short, keep it secret. If he or any of his patients became the source of a leak, ever, his career, and most likely his life, would face but one alternative—termination. "Miss Stoica, I have the results."

Gretta jumped to attention.

The Doctor stepped back to look up into her worried eyes. "Good news. You made the cutoff for the second phase. And in fact, your score of 97.37 is so high that I can say with great confidence that you will be one of the candidates selected in the final phase."

Despite their strength, Gretta's legs seemed unable to provide their usual stability. She sat down and, through eyes that began to fill with tears, looked straight across into the Doctor's face. "I . . . I . . . thank you!" Water overflowed. Her head turned down as she fumbled for her handkerchief.

"We knew from the start that your size and bone structure would contribute to a high grade, that is, to your ability to properly carry a fetus of this size. But we also knew that your age, although thirty-three is not so old, would detract a little. However, what has really elevated your score is your current body chemistry, cardiovascular condition, and muscle tone. They've all improved markedly since your first screening. What have you been doing?"

Somewhat more composed, Gretta responded, "I guess I trained. I ate only natural foods, except for the supplements you gave me, and I exercised a lot after my chores in the field, and I slept a lot."

"It worked, Miss Stoica. Congratulations. I am happy that you will be one of those granted the privilege of bringing human excellence into the world."

"Doctor, when . . . when will I . . . ?"

"When will you become trustee for your component of The Gift? One week from today, on September fourth. The Gift, in total, will arrive at Earth next Thursday, the first, to start Phase Five. Then it will be brought here to Sovata and distributed over the next two days. You will return here at the same time next Sunday." The Doctor moved his face nose to nose with hers. "Miss Stoica, I cannot emphasize strongly enough that all security precautions—exactly as we have trained and tested you—still apply in full. Is that understood?"

"Yes, Doctor."

"Excellent. After The Gift's implant, you will receive all necessary instructions to carry you through your pregnancy and the first six days of The Gift's life, at which time you will return The Gift to PRECISE and be paid in full. Understood?"

As Gretta stood and nodded, instinct compelled her to push for more. "Doctor, will I be able to do this a second time and maybe even more?"

"I admire your willingness to contribute, Miss Stoica, but that will not be possible. After this phase, all subsequent contributions of The Gift will be gestated in a more controllable mode."

"A what?"

"We have made a few enhancements to the artificial uterus that has been developed to provide the conditions necessary for embryo development to full term outside of the human body. As you know"—the doctor glanced up at Gretta who still looked down on him with a confused face—"this is the core of the incubator system that functions as a surrogate womb. That is, it not only provides the same chemical and thermal environment as a natural mother, but it has been made to also re-create her breathing patterns, movements, speech, and even her emotional states."

"Oh . . . but why would anyone do that?"

"Have you not heard of Life With Choice?"

"Life With . . . ?"

"Yes, Life With Choice, the movement that has tried to reconcile both the Pro-Life and Pro-Choice forces in many industrial nations. The surrogate womb was developed with funding and pressure from both sides . . . along with a lot of useless controversy. The ability to transfer a fetus from a woman with an unwanted pregnancy to this surrogate womb now provides a second option for the preservation of life. In essence, it augments the range of choices available to the mother. Except in a few underdeveloped nations still having an urgent need for population control, it has proven to be an acceptable alternative to a growing number of women who do not wish to be mothers but who find themselves pregnant."

"Find themselves . . . but how could that happen?"

"Ahhh. . . ." With an open mouth, the Doctor squinted up at Gretta, then blinked several times, looked down, scratched his head, and continued. "Let us just say, Miss Stoica, that even in this day and age, it does happen. As I said, we favor the use of the surrogate womb because it provides a much more controllable environment than the natural womb. Thus, we have made a few special, ahhhh . . . enhancements to the Life With Choice system and now have it in mass production. We will have the required number installed, tested, and ready for use in the next phase. So, Miss Stoica, you should feel especially honored. You are one of a select group that will never be enlarged."

"Oh. . . . I guess so. I—"

"Miss Stoica, good day."

Gretta rose, fumbled her way to the rear exit, and paused, "Thank you, Doctor. . . . Thank you!" As she walked toward her bicycle, a warmth filled her body. I'm not just another old maid, not just another oversize woman without a man. I'm important. I'm part of the future. Soon I'll have another human growing inside me—the best ever!

Only one acceptable solution.

Otto drew himself up to his full height and looked down but a shade into Face, into Surprised Face. "From here on, Gift Case Two is Gift Case One and I will deliver it."

"What?"

"And Gift Case One is now Two. Kurt will replace its connector and will probably have it ready in time for you to follow me."

"Why?"

"Because I cannot risk that I will not go first."

"But what difference does it make which one of us goes first?"

"What difference does it make?" Otto's eyes burned into the face opposite his, into Questioning Face. "The difference is that I have always been first and will continue to be first!"

"What? First or second or last, it's irrelevant." Confused Face sat in Rover's seat to think. "With us, those concepts no longer have any meaning. All this is opposite to everything bestowed by The Gift. . . . The answer is *no!*"

Otto paused. Inside, Reason and Rage struggled. As always, Reason laid out the logic of their equality, the precision of their parity—red carpets for all thought and action. But from some secret source farther down, Rage exploded and engulfed Reason, surged up and swamped outward to cover and smother all but itself.

Otto lunged forward, clamped his hands inside the neck ring below Surprised Face, wrenched backward, jammed his feet into ribs opposite his, and thrust his legs upward. One-sixth gravity offered little resistance and body arced high. Legs kicked. Arms flailed. And, in time, head impacted lunar concrete. Surprised Face turned into Passive Face for a moment, then yielded to anger.

Angry Face charged into Otto's stomach with a tackle unmatched by any WFL linebacker, yet, and smashed Otto's back into the airlock's wall.

Jolt emptied air from Otto's body. Rage refilled it.

Otto's biceps bulged into Angry Face as he wrapped a hammerlock on its head. In slow motion, he dropped toward the concrete. Then he twisted—hard! His body and ears sensed the snap, sensed Life, in its entirety, being lost by one; from the depths of his mind he sensed a bit more Life being gained by him and others. He stood, released head, stared at Face, now Passive Face once more, and watched it float toward the concrete for a second time. Ears heard the smack. Gut issued pain. Otto winced, then froze as he studied Passive Face. . . .

Identical Face!

In time, Otto turned toward Rover, shuffled toward it, strode toward it. He disconnected Gift Case Two's umbilicals, snatched it off its magnetic support, christened it Gift Case One, and headed toward *his* Rover with *his* Gift. His mind churned. His legs churned. No, not now, not ever—Number One would not be stopped—the best could never be stopped!

Many pondered, but rarely Wolf. . . .

Life, who's in control?

Life, the evolution of human DNA, its expression, its use, and its home—who's in control?

Life, a precious product nurtured over millions of years by a Power far greater than itself, a product in awe of its Creator and His creations, a product that feels an urgency to know— who's in control?

Life, a force now able to slice through its gravity cocoon, surges outward from its home to explore, searches for more like itself, or for those with different codes of DNA than itself, or even for those with far different chemical structures than itself, for any other Life that may help it to know—who's in control?

Life, now trusted with the secret of its own existence, the secret of its own DNA, a secret it now explores and details to find ever-greater understanding, a secret it can use to heal or alter its very essence, a secret from which it seeks to extract the ultimate answer—who's in control?

Life, able to think, to direct its actions by choice, to move toward perfection in every endeavor, to debate and dispute at what point does it start to usurp the authority of its God, to wonder and want to know—who's in control?

Life, a rich diversity that manifests itself in billions of beings each with their own distinctive set of attitudes and abilities, their own history of actions and accomplishments, their own pride in their originality and uniqueness, and certainly beings all at least a little like the one who now turned to his neighbor. . . .

"How about a little spot of tea there, Shiva?"

"Comin' your way, Joe?"

Joe released his spork in space where it hung at arm's length stuck into a fist-sized glob of mashed potatoes. He opened his hand to catch the soft plexan tea container that glided to him from Shiva's direction, snapped off the container's can with his front teeth, and squeezed its accordion-shaped body. Warmth flowed down his throat and into his gut. Good flavor. Almost like home, but not quite. Maria puts in just a bit more honey. He mated the container's Velcro base with the Velcro on the table, plucked the spork from its midair stowage, and dabbed the potatoes into an open can of dark brown viscous fluid that clung to whatever it touched. He pulled the potatoes to his lips, then moved his head to lap up a small fluid ball that floated free. "Not bad gravy." Rox and Hunter nodded. "Whip it up all by yourself, Chef?"

"Sure did. A few squirts of hot water, shake, and you got it."

Joe flashed his max grin. "Chef Shiva. Got a nice ring to it. You run a real luxury liner here. All we need now is a little entertainment."

Shiva's eyes lit up as he reached into the stowage compartment over his shoulder. "Got that too. You're all gonna love this—the Dynamic Acceleration Reference Trajectory System."

Rox squinted. "The what?"

"The Dynamic Acceleration Reference Trajectory System—DARTS."

Rox's squint intensified. "Darts? That's our entertainment?!"

Hunter yawned. "No, I do not believe this will be an adult party."

"Give it a chance," said Shiva as he stuck the Velcro target to the food lockers. "It's a real challenge. In fact, I bet none of you can hit the bull's-eye."

"You're on," said Rox as she ripped a dart out of Shiva's hand. She took careful aim and fired. The dart's Velcro tip bounced off the wall two feet above the target positioned only eleven feet away. "What the . . . ?" Rox flew after the dart, snatched it out of the air, and returned. "Something's fixed." She fired again and repeated her first performance. "Shiva, where's the magnet?"

Shiva only smiled.

Hunter floated down next to Shiva. His fingertips relished a few more passes over his chin before they gripped a dart. He aimed two feet below the target, concentrated, and fired. Bull's-eye.

"Now I know it's fixed!" said Rox.

Joe floated up to the firing line. "The only fix is in our conditioned reflexes we each brought up from Earth."

"That's right," said Hunter. "You can't help but throw just like you would back on Earth, to loft it, but there's no gravity to pull the dart back down after you release it. So, you have to ignore your impulse to aim directly at the target, but instead, aim below it."

Joe fired. The dart hit the target one circle outside and above the bull's-eye. "It's easy to understand intellectually, but it's another thing to completely control your impulses."

Rox, in a more deliberate fashion, floated forward again. "Gimme that sucker!"

Joe looked down at his wrist as his CommWatch vibrated his skin, pulsed its high-pitched tone, and flashed its electric blue light. "Troops, my call's come through. And they're giving me only a few minutes. Gotta hustle. See you shortly."

In his sleep compartment, Joe positioned himself in front of his communications unit and hit CALL ACCEPT. Maria's smile and happy eyes bloomed outward from the blank screen.

"Hi, Maria."

"Hi, honey. Glad you called. Any special reason?"

"No, other than I like talking to you."

"That's always good to hear. Everything okay up there?"

"Yep, no problems, other than things are a little slow."

"Somehow I think you'll change that."

"Wish I could."

"What's your hurry?"

"Not sure. Maria, you're really looking good today!"

"Thanks, but I feel a little hassled."

"Oh?"

"I had to go up to preschool today. Seems *your* son refused to practice writing the alphabet because he says he's invented another one, one that's better."

Ricky's face squeezed in beside Maria's. "It is, Daddy, it really is!"

"Hi, Ricky! I bet it is. But you still have to first learn what everybody else uses and conform to that or no one will understand you. Then you can work on your own."

"Nice try, Joe. I'm glad I got a recording of this."

Joe felt the skin of his wrist vibrate again. "Our time's about up. Sorry it's such a short one. They need the link. I'll give you a call from Unity."

"Talk to you then, Joe." Maria paused as her smile faded. "Honey, please try to relax and enjoy the flight for a change. Don't be so impetuous. You know how it always gets you into trouble."

"You're right, Maria. That's good advice."

"It is!"

"I love you both. So long."

"Love you too, Joe."

"Bye, Daddy . . . you'll see!"

• • •

Left alone, he made ready.

Each built-in test and checkout nanochip responded to its stimuli, stimuli initiated by his command SYSTEMS TEST. Every EMTV had 2,097,152 of them, and though each nanochip could not be distinguished one from the other, different inputs resulted in different outputs, different inputs from a centralized computer that also analyzed their different outputs and made decisions on each and every component, element, system, and then the total spacecraft. As in the previous two cases, the result came out the same: No anomalies. EMTV-3 operational. Perfect.

One more to go. He reconfigured each system to standby and moved from the spacecraft cabin into the Hub at the center of Equality, PRECISE's Moon-orbiting space station.

That's when it happened . . . not really much, just a Class-Four Alarm, an alarm of the lowest priority. He lightly bounced once in Equality's near-zero gravity, floated to the Hub's Data and Command Work Station, and read the display:

NEW OBJECT IN SAME ORBITAL PLANE—
POTENTIAL RENDEZVOUS

He studied the OBJECT TRACKING display as it diffused automatically onto the split screen. Must be just another WSF EMTV going to Unity. No, better not assume anything. Better enable the alarm to tell me if its rendezvous potential increases. He poked a single key, turned, and bounced away.

Adjacent to one of the Hub's 8 windows, he glided by an optical tracker, a sighting device that guided a pencil-thin X-ray laser beam, a beam that 13 years before had melted through a 0.38-inch steel plate in 43 milliseconds at a distance of 743 miles. Relative to the demonstration plate, the wound plexan of spacecraft walls offered negligible resistance. So far, the beam had never fallen on a real spacecraft, but it had been continuously refurbished, tested, and serviced to maintain its fully operational state. He paused by the tracker and pulled himself back. Why not check?

He commanded auto track and brought his eye to the sight, an eye buried deep within its socket. Tracker swiveled to a new direction. He slid his finger around a trigger, nuzzled his eye closer to the sight, and smiled. A natural feel. A natural fit. But he saw nothing. Must still be too far away. Let the alarm do its job.

With reluctance, Kurt released the trigger and continued on to EMTV-4.

23

□□□□□□□

detour

"You did what?!"

"Hold on Shiva," said Joe. "Watch what we're doing. Engine goin' to ENABLE. . . . Four . . . three . . . two . . . one . . . ignition."

Again, EMTV purred and pushed. With a force of 0.63 G, four couches each swallowed the body that floated above it.

"I changed the target."

Eyes above Shiva's open mouth blinked several times, then bulged as they shifted back to Joe. "You changed it? To what?!"

Joe's eyes continued to prowl spacecraft displays. "We're makin' a slight detour—to Equality."

"Equality? We're supposed to rendezvous with Unity. Going to Equality gets us into lunar orbit all right, but it won't get us to our LADSs or down to Karov!"

"True."

"Then how do we get back to Unity?"

"No sweat. We'll have just enough propellant to get back with a two-orbit rendezvous. Unity's almost in the exact same orbit as Equality but just a little ahead. And the phasing looks good."

Shiva's eyes continued to jump back and forth between Joe

and the RENDEZVOUS TARGETING display as the burn progressed. "Not sure if we can make it."

"Comin' up on 2:58."

Shiva scrutinized the display. "Looks like we've got just enough propellant. But why?"

"Two . . . one . . . cutoff. Perfect burn."

"Right, perfect. We're just headed for the wrong space station, that's all." Shiva shifted his scrutiny to Joe. "Lopez now expects us at Unity a full three revs early."

"Ahhh . . . yeah. No doubt he won't quite view this tiny detour as a sagacious maneuver. But it's the right thing to do."

"Right?"

"Look. Otto's ahead of us, and he may've already left Karov to return to Equality in one of those four LADSs. If so, Equality is where we should also be. Otto's key."

Rox's voice thrust forward over their shoulders. "I agree with you, Joe. Otto, by far, has to be the best they have. If PRECISE is doing anything really important, Otto's at the center of it."

"In any of your time with him, Rox, did Otto ever tell you the real nature of his mission?" asked Joe.

"No. Nothing. But under the surface, I sensed a lot of tension and turmoil about something coming up, something you don't sense at first, but something real that he can't seem to open even himself up to."

"Yeah, I got a hint of that too, like he's almost human," said Joe.

Rox's voice softened as she smiled. "Oh, he is that."

Hunter's smooth, logical tones floated forward. "Okay, even if we assume that Otto is the key in these ill-defined operations, what can we do about it once we reach Equality?"

"We'll fly around it, inspect it, and only request boarding if we determine Otto's there. Then we'll just take it as it comes."

"None of this is too rational, Joe," said Hunter. "We'll have a tough time explaining it to anyone, especially to PRECISE."

"We can handle them." Joe offered a tentative smile. "We'll just explain our presence with a creative systems problem or two."

Shiva shook his head. "I'm glad you're the Commander. If and when we ever do get to Unity, I'm going to hide inside a stowage locker till after Lopez runs out of steam."

A frown registered on Joe's features for but a second. "Can't always be neat and clean, troops. Sometimes you just have to do what feels like the right thing to do."

"Feels?" asked Hunter. "I'd rather have more knowledge than that."

"But if it isn't available, you still have to act."

"Act without full knowledge?" Hunter leaned forward. "In this business, that tends to get one killed."

"Otto, do you have no regret for my loss?!"

"I have to remain first, so when he refused to cooperate—"

"First? You *all* will be first!" Wolf's palms sped over one another in ever tighter circles. "It makes no difference which one of you actually *is* first—absolutely no difference at all!"

"But why do I feel it necessary for *me* to be first? Hasn't the first position always been *mine*?!"

"*You? Yours?* How can you entertain any of these thoughts? Where'd they come from?"

"They just . . . just come naturally. They seem a natural part of perfection."

"Well, they're not! They're the opposite, irrelevant, and outmoded." Black pits bulged as they glared up from their yellow matrix. "Get rid of them!"

"Yes, sir!"

"Otto, I ask you again. Have you no remorse for your crime—for your atrocity?"

"I didn't really mean . . ."

Wolf's palms accelerated. "Don't you understand and regret the depth of my loss?!"

"Your loss, sir?"

"Yes, my loss—*redundancy*! Only you four were trained to fly the LADS. Now, because of your desire to be uniquely first, I no longer have redundancy in all of The Plan's operations!"

Otto's face reddened. "I'm sorry, sir." He reached down and gripped Wolf by the shoulder. "I really am sorry." Then a snarl replaced his low rumble. "But I will make up for it. I promise!"

Otto squeezed.

Wolf yelped.

Otto released.

"I know you will. You are, after all, our best."

In a few strides, Otto entered the airlock and reached *his* Rover and *his* Gift Case One. He turned. Arms quivered as fists clinched. "From here on, Wolf, nothing will go wrong!"

"It's like a gigantic bicycle wheel," said Shiva.

Joe's fingers slipped over sweat-covered controllers. "But one with only four spokes."

"Even from a mile out, it looks huge!"

Joe peered out the window and down at Equality, the rotating space station operated by PRECISE, as it sped over Big Rock's gray dust and dirt. "It is large, Shiva, considering how long ago the Soviets assembled it."

Shiva handed the binoculars to Joe. "How large?"

"The advertised diameter of its wheel is 336 feet. But remember Independence? When it was operational in Earth orbit, its diameter was 973 feet, although that was mostly just modules strung together on tethers and spun up." Through the binoculars, Joe saw Equality highlighted against black lunar sky as it rose above the horizon. Sunlight bounced off Wheel's gray surface but gave no clue of what lay inside.

"In all the Earth–Moon transfers I've made," said Shiva, "this is the first time I've seen it. It rotates slower than I thought it would."

"Takes about thirty-five seconds to complete a rotation. That gives them about one-sixth G at the outer edge of the Wheel." As technical data flowed out, Joe sensed some of his tension entrained with it.

"I wonder why they don't stop its rotation and use it in a zero-gravity mode like all other stations?"

"PRECISE claims that they want their artificial gravity to be the same as lunar gravity so they can use the station to further develop engineering processes for the production of building materials on the surface. They say that's why they bought the station from the Soviets back in 2023 in the first place." Joe's neck and shoulders began to loosen. "Actually, when the Soviets built it in 2008, its original purpose was the same as most other rotators, to study and prevent bone decalcification of their crews, although they spun it faster to get closer to one gravity. But when we came up with biochemical means to prevent the calcium loss, they sold the station to PRECISE for a fraction of its development cost."

Silent for many minutes, Hunter's logical monotone floated forward again. "However, Joe, when the UN Facility Inspection Team last went through Equality three years ago, they found that PRECISE still uses it for biomedical experiments. I never understood the focus of their work."

Joe squinted through the binoculars. "Me neither."

"See any spacecraft or evidence of anyone onboard?" asked Rox.

"No, not on this side. No LADSs or EMTVs. It looks in standby . . . everywhere. The doors of the four Servicing Garages on this side are open but there's nothing in any of 'em."

"Strange. I do not see a reason why they would leave them in that configuration," said Hunter.

"Check the frequency, Shiva, and give 'em another call."

"373.0, that's the right one, Joe, the International Contact Frequency." Shiva pressed his mike button. "Hello, Equality. WSF EMTV-7. Over."

Silence.

"Sounds like nobody's home," said Joe. "Let's go around to the other side."

"Then what?" asked Hunter.

"We move in closer if it looks the same."

"I bet it won't," said Hunter. "If they have four LADSs on the surface, it is only logical that they have at least one EMTV up here."

"We'll see," said Joe as he returned the binoculars to Shiva, wiped his palms on his thighs, and gave the TRANSLATION CONTROLLER three forward and three up pulses.

Silence returned as Joe guided EMTV on its drift up and over Equality. Stop drift up. Three pulses down. Rotate nose down. Joe's eyes never blinked as they locked on Equality. Seems to have a life of its own. Must be its motion . . . yeah, must be. Uh-oh, its disappearing. Equality's gray blends into lunar background, a cold gray that shows nothing, tells nothing. Hides everything that . . .

"Wonder why they ever chose the name Equality," said Rox. "It doesn't seem to fit PRECISE."

"Right," said Shiva. "The only other station they own, their Earth orbital station, is named Excellence. And that's another one that I've never been to either."

Joe paused when Equality's gray popped into view as it

sped over a black shadow that hid half the floor of a large crater. "They must've gotten caught up in the swing of things right after the turn of the century when every new station got named after some kind of human goal. It started with Freedom, then we had Liberty, Independence, Opportunity, and the others right on up to Unity. Then everybody went back to names of space pioneers. They're easier. There's more of 'em." Equality disappeared again.

Joe bumped the hand controller three pulses down. With the Sun low behind them, Equality again edged above the horizon.

"Joe, I can't see any spacecraft on this side either," said Shiva. "Or any other sign of life. And I'm zoomed in to full power."

Moist fingertips tweaked controllers. "We're moving in for a closer look."

Joe studied the distant station. Wheel inched closer, larger. No longer smooth and continuous, Wheel's facets glittered as it rotated. Each of its sections, a straight cylindrical shell almost in line with two of its identical brothers joined to it on its either end, glittered as it rotated through its place in the Sun. Four Spokes, only a quarter the thickness of the Wheel, ran from Wheel to Hub. As they intersected Hub, they bulged with eight spacecraft Servicing Garages, two per Spoke, four on each side.

EMTV drifted closer.

Equality towered and filled Joe's window as they approached its Wheel. He looked up toward its Hub as a Spoke flashed by. From dark recesses, an image emerged and spurted forward, one implanted in Joe's brain thirty years before, an image of a Ferris wheel that towered above wide eyes as little legs propelled him toward its base. But now, no electronic music filled his ears, just the rasp of an occasional deep inhalation; no cotton candy covered his fingers, just the stickiness of his own sweat; and no father caught up to him and hugged him and loved him—no, that remained lost, forever. But now, as then, explosions pounded the walls of his chest.

Joe unclenched the controller and they continued to drift.

Close enough. Joe used EMTV's noncontaminating jets of cold gas to bring them to a stop at the edge of Wheel. EMTV froze. Joe froze. Only Wheel's motion remained. Section after section glided by, each a straight cylindrical shell of a station module, each the international standard twenty-one feet in diameter and fifty-three feet long, and each identical to its brother. Joe stared, hypnotized by the parade of uniformly spaced portholes cut like precision eyes in the continuous string of nondescript gray faces. Had Wheel made a complete revolution? Had the same face come by twice? Did it make a difference?

"Nothing in there, Joe."

"Right, Shiva. At least nothing we can see from out here. Let's look at the rest." Joe pulsed his controller and started a drift up toward the station's core, up toward Hub. Then he stretched. Stiff muscles jerked as wet cloth brushed against frigid skin.

Below, long shadows consumed disheveled gray dirt. Only lighted peaks survived. Joe watched their own shadow pulse on and off the Spokes, then scrutinized each one as it drifted by. "I think we've got a friend watching us out there. See him?"

With every fourth flash they saw it—a hand-sized robot shaped like a spider that scurried along the Spoke's surface; a mass of plexan and electronics whose eight legs propelled it along at a speed exactly equal to theirs; an extension of its maker that followed the reason of its own intelligence except, on occasion, when it accepted assignments from intellects outside; a device of many capabilities that now seemed content just to observe with its electronic eyes, and possibly report back to somewhere beneath Equality's gray surface.

"Looks something like one of our RoboServicers, or at least their version of one," said Shiva.

Joe nodded. "Yeah, it's one of their Servicing Spiders designed for servicing electronics in vacuum."

"It's got some mean-lookin' pincers on its forward legs. Wonder what else it does, Joe."

"Don't know. And with any luck, we won't find out."

They continued up toward Hub until each Spoke widened into a Servicing Garage. Again, Joe stopped their motion and studied the scene. Spider had disappeared. "Shiva, there's not much light in there, but don't you see what looks like the open cabin hatch of an EMTV in every Garage?"

Shiva squinted through the binoculars. "Yeah, I do . . . and I can see the webbing of a Commander's couch in every one. Yep, there's an EMTV in every Servicing Garage!"

Joe flexed his ankles to force his nose forward against his window. "It's not dead in there, it's just in standby. Why isn't there anyone minding the store?"

"They must all be down at Karov," said Shiva.

"No, I do not believe so," said Hunter, "for it is prudent not to leave a station unattended, especially one that is as old as this one and not highly automated."

"I agree," said Rox. "There's gotta be someone lying low in there giving Spider commands. And whoever he is, I don't think we should trust the little sneak."

Hunter nodded at Rox. "Yes, I do believe that is also prudent."

Joe continued their motion upward until Hub's central docking port glided front and center. Then he stopped all translation and started a rotation to match that of Equality. His fingertips rested on the controllers as he studied the docking target that now sat stable in front of him.

"Don't do it, Joe."

"I won't, Shiva, but it's tempting."

"Wish we could," said Rox.

"Dismissal, a $250,000 fine, and a minimum of five years is standard," said Hunter. "Yes, docking at a station without permission is definitely frowned upon."

"That's one helluva frown," said Joe as he studied Hub's skin, then the robotic arm used to move spacecraft to and from each Servicing Garage, then Hub's four windows. Through each clear slab, he saw no one, no evidence of life. Yet something hung there, alert and alive. Only two spacecraft windows and the vacuum of space separated him from something only feet away, from something that seemed dark and endless, electric and poised. Joe's eyeballs glazed as he peered at the docking target, the only target he could see. I know it, it's there, *something* . . .

An eye snuggled against a sight. A trigger clicked.

Radiation entered a lens, infrared sensors processed it, electronics encoded it, and an onboard bubble memory recorded it. In time, the result, a data bit stream, would race at the speed of light to Karov where images would reappear on a screen, images of faces pressed against the windows of an EMTV.

• • •

"Joe. . . . Joe!"

"I'm awake, Shiva."

"There's not much else we can do here."

"Yeah, you're right."

The horizon at their backs blotted out the last remnant of sunlight. Joe flicked on EMTV's floodlights, then blinked and stared. "Shiva, did you see a flash inside the window right in front of us just now, like something jumped when I turned on our floods?"

"No, I didn't. If anybody is in there, they would've answered our calls."

"Maybe."

"C'mon, Joe. Let's get on to Unity."

"One last look." Joe stopped their rotation, scrutinized each window as it drifted by but saw nothing. He looked down into blackness. Or was it up? Must be down. No stars. But no matter. Nothing all over.

"Joe? . . ."

"Okay, onward to Unity."

Wolf studied the image on the screen. "There, freeze it."

"Yes, sir," said Otto.

Wolf squinted, then exploded. "Rebello again? Damn him. What's he doing there?"

"I don't know, sir. He was supposed to go straight to Unity."

"Rebello's getting to be like a fly buzzing in my face. Who's that with him?"

"Rakesh Shivakumar, sir, their EMTV Pilot, and Hunter Middleton, their Lunar Base Engineer, and . . ."

"Yes, Otto?"

Otto's gut quivered but his voice remained steady. "And Roxanne Jama, their Astrogeologist."

"Kurt, where are they now?"

"They're closing on Unity now, sir," said the face in the corner of the screen. "But because Unity's ahead of us by 613 miles, which is just over the horizon, I can't reach them."

Wolf put his head down and, with his fingertips, massaged

his face through its fur. "That's all right, Kurt. They don't know any more now than they did before."

"Without your instructions, I thought it best to just let them go away."

"Yes, without my instructions and with only you onboard, that was the right thing to do."

"Thank you, sir. What if they come back?"

Wolf shook his head. "They won't. Rebello's mission is to land at the WSF site and then lead an expedition to over here. We have coordinated their itinerary with their Karov Base Commander."

"Good, then they will be handled there?"

"Because of their deviation over to you, that may not be necessary," said Otto. "By the time they land and get over here, we'll already be back up with you, maybe farther."

"True," Wolf smirked. "They've taken themselves out. Rebello and his crew are no longer a factor."

24

□□□

inform

Soap and suds drift and float, cover and cling.

So far, so good—no Lopez!

Beads and spheres waft and coast. Foam and water fly and glide, hit and stick.

Maybe he won't even say anything.

Point and press, hum and hiss. More water. Stops and seals. Open eyes. Glazes of light glimmer and shimmer. Nothing to see. Close.

Yeah, maybe he's mellowed.

Spread soap, smooth soap. Hands glide over skin. Foams and tingles. Feels fresh and clean. Point and press, hum and hiss. Water covers and smothers.

Maybe he's got other things to do.

Creeps up nostrils. Snort. More fills in. Perfume soap, iodine water, all seeps and sneaks in, slinks and slithers in. Shake. Snort. There, clear. Open eyes. Point and press, hum and hiss. More water, hangs on skin and shivers and quivers. Warm, soft. Hot, snug.

I bet we can just hop right in LADS and descend. No fuss.

Fills in ears. Blocks all sound. No, faint noises come through. Shake. Water drifts off. Voice, strained voice, invades. Shake. Water flies off. Shake hard. There, make any dog proud. Ears open. Shouts. Loud shouts. What?

"Rebello! Get out of that shower!"

Damn, he found me.

"Rebello!"

Dread surged and sickened. Should have hid with Shiva in the stowage locker. Can't put it off.

"We have to talk—now!"

Joe cracked open the door to the cylindrical shower stall.

"Nice of you to finally show up, Rebello. Open up!"

As Joe swung the door open, a slug of water and suds broke loose from its inside surface, floated and coasted, then hit and stuck. Within seconds, only traces of foam and soaked cloth indicated its area of impact. Joe stretched the hose of the vacuum cleaner as he handed its nozzle out to a soggy Commander Lopez. "Yeah, we were sure glad to see the WSF flags, Lopie. Knew we finally got to the right station."

"I want some answers!" The engine on the cleaner whirred as Commander Lopez scrambled to vacuum off what soap and water the nozzle could reach. "Why did you deviate from the flight plan?"

Joe floated out the shower door. "Our objective is to understand what PRECISE is up to."

"First you make a one-orbit rendezvous with Von Braun." Engine strained.

Joe turned and grabbed the towel under the bungee on the back of the shower door. "And now PRECISE has four LADSs at their Karov operations that indicates that—"

"Then you move your arrival time here ahead by three revs." Engine jumped to a higher pitch.

Joe inserted his feet under the elastic loops on the floor. "The possibilities are that they are doing something down there, or that they are coming back up and on to—"

"Then you deviate to Equality without my permission or coordination with WSF Flight Control." Engine whined, then coughed.

Joe dried his face and hair. "I thought it best to work our way back down toward Karov to see what they are doing or where they are going. That's why we went to Equality first in order to—"

"To say nothing of clearance from PRECISE." Commander Lopez pulled the nozzle off his chest and let the engine grind back up to speed.

Joe moved his towel onto his upper torso. "And I believe that Otto Stark is a key to—"

"Without much effort, I can write you up for at least four violations. That'll turn your career into history!" Within seconds, engine whirred, whined, and coughed again.

Joe released his feet, floated free, and performed a slow tumble before Commander Lopez as he scrubbed his feet, then shins, then knees, and then thighs with his towel. "The time is getting short and an aggressive approach to getting into their operation is required in order to—"

"Damnit, you just don't care at all about—"

Engine coughed, sputtered, and died.

Joe moved his towel action to his buttocks and crotch. Oooops.

"Since your mission has been assigned Priority One, I must let it proceed." Commander Lopez took in another deep breath as he glared at the nozzle, then at Joe's backside that floated and rotated four feet from his face. "However, since I am in command of this station, I can and now *do* require that before you are given clearance to undock, you present your flight plan to me for my approval." He started to jab his index finger forward, but having only buttocks to lecture, he paused, grimaced, and clenched his fist. "And I can assure you that you shall conform to *that* approved flight plan—with no more deviations initiated on your whim or fancy—or your career with WSF will be terminated—on the spot! Is all of this perfectly clear, Rebello?!"

Joe dried his ears as his face floated toward Captain Lopez. Worse than I imagined. For him, conformity is the accomplishment. And I'm on his turf. No choice. He flashed his wide grin. "Yes, sir. I'll present our flight plan to you in your quarters in eight minutes."

Though not in zero gravity, he drifted and floated.

Otto tried to sense vibration. He felt none. He tried to pick up sound. He heard none. He looked down at the cold gray shaft of the monorail—all smooth, no grain, no perception of motion. Yet, he knew he moved, for enclosure after enclosure shot by, white box after white box zipped from before to behind him on either side. And the breeze, a steady flow of cool air against his face, indicated swift motion forward.

Otto looked ahead. As when he first entered the Production Tube with Wolf, he could see no exact end, only a vanishing point where white strips, gray rail, and black walls ran together and disappeared. He turned and glanced behind. The same. *I just float forward but never seem to get closer to or farther away from either end. Like speeding from one infinity to another . . . ridiculous. I should reach the end in less than seven minutes.*

Otto thought again of his entrance into the tube only minutes before and the open space next to the car he now rode. *Wolf must have the other car up there. Couldn't he sleep either? Lift-off prep is less than two hours away. What's he doing? My last chance to see Wolf's "private laboratory." Why's he still need one? He's completed all his research and development . . . hasn't he? Of course.* Otto's features yielded a smile. *And I won! All we have left to do now is crowd out the weak.* Otto's jaw tightened and eradicated even a microsmile of pride. *So why's he need a lab?*

His eyes glazed as white boxes, identical boxes, blended into continuous strips. *Tube reproduces one of me every twelve minutes*—Otto's fists balled and tightened—*with just a little "spoilage."*

Otto's vision snapped back into focus. *Almost there. The end's no longer a black point. Looks more like a rectangle—a door.*

Vaulter, a well-muscled Adonis, glanced up.

The bar, an official 23.037 feet above the ground, as determined by continuous laser meter measurement, sliced white across the razor blue sky. Vaulter nodded. He bent down, tweaked out a pinch of grass next to the runway, and released it from seven feet up, just a shade above eye level. Grass fluttered and drifted down, straight down. No wind. *Good, this'll be nominal.* He turned, and, as he did half the time, let Pole, his servant and supporter, hang from his left hand as he paced back up the runway.

Vaulter probed the surface through his form-molded track slippers as he stalked by his checkpoints. The sole function of his lean lower body, which moved with a ballet dancer's grace and precision, appeared to be the transport of his well-muscled upper body. At the end, he turned, positioned his left foot by his start marker, and shifted his hands to the end of

Pole, an Antonescu 700/122 PlexiPole, his 7-pound flexible spear designed for his 273-pound frame, a 23-foot plexan shaft that glistened gold in the noon Sun except for the blue and red tape that spiraled around the end he gripped. He positioned his hands three feet apart, and, with his rear hand by his hip, brought Pole's distant tip up to eye level. He studied his approach, then the bar.

Other eyes also studied the bar, but they sighted straight along it from the elevated commentator's booth seventeen feet to the side. Commentator's eyes darted between bar and Vaulter as his words flowed in a smooth, steady cadence. ". . . clear that most spectators are taking this as a joke. But I think he's serious. He behaves just as he did when he cleared the bar on his first two vaults with little strain. And when he glanced at the bar just now, he did not look at all intimidated. Yet, why would this unknown move the bar up a full foot, and then some, above the world record? He's already won the event. Wait . . . This has to be a joke. . . . He's going to try it right-handed! The other two vaults he did left-handed. He has the right, but a world meet is not the place to play games or embarrass one's . . ."

Eyes scanned, then focused on the vaulting box. Neurons measured and clicked. . . . Nominal—go.

With a single hop, then a slow jog, Vaulter started down the runway. Blond hair bounced. Beard held fast. At checkpoint one, he accelerated; checkpoint two, he shifted to a knee-high sprint; checkpoint three, he raised his rear hand past his ear and straightened his arm.

Pole speared its target.

Vaulter drove forward another two steps. He flexed Pole into an extreme arc as he rammed energy into it, a precise quantum of energy. His chest, hips, and right knee continued forward as he stepped into the air.

Once again, Brain cycled through nominal commands: push left hand forward, keep Pole away from chest, rock back, pull up, bring knees to shoulders, keep feet together, push down, uncoil, twist, handstand, look straight down Pole, look down on everything, rotate body, fold over bar, throw up hands, drop, loosen, land.

". . . high enough. He cleared it! With a speed, strength, and agility never seen before in the history of pole vaulting, he's broken the record by over a foot and three inches! Where has Rumania been keeping this man?! Why haven't we seen him vault before? Will we see more of him in the future? What will he . . ."

Nominal. Exit east side of pit. Move on to the shot.

"Karov in four minutes."

Joe popped up through the hole in the floor and squeezed in next to Hunter. "Are you going to look at visible light only?"

"Oh, hello, Joe," said Rox. "We gave you up for lost."

"Not really lost"—Joe beamed into the darkness—"just a friendly little discussion with the good Captain Lopez. Are you going to look at the IR as well?"

"Yes, we are," said Hunter. "If the LADSs have any electrical power being applied to them, we should be able to pick up their thermal signatures in the IR and verify that they are still there, just in case we can't see them in visible light. Is that what you had in mind, Joe?"

"It's coming over the hill," said Rox. "I'm tracking it."

"No, Hunter, I didn't. But that's a good reason also. I just remembered that Dieter thought he could learn something about Karov by looking at its IR emissions. That's what he was trying to get to the Friday before he was . . . the Friday before the sub accident."

"Sensors on," said Rox as she squinted through the telescope eyepiece of the terrain tracker. "I'll center the scans on the crater."

"That is certainly logical," said Hunter, ". . . even for a geologist."

"Got it! Goin' to IMC." Rox's fingers slid off the tracker joy-stick onto the switch labeled TERRAIN TRACKING—IMAGE MOTION COMPENSATION and flipped the switch from MANUAL to AUTO. "I'm going to continue to look for the LADS in the tracker sight. Hunter, you can watch the images build up on the monitors. That should be a feasible task . . . even for an engineer."

Joe and Hunter looked up as they pressed their backs against the rear wall of Unity's Lunar Terrain Observatory, a facility one-seventh the size of its counterpart on Armstrong, WSF's lunar polar-orbiting station, and just large enough to hold two workers and one observer. A faint gray image appeared and strengthened on one of the two chest-sized screens over Rox's control station.

"I see 'em," said Rox. "There's four of 'em down there all right."

In silence, Joe studied the red IR image before him at arm's length as it intensified and sharpened.

"They're not obvious on the visible light monitor yet," said Hunter as he studied the display. "But a single flat picture that's frozen in time is obviously not as good as seeing the scene directly in real time through the tracker. Our orbital motion gives you the advantage of a three-dimensional, time-lapse, stereoscopic effect—*Rox!*"

"Nope, it's just the good eyes of a geologist—*Hunter!*"

Joe squinted and blinked, then stared again.

"Still don't see them, but the contrast is getting sharper . . . and my eyes are twenty-fifteen," said Hunter.

"Then if you can't see them by now," said Rox, "you have to admit that the problem lies downstream of your eyeballs somewhere in the signal processor between your ears."

"No, I can see each pixel on the display, and each one represents 1.7 feet on the surface, so if the LADSs are there, I should be able to . . . got 'em! Coming in sharper now. There's four all right. They cast a good shadow. And I still say that you saw them first because our orbital motion gave you the advantage of—"

"Nope. Just better eyes."

"No. Orbital motion."

"Better eyes."

"Orbital motion."

"Eyes."

"Motion."

"*Eyes!*"

"*Motion!*"

"Will you kids knock it off! Look here. The four LADSs show up on the IR, which means they must have power to them. And something else shows up as well." Joe crowded to his left farther into Hunter as Rox left her optical tracker and wedged up on his right. He reached forward and ran his pencil over the screen. "Here's LB-13, the four LADSs, their Observatory, and . . . What's this faint line that runs straight south from the Observatory?"

Rox's eyes darted back and forth between the displays. "It's real all right, and it coincides with this surface rille." Rox pointed to a linear feature that ran straight south from the

Observatory and disappeared off the edge of the white light display. "It couldn't just be the rille. Perhaps it's a subsurface lava tube that caused the rille itself."

"If that is the case, why would it be warmer than the surrounding terrain?" asked Hunter.

"It's gotta be related to the presence of the Observatory," said Joe.

Hunter leaned forward around Joe, looked at Rox, and stroked his chin. "Could it be a sign of current volcanic activity?"

Rox leaned forward, glared at Hunter, and gave her head a few strong shakes. "No! Volcanic activity is out of the question. The Moon is volcanically dead."

Hunter stroked again. "Yes, I do believe you are right. But also, logically, PRECISE would not stay there if any activity was present."

Rox frowned and also stroked her chin. "That's a tad bit on the obvious side, Doctor."

Hunter stroked harder. "It could very well be they are using the lava tube for something and have it heated."

Rox too escalated the vigor and pace of her strokes. "Well now, ain't that just supersmart?"

Hunter stroked his face with both hands. "It might even be the reason they chose that site to begin with."

Rox's fingernails dug into her skin as she dragged them down over both cheeks. "Indubitably, Doctor, that too is a plausible postulate."

Hunter stopped his stroking just long enough to fix his grin and give Rox a firm nod. "Yes, I do believe that proposition possesses merit. Thank you."

"Damn you, kids, knock it off!" Joe thrust his head forward and turned his face left and right several times. They both smiled. Joe moved back. Within seconds, Hunter stiffened as Rox dabbed at her chin with her little finger.

Joe sighed. "Look. If that heat does come from something PRECISE has under the surface, that's all the more reason to get down to that Observatory."

"Exactly," said Hunter.

"And that's what our mission plan says we are going to do—without fail. Commander Lopez has clarified that point for me."

They both turned inward to Joe and laughed. "Oh, did Lopie rain all over you, Joe?" asked Rox.

"More like a monsoon. It's clear that from here on, I will follow the flight plan—exactly!"

"That is always the best procedure," said Hunter.

Rox nodded a second time. "Do you think Dieter also saw this IR signature?"

Humor evaporated.

"If it was in the IR records he searched that day, he must have," said Joe. "And as a result, PRECISE might have viewed him as a threat. It may be what cost him his life."

"But could there have been anybody there from PRECISE to know what he did or didn't see?" asked Hunter.

"Just one that I know of," said Joe. "Otto."

Pain surged into Rox's eyes as she stared at Joe. "Otto?"

Joe's somber face stared back. "Yes, I'm afraid so."

Hunter stared at the empty screen. "It is abundantly clear that their Observatory and whatever is south of it are central to their plans. Therefore, that is where we should be."

Joe floated down through the exit in the floor. "Yep, make no mistake about it, troops, that's exactly where we're going."

25

◻◻◻

energize

The Grand Cultivator—could anyone usurp His might and right . . . even Wolf?

A little hydrogen, a little helium, Grand Cultivator didn't start with much. But He wielded a powerful tool—Evolution—the combined might of mutation, selection, and time, lots and lots of time.

With stars and elements, explosions and molecules, Grand Cultivator commenced.

Bases and acids, plants and proteins, Grand Cultivator continued.

Bodies and brains, flesh and feelings, Grand Cultivator created.

Then with mutation and selection, modification and election, Grand Cultivator honed his living products. The adaptable, He accumulated; the inadequate, He executed.

And in one survivor, He evolved a brain of superior size and complexity. This flesh of chemical and electrical thought supplied reason and spirit that dominated speed and muscle. This premier product, as Man judged himself to be, refined his logic and hoarded his knowledge as he developed his skills from one generation to the next.

And over time, lots and lots of time, Man developed the

inevitable, the skill to alter himself—and, like Wolf, the arrogance to attempt it. He broke the code of his existence and learned to manipulate his material essence. He deciphered the rules by which he could recycle the stuff of stars to reproduce, then alter his own DNA, his flesh, the physical essence of his life.

For at last, Man no longer needed to depend on the chance of natural mutations and endure the frustration of time, for in one sitting, of the kind that now so engrossed Wolf, he had the might to manipulate the smallest components that defined his physical self. Finally, he could self-direct His gift from eons of the past. At last, he could flash over that unique path that Evolution placed before him for eons into the future, if he could ever predict what that path was to be. Or, more likely, as Wolf now attempted, he could accelerate down one or more of all those many other paths of which he could only start to conceive.

But in the process, Man wondered. Was not this skill to self-direct and accelerate his own change just an inevitable result of the Grand Cultivator's evolutionary process itself? Was not His premier product and all this newfound ability still just a part of His Grand Scheme of Evolution?

But if so, was Man therefore not absolved of all responsibility? Did not ability simply confer right? Or had He cultivated Man, His premier product of premier thought, to bear the weight of freedom of choice, that ever-present burden to balance power and privilege? Most moral men thought so.

But if so, where did Man's technical reason leave off and his moral wisdom begin? Was his genetic engineering wrong for the species as a whole but right for its individual sick? Most moral men thought so.

But if so, and relative to what Man could someday engineer himself to be, were not all present members of the species also, to a degree, sick? Wolf thought so.

But Wolf, a man with considerable motivation and mental might, let the philosophers and theologians wonder and ponder all the nuances of right, the politicians and journalists deliberate and debate the proper uses of might.

Wolf acted.

At his MicroBiological Manipulator, his MBM, Wolf glanced at the holographic image that hung vertical before him like a headless, helical, green and red snake, a green image seen by an electron microscope that overlay a red image inferred by a computer, an image the size of a python that Wolf now assembled as he added one rib after another at the top. And as a pair on either side of each rib, two letters resided: either a C paired with a G, or an A paired with a T, letters that labeled the bases that distinguished each base pair, each nucleotide, the basic building blocks of DNA. For but a moment, and just a moment, Wolf also deliberated and debated as his attention returned to the TV screen to his right:

TARGET AND REFERENCE DNA STRUCTURES

Gene: 313   Chromosome: 21q   Reference Specimen: 0–14.738

Target	Reference	Amino Acid	Position
—> ? <—	A		
G	G	arginine	4337
A	A		
T	T		
C	C	threonine	4336
A	A		
A	A		
A	A	glutamine	4335
C	C		
.	.	.	.
.	.	.	.
.	.	.	.

The "?" flashed at the cursor. It demanded an input.

Wolf lowered his head and rubbed his eyes. How to know? Is this where I went wrong before? Do I want C rather than A, serine rather than arginine? How to know? For sure this is the right gene. And it's right along in here that my structure and that of all other high IQs differ from the norm. But what positions really define neural size, complexity, and growth. Damn—if I only knew for sure! But I don't, so I have no choice . . . no choice. I'll just have to program or not program each of the five possible positions for enhanced growth and observe the results. That's thirty-one more possibilities, thirty-one additional embryos I'll have to carry into the Reproduction Phase. And, no doubt, I'll get more spoilage. That's always been a real nuisance . . . but it couldn't ever be worse though than my first experiments at Sovata. If I can program for optimum natural intelligence, it'll be worth it. And why limit myself to what's on nature's menu? Program not only for optimum intelligence now, go for its explosive growth!

But it'll take years to get a reliable answer, just as it's taken me years to arrive at Otto. That's another problem I need to solve—how to accelerate the growth of the human system to reach maturity in months rather than years. No matter how you look at it, childhood's a waste of time. But that's another day. Better get on with it, make a choice.

Wolf studied the snake. Okay, C it is. He spit his words into MBM's receiver. "Add cytosine, pair it and cap all but three prime."

Inside MBM, Wolf's target DNA encountered a microdrop of cytosine molecules plus an enzyme that added one of its molecules to the chain, then one of guanine and an enzyme that paired one of its molecules with the cytosine to form the nucleotide base pair, and lastly an enzyme that capped off all potential sites for reaction on the DNA strand except for three prime, the one to receive the next base pair of Wolf's choosing. Both electron microscope and computer confirmed—the snake had another rib.

Wolf spoke again. "Insert proline, then phenylalanine, then construct the remainder of the target to equal the reference in automatic mode." He leaned back to watch the snake restart its growth, then looked down and selected "713" and "PLAY" on his hip-mounted PSL, his Personal Sound Library. As another data stream in the form of radio waves flowed from his PSL, entered the laboratory's receiver, and exited the speakers built into the walls around his MBM, Mozart's *Idomeneo* reverberated throughout his laboratory. Wolf rubbed his palms together in slow circles and smiled as he watched the snake lengthen. Within only another fifty-two base pairs, his eyes closed.

Otto opened the door. Mozart filled his ears.

Although Wolf sat at his MBM with his back to Otto, his posture gave him away. Good ole Wolf. Gets up in the middle of the night to come out here and work, then falls asleep. Otto started forward but stopped as a virile voice boomed from the MBM. "Automatic sequence complete."

Wolf flexed his neck out of his shell, sat up straight, rubbed his eyes, lowered Mozart's volume, and spoke. "Move Target Gene 313 to hold. Secure and thaw Otto DNA 14.1. Remove Gene 313 from Otto Chromosome 21q and save. Splice Target Gene 313 into Otto Chromosome 21q in the 313 location."

Otto stopped, blinked, and stared at the TV screen that echoed Wolf's commands. Splice Target Gene into Otto Chromosome?

Wolf continued. "Insert Altered DNA 14.1 back into Otto Cell 14.1. Insert Otto Cell 14.1 into Prepared Zona Pellucida 2764 and save."

Otto's shoulders, back, and buttocks tightened. His jaw and neck quivered. Altered Otto DNA into Otto Cell? Wolf's engineering another me, a superior me . . . but no, it won't really be me, no—not *me!*

Wolf returned Mozart to its original volume and leaned back, his head only a thrust away from Otto's hands.

It ignited somewhere in his bowels, not in his mind, and it burned upward and consumed. Arms shook and thighs trembled. Toes tightened into clumps and hands clenched into hammers. Wolf's head—only a swing away. Otto could hear it crack. His neck—only a twist away. Otto could hear it snap. Water filled his eyes. Wolf, why? Am I not good enough for you?

Otto took a half step forward and flexed his fingers. Blood flowed from slits in his palms. He sucked in a breath and reached out. Just one motion and that brain would be stopped. He exhaled. Will you still make me the dominant one? No, you won't because—I'll no longer be the best. Otto's eyes and fists clenched again, his rigid body convulsed. And then I'll no longer even deserve life!

Otto's energy peaked and plummeted. Drained, Otto stared down at the frail figure, that tiny torso that supported that huge intellect. He chose me, but now what's a *me*? Will I be the same as *he*, the new *me*? One more time, MurMur spread upward from the base of his brain, rose in clarity and volume to a high-pitched warble, exploded in a cacophony of noise, then waned and withered.

He strained. Control, have to hang on to self-control, to think this out. He turned and forced himself toward the door. Maybe if he sees our superiority, he'll . . . no, he won't. He turned and studied the screen again.

ALTERED OTTO DNA INTO OTTO CELL—AND SAVE!

Once again, it exploded in his gut and surged. Otto thrust his rigid body through the door, flung it into his car, and accelerated. And, like before, he felt no vibration and heard no sound as enclosure after enclosure, Otto duplicator after Otto duplicator, flashed by. But now, air blew cold against the moist skin of his eyes and cheeks. And he sensed it stretch—there's only one way I can do it . . . sensed that invisible link back to Wolf tighten and pull—have to become dominant first, just as he planned . . . sensed that heavy black rein between executioner and condemned elongate and store energy, that all-consuming energy in his passion for survival—have to deliver The Gift first and let it grow . . . sensed that thick black cord stretch and strain, tug and pull, that gross grisly cord that no longer masqueraded as lifeline between creator and son—I have to become dominant first, then I'll deal with Wolf!

As Otto sped away, the leash back to Wolf continued to stretch and pull, continued to store an energy that built without bound, cocked a limitless energy that craved release. . . .

". . . two . . . one . . . cutoff!" Joe watched as the numbers on his display froze. "We're in a 37.21- by 7.13-mile orbit—exactly as targeted."

Hunter nodded. "Yes, the system does exhibit a touch of faultless precision."

Joe punched two keys and their LADS flipped halfway around to point its engine in the direction it would fire in a little less than an hour to start its powered descent to the lunar surface. The scene out the window remained unchanged—a heavy darkness, softened only by a crescent Earth, pressed into the cabin.

Joe absorbed the darkness in silence, a pensive silence. He drifted and waited, observed and thought as his physical world marched forward with the rigor of physical law. Can I control or even just predict Otto anything like I can my orbit? Orbit's easy. Just give it an impulse, a well-quantified impulse, and it yields a well-quantified change. In theory, I should also be able to give Otto an impulse and predict the result. Brains follow physical laws just like everything else. But get real, they're just too complex. Can't predict them now, maybe never. It's all too random, too uncontrollable, especially Otto.

Joe stared at the threads of light that reflected from crater rims. Can I predict Otto well enough to stop him, or even just survive him? Hell no, Rebello—you can't even predict yourself.

"We're holding at thirty seconds, sir."

"Have we picked up Equality yet?" Otto's voice reverberated in their LADS's cabin.

Copilot glanced at Otto again, then ducked behind Gift Case One that hovered on its magnetic suspension between them. "We've had a good radar lock on Equality for three revs, sir, and each time have experienced zero dispersions in its state vector."

Otto's voice boomed again. "And the systems?"

Behind Gift Case One, Copilot shrank farther into his corner of the spacecraft. "We have no system anomalies so our exit from this hold will be automatic, sir. And in . . . ahhh . . . mark! . . . exactly two minutes we'll pick up the count."

A third voice, the laconic voice of their launch monitor, slipped in through their audio. "Evolution One, for your information, we're tracking a LADS spacecraft approaching Karov from the east. Its trajectory indicates it will overfly us and land at the WSF complex on the west rim. It should touch down in approximately three minutes. No interference is predicted."

"Roger, Control."

"That must be Rebello and his engineering team," said Wolf who sat in the first of the six passenger stations behind the crew.

Otto nodded. "They're about two hours early. But they're still not a problem. By the time they get over here, there'll be nothing left to see."

Wolf chuckled. "That's right. All they'll be able to do is sniff around and argue with our engineers again. And if they do blunder on to something, I'll call in Kurt."

Copilot peeked around Gift Case One. "Why let them come at all?"

Wolf glared at the inferior intruder, but appeared to also welcome the opportunity to continue expounding. "I have no choice. It is to be their facility, someday, and by international law they have the right to inspect its construction. They're just frustrated by our delays. And the only outlet they have is to send incompetents like Rebello. It keeps them occupied."

"Won't they only send another team if Rebello doesn't go away satisfied?" asked Copilot.

"No, they won't. WSF's under a lot of budget pressure and these hunting expeditions are expensive overhead. They don't have the—"

"Mark, thirty seconds to ignition," Otto interrupted with a voice that thundered into every corner of their spacecraft. "We're out of the hold and counting."

"Evolution One, we wish you continued success. We're proud to have contributed."

"Roger, Control. Thanks." Otto's face solidified into a passive gaze forward. Cabin's silence absorbed his thoughts until Copilot counted.

". . . five . . . four . . . three . . ."

Fingers crept up and around the hand controller.

". . . two . . . one . . . ignition!"

LADS pitched down. Perfect aim.

Joe squinted as he looked below the Sun, which hung forty degrees above the horizon, to the four 90-foot circular WSF landing pads on the farthest and western rim of Karov Crater. "Karov, we're at high gate and comin' down through seventy-three hundred feet. And we have the pads in sight."

"Roger, LADS-7. Your out-of-plane error's zero and your altitude's right on the money. Land on Pad Alpha."

"Will do, Karov. I'll overshoot the pads a bit and come in from the west to put the Sun at my back."

"Sounds good, Joe. We're looking forward to having you down here—and your spacecraft!"

"Roger."

"Joe, at pitchover I got a glimpse of PRECISE's pads on the

east rim," said Hunter. "And just as we've seen before, they still have four LADSs, parked there."

"Yep, still a full house," said Rox as she squinted through her binoculars out LADS's aft window.

Joe beamed. "Good. We're in time."

Rox handed her binoculars to Hunter who unbuckled his restraints and also moved to the aft window. "Here, these may help . . . especially the eyes of an engineer."

"Still just a tad touchy, I see," said Hunter as he refocused the binoculars. "I guess emotionalism is all we should expect from one who's never had the mental discipline to learn anything beyond the soft science of geology."

Rox ripped the binoculars back out of Hunter's hands, thrust them to her eyes, and refocused. "Screw it then, I'll use 'em. Get back up there where you belong and keep your eyes on the control panel—it's close enough and mechanistic enough for even you to understand."

Joe fired a frown at both of them. "Kids, not again, not now."

"It's a real contrast," said Rox as she looked aft, then forward. "Their pads are full, ours are empty."

Joe pushed his face forward toward the window. "Yeah, and just like Lopie said, our folks down there can't wait till we get a LADS to 'em. Captain Aslett and three others have to get back up to Unity. They just got assigned another Priority One mission and have to get back home." Joe glanced inside at this panel. "There's seven hundred feet. I'm going to MANUAL and set us up for our approach from the opposite direction so we'll have the Sun at our backs."

LADS leveled, glided over the WSF Landing Pads, pitched up, stopped, pirouetted halfway around, pitched forward, and started down again.

"Perfect position, Joe."

"Right, Hunter. Keep an eye on the radar altitude and give me call-outs."

"You have it, Joe. We're at five hundred feet and coming down at fourteen feet per second."

"The approach corridor to our Pads looks great." Joe felt Rox's elbow graze his back and her binoculars hover by his right ear.

"Four hundred feet and coming down at thirteen."

"No boulders, very few rocks. It's really clear." Joe glanced up ahead into Karov Crater, into what appeared to be a bottomless hole that separated the western and eastern rims, a chasm

between WSF and PRECISE, an abyss that. . . . Joe pried his
eyes off the crater and back to the approach.

"Three hundred feet, coming down at ten."

"Looks like someone swept the approach path. Hardly any
dust left down there. Must've all been blown off into the tulles
by all the other approaches."

"Two hundred feet, coming down at seven."

"Even the Pad looks spotless." Joe glanced inside at the
attitude ball at the center of his display panel. Attitude's level.
Easy to do with no dust. Perfect setup. But don't get cocky—
that's always when something goes wrong.

"One hundred feet, coming down at four. Joe, you're
making this look too easy. I bet your touchdown is the
smoothest ever recorded."

"I'll try."

"Fifty feet, coming down at three."

Rox put her hand on Joe's shoulder. "Joe, there's dust
comin' up on the other side of the crater . . . a lot of dust
shooting up right from PRECISE's Pads."

"Forty feet and you're leveled off. Keep it coming down."

Rox's voice shifted an octave higher. "One of their LADSs
just lifted off!"

Hunter turned toward Joe and shouted, "You're at fifty feet
and drifting up—Joe, keep it coming down!"

Rox shook his shoulder. "Joe, I don't believe it! That LADS
just . . ."

Hunter screamed into Joe's ear. "Keep it coming down!"

Joe glanced toward the dust on the horizon. "It just what?"

VI

ᗡᗡᗡ

FLEE

At times, nature provides logic difficult to refute—stark terror.

26

□□□

abort

"It did a victory roll, two of 'em just as it lifted off—just like you did in the simulator!"

Ears heard. Brain received. Mind questioned.

A roll?

Joe scrutinized the horizon. Clear. Static. Lifeless. In the vacuum of space, the dust, like the LADS that'd just lifted off, had not lingered.

"Joe, you're back up to seventy feet. Land!"

Intellect reviewed. Neurons recoiled. A roll. Who in PRECISE would do a roll? Only one person—*Otto!*

"You'll run us out of gas. Land!"

"Joe, there's more dust on the horizon!"

Nerves jolted again. Body froze. Have to land—promises, demands, career—have to land! Cold hands again clinched wet controls. But we'll never catch up, never stop 'em. No . . . no choice. Sorry, world, just one more time.

"Land!"

Decision made, body loosened. Joe's fingers slipped off the ATTITUDE CONTROLLER and flipped up a cover to expose one of the few push-buttons left in the cabin that, over the years, hadn't been swallowed by the keyboard. He pressed it.

—ABORT—

Currents flowed. Pyros exploded. Bolts disintegrated. Fuel storage, oxygen storage, propulsion system, power supply, landing legs—the whole lower stage of LADS—separated from the upper stage and started a slow . . . relaxed . . . lazy . . . drifting . . . tumble down . . . down toward the lunar surface.

Within the upper stage, intended for solo use only in emergencies, currents also flowed and the ascent engine ignited. LADS's cabin, minimal propellant, minimal oxygen, minimal system support, and three crewmen with minimal forethought accelerated straight up.

Hunter rammed his face up to Joe's. "What the hell did you do?!"

Joe glanced at Hunter. Crimson face. Golf-ball eyes. Guess I finally got him a wee bit excited. Relaxed words slid out. "We aborted."

"WHY!"

In silence, light exploded below as LADS's lower stage impacted and its propellant tanks ruptured and ignited.

Joe again took manual control and rolled the spacecraft to face west. "Hunter, give me a minute to get us set up."

Rox's whisper pierced forward over his shoulder. "Go get 'em, Joe."

"We hovered too long. We'll never make it." Hunter studied his displays. "It'll take at least five orbits to catch up to Unity. We've got enough oxygen for only three!"

Joe continued LADS's vertical ascent as he scanned the lunar sky. "We're not going back to Unity."

"Then where?"

"Equality."

"Equality? But its state vector isn't in our computer. And we don't have time to get it!"

"We don't need it."

"Don't need it?"

Joe continued to scan until his eyes found and locked on a bright dot. He pointed. "Hunter, there. We're looking right up Otto's nozzle. Set up the rendezvous radar for a passive target, scan, lock on, and give me range and range rate readings."

Hunter pondered.

"Do it!"

Hunter responded.

"LADS-7, we see your abort! What're your plans?"

Joe pressed his external comm control. "Karov, we're going to exercise our only option—rendezvous and dock with Equality. We'll follow the LADS that just lifted off. We have him in sight. Our thrust-to-weight is much greater than his. We'll catch up and trail him up to Equality. I request that you call over to their control and get their comm frequency for us."

"Roger, LADS-7. In work. What happened?"

"Stand by, Karov."

"Got a lock, Joe. They're plus 47 degrees in pitch, minus 3 in yaw, 2.7 miles out and moving away at 343 feet per second. Recommend zero yaw and minus five in pitch to initiate catch up."

"Good data, Hunter. Will do."

"LADS-7, you with us? What happened?"

"Rog, Karov, we're here." Joe took a deep breath and rolled his eyeballs. "We had a fire warning in Oxygen Storage Bay Alpha in the descent stage. Three seconds later we got one in Beta. Had no choice but to dump it."

"Roger. That's a first. Glad you got off it in time! We're working on that frequency."

"Thanks." Joe checked his display. "He's 3.1 miles out and moving away at 152 feet per second. We'll catch him."

"LADS-7, our lunar satellite comm network is still down. Also, since Unity is just over the hill from Equality and not in their line of sight, they can't talk with each other. We'll notify Unity in another hour and fifty-three minutes when we have contact with them again. Then we'll see how Commander Lopez wants to work your retrieval. Do you want to try to give him a call?"

"No, I think we'll always be just a little beyond his range." Joe's eyeballs rolled a second time. At least, I sure hope so.

"Okay, Joe. You can use us for a comm relay as well as Armstrong or any of our other bases on the front side."

"Thanks, Karov. We will. Tell them that we plan to get resupplied at Equality, then return to Unity, ahhh . . . just as soon as practical."

"Roger, we will."

Joe's eyes focused on his displays as he adjusted their pitch, then their acceleration. "We're catchin' up, 2.7 miles out and closing at 134. I'll hold this closure rate till we get a little closer."

"LADS-7, it looks like you just created another good-sized crater down here. There's not much left of your lower stage. We might not ever find out what went wrong."

"Roger, Karov. That's too bad. We'd sure like to know." Joe felt Hunter's glare irradiate the right side of his face. "Got a frequency yet?"

"No. Neither PRECISE Control nor any of their LADSs are answering our transmissions even on 373.0. They must have powered down after their launches."

"Launches? How many?"

"Two more of their LADS lifted off after you aborted, three in total. They have only one left down here."

Joe studied the LADS in the overhead window, then his displays again. "We're 2.1 miles out and closing at 137. Once we're about a mile behind, I'll null our closure rate and wait back here for their engine cutoff. Then we'll move up next to 'em."

Hunter's glare broiled Joe's skin. "Was I in the same spacecraft as you, Joe? I didn't see any fire warning lights!"

Rox's voice wedged between them. "I saw 'em, Hunter, but as you might say, they were just a wee tad faint."

Joe turned and took Hunter's glare head-on. "This is the only way that we can go after Otto. Hunter, I understand how you feel, but we had no time for debate. When we get back, I'll explain the whole thing to Dr. Daro. Then I'll take my lumps, but not until then."

Glare abated but a touch. "We certainly have wagered a great deal that we'll, first, even get to Equality, second, uncover something of enough significance to justify the abort, and, third, even be alive after all this is over."

Rox leaned forward with a wide smile. "Yep. We're sure bettin' our hat, ass, and overcoat on this one."

"LADS-7, you're about to go over the hill on us. Sorry we can't get you a good frequency. We'll talk to you in about an hour and forty-three minutes. Good luck!"

"Thanks, Karov. So long." Joe turned again to Hunter. "Our inertial velocity is going through forty-seven hundred feet per second. Cutoff should come at about fifty-five hundred. Give me calls at fifty-four and fifty-five even. I'll cutoff at fifty-five or as soon as you see our closure rate on them jump or I see the light in their nozzle go out."

"You got it. It's coming up fast, Joe . . . fifty-four on my mark . . . mark! . . . Now fifty-five. . . . Stand by . . . mark!"

LADS's acceleration ceased. Its occupants lurched up against their straps. The spacecraft ahead loomed and billowed in the windows.

"Damn . . . overshot! We'll smoke right by 'em like a blazing bear." Joe fired the forward reaction control jets as he sought to stop their rate of closure. "C'mon . . . almost . . . got it! We're seventy feet back and our relative rates are nulled. Now all we have to do is creep up alongside of them."

"Then what?" asked Hunter.

"Then we ask them for directions to Equality."

"And what if they don't want us along?"

"They really have no choice."

"No choice? Neither do we!"

The entire lunar horizon sped across their windows—twice.

Wolf blinked, then screamed. "Otto, what did you just do?!"

"I did a complete yaw, a victory roll, two of 'em in fact." Otto's voice boomed with even more intensity than before lift-off.

"Why?!"

Otto shrugged. "It just seemed like a good way to look over Karov on the way up."

"Seemed? Look over? That's not a requirement. It's never been in any of our procedures!"

"It really doesn't make a difference. It consumed negligible propellant."

"Doesn't make a difference? Nothing is negligible if it can be measured!"

Otto did not respond as their LADS pitched and started to bend its flight path toward the western horizon. Instead, he studied the WSF LADS as it approached its landing pad below. A light layer of dust fanned out below the spacecraft, dust that turned invisible as it spread outward and dissipated.

"Otto, that procedure was not optimum, not the same as we have developed. Why did you do it? I have never observed that behavior in you before. In fact, it is unique."

A smile slipped onto Otto's face before discipline erased it. He continued to study the scene below.

"I do not understand it. I could not have predicted it." Worry seeped into Wolf's eyes. "Otto, when we reach Equality, you and I need to talk."

"Certainly, sir." Otto watched the LADS below draw to a halt over its pad and hover. Dust ceased. "But, don't worry. From here on I'll follow The Plan exactly." He turned. "Rebello just touched down."

"Good. As I said, he's no longer a factor."

A flash caught Otto's eye as he turned back to his window. "What was that?"

Copilot, absorbed in Otto and Wolf, also turned back to his window. "I didn't see it. It must have been sunglint from something at the WSF site."

"Let's pay more attention!"

Copilot blanched. "Yes, sir."

They continued in silence. Otto studied his displays, Wolf studied Otto, and Copilot studied them both while LADS accelerated to 5513.373 feet per second.

Otto spoke in a matter-of-fact voice. "Engine cutoff. We're in a 9.13- by 27.37-mile orbit. Exactly as planned."

Reassured, Wolf nodded and sat back.

Nine miles below their spacecraft, the placid, peaceful surface of the Moon sped by. Otto gazed out and drank in the stream of bright peaks and shadowed craters, let his eyes relax and defocus the scene into a gray blur that lulled and mesmerized, let his mind loosen and roam back to Earth and the time, so soon now, when he'd deliver The Gift, then ahead to his recognition, his dominance, his supremacy, his . . .

Something, not a blur but something rigid, crept into the bottom of Otto's vision. Something, not distant but something close, coasted up to block out the gray blur below. Otto's eyes focused.

Another spacecraft!

It glided up to the center of Otto's vision and came window to window with him a bare seven feet away. A face with an ear-to-ear grin stared out.

"Rebello!" Wolf's scream shot over Otto's shoulder. "It's that damned Rebello again!"

Joe jabbed his finger at his ear. Otto nodded and jabbed his finger at his keyboard. Their radio communications came to life on frequency 373.0.

Joe's eyes flashed and his smile broadened even farther as he spoke. "Hi, guys!"

"Joe? What are you doing up here?!"

"We had a fire warning in Oxygen Storage Bay Alpha in the lower stage just as we were touching down. Three seconds later we got one in Beta. We really had no choice, none at all. We had to abort."

"But what are you doing here?"

"We have to go to Equality with you."

"What?!"

"Before our touchdown, we hovered long enough that a rendezvous with Unity moved out to at least four and a half revs away. We have only enough breathing oxygen on board for three. We request permission to follow you up to Equality and that once there you give us a full load of oxygen, including an extra tank for good measure. Then we can return to Unity."

"Stand by." Otto returned to Wolf. "Do you think he aborted on purpose?"

"Most likely he did. He's always buzzing in my face, just won't go away!"

"Unlucky timing. If we'd lifted off just a little later, he would've been down for good." Otto cringed. Or if I hadn't done that roll "for sport" that he showed me, he wouldn't have known it was me. Is that why he did it? He came after me?

"Otto, now he gives us no choice."

"Kurt?"

"Yes, but at Equality. I can best deal with him there. Besides, their Karov Control must know they've aborted and are up here with me. That really gives me no option. I have to let him come along. I can't give the WSF any further reason to get in my way."

Otto gave Joe a thumbs-up. "Okay, Joe. You can follow us up to Equality. I'll give you the burn information as we set up for the Terminal Rendezvous Phase in an hour and thirty-eight from now."

Otto looked in the adjacent window where Rox winked at him, smiled, and waved. With Wolf looking over his shoulder, Otto managed a soft smile but kept his hands on the controls. Within, emotions swelled and surged, other emotions strangled and suffocated. "Joe, you'd better back off to three hundred feet."

Joe and his distraction backed away.

Wolf's voice hissed into Otto's ear. "When I get him onboard Equality, I'm going to find out if this stunt is his own idea or if he's acting with the consent of others in WSF—then he and his crew shall be excised from any further participation."

Rebello's voice intruded into their cabin again. "Otto, can we get the services we need at Equality?"

Wolf's smile hovered over Otto's shoulder. "Tell him the truth. We'll make sure that he gets all he needs at Equality—and then some."

27

□□□

welcome

"Joe, you'll be the last to dock."

"Understand, Otto. How long till you're ready?"

"Another eight minutes and forty seconds, that's when our last LADS will be docked and moved into its servicing bay. Then you can dock and remain at the central docking port. We'll get your oxygen resupplied as soon as you exit."

"Thanks, Otto. For your info, we've got enough oxygen left to keep our cabin at comfortable levels for about another twenty-five minutes."

"More than enough time, Joe."

Rox glared at Hunter. "That's as long as we don't get too excited and suck it up faster than normal."

"Please be patient and remain well clear of the approach to the central docking Hub."

"Okay, Otto, will do."

Joe flipped their LADS around to look behind them. Like chicks trailing a mother hen, two identical LADSs glided along behind Otto as all three drifted toward Equality's central docking Hub.

"Hmmmm . . ." Hunter frowned at Rox as his fingertips massaged an ear. "Curious thing there, Cool One. Why do you think three of their spacecraft are engaged in a simultaneous Moon-to-station transfer?"

Rox yanked on both her ears. "Right, what the hell are they up to?"

"Hang on for just a few more minutes, kids. Once onboard, we'll have our chance to find out. Till then, let's do just as Otto asked—stay out here and relax." Joe tweaked the controllers, drifted out to the edge of the space station, and slid to a hover five feet from the interconnected, gray, cylindrical modules that formed Equality's rotating Wheel. He rolled a half turn to put their head toward Equality's Hub and their feet toward the direction of Equality's induced gravity. "Let's stay out here and see what comes by, see if anything's changed." In silence, and in a little less than two seconds each, each one of Equality's twenty modules streaked by from right to left. And with each module came the familiar string of nine 2-foot windows. Joe's eyes glazed. "Oops, too close. Better back off."

"Yeah, it's like tryin' to see into a train barrel-assing through the station," said Rox.

Again, Joe tweaked the controllers. "This oughtta do it."

"Much better," said Rox. "But it's still hard to see much. Sun's too bright, except in our shadow. And it still looks like there's nobody home."

Almost as if by command, the Sun's bright ball behind their backs rested on the Moon's edge for an instant, then broke through and plunged below the surface. Equality's gray tube continued to glide by and dissolved into a mellow blackness. Joe flipped their searchlights on to low power to keep the outline of the station in sight, then tried again to peer into the meteoric procession of windows. Black, every one's black, impenetrable, impervious . . . no, some light, partial light . . . bright light . . . intense light . . . windows flash like a strobe . . . crewmen, only a few—no, *can't be!*—oh, no, back to partial light . . . no light, darkness, light's gone, crewmen are gone, only gray outlines of modules again. Joe continued to stare into the darkness. "What'd you folks just see?"

"Not much," said Hunter, "except for those few lighted modules, about five of them, one quarter of the total, and some crew. Just one quadrant of the Wheel's lighted and looked occupied."

"But the crew? . . ."

"I, ahhhh . . . saw only about three or four in there," said

Rox. For the first time in the flight, Joe sensed tension strain her voice.

"And? . . ."

"Thought I saw . . . forget it, Joe. I must be too keyed up."

"Here comes the lighted quadrant again," said Joe. "Let's take another look."

Three pairs of eyes inched closer to the windows. Light flickered over their faces, mesmerized their minds, then faded again into blackness.

"They're gone," said Rox. "They moved out of sight."

"Try again."

They waited. Light flickered. Eyes absorbed.

"Not there," said Rox.

"Keep watching."

Otto's voice blared from their cabin's omni-sound speakers. "Okay, Joe, we're ready for you. You can start moving up to the Hub for docking."

"We're on our way, Otto."

"By the time you're ready for docking, all of the vehicles will be in our Servicing Garages."

"Thanks, Otto." Joe turned his spotlights to full power, started upward, glanced up at Hub and the last PRECISE LADS as it glided in for berthing, then looked straight ahead into the blackness that again replaced the Wheel's gray outline, a blackness interrupted only by the flash of one Spoke every nine seconds, flashes that gave only brief glimpses of the four gray surfaces and one Servicing Spider that again scurried along to keep pace.

They drifted in silence until they reached the floodlit area of Hub. Joe lined up on the centerline of the central docking port and, from sixty feet out, studied the four windows in Hub as they rotated. No faces. No clues. He started a rotation to equal that of Equality, then tweaked it to align his sight on the docking target. Before him, a LADS's snout nudged into a berthing fixture.

A thirty-eight-foot Robotic Arm Manipulator, as named by its designers but called RAM by its users, reached out from the side of the port, gripped the LADS attach ring on its back, and maneuvered the vehicle to the docking port in one of two vacant Servicing Bays. In an adjacent Servicing Garage, clam-shell doors closed over its occupant. Joe looked ahead.

Like a solo eye socket, only the dark open cavern of the central docking port gazed back. It furnished no answers, no clues, no options. You've got no choice now—worked yourself and your crew into a corner again—don't get 'em killed!

"Ready for your docking, Joe."

"Roger." Joe focused on the docking target above the dark cavern. All of the standoff circles lined up precisely on the centerline. Taut muscles shoved the controller forward.

LADS accelerated. Dark cavern loomed.

Inside, Wolf calculated.

They hit.

Joe jolted. No, not even a flinch. Equality absorbed us and didn't even budge. A more rigid docking system than I'm used to. That's gotta be it. Ahead, only the docking target filled his vision. He looked out his side window into the LADS that had just docked. For a moment, the torso of a crewman blocked the window, then glided forward to expose a white sphere, about the size of a basketball, as it quivered in its magnetic suspension. Hands reached back several times to accept a food pack, a mission-planning computer, the white sphere, a trash bag. Servicing Bay doors swung closed and cut off any further view.

Mechanically, Joe started through his post-dock checklist, but his mind remained in the other spacecraft. What's that white sphere? Not ever seen one like it. Had electrical and instrumentation connections. They're not wasting any time. Better hustle and get our hatch—click—open. They've just plugged into our intercom system. They're hustlin'. Delta pressure's good.

"Hello, Joe. We're standing by for your hatch opening."

"In work, Otto."

Joe unlatched the hatch and had no sooner pushed it open than Otto poked his head in and smiled. "We'll have a technician up here in ninety seconds to service your vehicle. Until he's finished, please be my guest down in our wardroom." Otto beamed again.

Joe reached forward and grasped Otto's hand. "Thanks, Otto. We'll be glad to." Under the negligible artificial gravity at Equality's center, Otto's tug hurled Joe through the hatch, into Hub, and toward the central docking port cover on the opposite wall. Joe smacked into the cover's rigid surface. Otto's really fired up. How come?

Joe grabbed a handrail and turned to study the inside of Hub. From the outside, Hub's disklike outline had reminded Joe of a huge hocky puck. Being on the inside didn't change his impression. Three secured hatches to the Servicing Garages where the LADS had just docked and one hatch to an empty Garage were evenly spaced around the outside of the opposite flat disc-shaped wall, the wall through which he'd just been yanked by Otto at its center. Four additional secured hatches were located in the same relative positions on the flat wall to which he now clung, hatches that he knew led to four EMTVs in the Servicing Garages they'd seen in their previous visit.

"Welcome aboard, Hunter." Otto beamed again as he shook Hunter's hand and ripped him through the tunnel into Hub where he impacted next to Joe. "Glad we can help you people out," Otto said through another wide smile as he yanked Rox into Hub. Rox clung to Otto's hand as his arm extended, then pulled herself back to him and radiated warmth and affection into his face. Surprise, then confusion pulsed on and off Otto's features before he continued. "Please follow me."

Around the outer cylindrical wall of Hub, four evenly spaced hatches covered the four Spokes and presented four choices like those at a crossroads: north, east, south, and west. Otto grabbed a handhold that circled the exit from their central docking port and, with a flick of a wrist, shot to the opening labeled east. Rox and Hunter followed.

Joe pushed as he continued to study Hub's interior. Each of the four quadrants are identical: a hatch to a Servicing Bay on either side and another hatch leading to a Spoke . . . yep, exactly identical. And Otto sure is more enthusiastic than I've ever seen him. What's got into him? Joe grabbed the handhold, yanked, and landed behind Rox and Hunter who didn't budge as they stared up at Otto.

"We'll take an elevator down the shaft inside the Spoke to the Wheel's east quadrant, the only quadrant that's active now. The ride going down takes exactly seventy-three seconds, a third of what it takes coming back up." With a single pull, Otto swung open the three-foot hatch and held out his hand to Rox.

"Please enter feetfirst." He laughed as he tossed Rox's torso through the hatch. "There ya go!"

Joe watched Rox's surprised face disappear, then Hunter's. *Otto must think he's loading sacks of potatoes. My turn. Here I . . . go!*

Joe shot into the elevator pod and landed feetfirst between Rox and Hunter. Like a javelin, Otto also hurled himself in between Rox and Hunter but on the opposite side. Then, with a single swipe of his hand, Otto pulled the hatch closed above him—and confined the four of them in the pod. Joe closed his eyes.

Otto hit the button marked WHEEL.

Slap! Pod jerked.

Whirrrr. . . .

They started down.

Joe opened his eyes. The pod seemed to have shrunk in size, to close in, to collapse around them. He concentrated on Otto. *No doubt about, he's fired up about something. What's he got lined up for us? Damn, this is tight in here. Relax, don't fight it. But this is tight, way too tight—I'm confined!*

Within Hub, a hatch from one of the four PRECISE LADSs opened. A technician floated out and headed for the WSF LADS, the spacecraft at the central port that required servicing and, according to Wolf, a special Software Enhancement. In less than thirteen minutes, he would accomplish his task. For the technician, Kurt, knew his job well.

28

☐☐☐

comprehend

Confined! It welled up. Joe forced it back down.

Four backs and buttocks pressed against the cylindrical outer wall of the elevator pod. Four chests and faces pressed against the cylindrical inside surface, a ten-inch pole that ran down the center of the pod from top to bottom. Otto's head butted against the ceiling.

. . . *Whirrrr* . . .

In the dim illumination, Joe stared at the nicks and scrapes in the gun-metal gray surface inches from his nose as he listened to the elevator's voice that gurgled and grated within the pole, from something that whirred and scraped. He felt its vibration through his chest. It's mechanical and in motion . . . must be the cable that drives the elevator. But God this is too close, way too close. Relax, concentrate on Otto. Get him talking. Figure out what he's up to. "Otto, what's moving inside this pole? The cable?" No answer. Joe glimpsed around the pole to his left. Humor gone, Otto blushed as he held his arms to his sides and stared down his nose at Rox who rested a hand on his elbow and stared back up at him with eyes that questioned. As if relieved to see Joe's face, he talked straight into it.

"No, it's not a cable, Joe, but a chain, the return loop for the elevator's drive chain. A superconducting motor in the Wheel drives a chain hooked to the top and bottom of our pod. The chain's return loop passes through this pole in the opposite direction we're moving. The chain would've been put outside the pod except that the spoke is too narrow. Have any of you ever been in a rotating space station before?"

As Rox shook her head no, her eyes never left Otto's, never stopped searching.

"Just Independence," said Joe. "But that was larger than this and interconnected with tethers."

Otto nodded once, then looked relieved as Rox withdrew her hand and eyes. "That's right, almost three times larger. But, this serves us well for our mission."

"Which is? . . ."

"Just what you see . . . the same as Unity's, a transportation node, a place to trade lunar vehicles for Earth–Moon transfer spacecraft, LADSs for EMTVs. And a place to get them serviced."

Joe studied Otto. Strange, he's turned bashful, almost timid toward Rox. But why the shy act now? Maybe he's still enough off guard to let something slip. "Otto, you said that only the east quadrant's active. Do you ever use the others?"

"Not anymore. Up to just two years ago, we used the west quadrant for some research on engineering construction, but all that's done down on the surface now."

. . . Whirrrr . . .

Elevator continued out toward the Wheel, out to where the artificial gravity of centrifugal force would grow to equal that on the Moon's surface. Joe's feet began to brush against the floor as the pod's centrifugal force intensified; his body pressed to the side against Hunter from the acceleration of the pod's circular motion as they moved farther out the Spoke. "Otto, if you don't need lunar gravity here anymore, why do you keep this rotating? Don't you use Calblock to prevent calcium loss from the bones?"

"We do. But this station's prime mode of operation is rotation, so that's what it does."

"Prime? Do you have any other modes?"

"No." Otto looked confused. "Why should we?"

"What happens if you do stop the rotation?"

Otto shrugged, then glimpsed down his nose at Rox who looked up again and scrutinized his face with eyes filled with hurt. "A few of the systems won't work in absolute zero gravity, systems like thermal control, fluid distribution, and this elevator, for example. But that's the way it is. When we purchased Equality from the Soviets back in 2023, we modified it to be as efficient as possible in it's Prime mode and eliminated all other modes that only compromised the Prime."

Joe's feet pressed against the floor with enough force to indicate that they'd almost reached the Wheel. When these guys at PRECISE get their mind locked on one way of doing things, they can't seem to accept anything else.

Otto continued: "The best mode is simply just that—the best."

. . . *Whirrrr*. . . .

Slap!

Whir inside the pole ceased as the chain slapped against the pole's inside surface and pod jolted to a stop.

Otto appeared relieved. His body loosened. "We're at the Wheel." He looked down and away from Rox and pushed a release with his foot. A hatch opened downward in the floor between him and Hunter. Bright light flooded back up. "Let me help you out. You'll find yourselves in the wardroom." Otto held Hunter's hands and lowered him through the hatch.

With a sense of relief, Joe followed.

At last, alone with Otto.

Rox slipped her hands around his waist, then up his back as she snuggled up to him. "Otto, why are you acting shy in front of them." She nuzzled her head into his chest. "They obviously know."

"Know?"

In the one-sixth gravity, she sprang up, put her hands around Otto's neck, pulled her eyes even with his, and laughed. "Yes, they do!" Her eyes probed in silence for those special messages that'd flowed so freely before, primordial messages of oneness and understanding, of need and desire, of . . . Lips brushed. Passion erupted. Rox pressed forward. Surprise . . . comprehension . . . then a smile flickered on and off Otto's features just before her open lips met his, her tongue probed and explored, awakened and aroused. He returned her intimacy—at last—with his normal finesse, his normal fire. He opened his armor—at last—and exposed the Otto she knew, the one that accepted her, understood her. Arms wrapped around her as they had before; one hand ran up and down the curves of her back and hips and induced that familiar quiver, the other slid over her buttocks and leg and again began to stir desire.

"Otto, I'm sorry, but I just had to feel your closeness again."

"Don't apologize, Rox," said Otto as his hands continued to awaken her urges. "I understand . . . now I really do. But this will have to wait."

"Of course, I know. You just acted so aloof, and I didn't know why."

"Don't worry, Rox, nothing's wrong."

Rox beamed at Otto, conduits opened and again messages flowed. "I wish we didn't, but we have to go below. They're waiting—"

Again, passion surged.

Rox lingered, then tried to force herself away. "Otto, this is not the place. . . ." But just once more—yes, this has to be the last—she let herself fall back into that unique glow of warmth and security she sensed only Otto could provide. "Otto, I've been thinking about what you said before? I know you're right. We do have something special, very special—you and me. . . ."

Joe dropped to the floor into an ocean of brightness.

His eyes clenched and blinked as his pupils collapsed inward, then slowly adjusted to the intense white light that came from the flat lights embedded in the perimeter of the flat ceiling and the reflections off every smooth, glossy white surface.

He surveyed the wardroom, a spacious volume that utilized the entire module for its function. A seven-foot-wide table stretched almost to the end of the module twenty-six feet to his left. Behind each of the eight chairs on either side of the table, waist-high individualized pantries extended to the wall except for gaps that permitted access to the four windows on either side. Ovens, food warmers, refrigerators, freezers, and food-storage compartments lined each wall to his right. More stowage compartments covered the flat, smooth, glossy white surface of the ceiling eight feet above as well as the surface of the flat floor of similar appearance under his feet. Other than the windows, Joe saw only a few dark specks in the sea of white—small cold lenses, tiny ice-blue lenses of holovision cameras ever ready to poke and probe and pry. Who's on the other side? Have to find out. Have to get into the other modules.

Hunter rubbed his eyes with his fists. "A touch lighter than your standard pastels."

Joe grinned as he bounded to the end of the table where steam rose from five white plates each covered with identical portions of steamed onions, mashed potatoes, and white fish covered with cream sauce. "Can't ask for more hospitality than this."

"Nice of them to let us drop in, but where are they?"

"Don't know, Hunter, but it smells good."

"Wonder if they have any black-eyed peas."

Rox descended through the ceiling followed by Otto. They both appeared relaxed and invigorated.

"I took the liberty of having a snack prepared for us while your spacecraft is being serviced." Otto blinked as he motioned to the chairs by the plates. "I hope you're hungry."

"Thanks, Otto. We are." Joe looked around. "Can we thank the chef?"

"No, he's elsewhere."

Rox slid into the end chair opposite to Joe and Hunter and Otto sat next to her. "Please eat before it gets cold." Otto focused on Joe. "Would you please tell me how you—"

Joe interrupted. "What do you have in the other modules?"

Otto motioned to his left at the closest bulkhead beyond Rox. "The next module contains the lavatories and sleep compartments. Beyond that is just a storage module." He motioned to his right. "The two active modules there contain a laboratory and an exercise facility." Under the table,

Rox's hand rested on his thigh. "Ahhh . . . please tell me how—"

"How about the modules in the other quadrants?" asked Joe.

"Most are laboratories, but they're all inactive now." Otto slipped his hand over Rox's. "Joe, tell me how—"

Joe pressed again. "How many crewmen are onboard?"

"We have a total of seven pilots, no . . . six now, eight copilots, and seven technicians. Joe, how—"

Hunter picked up the interrogation. "Where are they all?"

"They're up working on the preflight test and checkout of our EMTVs and post-flight servicing of our LADSs."

"So, that's why we didn't see them," said Hunter. "They're all up behind those closed hatches."

Joe started just as Hunter finished. "Otto, after we're done eating, could you extend your hospitality to show us some more of Equality?"

Rox's hand freed itself and her fingertips began tracing small circles on the inside of Otto's thigh. He tried to speak one more time. "Joe, maybe we can—" He paused, as if he listened to a silent voice, then jumped up straight. "Excuse me for a moment." He turned and charged through the slit in the pliable white flexolex that served as the door in the bulkhead.

Joe frowned as the flexolex guillotined closed behind Otto. Acts like he got a command from somewhere. Think we got him opened up. Have to press him harder when he comes back.

"Where'd he go so fast?" asked Rox.

Hunter stroked his chin. "Nature's call?"

Joe looked up and swept his eyes across the clear lens in the opposite wall. No, not nature's—but someone's. . . .

"He's not getting the job done!"

Wolf sat at his command and control station and studied the holographic reproductions that hovered in space before him. In one-seventh size, four figures sat at a white table. Their voices reached his mind through molded ear micro-speakers, the same kind of speakers that also resided in Otto's ears. Wolf torqued a joystick with his fingertips and the holographic scene rotated to provide an end view of the table, a view that showed fingers making circles on a thigh.

As thigh's owner spoke, Wolf scrutinized the audio frequency analysis on the display over the joystick. A line at the bottom summarized the last seven seconds of data:

STRESS LEVEL = 73; ABNORMAL AND INCREASING

Damn! He's lost concentration. Too busy playing handsies under the table with that unworthy wench. What's wrong with him? Anna's everything he needs—the best. What's he see in her? Now he's unreliable. That will change! Wolf pushed a button on top of the joystick. "Otto. Exit. Now!"

Wolf rose, accelerated, and moved at maximum hobble-hop speed through the pliable flexolex slit that separated him from the next module.

Again, at the speed of light, Enhanced Software flowed.

The last packet of data, electronic data that contained Enhanced Software to "improve" the operation of a few spacecraft systems, coursed through optical fibers from Kurt's work station in Hub into the computer memory of the LADS at the central docking port, the LADS that had previously spurned its lower stage. Always a dependable performer, this Enhanced Software designed by Wolf had been developed as a natural outgrowth of the viruses that infected computers for many decades before. Without fail, it precisely performed Wolf's assigned tasks, erased itself, and vanished completely much like the hole left by a finger plucked from a pool of water. And now, once again, Enhanced Software slumbered in wait for its scheduled wake-up call.

A second, smaller packet of data returned to Hub. Kurt reviewed it and, satisfied with the perfection of his performance, shifted mental focus to his next task.

Fully serviced—its tanks filled with oxygen, nitrogen, and propellants and its computer programmed with Enhanced Software—LADS waited for the return of its crew.

• • •

With anticipation, Rox looked up.

Otto rejoined them at the same speed he'd left. With eyes again cold and aloof but now of greater intensity, he glanced at Rox only once before he snatched the extra plate of food from the table, scraped its contents onto his plate, and took a bite from his fish, his first one—a large one.

"Otto, when you left, I was just asking if you would be so kind as to show us some more of Equality when we finish here. Is that possible?"

Otto continued to chew, then gulped once. He looked up as his spork tore into his fish again. "Joe, what really happened when you aborted?" His eyes remained locked to Joe's as he took Rox's hand off his thigh and flung it back into her lap.

"Otto, we went over this already. Just before touchdown, we got two fire warnings in the lower stage and punched it off."

"Joe, you really didn't see any warnings and you aborted on purpose so you could follow us up here." Otto leaned forward and glared at Joe. "Isn't that right?"

Joe leaned forward and matched Otto's glare. "Why would we want to come up here rather than complete our mission at Karov?"

Otto hurled Rox's hand away a second time. "And did you alone decide to do this, or is there anyone else in on your fake abort that instructed you to follow us?"

Joe pushed himself nose-to-nose with Otto and snarled. "You've gone out of your mind!"

"Answer the damn question, Joe!" Otto paused as if he listened again to a silent voice, then chuckled. "Actually, Joe, you just did."

Rox stood and started to massage Otto's neck. "Otto, what's got into you?"

Otto flung her hands aside again.

"Otto?!"

"Keep your place!"

"My place? What's that?"

"On your back!"

"What?!" Embarrassed and hurt, Rox ignited, charged into Otto, and pummeled his back with her fists. "What do you think I am, just some roll in the hay to use and abuse?"

Otto turned, growled, "Shut up, whore!" and took a swipe at Rox with the back of his hand.

Rox felt the impact, then her body spun and bounced across the floor and cracked into the end wall. Dazed, she jumped to her feet. Tears overflowed and ran. Her voice quivered as she stumbled forward with her arms outstretched. "Otto, why?"

As Otto rose out of his chair and cocked his hand again, Joe and Hunter flew into him.

Rox turned and dove through the flexolex slit into the next compartment. Her face skidded to a stop on another cold, smooth, glossy white surface.

Pain throbbed on her face, flooded her body, and inflamed her mind.

Silence hung.

She heard only her own whimpers, then the scuffle of feet, feet that seemed to shuffle closer and crowd around her. Rox smelled a familiar smell and lifted her eyes.

She looked at the feet straight ahead, then up—*Otto!*

Then into the face to his right—*Otto!*

Far to his right—*Otto!*

And to his left—*Otto!*

Far to his left—*Otto!*

And to the face that poked through the door—*Otto!*

Faces merged into one, then parted again. Otto—all *Otto!*

Rox felt a scream tear at her throat, heard it echo until she ran out of breath. Her mind tried to turn her world black, to lock out the swarm of friends and strangers, to cloak the reality of lovers and enemies that all merged and parted . . . merged and parted in same yet different forms— *Otto!*

It failed.

"Quality through equality?"

"Yes, Mr. President. Quality of life through equality of excellence. All of our corporate objectives, all of our corporate achievements stem from this one fundamental principle."

The President straightened as a quizzical look consumed his face. "Professor Closca, please explain."

The Chairman of the Board of PRECISE, Professor Dinu Closca, a careful man, a man who knew his own limitations and the strengths of others, barked across the coffee table to Lothar Lopescu, his Director of Public Relations. "Lothar, please respond to the President." His command echoed in the oval volume of the White House's Diplomatic Reception Room.

"Yes, sir, Chairman Closca!" Lothar turned to President Privara who sat to his right at attention on the couch against the wall. Lothar's face glowed empathy and warmth as he leaned forward and beamed his expansive smile into the President's eyes. "Mr. President, we, the proud team members of PRECISE who are being so graciously honored here today, who I feel so privileged to represent, and who perform under such inspirational corporate leadership"—he paused to motion and smile at Chairman Closca—"have demonstrated in areas from science, technology, and medicine to social action, education, and athletics that we have made a rigid commitment to the equality of excellence. Achievement of the highest levels of excellence blankets all sectors of our Corporation. Perhaps not surprising, we have experienced that with each new achievement of excellence, there comes a commensurate enhancement in the quality of life of each of our employees. And, in turn, each enhancement in the quality of life has created within our people a renewed commitment to excellence and to its equal distribution. Thus, the quality of life and the equality of excellence that pervade our Corporation are mutually dependent and, together, continue to spiral upward. We have achieved quality of life through equality of excellence. Or, in short, quality through equality."

The President rubbed his eyes, then scrutinized Lothar through a squint.

Lothar leaned back and made a micro adjustment to his red silk tie as he stretched and wiggled his neck. Then he continued. "But our actions are neither myopic nor self-centered. For not only do we consciously serve as THEE role model for all responsible corporations of the world, but through our leadership in space, our worldwide distribution of products and services of unsurpassed excellence, and our humanitarian initiatives, we intend to improve the quality of life for all those who share this planet with us!" Lothar tightened his jaw and peered upward, then looked again at the President who had put his head down, grimaced, and swallowed hard. "Yes, simply put, our gift to humanity is enhanced quality of life through enhanced equality of excellence. Quality through equality"—Lothar's eyes glazed for a few seconds—"quality through equality . . ."

"Lothar?" The Chairman raised an eyebrow as he studied his subordinate.

President Privara squinted again at Lothar before he sat up and blinked several times. "Thank you for the explanation, Mr. Lopescu." Then he turned back to the Chairman and leaned forward again. "Now, in addition to the reception to honor your Corporation's contributions to world prosperity, there is a second reason I have asked to meet with you today. Professor Closca, I would like PRECISE to act as the corporate leader within the East European business community to assure support from your UN representatives for our Human Replication Initiative. This Initiative comes to a vote in the General Assembly next Thursday morning, and at this point, it appears too close to call."

The Chairman began, "Most certainly, this issue penetrates right to the very core of our Corporation's, ahhh . . . moral fiber." He paused.

Lothar pounced on the opening. "Yes, Mr. President, we feel as strongly as on the limitations imposed by this Initiative as we did when we lobbied for the Right to Life Initiative back in '32, which, unfortunately, still has not passed. If you will recall, once Life With Choice became available, we supported an Initiative to rule the willful destruction of a growing human fetus universally illegal—just as we have always asserted it to be universally immoral. For once a growing embryo exists, regardless of its origin, it deserves an excellence in its treatment equal to that given to any and all other living humans; that is, although unborn, a fetus must be accorded a full and equal opportunity for a quality life and, in fact, be treated to the same and equal opportunity for a quality existence as we, the already born, claim for ourselves. That is, quality through equality . . . again, quality through equality . . . quality through . . ."

"Lothar!"

"Yes, but what about our Human Replication Initiative?" asked the President.

Lothar blinked, rubbed his face, blinked again, then continued. "Yes, we will strongly support this Initiative that maintains the human duplication limit at one. In fact, we intend to also support the French amendment for even more meticulous on-site inspection of all biological facilities. We must assure that no illegal or immoral human genetic engineering is found anywhere on this Earth!"

"Good. Significant corporate support should make the difference. We appreciate your backing." The President, a man whose mission had been easily accomplished, leaned back, stretched his arms along the top of the couch and his feet forward to toy with Connecticut and Cuba, two of the fifty-two state seals on the border of the gold and light blue oval rug. He beamed at the Chairman, then at Lothar. "Gentlemen, please also let me comment that our nation has been heartened by the dynamic growth of entrepreneurial corporations in Eastern Europe since the turn of the century, and, led by PRECISE, by their contributions to responsible world government."

The Chairman, always ready to make the most of a tribute, responded. "Thank you, Mr. President, but much of the credit for our growth should be given to your nation for its continuous leadership and generous support to the much-delayed revitalization of Eastern Europe."

Also of a mind to enhance the positive mood, the President nodded and laughed. "Yes, you are right. Together we have done it." Then he turned serious. "But, gentlemen, these are still dangerous times. We have but one Earth. And it is up to the stronger and more prosperous nations to uniformly assure and, if necessary, uniformly enforce the development of humanitarian and globally responsible governments within each and every country, especially so now in the Southern Hemisphere."

Lothar saw and seized another opening. "We agree wholeheartedly, Mr. President. As we have pledged before, we will continue to work for 'One World, One People.' All nations of the world should be assured a quality of life equal that of other nations, a quality of life that can only come through an equality of excellence." Lothar focused on the President and nodded. "Yes, Mr. President, quality through equality." He then focused on the Chairman. "Quality through equality." Finally, his glassy eyes gazed at the wallpaper behind the President's head, a depiction of early American life at Boston Harbor, and began to jump from one settler to the next. "Quality through equality . . . quality through equality . . ."

"Lothar!"

With many settlers yet to receive the word, Lothar continued. ". . . quality through equality . . . quality through equality . . ."

The Chairman leapt from his chair and shook Lothar by the shoulders. "Lothar!"

Yes, so many, so many. ". . . quality through equality . . . quality through equality . . ."

The President stood in confusion and studied Lothar. "Can I help?"

". . . quality through equality . . . quality through equality . . ." Oh, my, so many settlers yet to hear.

"No, he's just been working too hard. It's caught up with him. Fresh air will help. Please excuse us." The Chairman helped Lothar from his chair and turned his back to the wall.

Lothar looked down. Maybe the settlers can spread the word among themselves. ". . . quality through equality . . . quality through equality . . ." Only fifty more states to go. The Chairman pulled Lothar out through the double doors, along the plexcrete walk toward the South Lawn, and past the six-foot ten-inch Marine guard braced at attention in his dress whites. Lothar looked up and spread the word to each of his shoulder boards. ". . . quality through equality . . . quality through equality . . ."

"I'll summon the White House doctor," the President called out.

A second guard. ". . . quality through equality . . . quality through equality . . ."

The Chairman stopped and shook Lothar one more time. "Lothar! It's Mindlock, damnit, you've gone into Mindlock again!"

". . . quality through—"

The Chairman slapped him with a roundhouse. Lothar spun twice and came face-to-face with an eight-foot rhododendron. Much work to be done here. ". . . quality through equality . . ." His eyes jumped to another flower as his mind defined his targets and pattern of scan, and his voice picked up the tempo. ". . . quality through equality . . . quality through equality . . . quality through . . ."

29

trap

Otto, which is Otto?

All are. . . .

None are!

Rox collapsed on her back and gawked upward. They towered.

Each body—identical!

Each head—identical!

Each face—identical!

Eyes questioned, eyes ignored, eyes threatened, eyes eluded, eyes . . . Is there one that really sees me, understands me . . . loves me?

Lips moved, they all moved, all made the same sounds, all fluttered in the same way, all blended into the same buzz. Does one really speak to me, to *me*?

Shins and knees, all identical, crowded.

Arms and hands, all identical, pointed.

Faces and eyes, all identical, gazed.

She searched form after form—is there one that's really different? All Ottos merged and crowded together into a sea of one; human flesh blended into a solid grisly uniform mass. Rox turned away as she retched and gagged.

Light from above faded.

Rox glanced back up—a different body!—one that soared over Otto heads, scrambled over Otto shoulders, fell through Otto torsos, reached past Otto legs. . . .

Hunter's voice screamed from the side. "Otto!"

They all turned.

Joe grabbed Rox's hand, pulled her to her feet, and jerked her from the Otto sea. He ripped her through the flexolex slit just as Hunter called from the elevator hatch, "Rox, up here!"

As Joe started to lift Rox up toward the hatch, a hand landed on his back and lifted him off the floor. He looked into Otto's face, then across at Rox. Like kittens, Otto held them both by the napes of their necks. Hard eyes drilled into him, then Rox. Eyes flinched. Then softened. Hands released.

Joe flung Rox up to Hunter, hesitated but a second, then sprung through the elevator hatch after her. He glanced down at the Ottos who paused as they collected around Otto—the paralyzed Otto. As the Otto mass sprang toward the hatch, Joe backed away and ripped it closed. Hunter commanded the pod's ascent to Hub.

Pod jerked.

Slap! Chain hit the inside of the pole before Joe's face. *Whirrrr* . . . that welcome whir.

We're moving! Joe knelt down next to Rox who sat on the bottom of the pod with her head on her knees. "Rox, I'm sorry. I had a suspicion, but I never knew."

She looked up. Teeth dug into her lower lip and restrained its quiver. "Oh, Joe, I never even suspected. I had my mind closed to everything but him."

Joe put his arm over her shoulder. The sadness of his eyes seemed to absorb some of her pain. "Rox, I'm sorry, really sorry."

Tears welled as she choked, "All those Ottos . . . is one different, one my Otto? Which is the one?" Rox looked at Joe through tears, her mouth open. ". . . one? . . . or *all*?" She shuddered. "Does it even make a difference?"

Hunter gripped her hand and looked into her face with an empathy she'd never seen from him before. Her eyes accepted.

Joe stood and pulled Rox up by the hand. "Let's get ourselves pulled together. What's important now is that we get back into our LADS. Then we can call down to one of our stations, give them a report, and get ourselves back to Unity."

"Yes, but clearly we can only get to Unity if they have resupplied our LADS," said Hunter.

. . . *Whirrrr* . . .

Joe felt his face pressed into the pole as his weight started to lighten. "For now, we'll have to assume that they have serviced our LADS. But our first problem is to just get to it."

Hunter rubbed his neck. "Yes, it would appear that we have now learned enough to die."

"More than enough, yet I'd like to know the whole picture, then find a way to bring it all to a stop." Joe flinched at his own words. Get out of here—don't get us killed!

. . . *Whirrrr* . . .

Joe listened to the chain race through the pole, felt its vibration through the tip of his nose. "They could stop this pod any second."

"And if they do?" asked Hunter.

Rox looked up. "I'm going out that top hatch and crawl up the chain. Anything to get outta here!"

"Even if they don't stop the pod," said Joe, "they're probably calling up to the Hub right now and arranging one helluva reception."

"Then what do we do?" asked Hunter.

"If there's not too many of them, we take them on any way we can." Joe frowned at the futility of his own words.

"And if we're outnumbered, the ball game's over," said Rox.

"I wonder how many of those things, those Ottos, there are," said Hunter.

"No way to tell," said Joe, "but I saw at least six."

"Those 'things' are human," Rox snapped. "They may each look the same, but they're each human, just like any one of us . . . they must be . . . and there's one that's special, the one that let us go—mine!"

Hunter pondered. "How could you ever tell for sure?"

"I don't know. . . ." Rox clouded. "As yet, I just don't know."

. . . *Whirrrr* . . .

"Seems possible there could be many more down there at Karov," said Hunter.

"Yeah, and who knows how many more they're breeding."

Joe's viscera fluttered as a limbless twisted human torso with an infant head on either end flashed forward in his mind. More infants flowed behind the first, a gross parade of distorted anatomies produced in the Sovata bioengineering experiments of '17 by undefined persons, anatomies that awakened the world to the horrors hidden on the bottom side of the bioengineering coin, anatomies far too well documented on late-night X-Holovision. "Or they could be doing worse."

"That's most likely why they've always kept us at arm's length at Karov," said Hunter.

Rox nodded. "We'll stop that! Our testimony will be far more than enough to order a full on-site inspection."

"That's if we get back," Hunter sighed.

Slap!

Whir stopped.

As a unit, they floated off the floor, mushed into the ceiling, and pushed themselves back down.

Joe sneered up at the hatch, then at his crew. His eyes ignited and radiated fire from an inferno within. "We'll do it—we *will* get back!"

"Kurt, define the configuration of their spacecraft."

"Their tanks are fully serviced, appropriate systems have been modified, and the Enhanced Software is fully loaded and verified."

Wolf's voice again hissed over Kurt's command loop up to Hub. "And undocking control?"

"It's *internal*."

"Change it."

Kurt pictured Wolf's palms rubbing together in ever-tighter circles. "Yes, sir." He stroked his keyboard. "It's back to nominal."

"Good. There has been a change of plans."

"Sir?"

"Rebello and his crew are not to leave just yet. Otto will retrieve them."

"And my actions, sir?"

"Stand by."

Kurt placed the FIRE CONTROL switch to STANDBY and scratched his index finger across the trigger. "Yes, sir. Standing by."

"I'll open it just a crack," Joe whispered.

"Why not go out just like everything is normal," said Hunter. "That should confuse them."

"No," said Rox, "let's charge out. Maybe we can get through."

"Perhaps we should go back down and try coming up another spoke," said Hunter.

"No, let's . . ."

Joe cracked open the hatch and peered into partial darkness. Forward, left, right—nobody! He lifted the hatch and looked up, then down—nobody! "We're in luck. Let's move." With Joe in the lead, they floated out and glided to the central hatch.

Joe reached in, flicked his wrists, and coasted through the hatch, tunnel, and central docking port, then into their LADS. "Looks just as it did when we left." Rox and Hunter followed as Joe moved to his Commander's station, strapped in, and started an abbreviated power-up and checkout. He checked the oxygen first. "Someone *has* serviced us!"

Hunter's fingers stroked. "Let's hope their training was not in animal husbandry."

"Full tanks?" asked Rox.

"Yep, full tanks—oxygen, nitrogen, and propellant." Joe put up his hand to block the Sun that shafted onto his displays, then glanced out and down at the uniform, washed-out gray features of the Moon's surface at lunar noon. "We're coming up on the near side. We'll try to contact Houston first, then Armstrong." He entered commands that switched on every one of LADS's radios—two prime, one backup, and one emergency—then gaped at his displays. "No power!" He verified his commands. "They've done it to us. They've cut off all power to our communications."

"I do believe we should have expected that," said Hunter.

"I think we all really did." Rox reached up and started to close the hatch. "And I bet there's more."

"Rox, wait. I saw something outside we might need. Hunter, keep working on the radios." Joe floated back into Hub as his eyes scrutinized the walls. There! He pushed off, drifted over to a hatch that led to an EMTV, reached over to a box labeled FIRE, flicked open its cover, and made his retrieval. As he pushed off again, he glanced out the window adjacent to the hatch and into the EMTV. Nobody home, but it looks stowed and ready to go . . . except for that empty magnetic suspension like I saw in their LADS. Joe continued his retrieval at each of the other three hatches and soared back toward his spacecraft. All of 'em have empty suspensions. Does each one hold one of those white spheres?

"What'd you get, Joe?" asked Rox.

"Insurance." Joe floated four oxygen masks and bottles, each set molded into a single unit, through the hatch. "Just in case we have a problem with the oxygen they gave us."

"A prudent precaution," said Hunter.

Joe coasted back into his position. "Let's press."

Rox closed the hatch between Hub and tunnel, then the one between tunnel and spacecraft. "Joe, why are they letting us leave? Something's wrong."

"I know, but let's not take the time to ask."

"Except for the radios, all systems appear good," said Hunter. "Ready for undock."

"Should I depress the tunnel, Joe?" asked Rox.

"No, leave it. The pressure in there will help give us an extra kick away." Joe keyed in his first command:

DOCKING LATCHES—ARM

then his second:

DOCKING LATCHES—RELEASE

Nothing . . . no change.

He reset and tried again.

Again, no change!

Joe listened. Only a faint hum emanated from the docking tunnel structure. "The motors are trying to drive the latches open, but the latches still have locks holding them closed." He negated his second command. Hum stopped.

"Their system must have a central control that does not authorize our release," said Hunter.

"Just like 'em," said Rox.

Joe unstrapped again. "We can't do any more from in here than command the latches open. Rox, open the hatches. I'll have to see what can be done from out there. Hunter, keep working on the radios."

"Comin' open, Joe."

Joe shot back through the docking tunnel and began an inspection of the area around the central port entrance. His fingertips glided over the smooth carbolon molding that concealed the latch mechanism underneath. No joints nor fasteners evident. He continued his search, continued to . . .

Slap!

Whirrrr!

"They're going up! Rox, throw me out a flashlight and your pick hammer." Joe's fingers continued to race over the surface.

"Coming out, Joe." Flashlight, hammer, then Rox drifted through the tunnel.

"Move back, Rox." Joe swung the pick against the molding. It bounced off. Again he swung, and again it bounced. He paused.

. . . Whirrrr . . .

"Hold the light here, Rox." Joe searched. "There it is. A slight crack. Interface between two sections." Joe swung again—but with precision. Chips flew. A small hole opened. He swung twice more, looked inside, studied the mechanism, then swung again and again as he hacked his way around the circumference of the hatch in a hail of carbolon chips. Finally, he paused again to scrutinize the mechanism and its electronics, then called back into the tunnel, "Hunter, throw out the bone saw. Hustle!"

"What'd you see, Joe?" asked Rox.

"Best I can tell, it's just like our docking rings that have a lock on every latch. But they've changed it so that the release command only frees the latches. It doesn't also free the locks like it does in our system. Our only hope is to use the manual release that goes straight to the locks. But they even have a clamp on that. I'll have to cut off the clamp just to pull the manual release—then we can hit the road."

. . . Whirrrr . . .

Hunter's hand reached out of the tunnel. Joe took the saw, a steel wire with a helical wrap of smaller titanium wire, and fed it behind the clamp and out the other side. He put a thumb in the ring on either end of the wire, pulled the wire taut, and began to work it back and forth on the backside of the clamp. A few filings drifted out. Joe's hand picked up speed.

Filings washed out. He glanced at Rox, Hunter, manual release, clamp . . . MANUAL release . . . damn! With pressure in the tunnel, both latches and locks are needed to hold the spacecraft on to the docking port. And the only way to use this release is from right here. One of us has to stay!

. . . *Whirrrr* . . .

Joe stopped. One of us. His eyes saw Rox and Hunter; his mind saw Yuri and Dieter. "I'm almost done. Rox, Hunter, get back in and be ready to undock."

Hunter remained still as he tapped his cheek with his finger. "Let's see, in order to use that release, someone has to—"

"You got it, Hunter." Joe released the saw and pushed Rox into the tunnel on top of Hunter. "Your job is to get back to Unity. If you don't, everybody down there will find out too late about Otto and his brothers—his clones!"

Hunter struggled up beside Rox at the exit to the tunnel. "Joe—"

Joe grabbed their outstretched hands and pushed them back. "Do it."

"Joe, we can't just—"

Anger and determination swirled, mixed, and erupted again. "I'm pullin' that release as soon as I get the clamp off and you'd better have your hatch closed—'cause you're goin'!" Joe slammed the tunnel hatch against their wide eyes and open mouths.

. . . *Whirrrr* . . .

Adrenaline flowed. Filings flew. Clamp broke.

Slap!

Whir stopped.

Joe glanced in the tunnel hatch window, verified the LADS's hatch closed, and pulled the manual release. It didn't budge!

He tugged. Nothing.

He grabbed it with both hands, planted his feet next to it, and yanked . . . then he yanked again—harder.

Pop!

LADS drifted loose as Joe shot across Hub and into the opposite wall. Now what? He stared back at the hatch over the east Spoke. Still closed—but not for long!

"Sir, they have just undocked."

"They what? That's impossible!"

"No, sir. They must've somehow gotten to the manual release."

"If they got off manually, then at least one of them must still be here."

"True."

"Kurt, accelerate the excision of those in the LADS, and assist Otto in finding whoever is still here and bring that person to me."

Kurt placed the FIRE CONTROL switch to ENABLE, slid his index finger into its familiar position on the trigger, and grinned. "Yes, sir!"

Joe kicked, then clawed his way along the wall to the hatch over the west Spoke. He ripped it open, wrenched himself through, yanked the hatch closed, then hovered in the darkness. Who's coming up? He cracked the hatch open again just enough to peer out. The east hatch on the opposite side flung open.

Otto emerged. Otto emerged. Otto emerged.

They spread out. Otto came toward Joe.

Joe nudged the hatch closed and held his breath as he floated in black silence. Will he open it?

Chest pounded. Throat throbbed. Ears pulsed.

Joe's head grazed cold hardness . . . the central pole of the elevator pod. His feet brushed the floor as his body settled under the light gravity. He straightened up and ran his fingertips over the walls—an elevator pod just like the other—one that contracts and constricts, cages and confines . . . cool it!

Cold darkness closed in as Joe eased his breath in and out, as body heat bled into the coolness of his flight suit, as the aroma of sweat saturated his air, as . . .

"Check each pod!" cried Otto.

"Right!" cried Otto.

"Right!" cried Otto.

Joe froze.

30

◻◻◻

violate

Pop!

Rox stared out the porthole in their LADS hatch, saw Equality's central docking port shrink, and searched for signs of Joe in the surrounding windows. She found none.

"Only did what he thought was right," said Hunter.

"One of the few that always does . . . no matter what."

Hunter punched a string of digits into his keyboard. "It's clear that we're now on our own."

"As is Joe."

Hunter extended his hand. "Best thing we can do is get back to Unity for help."

She accepted his hand and pulled herself back toward the copilot's station. "Yeah, let's get with it."

They exchanged glances with faces that hinted smiles: a silent pact, a truce—survival dictates it.

Rox's smile surfaced. "But we've gotta hustle if we stand a chance of getting back here before they leave or something happens to Joe."

"You're sure right there." Hunter beamed at Rox before he returned to stroking his keyboard. "I'm setting us up for the first phasing burn."

As they backed away, Sun plummeted below the horizon

and, once again, reached up behind and took its light with it. As their distance increased, the lighted windows in Hub and Wheel contracted to a rotating pattern of bright white points that cut through the blackness, sliced through the heavy black cloak that materialized from nowhere to envelope Equality.

Rox lifted her binoculars for one last look and probed each of Equality's portals. Again she saw nothing, nothing except body after body, crewman after crewman, Otto after Otto. She inspected each Otto for some extra-familiar look, some special recognition, some modicum of human communication, but they each moved through their tasks—cold, mechanical, identical. Her vision blurred as moisture seeped into the eyepieces. One last bright point to inspect, the only lighted module in the middle of the dark quadrants. Is that one of 'em looking out with binoculars, looking back at me? Is that *my* Otto?

For almost twenty seconds, cold lenses focused on cold lenses. . . . Rox waved and—the Otto waved back!

Otto!

A flash in the window of the Command Center at the edge of Hub drew Rox's attention. She shifted her focus. There's one that's different. For but a few seconds, she examined deep-set eyes before they slid behind an optical tracking sight.

Added insurance—almost always in order.

Unless the situation is perfect, one can always make an improvement. Obvious. And Kurt, a careful man like his superior, analyzed the current situation and also saw that it was not yet quite perfect. LADS's Enhanced Software might be enough by itself, but why take chances?

Yes, added insurance—almost always in order.

Kurt scanned his menu. Laser? No. That would leave its distinct mark, would leave evidence. Explosive-head projectile? No, too crude, too easily detected. What about . . . ? Yes. That's it. Perfect. He reached out and made his selection.

Added insurance—almost always in order.

Kurt sighted his target through his eyepiece, the broad flat surface of LADS's forward wall. His index finger depressed TARGET LOCK, then FIRE.

Currents flowed in superconductors. Magnetic fields surged in sequence. Forces thrust in response.

A pebble, a meteorite for all anyone would ever know, accelerated within its superconducting container at over ten thousand G's along a forty-foot rail. Pebble exited Hub at over five thousand feet per second and, with precision, found its mark.

Through his eyepiece, one that remained dry and clear, Kurt verified his work. A perfect hit, of course. And no one would ever be able to tell if the "meteorite" came from the heavens or from closer to home . . . like from Equality's rail gun.

But was it enough? Maybe a second one would be better, would move the situation closer to perfection.

Yes, added insurance—almost always in order.

Kurt's finger rested on FIRE. Instinct applied pressure, sought perfection; Reason held back. Didn't the first do enough? What is enough? Kurt's finger dithered in small circles over the surface of the trigger. Push or hold?

Inside the skull of Kurt Grimm, neurons continued to war. Enough fought more. Discretion fought excess. Judgment fought . . .

Him, part of it? Or it, part of him?

Otto gazed at Gift Case One as it hung in its magnetic suspension before him and in line with the other two identical spheres to its right. All the same, all those lives in there, each just like me, they're each just one more drop from that same endless sea created by Wolf.

MurMur rose. Otto blinked. MurMur faded.

Better finish up here. Only thermal systems left to check. He punched commands into Equality's central computer. Numbers, words, and figures flashed onto its panel. Perfect. Flows, temperatures, and pressures are nominal in Gift Case One.

His gaze shifted to Gift Case Two, then on to Three. He frowned. Each life string of DNA in there is the same, each one split from the same parent. What's different between them? Or between them and me, or all of us? What makes me me? A soul? But what's that? Something identical to all the others, something also split from the same parent? Wolf can't control that too . . . can he? Maybe none of it makes a difference anyway.

Otto blinked and shook his head. Move on! How's Two? He punched more keys. Sensors, signal conditioners, and processors reported back. More numbers, words, and figures flashed. Good. Two's thermal system is also perfect.

Gift Case One, Two, then Three again lured his eyes, mesmerized his mind. He scowled. Do I make a difference? . . . Of course—I'm the first of the best! That must give me special recognition . . . of some kind. Must make me special . . . in some way. Must! And when we complete the Elimination Phase, only we who are superior will remain, only we who are superior . . . but then, superior to whom? MurMur rose from the fuzz of Otto's mental background, jabbed upward into his awareness, peaked, then faded as he clenched his eyes and rubbed his face. And how long will it take until Wolf starts to disseminate a better *me*? Otto forced his ego and his anger back into storage, his attention back to his displays. Have to check Three and move on. He punched more keys, received more data, observed more perfection. What's next?

Otto glanced at the television checklist and keyboard on his wrist and depressed COMPLETE. The next block of procedures rolled up:

INSTALL SPHERES IN EMTVS

As his fingertips pressed the release at the base of One's magnetic suspension, a pop rang through Equality's structure. An undocking? No, it's too early, and I'm first. He glanced out a window. LADS drifted away from the central docking port. . . . Joe and Hunter—and Rox! No. Can't be. Latch locks are on. He grabbed his binoculars, his seventeen-power, auto-laser-focused binoculars, and steadied them against the window. That's Rox all right. What're they trying to do? Stop us? Impossible. Wolf won't allow it. The back of Otto's throat twinged as a fullness came to his eyes. His vision blurred. No, Wolf won't allow it.

Rox . . . why Rox? Why do I feel this way about her? Anna's better. Has to be. Wolf's right. She's the best. Familiar images of Anna flooded his mind, intimate images ground into his memory time after time after time. Energetic and entertaining, smart and stunning, luscious and lusty. Bred to be the best, trained to be

the best. They all are, all identical and all the best. But not Rox
Must see me. She's waving. Only one of her. Wave back. She's
open, then unpredictable; erotic, then aloof; happy, then moody
never the same, always different. And she's *only one*. Strange
existence, to have no other options. Wave again. She's unique
What if unique is best, then shouldn't everybody be the same
everybody be unique? There she is, she's back again. Once more
his vision blurred. No, Wolf won't allow—

Bang!

Structure resonated with the shock that emanated outward
from Hub. Sounds like the rail gun. LADS's cockpit clouded
Decompression! Otto closed his eyes. Kurt punched a hole in
their LADS. Air's bleeding out. He never fails.

Otto looked out again. LADS's cloud dissipated as i
continued its outward drift. All their air, their life, must be
bled out. They're gone. She's gone!

Otto pushed binoculars aside, squeezed useless moisture
from his eyes, and looked at his checklist. Two lines blinked:

STOW GIFT CASE ONE IN EMTV ONE; TWO IN TWO;
THREE IN THREE. 3 MIN, 13 SEC BEHIND

Otto's glassy eyes shifted to Spheres, back to LADS. . .
Spheres, LADS. . . .

Escape—but to where?!

Joe folded his body around the pole, reached down, and
groped the floor. His fingers grazed the foot release. He pulled
it. Hatch eased open. Joe glided through and pushed it closed
behind him.

From the darkness, a cold hardness brushed his face. He
grabbed it. The chain . . . no, two chains. He reached up to
where they intersected the pod floor. One hooks onto the
bottom of the pod . . . right here . . . and the other goes
up into the pole. One's ready to pull pod down, other to run
back up through it. Links're just big enough to slip my fingers
through. Smooth, slippery, but dry. Must be coated with
Slylon or Teflon. He reached out to the side. Smooth curved
wall, inside wall of the spoke that guides the elevator pod
encloses it, confines it. . . . Easy does it, hold it down.

Black air hung heavy, hung silent, hung still, yet it tore moisture from his wet skin. His face and neck cooled. And other than the shiver that rippled down his neck, along his spine, and out his extremities, he felt nothing.

Pod jolted. Chains jolted. Joe ripped his hands free. Calm returned. Then jolts came again as he heard the pod's top hatch slam shut. Otto must've looked in. How long will it take till they find me? If I could just get into one of their spacecraft, get away and back to Unity. No, won't work. All their docking latches must have locks just like the central port. And I'd have to get past the Ottos up there, maybe six of 'em, maybe more, all the same . . . what a nightmare for us—and for them!

But where else? Down? Follow the chains down? Like the other Spoke, this one must have a hatch out to the Wheel, out to the dark modules opposite the quadrant we were in. But then what? Might see something else, understand more of what they're doing. But could I stop it? Really makes no difference. You have no choice. Have to go down.

As Joe started to pull himself hand over hand along the chains, his feet traded places with his head. He peered forward. Damn it's black. Eyes are dark-adapted and still can't see a thing. Cold and gettin' colder. Relax, it's just a tube . . . just a tube. . . .

He pulled, accelerated, and glided.

His shoulder slid against the wall. He reached out to the chains. Links brushed by . . . rushed by! He grabbed them. They grated through his hands . . . grated . . . then finally seized and he wrenched to a stop. His feet continued down until they settled out pointing toward the Wheel. Pain shot from his palms. Artificial gravity's getting stronger. Accelerated me. Got going too fast. Better take it slow.

Bang!

A shock rang the hollow tube around him, resonated and reverberated up and down along its length, then faded below the neural noise of his mind. What was that? Felt like a gun's recoil. Can't go back up to find out now. Press.

Joe started down again, hand over hand, but with his feet down and clamped against both chains. Good. A controlled descent. Piece of cake. Feels better with my head up. That's crazy. But what's down there? He peered down into blackness . . . panic burst from the primeval sentry in his gut and rushed upward toward his brain.

Joe dropped another forty handholds, then stopped and clung to the chains with his arms, legs, and feet. With his fingers, he wiped beads of cold sweat from his face and neck, then started to slide.

Stop!

He grabbed the chains with his hands and pain again shot from his palms. He slipped his fingers back through its links.

Safe again.

Joe's frigid sweat-soaked shirt rubbed icy against his chest. A fullness pounded in his ears. Got at least thirty, maybe fifty feet to go. Gravity's gettin' stronger. Have to hold on to these chains. That's all I got. Nothing else to support me, guide me. Joe took a deep breath, tightened his grip. . . .

Chains snapped—one ripped up, one ripped down!

Arms snapped—one ripped up, one ripped down!

Whirrrr. . . .

Pod's coming!

Pain tore at his fingers, exploded in his shoulders, and seared his face, arms, and chest.

And he fell. . . .

He brushed the wall . . . tumbled . . . brushed the chains that ripped by—one up, one down. Chains tore at him, sliced and shredded him, spun him . . . then threw him free.

Blackness rushed by.

Bottom rushed up.

31

□□□

flee

"Everything looks good so far."

Rox turned away from the window toward Hunter. "Ready?"

"Yes, I'm up to the Separation Maneuver in the Rendez-vous Checklist."

"Let's do it."

Hunter looked down. "Jets coming on . . . 3 . . . 2 . . . 1 . . . mark!"

LADS's reaction control thrusters fired, nudged LADS to a lower orbital velocity to separate from Equality, then cut off.

Hunter continued to study his displays. "Main engine burn for the Phasing Maneuver is set for auto execute in seven minutes and thirty seconds. That'll put us in a seven- by thirty-seven-mile transfer orbit. Then, in another fifty-eight minutes, we'll circularize at seven and wait to catch up with Unity."

"Gotta make sure we do the burns right. If we overburn, we're headed toward lunar rock."

Hunter stroked his chin as he smiled and winked at Rox. "Ahhhh . . . good point. Could be a bit troublesome if we nick a peak or two."

Rox returned Hunter's smile and yawned—"Cabin feels stuffy"—then turned back to the window and gave Otto one last wave. . . .

Bang!

Pebble performed its function with precision—focused destruction—as it ripped through the exact center of LADS's lower forward wall, fragmented, and tore into Rox's shins.

"Owww . . . Hunter!"

Air rushed out the puncture and howled.

Air yet to escape expanded and cooled.

Water vapor condensed and clouded.

. . . *Beep* . . . *Beep* . . . *Beep* . . .

Lung vapor evacuated and fled.

The RAPID CABIN PRESSURE CHANGE oral alarm throbbed in unison with the red lights on the panel. Tanks spewed air back into the cabin but at a rate much lower than it fled out the puncture.

Pressure plummeted.

Rox doubled over and clutched at the pain that shot up from her shins. *Otto!* Fog traced the air as it streaked toward the puncture inches from her face. Hunter's hand landed on her shoulder. She turned, saw terror in his eyes, heard it in his voice.

"What?!"

"Puncture!" She gasped. "Must've been something shot from Equality."

"Gonna lose all our air." Hunter tried to inflate his lungs but their vapor continued to thin. "Gotta stop it!"

Rox turned back toward the puncture, back toward that howling, insatiable, black void that sucked away their air—their life. The world around the void started to fade. *Is this how it happens? Nothing more to it than this? Is this how I die?*

Joe tumbled.

Wall confined him, eased him back toward Spoke's center where the chains tore at him again and again and—

He hit.

Air jolted from his lungs. He gasped . . . then once again . . . and finally sucked in a shallow breath. *Can still think, good sign, finger hurts, shoulders throb, cuts all over face and arms and legs, cold, bottom's cold and hard, chains right next to my ear, motor right below me.*

. . . *Whirrrr* . . .

His ears heard it, his mind finally understood it. Elevator's coming! Gonna crush me, trapped, trapped like Dad—gonna die like Dad—*no!*

On his knees and right hand, Joe scrambled around the chains until he found the hatch. Pain exploded again from his left hand as he grabbed the handle. It felt cold and wet, slippery and sticky. He wrenched the handle toward him. Hatch fell downward and pulled him with it. He tumbled into the darkness of the compartment below and, for a second time, impacted hard, cold metal.

Again, Joe surveyed his pain as he pulled in a shallow breath. Shoulders feel torn out of their sockets, hands hurt, finger throbs!

. . . *Whirrrr* . . .

Escape, hide, think this out . . . Otto—all those Ottos. Stomach heaved. And more to come! Anger burst and gorged mind and body. Have to stop it!

He stood, stumbled, groped upward, found hatch, pushed it closed, latched it. Finger aches, have to hide, get to next module, go either way. He stepped forward, felt a sharp corner slam into his forehead, stepped to his left, then stepped again. A walkway? He put his hands out, felt nothing, took a small step, then another, and another and—

Something hard, narrow, and pointed jabbed into his chest. He stepped to the side again, continued, hands rammed a surface—

"Ahhh!"

Pain, excruciating pain, exploded, rippled up his left arm, then tapered off to a throb. With his right hand he probed forward. A wall, edge, flexolex slit, exit, push through, force through—why's it so hard?—good, next module, dizzy, tired, flight suit's wet, left side, cold, sticky, gotta rest.

Joe staggered, then stumbled forward. Have to hide!

Again, on his knees and right hand, he crawled forward. Shoulder rammed an edge, hands flopped over object. Smooth, big as a desk. He fell against it, clawed it, groped it, crawled behind it, collapsed. Cold, rough objects pressed into his cheek. He pawed. Like foot pedals, work station of some kind, what kind?

Joe lifted his head, cocked an ear, froze his lungs . . . still there, but faint.

. . . *Whirrrr* . . .

Still coming!

In darkness, Joe probed with his right hand—left side, left arm, left hand—all wet, all cold, all sticky, finger hurts, must be cut.

Right hand probed left . . . soft slippery flesh.

Fingers sent Impulses to Brain . . . bone sticks out.

Brain turned sensations into Meaning . . . open slot.

Brain jolted and jangled Nerves . . . no, not right!

But Fingers and Brain reviewed . . . one, two, nothing, four . . . confirmed—*Gone, Ring Finger's gone!*

Joe's head dropped, cheek slammed into foot pedals, mind raced. Finger's gone, ring's gone, gotta go get it, go back to Spoke, find it, can't, then have to go home, get another ring, get home to Maria and Ricky, be together, can't, life's bleeding away, sorry, Maria, sorry, little guy, can't let it happen to you too. . . .

No—I'm gonna do it!

But how?

Done it all wrong so far, have to think, to change, but can't now, too late, too sleepy.

In his mind, Joe stepped back and looked down at himself. He giggled. Ridiculous, cartwheeling around Moon in this damn contraption, let life spurt out, now just lay here and let it ooze out. He shifted his cheek to rest on the cold stickiness of his shoulder. Body warmth evaporated fresh fragrances of spent blood and musty metal. Don't die. What do you mean don't die? He giggled again. Rebello, that's exactly what you're doing—and you can't stop it!

Whir stopped.

Joe cocked an ear. They're here!

Head dropped.

Awareness dissolved.

Energy surged.

Otto reached out to two of his brothers. They smiled, locked hands, then laughed in unison as they each issued a single shake and squeeze.

"At last, it's started."

"Thought this time would never come."

"Me neither."

"I have all the Gift Case Spheres checked out and my EMTV's ready for installation."

"So's mine."

"So's mine."

"Let's do it."

"Let's."

"Let's." .

Otto unfastened Gift Case One from the pallet, wrapped an arm around it, protected it with the other, and glided into EMTV One.

As in their LADS, the gift-case magnetic suspension resided between the Commander and Copilot stations. With one hand, Otto held Gift Case One in its proper location and entered commands with the other. Magnetism snapped awake and froze the white sphere in position. With the tip of his tongue at the corner of his mouth, his fingertips mated first Gift Case One's power connector with the spacecraft umbilical . . . the instrumentation connector next . . . then the test and validation connector. Perfect. Never a problem if you're careful.

Otto slid into the Commander's position. It felt natural. Yes, his position—the position where he belonged. After a single command entry into the keyboard, data diffused onto EMTV's displays. Nominal. All connections are perfect and all Gift Case One's system parameters are perfect. His smile broadened as he pumped his clenched fists. It's ready. I'm ready. Let's get powered up and go!

"Otto!"

Otto winced at the shrill voice as he reached for the intercom key. Wolf sounds excited. "Yes, sir?"

"Yes, sir?"

"Yes, sir?"

"Come down to the East Medical Facility. There is someone here I want you to see."

"Yes, sir."

"Yes, sir."

"Yes, sir."

VII

DIFFER

To be a difference—make a difference.

32

□□□

finish

Light. Too much light. Joe's eyelids drifted closed.

Was that Otto? He cracked his eyes open again. Otto's face swam over him, then broke into three. With effort, his mind merged them again. Sensations wormed back into his flesh. Dull sounds sharpened. He struggled to understand the words.

"But he's a mess."

"But he's one of their best."

"But he's inferior."

Pain throbbed up his left arm, sliced through the fog, and prodded him awake.

"Wolf wants him alive to question."

"Wolf wants to see what WSF knows."

"Wolf wants to work on him personally."

As Joe lifted his head, pain snapped his world into focus. A bandage covered his left hand. He wiggled his fingers. Gone— still *gone!* Two inches above his wrist, a red tube led to a needle that stuck into a vein. He traced the tube back to a clear lucilex bag that hung above his feet, contracted and empty. Good, they gave me an IV. Sounds like they want to trade blood for answers.

"Let's not get behind."

"Let's not forget the clock."

"Let's not lose our seven-minute pad."

Joe looked straight up. Two feet away, Otto's face split into three again—and stayed split. Like a snared animal, he scrutinized his three captors as they glared down and scrutinized him. Don't be defensive. Weakness never works. Go after their soft spot.

"Wolf said he'd be a sight."

Joe snickered. "Hey, don't you guys know you're doubly redundant?"

"Wolf said he wasn't too bright."

"Have you guys figured out yet which two of you are superfluous?"

"Wolf said he'd think he was always right."

He glanced at each one individually. "Twiddle Dee, Twiddle Dum, and Then Some." Each one, neither young nor old, happy nor sad, just identical. And their eyes look the same—determined, hard, and empty. No warmth. No recognition. Where's the Otto I know?

Light switched off as they stood up. Their heads backed away to expose a curved mirror with a darkened light at its center. Joe looked into the mirror—an operating table light—and moved his head side to side. His reflected features stretched and distorted; only his colors remained clear: pasty white face, tangled black hair, and light blue flight suit caked with rust-colored blood. They're right. I am a mess. And I still look a pint low. "Thanks for patching me up. Now what?"

A new face, a grim face, leaned over him. Kurt! "Now we wait for Wolf to return. And after he is through, you are to become my guest." Grim face leaked a smile—"And I promise to make it, ahhh . . . interesting for you"—then backed away.

Joe tried to lift his arms, but pain shot up from his left hand, and neither arm moved. He tried to sit up, but pain shot through his shoulders, and his chest wouldn't budge. He tilted his head up again and looked down his nose at shredded cloth caked with dried blood, crusty cloth softened only in spots with sweat. Its smell, an aroma of injury, a stench of death, assaulted his nostrils. He shifted his focus to the three-inch-wide blue strips around his chest, then to similar strips around his wrists. Conductex strips. Locked down by superconducting auto-tightening strips. Standard patient restraints. At least my legs are free. Joe wiggled his right wrist, and in response its restraint cinched a bit tighter.

He lifted his head and frowned as three more figures filled in the semicircle before him. Damn, it's like double vision—six Ottos! Same ones we saw before? "Aren't you guys taking the requirement for backups a bit too far?"

"Dumb question." Five heads nodded in agreement. "Yes . . . Dumb . . . Yes . . . Yes . . . Dumb."

Joe let his head drop. How many more are there? Is one of 'em the Otto I know? He's my best bet on getting out of this. He lifted his head again. "Otto?"

Six figures stepped forward, wedged into one another, and blended into a chorus. "Yes?" The one second from the right stepped a bit closer. His eyes danced, seemed to laugh for a split second, then question before he edged back even with the others.

"Hey, which one of you guys is the best?"

As they nudged forward and wedged into each other a second time, the Otto chorus sang again in multipart harmony. "Me . . . Me . . . I am . . . Me . . . Me . . . I am."

The semicircle broke to let in a new figure, a small frail figure that resembled a deformed dwarf next to the Ottos. Dwarf continued to hobble forward until it wavered to a stop at Joe's feet where a rhythmic flash caught Joe's eye. Dwarf's hand twirled a pencil-sized object down and around each finger, then back up again to begin the cycle anew. Above, gray fur covered its face except for a patch of gaunt yellow skin stretched over its wrinkled forehead, protruding cheekbones, and sharp nose, a spike of a nose that now pointed directly at Joe. Intense black pits in a yellow matrix flicked up and down Joe's body beneath heavy gray brows.

Joe pushed up as far as he could. "Who the hell are you?!"

"I am Doctor Thaddaios Alexandru Wojciechowski."

"Well that sure clarifies everything, Doc. Say it slow."

"Never mind, you'd never learn. Call me what others do, Wolf."

"That's more like it. Even fits."

"Enough time wasting, Mr. Rebello. You should realize that your life, as inferior as it is, is in my hands." Wolf's hunched shoulders ascended and swallowed the narrow neck below the triangle of fur. "Your presence here has created a real problem for me. But I am about to fix that." Lip fur bent upward as eyelids went into a spasm of flutters.

"Well, Wolfy ole buddy"—Wolf flinched at Joe's informality with even his nickname—"I ain't all that tickled about being here either. But thanks for the blood and bandages. What'd you find wrong with me?"

Wolf smiled. "In addition to your missing finger and low blood pressure, our flight surgeon also found torn shoulder muscles and multiple cuts and abrasions. He repaired the injury to your hand and replaced some of the blood you lost. But he was most impressed that you were both gutsy enough, yet also stupid enough, to make such a mess of yourself—all by yourself." Wolf's smile overflowed to a soft chuckle. "After a thorough examination, he attributes your condition to your anatomical configuration."

Joe squinted at Wolf. "To my what?"

Wolf's chuckle strengthened. "Your anatomical configuration, Mr. Rebello, one characteristic of the typical macho pilot." Eyelid flutter accelerated. "Big balls, small forehead."

Led by Wolf, the Ottos chortled and snickered. Then Wolf stepped forward. The rhythmic flash in his hand stopped. Joe stared. His innards tightened. A syringe!

Wolf's smile broadened as he looked at the syringe, then back at Joe. "Yes, for you."

"If it's all the same to you, Wolfy ole buddy, I'll just take another bottle of your best red and be on my way."

Wolf's anger exploded as he grabbed the bloody cloth over Joe's chest, "I am not your buddy, far from it. The name is *Wolf*. And I will command your respect!"

Joe paused. Good. Have a quick way to get under his skin. Use it wisely. "Okay, Wolf, I'll go along with that."

"You'd better! Now, as you desire, I shall let you be on your way . . . but only after a slight delay."

"Oh?"

"In truth, you have but one use to me—information. You are going to tell me exactly what WSF knows about our operation."

"What operation?"

Wolf shook his head, "Won't work," then thrust the syringe directly under Joe's nose. "Proneurodeltarol. Never fails to block all inhibitions and creativity and to stimulate speech.

You shall tell me the truth. In fact, in a matter of minutes after I inject this into your IV, you'll be screaming it at me."

"And then what?"

"Then, as you have requested, Kurt will help you leave." The puzzlement in Joe's face brought another chuckle from Wolf. "Yes, we have scheduled you for a space walk"—he brought his face down nose to nose with Joe's and spoke in a precise staccato—"without a suit."

Joe grimaced and pushed his head back. "Wolf, you've got foul breath!"

Wolf snapped up straight and raked his fingers through his hair. "Always the smart ass."

Joe wheezed. "Wolf, if you don't loosen these strips, I won't have enough breath to tell you anything."

"Of course." Wolf looked at Joe with mock concern as he moved to his feet. "I do not want to cause you any discomfort." He reached down, pressed a control, and the restraints started to loosen. He pushed the control a second time and the restraints locked again. "That's all you get."

"Thanks." Joe raised his head and peered at the semicircle of Ottos as they continued to peer back at him. "Wolf, looks like you've extended the concept of twins a bit."

"Had to. There's no real value in just twins."

"No, there is. If only two are identical, they have a lot of value. As a pair, they're rare in themselves, yet each one can still be unique. I see no value in this nightmare you've assembled here. Wolf, what're you going to do with all of these guys?"

"These *guys*? What you see is my Otto, the Otto I have perfected, the result of eons of random evolution, and now fifty-three years of my controlled and selective evolution, the pinnacle of our species—and our future!" Wolf swept his hand over the six bodies behind him as he puffed and beamed like a proud father. "And almost all of my current Otto is right in front of you."

"Almost . . . ? Sounds like you have some private stock bottled away somewhere else."

Wolf smiled. "In a fashion, that too. But I've also left one part of my current Otto on Earth to lead into my next phase, the Recognition Phase where I will demonstrate Otto's superiority. Already Otto has made a shambles of the World

Games. In every event he's entered, the only competition wa
for second place."

"And does each one of your Ottos have the same abilities?"

"Not 'each,' just simply 'Otto.' You see, all is one, and on
is all. And of course Otto has the same talent, for he is identica
to himself."

Joe squinted again. "What?"

"Yes, all Otto—Otto of today and Otto of tomorrow—all ar
identical for all are the best and therefore the same."

"Otto of tomorrow?" Joe studied Wolf as he hobbled to Joe'
side and danced in place. Finally has some color in his face
Eyes darting everywhere. Proud. Excited. Wants to talk, t
brag. Gonna wet his pants. Keep 'em going. "Wolf, are yo
brewing up more Ottos?"

"You are a slow learner, but eventually you do catch on
Yes, that's what this is all about. I'm returning to bestow m
Gift—my Gift of Otto. In three separate flights, I'm returning
4096 Otto embryos. And that is only the start."

"Thousands of Ottos, then more? Why?!"

"Obvious"—Wolf shrugged—"to create the optimum hu
man condition."

"Optimum condition?"

"Yes, much human conflict and most wars have been drive
by the hunger for either equality or supremacy. But I hav
arrived at the ultimate answer—supremacy and equality bot
in one—in Otto! Thus, it will soon be my pleasure, and mos
certainly my responsibility, to bestow my Gift."

"Sounds like you're trying to create another whole race."

"No, not just *another* race, for when I share Otto's supe
riority, it will pervade and eventually replace all that i
inferior, that is—all that exists down there now. In time, Ott
will *be* humanity!"

Nausea swept over Joe. "Crazy, Wolf, that's genocide—
you're the ultimate racist!"

Wolf's eyes widened. "On the contrary, it will not at all b
genocide, for I display no prejudice whatsoever toward an
one race nor ethnic group . . . they *all* will be eliminated!"

"All will be . . . ?"

"Yes. I will distill humanity down to the ultimate classless
society, to nations of equals, to one world with one people—all
superior people—all Otto!" Wolf appeared to climax, then
wilt.

"Right, Wolf. Then everybody lives happily ever after?"

Wolf motioned, a stool materialized, and he sat down. "Exactly." He put his head down and paused to let his energy return.

"And then after this crowning achievement, Wolf, what are you going to do when you wake up some morning and hear the whole world singing, 'I gotta be me, oh, I just gotta be me'?"

Wolf remained still, as if semiconscious and oblivious to Joe's senseless sarcasm, disrespect, and terrible voice.

Joe studied Wolf's slumped body. A grandiose plan like this one can only come from someone who's extremely egotistical and lost all contact with reality . . . yep, this guy's nuts. But he sure takes himself seriously. Love to slip a whoopee cushion under him. Stop it, Rebello, you'd better get serious yourself. Think! Joe shifted his eyes to six identical blank faces, six identical impassive masks. Do they really buy this crap, the ultimate conformity? Zero diversity means zero chance for survival as a species. Haven't they ever thought this out for themselves? Have to reach at least one of 'em—*my Otto*—get him to think for himself. "Wolf, please let me ask Otto a question or two to better, ahhh, appreciate your brilliance."

Wolf lifted his head and nodded.

"Otto, how can any one of you be the best if none of you are the worst? Superiority can't exist without inferiority." The Ottos returned only blank stares.

Wolf shook his head. "You're not making sense, but then, I never expected you to."

"Do you all really want to be one and the same? Don't any of you want to be different? Don't any of you desire difference, really crave it?" The face of the Otto second from right flinched.

Wolf spoke above low-level Otto mumblings. "As I've told you, Otto is one because the best can only be one." He swept his eyes over the Otto ring behind him. "Would you want to be anything other than the best?"

Six heads waggled and sang in unison. "No!"

Joe tried again. "Don't you want freedom of choice?"

All six faces looked equally confused.

Wolf spoke again. "Otto has not only freedom of choice but the superior intelligence to always make the best choice."

"But they all make the *same* choice."

"Of course, there can only be one best."

Joe's eyes moved from one Otto face to the next . . . studied every one . . . sought communication with each. "Even though you're identical, each of you is unique." The Otto face second from the right flinched again. "Your spirit is not like your flesh. Wolf can't just fill his syringe with soul fluid and inject an identical dose into every identical container he produces. Don't you feel it? You're each unique!" The second-from-the-right Otto face flinched again.

"Soul fluid? Human spirit? It's clear that your inferiorities also extend into mysticism." Wolf stood and pushed his stool back. "It's time to close the book on you, Mr. Rebello, time to move on."

"Wait, Wolf. It looks like you run the whole show, you decide what every Otto should do. If they're such superior thinkers, why not let them think for themselves?"

Wolf glanced over his shoulder as six heads nodded, then pushed up to his full height to meet the challenge. "Of course I have to remain in control until I've established uniform order. Someone has to make it all happen!"

"Someone has to play God?"

"A meaningless concept. All I've done is use the tools in front of me."

"But where'd they come from?"

"Meaningless. We're wasting time." Sunlight exploded in the window over Joe's head and shafted on to Wolf as he moved to Joe's feet.

The Ottos glanced at their wrist computer checklists and spoke in one-part harmony. "It's time to continue the transfer."

Joe called out to the spotlighted Wolf. "Wait! One last question. Wolf, do you think you'll ever be able to stop trying to make a more perfect Otto?"

"Enough!"

The Ottos glared at Wolf's back but said nothing.

Joe sucked in a shallow breath against the strip that squeezed his chest ever tighter and screamed at the Otto second from the right. "And when you have something better, Wolf, will these inferior Ottos also be eliminated?"

"I said that's enough! I'll not have you infecting Ottos' mind with your mindless ramblings any longer." Wolf sneered into the light toward Joe. "After all, lie with a dog long enough and you'll get his fleas."

The Ottos stepped forward. "Wolf, I have to get to the

EMTV and . . . prep for undock . . . power up . . . finish stowing . . . reconfigure . . . target burn."

"Correct, Otto. We've wasted far too much time. I'll finish up here and join you in thirteen minutes."

Joe watched through his feet as the Ottos, moving as a single unit, turned and bound through the end hatch. Didn't stop 'em. I failed. And now I'm left with one ticked-off lunatic eager to work me over!

Wolf sprang forward to Joe's side. The few unfurred facial folds that defined his sneer deepened as he lifted the syringe and uncovered its needle. "Mr. Rebello, time to finish up."

Black void continued to guzzle. Air continued to thin. Alarm continued to sound.

Rox moved her hand toward the puncture, but it arrived an instant late. Hunter's hand slid in under hers as he dove forward. Rox heard a short hollow whistle as his palm slapped over the opening.

Flow stopped.

Emergency pressure regulators continued to spray gas into the cabin. Alarm stopped. Pressure crept back upward.

Rox looked at Hunter. Only his eyes screamed of the pain in his hand. "Hold on, Hunter, I'll get a patch!" She grabbed a handhold to her right, yanked herself over to the Emergency Equipment Stowage Locker, and ripped it open. Her eyes sped over the contents before fireflies danced in her fading vision. She gasped for breath and a gray world returned. "This should do it." She clutched the patch and yanked herself back to the puncture where Hunter gritted his teeth as he wiped water from his eyes. With his free hand, he grabbed the patch, a blister-shaped eight-inch circle of plexan, and held it while Rox huffed and puffed, then peeled the cover off the thick adhesive around its edges.

"Now!"

Hunter wrenched his hand off the puncture. Air howled. Hole guzzled. Alarm sounded.

Whomp! Rox jammed the patch back over the puncture.

"Good move, Rox."

"You too."

Gas continued to spray back into the cabin, and with the puncture now plugged, the pressure started to rise again; the environmental control system performed exactly as designed and as they understood it should—except for one fine point. Before undocking from Equality, Enhanced Software had been entered into the central computer, oxygen-saving Software that shut off all oxygen supply to the cabin—permanently. Now only nitrogen rushed back in to fill their cabin's volume, to return its pressure to normal, to further dilute the rarefied life-sustaining oxygen.

Rox held still to let her visual world brighten from black to gray, then reached for Hunter's hand. She saw the shape but not the color of the violet welt that had replaced his palm and continued to inflate.

"Pressure's coming . . . back up," gasped Hunter. "We just made it."

"Good . . ." Rox puffed thin air in and out of her lungs. ". . . but still dizzy."

"Me too." Hunter panted. "Glad you got . . . patch when you did . . . Couldn't have held much longer." Hunter withdrew his hand and bent over. "Your shins . . . took a pretty good hit."

"Hurt . . . need to . . ."

Hunter straightened up. "Right . . . need to patch you . . . but smaller patch . . . than you used."

Rox managed a weak smile.

Hunter floated over to his control station where a yellow ENABLE light flashed. He punched it off. "Burn comin'."

"Oh, yeah . . . auto burn . . . Unity rendezvous."

". . . two . . . one . . . ignition."

Engines fired, their velocity started to decrease, and they started to drop to lower altitudes where their angular speed around the Moon would be higher and they'd catch up with Unity. As long as they didn't overburn, their velocity would not decrease past a critical value. As long as they didn't overburn, their orbit would not attempt, in vain, to pass through the lunar surface.

Rox gasped. "Burn's . . . good." Her face and fingers tingled. Her vision narrowed down to a gray diffuse spot.

"Yeah . . . so far."

Soon they'd rendezvous with Unity and recruit help for Joe. Soon—as long as they didn't overburn.

33
□ □ □
fade

"You don't stand a chance of pulling this off!"

Wolf's eyes danced and facial fur twitched as his hands moved the needle toward the IV injection port. "How unfortunate that you will not be able to see for yourself." His smile vanished as his eyes ran back up the tube to the lucilex bag above Joe's feet. "Damn, empty!" He lowered his head and muttered to himself. "Proneurodeltarol won't go in without an IV flow. Inject directly? No, hard enough just to get a needle into him once. Easier just to get another bag." Wolf capped the needle, slid the syringe back into his vest pocket, and hobbled twenty feet to the stowage locker marked MEDICAL CONSUMABLES.

"Wolf, the world's not going to stand still and just let you do this."

"How right you are. They won't." Wolf threw his head back and laughed. "They will help."

"Help you breed human clones like we've done with cattle?"

Wolf spun toward Joe and his eyes narrowed, "Cattle . . . ?!" Then he softened and turned pensive. "Yes, in the beginning there will be a slight resistance." Finally, he smiled. "But in the end, they will help—they simply can't resist what I have to offer."

"And what's that?"

"Conformity," Wolf said as he opened the locker.

"That's crazy. People hate conformity."

"No, they don't, except for maybe a few like you. Most people are just sheep under the surface looking for someone to lead them, to give them answers, to imitate. And once they start, their minds have an affinity to lock on and lose receptivity to everything else. So . . . I will provide them with that someone they can imitate without reservation, someone their minds will lock on to and never want to release—Otto." Wolf returned a bag of synthetic blood to the locker, rummaged through its contents again, and muttered, "Why waste good blood? Use saline this time." Wolf opened a second locker and continued his rummage. "In fact, Mr. Rebello, even governments desire my product. That is how we've managed to find homes in several East European countries. For example, many years ago when Rumania felt it was time for them to assume more leadership, we promised to provide them with leaders of unmatched capabilities and they, in turn, have provided another base for our operation as well as extra resources when PRECISE was unable to do so."

"Rumania? No, they don't have delusions of grandeur on anywhere near the same scale as yours."

Wolf extracted a bag and, in several short wheezes, blew a thin layer of dust off its surface. "Let me just say that we have friends within the government that always see to it we get what we need." Wolf wheezed at the bag twice more. "Although I do fear that a few of the weaker ones are having a hard time with the planned scale of our operations."

"This whole thing's crazy in many ways, Wolf. Even if most people do cling to their conformities, they aren't going to let you just walk in with your army of Ottos and take over."

After two hobble-hops on his way back, Wolf paused to rest. "Wrong again. They will, but only because I am performing the process in well-thought-out phases."

"Phases?"

"Yes, in eight carefully planned phases, I am creating the optimum human condition. I've already completed the first three, Conception, Evolution, and Verification in which I've conceived The Plan, evolved Otto, and verified his superiority. Now comes the Recognition Phase I mentioned before. Within a few years Otto will be recognized as the best, by far, in every major field of human endeavor, fields as diverse as science, athletics, politics, law, symphony, and even rock. The people of every nation cannot help but all come to the same realization."

"Even with Otto, that's an impossible sell, Wolf. It's a competitive world out there."

"You're right, and that's just why I've developed Lothar Lopescu, our Director of Public Relations."

"What the hell can he do?"

"He's the master of the soft sell. And I've developed enough Lothar to assure that Otto will receive the proper recognition through an information program that I'm about to initiate, something you might call, ahh . . . a celebrity marketing blitz."

"Enough Lothar? You've cloned him too?! Wolf, you've been a busy boy. How many?"

With effort, Wolf reached up to detach the empty lucilex bag from the IV tube. "Enough . . . yes, let's just say far more than enough."

Joe's phantom finger awoke and again pulsed pain up his arm that rang in his head right behind his eyes. "Okay, suppose everybody thinks Otto is a great guy. So what?"

"Not just a 'great guy,' Mr. Rebello, but a leader, one who'll be indispensable to our world's society." Wolf paused to savor a smile. "I've developed a host of major contributions for him to 'make' in refined cancer diagnostics and reversal, environment restoration, a permanent drug addiction cure, international law for, of course, equity of human quality, and, certainly the biggest seller of all"—Wolf snickered as his eyelids fluttered—"novelties in the field of leisure recreation." His snicker overflowed to a laugh. "The desire to glorify and imitate is woven deep into the fabric of every human. In time, all people will honor and emulate Otto. And just as with any celebrated product of our commercial world, it is the people themselves who will actually *demand* more Otto."

"And you'll just happen to be there with your hand on the Otto spigot." Joe strained to lift his head and glare at Wolf. "But your plan is still naive. They'll always be those who'll figure out where you're headed and be in a position to stop you . . . journalists, judges, politicians, theologians, human rightists, just for starters. No, you don't stand a chance once they get wind of what you're up to. No way!"

Wolf smirked. "No way? No, it's you who is naive if you think I'm depending on the soft sell only. The hard sell is also indispensable to my ability to shape public opinion and action—the iron hand in the velvet glove, the scalpel behind the smile—Kurt."

"More Kurt? More clones?"

Wolf completed the connection between the IV tube and the bag of saline solution. "Let me just say that I have an ample supply of resources back on Earth and in my lunar facility below to monitor and excise every negative opinion before it can reach a critical level."

Joe strained to lift his head again and probe Wolf's eyes. "You plan to wipe out anyone who doesn't agree with you?"

Wolf shrugged. "Human perfection will, of course, require some sacrifices, and I stand ready to see that they are made."

As Wolf suspended the bag above Joe's feet with increased haste, Joe laid back and closed his eyes. Seems too familiar, too pat. Crazy man takes over world. Must've read too much fantasy fiction. There's no way he can pull it off . . . is there? Where's he headed with all this? "Wolf? Your Ottos, how long will you keep churning out more Ottos?"

Wolf snapped open the valve on the IV tube and snarled, "*Churning out?!*"

Cold fluid rushed up Joe's arm. "Okay, how long will you continue to bestow your gifts of excellence on humanity?"

Wolf nodded. "I will continue through several more phases. Along with the current Recognition Phase comes Phase Five, the Reproduction Phase, where, as I mentioned, I am about to gestate 4096 units on Earth. Unfortunately, I must still use the antiquated human womb. In the Domination Phase that follows, I will gestate millions of units using the more predictable and controllable surrogate womb. These units will assure Otto's complete dissemination into, then domination of all human activities and decisions. The second to last phase is the Elimination Phase."

Coldness continued its flow into Joe's body and invaded his core. "That's not hard to picture."

"No, nothing so crude as that, for after all, I am a humanitarian. With bias toward none, I will eliminate *all* human reproduction. That should be relatively simple"—Wolf could not contain another chuckle—"considering the air-borne contraceptive I've developed."

"You mean, if you breathe, you're sterile?"

"Something like that. It's painless but permanent."

"And your last phase?"

"Perfection, just one world, one people—nothing but Universal Human Perfection."

Joe's head fell back. "Guess it's like I always say, anything worth doing is worth doing to excess."

"There you have it, Mr. Rebello, eight simple phases to create order, then perfection out of this . . . this chaos!" Wolf spit the word out like excrement as he withdrew the syringe. "You should feel honored because you are now among the very few who know of all eight phases. Even many members of PRECISE and all of our supporters do not know of the true scale of the Domination Phase and nothing at all about the Elimination Phase. And, of course, they each have their own versions of the Perfection Phase. However, once it's rolling, there'll be nothing anyone can do about it, regardless of what they find out. Yes, you should feel honored."

Joe glanced down his nose at his bonds and bloody suit. "Right, a distinct honor. But tell me one last thing. What happens to you in this new world of Universal Human Perfection? You won't quite pass for an Otto."

"True, but it is enough that my intellect shall live on."

"I'm afraid to ask."

"Yes, I've located the neural genes, the sequences of DNA base pairs that define neural structure. From the Domination Phase forward, all Otto DNA will specify *my* brain's neural structure . . . plus a few enhancements."

Joe squirmed against his chest restraint. "You've really cooked up one helluva combo there, Wolf."

"I owe the world my best!" Wolf wilted.

Joe wheezed and gasped. "I still don't think, ahhh . . . you can make it all happen."

"That's it! Far more than enough. Now it's time for me to listen to you." Wolf uncovered the needle and, out of habit rather than concern for his injectee, pointed it up, ejected its residual air and a few drops of its violet fluid.

Joe gasped again. "Restraint . . . too tight . . . can't breathe."

"Yes, you will need your breath." Wolf bent down and, with his free hand, pressed the release control again.

Restraints started to loosen.

Fresh pain burst from Joe's shoulders and left hand as he gripped the sides of the table.

Restraints continued to loosen.

"Damnit, Wolfy ole buddy, you are brainless. You and your asinine flesh factory don't stand a chance!"

As Wolf's head jerked up and rage exploded on his face, Joe, in one motion, wrenched his body toward his feet, brought his knees to his shoulders, kicked out, and slammed his heels into Wolf's chest. In Equality's one-sixth gravity, Wolf flew to the end of the module along a flat arc that terminated when his back hit the sharp edge of the hatch with a soft thud and loud grunt.

Restraints continued to loosen.

Joe sat up, jerked his hands free, ripped the IV needle from his wrist, and slid off the table. In four stumbled steps, he reached Wolf who still writhed on his back as he gasped for breath. With his one good hand, Joe yanked Wolf to his knees, dragged him back to the table, and wrenched him up onto its surface. "I left the table warm for you, Wolfy. Now it's your turn."

Wolf sat up and coughed. "Damn you, Rebello—"

—*Oooof!*—

Joe sensed his swing to be far less than nominal, yet his fist made a solid connection with flesh beneath the fur. Wolf went silent as his head snapped back. Joe yelped as his shoulder burst with renewed pain.

Wolf teetered, then fell. Joe slipped the restraints around him and cinched them tight. "For one crazy little man, Wolfy, you're sure causing lots of big trouble. How much of what you told me is really true?" Wolf remained silent. "Do I have time to see? . . . Yeah, why not? Take only a minute, if you wake up."

Joe tightened a tourniquet on Wolf's arm and positioned the IV needle over his pallid, yellow skin. "Sick little man has no veins. No, there's one." Joe jabbed the needle several times into the flimsy flesh. "C'mon . . . got it. Hope you don't mind sharing a needle with me, Wolfy. Glad I was first." He taped the needle down, retrieved the syringe from where Wolf had landed, and through its bent needle injected its violet fluid into the IV port. "Wish you'd wake up, Wolfy. But regardless, I've gotta stop what you've started—I gotta stop Otto!"

He glanced around the module. "I only wish I knew how."

Otto One strapped himself into his station—the Commander's station next to Gift Case One in EMTV One.

"All systems are powered, sir. Automated checkout is ready . . . on your command, sir."

Otto leaned forward and glared around the Gift Case at Copilot. "Go ahead. Start it."

"Yes, sir!" Copilot only glanced out of the corner of his eye at Otto as he rushed to obey his command. "Checkout initiated, sir."

Otto straightened, turned halfway around to his right, and gave a thumbs-up to his three passengers: Otto, Otto, and Otto. As a unit, they simultaneously raised their left thumbs, then nodded and smiled as Otto nodded and smiled. Good, they're each as anxious as I am to escort our future brothers, our identical brothers back to Earth. Otto stiffened a bit. Identical . . . exactly identical? Well, not completely. I'm Otto One, commanding EMTV One, returning Gift Case One. Number One—I'm the Best of the Best.

Wimpish words slid around Gift Case One again. "All systems checks are nominal, sir. All systems are perfect, sir. No anomalies observed, sir."

"Of course."

"Ready to initiate automated system reconfiguration for Equality undocking . . . on your command, sir."

Otto leaned forward, looked around the sphere that hovered at his shoulder, and glared again at Copilot. Looks like a little rat, a scared wet little rat. Joe looked that way too, so defeated, so inferior. Wolf was right about him. Made no sense, just babbled gibberish. . . . *How can anyone be best if none are worst? Superiority can't exist without inferiority.* Otto looked behind him. As a unit, the Ottos looked back. Best? They all think they're best. But I know I am . . . don't I? What if I'm just another one of them? But then if we're all identical, we all can be best . . . can't we?

"Sir?"

"Proceed!" Yep, Joe sure had some strange questions. Never heard 'em before. . . . *want to be one and the same? . . . want to be different? . . . desire difference, really crave it?*

"Automated reconfiguration complete, sir."

"Good." Joe doesn't understand. It's obvious. It's best to be best rather than to be different and inferior.

"Ready for undocking . . . on your command, sir."

Otto put his head down and rubbed his eyes. Yes, obvious best is best. Why be different than that?

"Sir, undocking?"

"Proceed!"

Engine burned, and it burned, and it burned.

"Didn't the burn time"—Rox huffed and puffed as her eyes blinked—"count through zero?" Her gray world narrowed and swam despite her blinks and rapid breaths.

"Yeah . . . did." Hunter's hand flopped on the computer keyboard, a limp hand, a cold hand, a blue hand. It groped for keys driven by a mind unable to think, to analyze, to act.

In her dim world, Rox saw Hunter's hand flop and flail, saw his head roll and loll, their orbital velocity plummet.

Cabin pressure returned to nominal, all gas flow into the cabin shut off and hiss ceased. Rox analyzed by instinct. No more air flow. Cabin full. Must have enough oxygen.

Her skin tingled, her vision narrowed, her mind slowed. But still feel hypoxic. Something's not right. Still need oxygen. Her gray thoughts trudged forward toward a stop. Need help . . . and have something . . . something. . . .

34

□□□

falter

Thump!

Docking latches released. Separation springs uncoiled. EMTV One, Gift Case One, and Otto One drifted away from Equality.

"Undock complete, sir."

Otto pulled back on the translation controller; EMTV accelerated back and away. He pulsed the rotation controller counterclockwise; with crisp precision EMTV yawed left. He pulsed it clockwise; EMTV yawed right. He pushed it to his left; EMTV spun counterclockwise about his line of sight. A smile wedged into the firm flesh over his tight jaw. *At last, me . . . I have it again—total control!*

As their world spun, Copilot leaned forward around Gift Case One and gave Otto a quizzical look. Otto fired a scorching scowl back. Incinerated, Copilot shriveled back into position.

As Otto's scowl melted away, he turned around and glanced at his passengers. The Ottos, as a unit, shifted their eyes from Copilot as their scowls melted away and they returned Otto's thumbs-up. *They feel just as I do—and would have done the same thing—exactly the same. Yes, great minds do think alike.*

MurMur again percolated at the lower fringe of Otto's perception.

Otto saw the Ottos frown and look away just as he frowned and turned back to his displays. . . . *want to be the same?* Otto tried to force Joe's voice from his mind. Didn't work. Voice intensified. . . . *want to be different?*

MurMur, fed by Voice, simmered and fumed, hovered and waited. Otto's mind rushed from entrance to entrance, sealed each one off tight, went back and double-checked. . . . No, didn't work—Voice came from within! . . . *desire difference . . . crave it?*

MurMur boiled and bubbled, foamed and frothed, then pressed up against the tenuous membrane of perception.

. . . *Otto . . . Otto . . . Otto. . . .*

Otto stared outside and forced his mind to lock on Equity as it continued to shrink. I've reached it, right here, this is exactly the right distance away. . . . *You are each unique.* Otto rammed his palms against his ears. . . . *Unique!* Otto's arms shook as he tried to press the words from his skull.

MurMur pressed and pushed, probed and poked, found a crack and wedged it open. Otto released his head and shook it, but MurMur surged and gushed through the opening, overflowed and flooded. Otto looked to the Ottos behind, at the Ottos who now also shook their heads and looked at him. Otto banged his fists on his knees and shouted, "That's it! No more!" Voice faded. MurMur faded. And within seconds, the shouts of the Ottos faded.

Otto stopped EMTV's spin. Relative to Equity, EMTV One hovered thirty-seven hundred feet out, tranquil and waiting, waiting for the undocking of EMTV Two, then Three. Together, with precision, they would return to Earth and bestow their Gifts of Excellence. Together, with precision, they would take their next perfectly planned step toward Universal Human Perfection.

Universal Human Perfection—who would ever resist that?

Joe rubbed his face with his good hand. Wolf's insane, but he's not stupid. Some of what he's planned could happen. Can't let embryos get back to Earth and get implanted. Gotta stop Otto right here, right now!

But how?

Otto, our Otto, looks identical to the others, but underneath he has to feel the same as any of us, maybe as they all do.

Yeah, he's vulnerable. But how could I ever get to him? Not obvious. What else is vulnerable? EMTVs or station? Joe's eyes flicked around the module, then flashed as they settled on a blank wall. Yeah, that's possible. Might work. . . . No, I'll make it work!

His sneer flexed, then softened. Ottos, Kurts, Wolf, they're human—and it'll kill 'em all. I can't do that. But once they're headed for Earth, they can't be stopped. No, I don't have a choice. But can I survive? . . . Maybe. Wrong question—stop 'em first!

Joe paused as he felt explosions ripple fire deep in his chest, blood pulse outward through arteries to the stump on his left hand, and pain, throbbing, pulsating, palpitating pain, shoot back from mangled nerve endings—phantom finger pulsed and puffed with pain, bulged and bloated into a balloon of pain and threatened to pop, but no . . . it never would, never could burst and give relief.

He bound to the wall and inspected the surface. Makes no sense to try to go through it. But have to get to the jets outside. Take the normal route. Use the computer. He bound back to the work station seven feet behind Wolf's head, studied the menu, and marched through the selections. The monitor flicked through the hierarchy of displays he selected:

SYSTEMS MONITORING AND CONTROL
ATTITUDE CONTROL SYSTEM
ROTATION RATE

He moved the cursor to Z-AXIS RATE = +1.73 RPM, selected CHANGE, typed in +99.99, and hit ENTER:

WARNING—COMMAND EXCEEDS LIMIT!!!
OVERRIDE?

Joe typed in YES, then hit ENTER.

A single line popped up and flashed on the screen in reply:

PLEASE ENTER PASSWORD

Damn! No password. Am I locked out? . . . No, Wolf must have one. In one leap, Joe arrived at Wolf's side. "Wolf."

Wolf's eyes remained closed.

Joe pushed his own pain aside as he grabbed the fur on either side of Wolf's face and shook. "Wolfy."

No response.

He bent over and ripped on Wolf's fur as he banged his head up and down on the table. "Wolf! Wolf!"

Yellow slits opened. Black pebbles peered out.

"What's your computer password?"

Recognition, then understanding flashed within the yellow-black orbs. "Damn you, let me up—now."

"Your password!"

"Let me . . . let . . . fa . . . fa . . . Father, it's Father, Father. . . ."

"Your Proneurodeltarol really does work. Thanks, Wolfy."

Wolf's face turned passive as he continued to mutter, ". . . Father . . . Father . . . Father . . ."

Joe typed in FATHER and hit ENTER.

Bang!

The rocket thruster on the other side of the station's flat, drumlike wall erupted into life, just as did the other seven jets on the outside surface of Equality's Ring. Joe jumped, then leaned back into Wolf as the thrusters started to accelerate the Ring to higher rates of spin.

"Wolfy, how can I lock out all further computer inputs?"

"Father, then Clone. . . . Father, then Clone. . . . Father . . ."

"Logical. I should have guessed." After the second entry, Joe hit ENTER, and the display went dead. Good. *Now I can look for a way out.* "Wolfy, how can I escape?"

"You can't."

"Why?"

"Kurt's in the Wheel, Kurt's in the Hub, and Kurt's coming down for you now."

"Does Equality have any escape systems?"

"Yes."

"What?"

"PEARS."

"PEARS? Same as ours?"

"Personnel Escape and Rescue Spheres."

"Yeah, same. Where?"

"Airlock Module."

"Where's that?"

"Other side of the wardroom, three modules away."

"Anybody in the wardroom or the three modules in between?"

"Yes, the second shift of Kurt."

"What are they doing?"

"Getting ready for duty."

"How can I avoid them?"

"Go the other way, the long way around."

"Wolfy, you've been a big help. I really do admire an honest man. And while you're so full of truth, let me ask you one more. Do you really think you can replace all humanity with Ottos?"

"Of course. I've worked on The Plan all my life. It's foolproof. For sure—I am going to create Universal Human Perfection!"

"No, Wolfy, you won't. There're too many people who can stop you. And I'm first in line."

"There's no way you can stop it. No way. The Plan has no single point failures!"

"Yes, it does, Wolfy. Equality's going around faster and our gravity's climbing." Joe bounced on his toes and sensed the enhanced gravitational pull. "And soon this whole station's gonna rip apart and take your whole wild and wacko plan with it."

"No, Otto's about to undock, if he hasn't already. And besides, Kurt won't let it happen."

"It will, and soon. What's Equality's ultimate strength? About 3.0 G?"

"No, it'll take 3.73 G. But we won't reach it. Kurt's coming—more than enough Kurt."

Joe bent down eye to eye with Wolf and gripped his shoulder. "Wolf, I really do wish I knew of another way, I really do." For but a few seconds, their minds locked— empathy flowed, empathy that projected one inside the other's mind, that let one appreciate the other's ability, sense the strength of the other's determination, and feel the frustration of the other's plight—for but a few seconds. Then Wolf's eyes hardened. "You won't stop me because"—the fur below the spike parted and expelled a wad of spit—"you're inferior!"

Joe stood and wiped his face with his rust-colored sleeve, an action that only spread streaks of red over his forehead, cheeks, and chin. "Yep, that's what I like about you, Wolfy. As well as a humble humanitarian, you're a real fun fellow." Joe backed away and started toward the bulkhead opposite the one the Ottos had exited, toward the long way around Equality's Ring to the airlock and his only chance for survival. But he stopped short and glanced back as Wolf started to snicker.

"Inferior, and you lose." Wolf, still restrained on his back, amplified his snicker to a cackle. "There's no way you can stop us, me nor Otto nor Kurt." Wolf paused, then broke into a louder, more energetic cackle. "Yes, you're inferior—you lose!"

Joe sprung toward the bulkhead, but the strengthened gravity reduced his bound to a short hop. He stopped and grabbed a handrail as his vision blurred. *Gravity feels close to one G already. Didn't get enough blood. And feels like all I have is in my toes. Body's like dead meat. Gonna really be dead if I don't get to that airlock.* Joe pushed forward and staggered as he plunged through the flexolex slit into the next module. *Wolf thinks I won't make it. He's no dummy—and right now he's telling it exactly as he sees it!*

Wolf's cackle erupted into a roar that burst through the slit and followed Joe. "Mr. Rebello—*you lose!*"

Dead.

Display, the 3- by 3-foot, 64-color, 256-intensity-level display showed nothing. Normally, Display, the COMMAND, MONITORING, AND TRACKING display in the Hub, danced and scintillated with information on the health of each spacecraft docked to Hub or with the trajectories of every object within 730 miles of Equality. Normally, Display appeared to have a life of its own as it twinkled and glittered with its three-dimensional presentation of data. And normally, Display flashed and flickered as the operator commanded changes in the type or formats of the data he wished to see.

But not now.

Kurt punched the keyboard again, and again the anger that shot from his dark hollow depths was the only fireworks to appear. "I don't know how it happened, Otto, but the data system is locking out all our commands."

"Is it related to the firing of the spin thrusters?" asked Otto Two as he waited to undock in EMTV Two.

"Possible. But so far we don't know what turned them on.

Or it could be related to Rebello who's still in the Health Maintenance Facility with Wolf. Once we contact Wolf, we'll know."

"Hurry and get the system back up so we can undock. We're only seven minutes ahead of The Plan."

"In work, Otto. It won't take long. We've ordered the entire Kurt second shift to start working the problem." Kurt's fingers stabbed the keys again. And again, only his anger blazed. "Yes, I think the problem is Rebello. And within a few minutes, that's a problem that'll no longer exist!"

He scrambled and stumbled.

Artificial gravity pulled on Joe's body with ever-greater strength. Can't jog. Can't even walk. Just this shuffle. Feel twice my normal weight. Gravity goes up with the square of the speed. Not much time left till all this tears itself apart. Move!

By his count, Joe had struggled through twelve modules and had four more to go to reach the airlock and his only chance for escape. Sweat poured into his shredded flight suit as he shuffled and staggered through the sun-baked structure. He estimated that the 12 modules covered a distance of about 220 yards around Equality's Ring, the circular tube that contained 20 modules in all. Just 220 yards. Funny, I've come the same distance I sprinted in high school. Even then I wasn't all that fast. Coach moved me to the 440. Said it was my kind of race. "Joe, you're the only kid I've ever seen who sprints the first hundred yards, then tries to gradually increase his pace." He oughtta see me now.

Equality's joints stretched and strained, groaned and popped as tension in Ring climbed. My bones must've turned to lead. He paused, craned his neck, and looked out through an overhead window to the opposite side of the Ring over a hundred yards away. Do they know where I am? They . . . yeah, they . . . just how many Kurts are there?

Joe trudged through one Sun shaft after another that pierced through windows and heated the unlit, unfurnished modules, modules that appeared unused since the Soviets evacuated the station years before. Only stark white built-in fixtures remained to give any indication of each module's utility: empty equipment racks, computer work stations, maintenance and repair work benches, individual crew sleep compartments, food freezers, pantries, serving tables, lavatories, showers, crew exercise equipment racks, and one work station of unknown use, a white box smeared with random arcs and jabs of rusty red—surrealistic art groped out by Painter Joe just hours before.

He partly staggered, partly dove through the next flexolex slit. Three more to go.

Sweat, precious liquid, continued to squish in his boots and soak into drenched cloth. And as another of Equality's joints popped and pinged, his mind presented him a slow-motion picture of how it would all soon unfold, how his world would soon disintegrate in a flash without warning.

The weakest joint, for in the real world not every joint could have identical strength, would yield just a bit along one mirco-inch of seam. The seam on either side would be forced to take a higher load and, being close to its weaker neighbor in strength, would also yield. In about the same time the image could be conceived, the seam would rip open like a zipper, air would rush from Ring, and the zipper continue its dash until Ring had split apart. In but a few fractions of a second more, unsymmetrical loads would rip open other joints, then segments of Ring would twist and tear from Spokes and spin away. Electrical and data paths would pop and go dead; gas and propellant lines would rupture and ejaculate their fluids into empty space; and loose objects would smack against hard surfaces or fly off free to pursue their own individual orbits around Big Rock.

The net result? Big Rock's atmosphere would experience a momentary surge in density, just a blip, and then, in just a little time, bleed away.

Joe's mind heard the first mechanical screams of structure before air rushed away and took all sound away with it; felt air ripped from his lungs as his skin swelled, head puffed, eyes bulged, and ears popped; thought his last thoughts: Maria, her eyes and smile radiating, her warmth and joy consuming, and Ricky, his little body squirming and kicking, his voice laughing and screaming, "Daddy!"

Then black, all black, that empty hollow nothingness that flags the end to human life—time's up, Rebello—that void in sensation and thought that must be crossed before another form takes hold. Painful? No, probably not much, for the

Grand Designer used shock to insulate his creation from those final moments of horror, those moments that Joe anticipated now with far greater clarity than he could ever feel them when his time came.

Joe stopped. His chest pounded as it huffed. His body sagged as gravity pulled. He locked his knees as cold cloth chilled hot skin. Just two more to go!

He unlocked his knees and took half a step. They buckled. He folded to the floor into a clump of exhausted, painful, ponderous flesh. Don't die—move! As he rolled up on all fours and started to crawl, fresh pain burst from his shoulders and left hand and brought tears to his eyes but renewed clearness to his brain. He crawled through the module, wedged through another flexolex slit, and looked ahead.

At last—the airlock hatch—only fifty feet away!

Joe scrambled to the hatch, pulled his face up to its window, and peered inside. Good. Nobody there. He glanced at the pressure gauge, confirmed the pressure on both sides of the hatch to be the same, gripped the handle, and pulled down . . . and again.

Handle didn't budge!

Exhausted, he crumpled and lay flat on his back. As he tried to catch his breath, gravity farther flattened him against cold, hard structure. Just three feet above his eyes, Handle's shaft stuck out from the hatch, that fixed shaft that refused to budge, a frigid shaft that refused to even feel, that rigid shaft that separated him from life.

Again, he reached up and pulled—hard! Pain exploded as artificial gravity ripped him back to the floor. Handle, don't do this to me. . . . I want to live!

One more time he reached up. But now, hands shook and muscles could summon no strength as mind flinched in fear of more pain.

And one more time—Handle held!

35

☐☐☐

fail

Feels like three G—won't be long now.

Equality's ever-greater gravity flattened Joe against the floor and pinned his arms to his sides as structure wrenched and grated beneath his back. He stared up at Handle. Energy—I've used it all up. And time—there's none left. Too weak, hurt too much. Handle's too strong, too far away. But have no choice. . . . Rebello—*do it!*

Joe pushed to his knees, worked his feet under his body, and gripped Handle again. He pulled, pushed, and wriggled vertical, then locked his knees. His world dimmed . . . then returned. He worked his right elbow over Handle so that the end of the rigid shaft stuck under his arm, then grabbed his right wrist with his left hand, closed his eyes, clenched his teeth, tightened every muscle, and—one . . . two . . . three!—yanked his feet off the floor. At over two times his normal weight, his body accelerated downward.

"Ahhhh! . . ."

Sharp, rigid, cold shaft rammed into his armpit, and pain, excruciating intolerable pain, detonated in his shoulder, then rang through his body.

Handle budged, then flipped down.

Joe slid off and then onto the floor.

Hatch cracked off its seal.

On his knees and right hand, Joe moved to the side and strained and pushed and wedged the hatch barely one-third open against its heavy spring. He tumbled through and sprawled inside on his stomach. As blood rushed back to his head, he lifted his chin and searched the airlock, an enclosure about the size of a one-car garage. Opposite the hatch he'd just entered, another identical hatch opened outward to the continuation of Equality's Ring. He glanced at its window. No face appeared— yet. At the outer wall of the airlock, a six- by six-foot door to the outside waited, a door ready to expose the room's innards to the vacuum of space. Along the wall above his head, a row of stowage compartments ran from corner to corner. His eyes jumped from one compartment to the next, one label to the next:

JET GUNS (3)

VISORS (7)

RADIOS (3)

STRAIGHT TETHERS (7)

LOOP TETHERS (21)

TOOL KITS (3)

PEARS (10) . . . PEARS!

Joe wiggled and writhed on his elbows and knees to the floor under the compartment labeled PEARS. He reached up, gripped compartment's latch, and pulled.

It gave.

Compartment's door swung down and its contents tumbled out. As Joe lay on his back, he inspected the PEARS that landed on his chest. Its form resembled a large partially inflated beach ball, but the material of its membrane felt much thicker, more rugged. Next to the built-in oxygen tank, he found the three-foot-long airtight zipper in the four-foot-diameter membrane. He zipped it open and slipped his hand inside. Its inner airtight layer of milky-white, rubberlike Marulan felt smooth and tough. He inspected the folds of the zipper. Seems like an adequate enough pressure seal. He massaged its outer surface of white Gamma Cloth that provided thermal reflectance and insulation as well as a cushion of abrasion resistance. Yeah, strong enough to do the job, but it's not as thick as ours. Damn, don't question it, just trust it and go!

Joe glanced around at the other PEARS. Leave 'em. They'll inflate too. Might make good decoys . . . if I need 'em.

PEARS, Personnel Escape and Rescue Sphere, had been a standard piece of space emergency equipment since well before the turn of the century. Designed to require minimum volume and air yet still protect a crewperson from the vacuum of space, just like bulkier, heavier, and more expensive space suits, the membrane of the PEARS encased a crewperson in the fetal position so that he or she could be transported from a damaged or toxic spacecraft to an external location of relative safety. Its only systems support was a built-in oxygen supply and a carbon dioxide scrubber; its only connection to the outside world, a five-inch porthole. Although PEARS had saved the lives of WSF crewpersons on six different occasions, the impertinent and irreverent astronauts still referred to it as "The Womb Tomb."

Joe pulled his knees to his chest, pushed his feet into the membrane's slit, then stopped. No, wait, need something else—have to have it. Once again, he forced himself to his knees, wiggled, writhed, reached up, pulled, fell back, and sorted through the second compartment's contents that'd rained down around him. There's one. He clutched a radio, snaked back to his PEARS, and threw it inside. That's it. Enough diddling.

Go!

As he slithered toward the airlock door, he glanced at the window in the hatch through which he feared they would come, where he feared he'd see a face—where a face now slipped into view.

Face glared at Joe.

Kurt!

Rox panted, but her vision remained narrow and gray; her head, light and dizzy.

Engine continued to burn.

She focused again on the cabin pressure readout. One atmosphere . . . as it should be. But still feel hypoxic . . .

need oxygen. Yes, I know I do . . . but how? Joe . . . *oxygen masks!* He threw some in . . . where?

Rox stumbled toward the hatch and saw the dim outlines of objects on the floor. She fell to her knees, fumbled for one. A mask! She pulled the release and jammed it over her face. Within seconds, her mind sharpened, her vision cleared. She grabbed the second mask, activated it, and flew toward Hunter.

Within seconds Hunter's blue skin started toward pink. Still on his knees, he smiled up at Rox as his half-opened eyes locked with hers and he squeezed her hand. "Thanks. I. . . ." His eyes snapped wide open and he sprang toward his work station. "Engine's still burning!" He jabbed at his keyboard, Engine stopped, and he gawked at his display. "We're in a thirty-seven-by *minus* thirteen-mile orbit."

Rox started to poke her own keyboard.

Hunter turned his gawk toward her. "We're going to hit!"

As Rox made one last poke, their LADS swapped ends and Engine erupted again.

"Well done, Rox. Maybe we've got enough propellant to get perigee back above zero." Hunter looked back at his display. "Perigee's coming back up to minus 12.7 . . . 12.5."

"But our propellant remaining is down to only 3.7 percent . . . now 3.6 . . . 3.5."

"May not have enough to keep from hitting . . . no . . . maybe . . ."

"Right . . . can't tell," said Rox.

"10.2 . . . 9.4," said Hunter.

"3.1 . . . 2.9."

"Might make it. . . ."

"Might not!"

Go!

Joe rolled the rest of the distance to the airlock door, ripped out the handle's lock pin, and gave the handle a nudge. Thank God, easier to move than the handle on the hatch. But you're supposed to dump the airlock to vacuum before you unlatch the door. Screw it, no time. And what difference does it make? Just a faster exit.

Go!

Behind him, he heard the hatch with its heavy spring

smack the module wall as Kurt flung it open. Joe slipped the PEARS around his legs and torso and, through the membrane, positioned his feet against the ledge of the door. He grasped the handle at his chest with his right hand and, with his left, searched for the zipper.

A grunt barked from behind. Joe turned. Kurt, a fireplug of muscle and gristle, thrust himself upright against the nearly three times gravity and trudged forward.

Joe tightened. Fingers fumbled. They clutched for the zipper again . . . and fumbled again. Before he could make a third try, Kurt's weight times three landed on him, flattened him, smothered him.

Joe strained to lift his face off the floor, to turn it, to gasp, "Kurt. . . ."

Weight shifted forward.

"Why don't you look like the others?"

A guttural growl gnawed at his ear. "I do."

"No—you look better!"

Weight rolled off to his right. "What?"

Joe pushed up on his knees . . . faced straight ahead . . . rotated eyes hard right . . . calibrated with peripheral vision . . . grabbed left shoulder with right hand. . . . *Now!*

Right elbow slammed down and back, quick and hard. "Ohhh!"

Joe glanced but once at Kurt who toppled to the floor holding his crotch before he again reached for the zipper. He ripped the edges over his head, around his ears, then . . . then . . . over his face—no space! Force it back, hold it back. No air! He groped in darkness, found zipper, sealed membrane up from within, felt door ledge with feet, fell forward on handle, grasped it through membrane, started to push up, to push handle over center, to push it up and open, to . . .

Weight crushed him again. Through membrane, he heard snarls, the savage sounds of a human animal bred to butcher. Bands of muscle and gristle wrapped around Joe's arms and chest, squeezed and smothered, compressed and confined. . . .

At last—my turn!

Inside EMTV Two, the flutter in Otto's gut strengthened.

He savored it as he savored the sensual feel of the hand controllers his fingertips now caressed.

Almost time to undock with Gift Case Two. Almost time to separate from Equality and return to Earth with his brothers, born and unborn. Almost time to bestow The Gift, to make his contribution to the perfection of mankind, to play his role in making humanity all that it ever could be—himself.

Yet underneath he felt a second joy, a joy he sometimes sensed but never completely understood, a rush of joy that now swamped his intellectual pride.

A second joy.

What?

Irrelevant. Other matters demanded attention.

Why did the station have to have this problem just now and put a hold on the operation? Why hadn't they just reversed the jets, slowed the station, and let him undock like he should have minutes ago. And why couldn't they just let him leave in spite of the problem. After all, being at the center of rotation in Hub put no forces on EMTV Two. He could easily undock, back off, then kill off his own rotation.

Another thought flicked. His heart pounded with added force, reached higher in his throat for a few beats. Why not just undock anyway—without clearance?

No!

He couldn't act without permission, for he belonged to the whole, and as a cell in this larger body, he contributed to it, received from it, and always acted in full concert with it—never alone. For independent action indicated a cancer, a growth to be excised from the body without delay or question. No, he would wait.

Besides, soon he'd have the best of both worlds for those few days it would take him to return to Earth. Otto smiled as he pictured the world of his *own* spacecraft, the world that he *alone* would command, the world where he would be *free* of his brothers and Wolf—independent, different, unique. A grin burst on his face as his hands wrung the controllers. Joy, that second joy rushed again.

Grin soon faded. Independent, different, unique? Not really. For EMTV One preceded him and EMTV Three followed. And he must perform the exact same functions in the exact same way as each of them.

But, of course, some conformity is always unavoidable. Yet

wouldn't it be easier to take if I were Commander of EMTV One? Forget it. Irrelevant. Better review the flight plan one more time.

As Otto's vision flashed past the hand controllers on its way to the checklist, a blip of joy, just a tiny blip of that second joy, rushed again.

Weight squeezed and crushed. Joe pushed.

Weight wrestled and wrenched. Handle slid.

Whuuump!

Door exploded open.

Propelled by the rush of air and Equity's centrifugal force, ten PEARS rolled over the edge of the door and the outer surface of Equality and hurtled outward, nine empty spheres and one filled with Joe and wrapped with Kurt.

Squeeze weakened. Joe scrambled against the inside wall of the membrane, pulled his face to the porthole, and looked out. Kurt looked in, a red Kurt, a swollen Kurt. Kurt's eyes, at last visible, bulged and screamed with terror—human terror. This copy, this machine, this excisor par excellence, finally felt something personal and unique to himself—his own death. Joe's mind sickened.

Eyes softened, then defocused.

Squeeze relaxed, then released.

Kurt clutched, then, with Servicing Spider still dug into his back, spun away and sent Joe spinning in the opposite direction.

Joe paused—he was human; God, I'm sorry—then started to search for his radio. The porthole slid to the side and his shoulder now blocked out almost all light. But, no real worry, for rescue should be simple from here on. All Joe had to do, as he sped at nearly thirty-seven hundred miles per hour over Big Rock thirty-seven miles below, was contact one of the seven WSF lunar bases, have them acquire a radar fix on him, then wait for rescue from Unity, a rescue that should be only two or three hours away.

As he groped for the radio, his vision faded. Lack of light? He fumbled. His mind hazed. He thrashed, but he couldn't seem to catch his breath. He ceased all movement, but his mind wouldn't clear. Elbow and shoulder joints pierced with fresh pain, one different from what still throbbed underneath and he'd come to accept as his baseline pain, one that seemed to stab and lance and shoot, one he'd felt only once before in high-altitude training—pain from the bends.

His sun-heated membrane softened, wrapped around, and clung to the soaked cloth of his flight suit. In the darkness, its hot slippery surface enclosed and pressed against the warm, wet skin of his neck and face. He tried to draw a deep breath but couldn't. Air's too thin, pressure's too low. I'm not getting any oxygen . . . membrane's not inflated!

The spinning membrane continued to soften and seemed to draw in closer as it scrubbed out Joe's exhaled carbon dioxide and gave him no oxygen in return. It can't collapse—there's no air outside—but it is! He smelled only fresh sweat mixed with stale foulness, heard only the back of his head scrape against the membrane and his own gasps in thin, wet air. His world grew hotter and wetter, smaller and blacker. Membrane enclosed . . . clung . . . confined. . . .

His limbs thrashed against the walls—no space!

His panic boiled and erupted—no air!

His mind fogged—Dad, we're gonna drown!

How much longer will it take.

Inside EMTV One, Otto watched Equality's Ring spin and tried to relax, tried to force his mind into the same state as the mission—hold. He reached for his PIP, set it to the timing mode, and measured Equality's period of rotation, twice, and obtained the same result. 7.91 seconds. A few strokes of his keyboard later, a second result appeared. That's 3.27 G at the Ring. Destructs by 3.73. Won't be long now if they don't get the jets off.

Otto smiled to himself. It's good I undocked when I did. If it comes apart, at least I'll be able to return to Earth. I have only one third of The Gift, but it's still enough to go into the next phase. And I'm on the axis of the station's spin, so when it comes apart, none of it will come my way. His face snapped to a frown—Otto Two and Otto Three won't make it; then it inverted into a smile—nor will Wolf. I'll be not only the first but the only commander that bestows The Gift. I'll remain the best, me—me alone!

He slipped his PIP in the lower pocket on the left leg of his flight suit, zipped it closed, and turned around. The Ottos returned his stare as they each finished slipping their PIPs into the lower pockets on the left legs of their flight suits and zippering them closed. Otto wondered what happened back there in Equality? Then he said aloud, "Must have been Rebello." He faced forward again as a babble of "Rebellooo . . ." from four identical voices faded away.

Once more he stared at Equality. Its rotation mesmerized him, relaxed him. His mind loosened, then his muscles. MurMur, still present, sunk a bit deeper yet still hovered close to the limits of perception. The Sun, about ready to set behind him, still illuminated Equality as it rested on the horizon. That's when he saw them—about ten white dots up and to the right of Equality. Could be PEARS, but they're too far away to tell.

Otto One unstowed his binoculars and pulled them to his eyes.

Gonna drown!

Joe pushed it to the back of his mind . . . just as far back as he could.

His hands groped for the oxygen control. Inflation's not automatic, not like ours. Feel it, a bulge, a small lump against the upper left side of my back. That might be it—must be it!

He tried to pull the membrane around, but its wet, smooth, slippery surface slid off his hands and clung to his suit. He stretched behind his back with his right hand, but he couldn't come close; he stretched behind with his left, but pain shot from his shoulder, spiked from his elbow, and burst from his hand and phantom finger. He put his left hand behind his back again and pushed up against the pain . . . no, still not there. He paused and huffed, his world remained fuzzy and black. Once more he pushed his hand behind his back . . . and thrust up hard. Agony forced a scream. Didn't reach. He collected his strength and again rammed it up toward the bulge—rammed it, rammed it, rammed it, rammed it—*reached it!* His first and second fingers grasped a handle, a lanyard.

Fingers yanked and . . . air hissed!

Cool, dry oxygen, life-bearing oxygen flooded in and stretched the membrane open to a taut sphere. He sucked in a long, deep breath . . . his vision returned and sharpened, his mental and physical worlds focused. Joe pushed his thighs off his chest and his arms away from his sides, then stretched his knees all the way out to half-bent and his elbows out almost straight. His back came off the porthole and his world turned light, then black, light, then black, turned stroboscopic as the porthole in his spinning sphere accepted sunlight in even spurts.

Joe analyzed. Tumbling—Kurt's lasting legacy. Not really a threat to life, just to comfort. Dizziness and nausea, not my favorites, but they won't kill me either. Just don't throw up; you can't hose it down. His stomach fluttered. He clenched his eyes and teeth. Don't even think it! Nausea ebbed . . . that's better. What's happened to Equality? Joe looked out.

Nine spheres like his own, but inflated by the air they originally contained, all drifted within a couple hundred yards of Joe. Equality, about a half mile distant, continued to spin. Although he saw it on edge and got only a glimpse of it each time his porthole swept by, he tried to measure its rotation. Looks about like six to eight seconds a rev. Why hasn't it disintegrated? Can't hold together much longer.

On the next two sweeps, he studied Equality in more detail and saw that only two EMTVs remained at Hub. Nausea bolted through him a second time, stronger than the first. Otto's undocked! He's gone. Can't stop him. I failed—Wolf's hell is headed for Earth!

Joe looked inside and tried to calm his thoughts. Have to contact a ground station and tell them what I know. Maybe they can find a way to stop him. And for sure they can get someone headed this way—someone to get me outta here!

He reached toward his right foot, plucked up the hand-held radio from where centrifugal force glued it against the membrane, extended its ten-inch antenna, and flipped on its power.

Radio crackled.

Good. Works. Never had time to check it. Tune in WSF Common. Joe set in the first two digits of 373.0 megacycles, the frequency all WSF bases monitored, when his world turned black . . . and stayed black.

Sunset.

He looked out. With each sweep of his porthole in the direction of Equality, he saw only the flame of the jets as they rotated into view, jets that continued to accelerate the station's rotation. Should come apart any—

Jets disappeared.

Good, that's it. Equality's disintegrated. Some of its parts could hit me any second. But at least I stopped the rest of them, stopped—

No, jets are on again, but firing in the opposite direction! Stomach clinched.

They must've gotten to Wolf. Station's slowing. And once its speed is back down, the rest of 'em will undock and head for Earth. I failed. I haven't stopped a thing—Wolf or Otto or Kurt or any of it!

Stomach heaved.

It all's going to happen!

Stomach erupted.

36

□□□

understand

As a lamb strolling before a lion, a white sphere drifted into view.

In Equality's Hub, Kurt squinted through his tracking telescope, smiled, reached out to a switch labeled TELEVISION—RADAR TRACK, flipped it to ON, and turned his attention to the high-resolution television monitor above his control panel. The white sphere, illuminated by Equality's radar-controlled searchlight, wobbled as it spun. Looks just like the others, he thought. Could be the one Rebello's in, or the eccentric spin could be just from the oxygen tank on one side of an empty one. They all look the same, behave the same. As his eyes searched for other clues, a voice slipped from the intercom. "Just as we suspected, Rebello locked us out using Wolf's password. We've finally gotten to Wolf, used his password, and have the jets reversed. The rotation's coming down. Kurt, everything looks normal except for the airlock."

"What's wrong with that, Kurt?" asked Kurt, as the same words echoed in many voices but the same voice from his intercom speaker.

"When Rebello left in a PEARS, he left the external door open. We'll have to wait until we get the rotation rate down enough to close it remotely."

"Until I hear from Wolf," said Kurt, without an echo, "I'll continue to track the PEARS and try to determine which one Rebello is in. Right now they all look the same."

Kurt commanded the telescope and the searchlight to shift to another of the eleven objects that radar had detected. Sharp and clear, the image of a figure identical to his own flashed on the screen, identical except that its body appeared bloated as it drifted with its arms out straight and knees half-bent. Its face revolved toward Kurt and stared back, a face like his face, but a face with eyes and mouth wide open and an unfamiliar terror frozen on its features. Kurt turned rigid, his fists tightened, and his eyes and nostrils flared. Muscles entered a precisely controlled fine quiver as Wolf's shrill voice sliced over the intercom.

"Kurt, *abolish Rebello*, now!"

"Yes, sir!" Kurt opened a fist, slipped it around the handle of the laser fire control, and, with the other hand, commanded LASAR—RADAR TRACK. He shifted the tracker to the closest PEARS.

. . . Abolish Rebello. . . .

Kurt tapped the trigger of the fire control once. A single laser pulse spurted from Hub.

. . . Abolish Rebello . . . Abolish Rebello. . . .

He tapped the trigger twice more.

. . . Abolish Rebello. Abolish Rebello. Abolish Rebello. . . .

He tapped the trigger three more times as his thoughts began to accelerate and repeat.

. . . Abolish Rebello—Abolish Rebello—Abolish Rebello. . . .

Kurt shifted the tracker and spotlight to another sphere and tapped the trigger several more times in rapid succession before his thoughts resonated and amplified, his fingertip turned white as it locked the trigger down tight and a continuous beam of laser energy swept over the sphere.

. . . Abolish Rebello Abolish Rebello Abolish Rebello Abolish Rebello Abolish. . . .

Joe's body vibrated in one long, continuous shiver.

With no sunlight on Sphere, Joe's sphere, it'd cooled rapidly. The only source of heat came from Joe's muscles that now involuntarily shook and shuddered to burn energy and generate heat. He tightened and strained his muscles to burn additional energy despite protests of pain from shoulders and hand. Isometrics must've been designed for someone trapped in a rescue sphere, he tried to laugh to himself.

As well as his shivers, Joe had also tried to ignore the smell as he sought to clean up the inside of Sphere as best he could, which he judged not to be very well at all, and now again as he groped around for the radio. He found it and fingered the frequency control knobs. WSF common, 373.0. Already set in the 37. Have to set in the last two digits by feel. Last two knobs are straight up and down. Are they 0 or 5? Assume 0. Turn second to last knob three clockwise. That should do it. Transmit. "Mayday. Mayday. Calling any lunar station. This is Commander Rebello transmitting in the blind on WSF common. I'm in a PEARS a few miles ahead and below Equality. Request you relay my position to Unity for immediate rescue. Over. . . ."

He held the speaker next to his ear . . . all quiet. He transmitted again . . . and again, all quiet. How do I tell if I have the right frequency set in or if I'm even within range of a station? I must still be over the Moon's front side and should be within range of a station on one of these calls. At least this side's populated. But soon I'll be over the far side and have to wait till after sunup when I get back over Karov.

As he spun through the blackness over Big Rock's surface, Joe continued his calls. And other than his own raspy exhalations and soft grating of his suit, quiet prevailed. After the seventh try, he moved cold numb fingers back to the control knobs where they shook and trembled. Maybe one or both of these last two knobs started at five rather than zero, in which case I should rotate that knob halfway around. But which one, or should it be both? PRECISE's conventions could be different from ours. Does this transmitter really work? Or this receiver? Or neither? No way to know unless I get a response. It's possible I may never reach anyone!

Again and again Joe tried, and again and again he heard nothing. But he did begin to notice the stiffness in his flight suit. Parts of it actually crunched as he moved. Frozen, temperature's below freezing and my suit's frozen! How cold will it get before I reach sunlight again? Been in darkness for about half an hour and have about another half to go. This PEARS isn't insulated as well as ours. Does it even have enough oxygen for seven hours like ours?

For the first time Joe faced the real threat of death—and had a lengthy time to contemplate it.

He shivered.

He cringed.

Then he caught himself. His fists clenched and his face grimaced. Can't go out like this—I won't! There's gotta be a way. . . .

Controlled, Energy did its work.

Energy, ultraviolet laser energy, focused yet invisible, impersonal yet obedient, impinged on the Gamma Cloth surface of Sphere where it melted adjacent strands of a single layer of Cloth, then each successive layer of Cloth in its path. Energy ceased.

Energy pulsed on again, melted Cloth, penetrated through to Sphere's Marulan bladder, then ceased again.

Energy pulsed on once more, melted a neat hole in both Cloth and Marulan, and exposed Sphere's air to the vacuum of space, the thin air that had expanded Sphere as it tumbled from Equality's airlock. Air fled and accelerated Sphere's spin.

Energy, as if guided by intelligence, moved on to another sphere. But this time it pulsed several times, then came on steady and melted a long strip through both sides of the sphere. Again, air fled.

Energy moved on to yet another sphere, pulsed on, stayed on, burned and melted, burned and penetrated, burned and charred . . . burned and . . .

Gotta be a way . . .

Joe pushed his nose against the porthole and, with each sweep past Equality, studied the orange exhaust flames from the eight jets as they each rotated into view, rotating flames of a gigantic pinwheel of fireworks seen on edge. And other than that? . . . Blackness—total blackness.

Light—bright light!

Sphere, only fifty yards away, exploded in white light, went limp, spun faster, then vanished as it faded back into darkness.

They're shooting at the spheres. . . . Am I next?!

Joe closed his eyes and shivered. I'm going to die, right here, right now, all alone. But would it make a difference if I die in a crowd? No, dying's an individual act. But is it my last? Maybe in death I'll be ripped and shredded, then mixed and blended, stirred in and spread out with all others—never to be individual again. . . . Rebello, stop all this brainless bullshit. Just don't die, don't lose it. Fight!

Joe forced his eyes to focus outside again.

What's that?

Each time his vision swept past Equality, he found, then scrutinized a faint white light straight out from Equality's Hub. Another spacecraft? Who? Could've undocked from the Hub, moved straight back, and now is station keeping. Could be Otto, must be Otto still waiting for the others to undock.

But is it our Otto, the weak link?

Joe stared back into his internal blackness. If it's him, maybe I can get to him, make him realize what he's really doing. Just me and this radio, that's all I got. But what frequency would he be on. The one he used in the simulator by mistake? 237.3? Yeah, worth a try.

Joe fumbled the radio into his right hand. It shook out. He retrieved it, pressed it down against his thigh with his left hand, and pushed the fingers of his right against the frequency knobs. If I had 373.0 set in, I should be able to get to 237.3 from there. First knob goes counterclockwise one click . . . next one four clicks counterclockwise. . . . He sensed each spongy click of a knob's rotation, not through cold numb fingers that trembled and vibrated around each knob but through small mushy ratchets of his wrist.

There, that should be it. "Otto, this is Joe. Do you read?" Joe's receiver crackled as if someone had keyed a mike but not spoken. Must be him! "Hello, Otto. How're you doing this fine evening?"

"Joe, is that you?"

"In the flesh."

"Are you in one of those PEARS?"

"Yep."

"Why?"

"Just up here admiring the view."

"Joe, Kurt said you tried to destroy Equality. Why?"

"Simple, Otto. What you're doing is wrong."

"What is?"

"Cloning humans."

"No, what you did is wrong, Joe."

"Otto, cloning humans, especially if it's by the thousands or millions, is flat-ass wrong!"

"How could you ever be against upgrading human life? We're making it far superior to what it is now."

"In no way. Uniform superiority is inferior."

"What?"

"Absolute equality is not attainable, not desirable, and, most times, not even definable."

"Joe, being locked in that womb tomb must've cooked your brains. You're incoherent."

"Otto, being different is one of the rights, one of the joys of being human. And you or Wolf or anybody has no right to take it away!"

"Why be different, Joe? Tell me, why be different?"

Joe paused. Too impulsive. I'm not making any sense. Gotta find a better way to say it, to make him feel it. "Otto, the real value of being . . ."

Thirty yards away another sphere lit up and went limp as glowing ribbons crisscrossed it. Through sweep after sweep of his porthole past the sphere, Joe saw it glow, bubble, and pop with laser energy, shrink to a red ember, vaporize, and disappear. Am I next? He slammed his fists into the side of the membrane. Hell *no!*

"Joe, our conversation's about over. Kurt tells me your time is up."

Otto's lips tightened as he watched through his binoculars.

Sphere lit up, shrank to an ember, and faded. Was that him? Kurt never fails. Wish Joe hadn't followed us up here. He had lots of faults, but there's something I liked about him.

"Tough luck, Otto, my good man, I'm still here."

Otto smiled. "Yes you are, Joe." Then his lips drew tight again. "But not for long."

"Otto, have you ever thought about what you'll have after Wolf is finished?"

"Many times."

"After you destroy all diversity?"

"Diversity? Who wants diversity when you can have perfection?" Otto turned and smiled into the smiles behind him.

"Perfection? How can you feel perfect when you're just another grain of sand on the beach, even if you're exactly the same size and just as perfectly round and smooth as every other grain?" Joe's voice seemed to fill with confidence. "There you'll sit, Otto, buried in the depths just like the rest, just grain after grain after grain—Otto after Otto after Otto."

MurMur jumped above threshold. Otto paused a few seconds to let it subside. "Diversity is cruel, Joe. It means that all except a few will be inferior."

"Otto, if everybody is perfect, how can you ever be different? The only choice you have is to be inferior."

"But inferiors are to be excised. So, why be different, Joe, why be different at all?!" Otto turned again to exchange nods with the Ottos behind, nods that, like his, subsided as frowns reappeared.

"Otto, do you value your life, love life as I do?"

"Of course."

Joe now spoke like a man with a mission, one who'd had a revelation. "And don't you want your life to have meaning?"

"Sure."

"For your life to have meaning, Otto, it has to make a difference. *You* have to make a difference!"

Otto paused to inspect the quizzical faces that examined his, faces that seemed to know but still needed to ask. "Riddles, Joe, all riddles. What are you trying to say?"

"Otto, if you're exactly the same as everybody else, you and your life can't make a difference!" Joe's voice boomed stronger. "You could be plucked out of life and never missed, just a drop of water from an ocean, just an Otto in a sea of Ottos, just Otto after Otto after Otto."

MurMur intensified and echoed.

"Joe, to be different is to be imperfect."

"No, being different is not better or worse—it's the freedom to make a difference!"

MurMur strengthened and swelled, resonated inside Otto's skull and reverberated out to his ears. Otto tried to force words out above the internal din. "I. . . . I. . . ."

"'I'? What's that mean? After Wolf gets through, *you*, as an individual, won't exist because you'll be identical to the billions and billions of others, just Otto after Otto after Otto after Otto."

. . . *Otto after Otto after Otto after Otto after Otto* . . .

Joe's voice and MurMur resonated as one, fed on one another, and amplified themselves into one.

Otto heard the clap of flesh against flesh from behind just as he slammed his palms to his ears. Joe's voice cut through.

"Inside every identical body, you'll have a mind and soul interchangeable with all the others. You'll have no identity, no dignity—no *freedom* to be different, no way to *make* a difference—you'll be dead!"

"Dead . . . ?" Otto mumbled with the chorus behind him, then turned to the white sphere that hovered at his shoulder. Otto ripped his hands forward to his eyes but images of himself and his brothers, images of hundreds, then thousands of Ottos spewed forth united along a single helical string that danced and weaved, spiraled and corkscrewed through his mind's eye. MurMur exploded and accelerated.

. . . *otto* . . . *otto* . . . *otto* . . . *otto* . . .

"Right now you can still be different."

Joe's words pulled the cover off MurMur's reservoir, turned the key in its floodgates, let it push and rush, inflame and incite. . . .

. . . *otto* . . . *otto* . . . *otto* . . . *otto* . . . *otto* . . . *otto* . . . *otto* . . .

Bodies and embryos, all one, all the same, blended and poured and streamed together. . . .

. . . *otto—otto—otto–otto–otto–otto–ottoottoottootto* . . .

"Otto, right now as never again, *you* have the freedom to make a difference!"

MurMur's cacophony swelled.

. . . *ottoottottottOttOttOttOttOttOTTOTTOTTOTTOTT OTTO!!!* . . .

"Before you die, Otto, live at least once—*make* a difference!"

Otto turned toward the set jaws that matched his. His wide eyes bulged as he searched for alternatives in the wide eyes of his brothers. As one, they saw none. Their thumbs came up with his in a final gesture of agreement, a final recognition of their conformity—and the first and final rejection of it.

Otto faced forward again. Tears filled his eyes but didn't run for they felt no gravity, no acceleration, yet. His hand shook as he commanded FLIGHT CONTROL—MANUAL, then steadied as he tweaked the attitude controller to point EMTV One directly at Equality's Hub. Yes, I will make a difference . . . will make a difference. . . . Make a difference. . . . Maka difference. . . . Maka difference. . . .

He commanded MAIN PROPULSION ENGINE—ON. Propellants exploded and EMTV One accelerated. Otto heads snapped back in unison, tears ran in unison.

At last, that invisible link drawn back to Wolf, that heavy black rein that tugged and pulled between executioner and condemned, that thick black grisly chord that had stretched and strained and stored unbounded energy, finally started to feel release.

Copilot, his face flushed red in contrast to the whites of his eyes, thrust forward around Gift Case One and screamed, "I demand to know what we are doing. Our flight plan does not call for—"

Otto's first karate chop slammed into Copilot's larynx cutting off all sound; his second, into the back of his neck cutting off all life.

Otto commanded the docking display onto the center of the panel and tweaked the pointing controller to maintain the two cross pointers over the dot at the center of the display, the indication that EMTV accelerated along the exact centerline of Equality's approach path. In unison, his sporadic shouts and those from behind settled down into the even rhythm and steady cadence of a locomotive's chug:

. . . Maka-difference . . . Maka-difference . . . Maka-difference . . .

With determination and precision, extreme precision, Otto One accelerated EMTV One toward the exact center of Hub's docking port:

. . . Maka-difference . . . Maka-difference . . . Maka-difference . . .

Otto's passengers, as a single body, looked over his shoulder at his display. Their hands twitched as if they too each held a controller. The chant of their identical voices escalated in volume and tempo:

. . . Maka-difference . . . MAKA-difference, MAKA-Difference, MAKA-Difference MAKA-DIFFERENCE MAKA-DIFFERENCE . . .

Also guided with determination and precision, extreme precision, laser energy impinged on yet another sphere.

37

□□□

impact

"Damn Rebello!"

Wolf grumbled and growled to himself as he reached for the hatch to Hub's Control Center and again felt the ache in his back, then in his jaw.

He ripped the hatch open and barked orders as he charged in. "Kurt! Get the hold removed. Get EMTV Two undocked. Get EMTV Three in position. Get every EMTV's guidance computer to reprogram itself back on schedule. And get Rebello!"

Kurt didn't in any way acknowledge Wolf's presence but continue to stare into his tracking telescope and squeeze the trigger of the laser fire control. Except for the turned-down corners of his mouth and his rock-solid muscles, he displayed no emotion. As Wolf flew over and banged into him, he heard a soft, steady chant that slipped through the faint flutter of Kurt's lips. ". . . Abolish Rebello Abolish Rebello Abolish . . ."

Wolf glanced at the television at the top of the COMMAND, MONITORING, AND TRACKING display. A red ember popped and sizzled as it continued to absorb laser energy. He tried to shake Kurt's shoulder—"Kurt!"—but his hand slid off Kurt's body as if it were carved from granite. The Kurt Granite remained rigid except for one rapid shift of the laser to a new target.

Wolf reached around Kurt, flipped on the audio switch to CONTROL ZONE COMMUNICATIONS, and barked more orders into his portable mike. "EMTV Two, undock immediately."

No reply.

"EMTV Two, wake up! You've got to move! . . . Okay, I'm undocking you from here." Through the computer, Wolf commanded undocking at the central docking port, heard the familiar thump, and saw EMTV Two drift straight away.

"EMTV Two, move out to Station Keeping Position One."

No reply.

"EMTV Three, move to the central docking port and prepare for undocking."

No reply.

"Are you asleep too? Damnit, I'll move you myself. Then I'll find out what's going on!" Wolf returned to the computer and commanded EMTV Three's robotic translation to the central port for release. "EMTV One, move farther out to Station Keeping Position Bravo and watch for EMTV Two moving out to position Alpha."

"I'm moving!"

"Good, at least EMTV One is awake." Wolf turned his attention back to the COMMAND, MONITORING, AND TRACKING display and the column of numbers that displayed EMTV Two's velocity relative to Equality: zero in two axes and plus 0.37 feet per second in the Z direction. "Damn, he's still drifting straight out," Wolf muttered to Kurt Granite beside him. "EMTV Two, accelerate out to position Alpha!"

No reply.

Wolf scrutinized EMTV Two's velocity readout again. Damnit, no change. Then something in the column to the left caught his eye, the column that displayed EMTV One's velocity. Zero, zero and . . . minus 313 feet per second? Must be an error. Too big. Wrong sign. Can't be. But it's never been wrong before. Now it's 327!

Wolf ripped at a handrail, flew to the window at Hub's edge, and looked around EMTV Three at the approach corridor. As he put his binoculars to his eyes and focused on EMTV One, an image of Otto hunched over his controls filled his vision, a familiar image of Otto flying his spacecraft with precision—extreme precision.

As the image bloomed and overflowed his binoculars, Wolf pushed them aside and saw EMTV One streak straight toward him for but one fraction of a second, one narrow slice of time that seemed to stretch and magnify, dilate and inflate to accommodate what he finally saw for the first time—the location and nature of the one single point failure in The Plan:

Otto!

Yes, Otto—his invention, his creation.

And, of course, Otto—the optimum, the best.

But also, Otto—a thinking, a feeling, an individual human.

"Otto, someone had to be the one, had to . . ."

In the first 0.00237 seconds, Otto's momentum rammed EMTV One into the rear of EMTV Two, pushed forward into its heat shield and propellant tanks, and compressed each of its rear compartments to much less than their original thickness.

Within another 0.0573 seconds, Otto's momentum rammed EMTV One/Two into EMTV Three, pushed forward into its heat shield and propellant tanks, and compressed each of its rear compartments to much less than their original thickness.

And within the next 1.073 seconds, Otto's momentum rammed EMTV One/Two/Three into Hub, pushed the rear of every crew cabin toward its forward end, and compressed each of its occupants to much less than their original thickness.

As a single mass, EMTV One/Two/Three/Hub carried Otto's momentum and ripped off Equality's four Spokes at the Ring.

Air fled.

Propellants mixed.

Explosions detonated.

Plexan, metal, and flesh, propelled by combustion products, reversed the compressions and accelerated outward.

". . . live at least once—make a difference!" What else can I say? Could only repeat myself. Yeah, only repeat myself. Otto must understand. . . .

Joe paused and took stock. Arms and legs don't feel so cold anymore. No, hardly feel them at all. He tightened and forced shivers through his body once again, but muscles resisted any movement. Should get back into the Sun soon. Must have frostbite on fingers and toes already. Another hour without heat and I'll be frozen solid. He tightened and tried to shiver one more time.

Light!

Light blinked in his porthole as he spun. Sun? No, it's the searchlight on me—the laser comes next!

He closed his eyes. Any second now. . . . God, I tried, I really did. Maria, Ricky—please take care of 'em—please. . . .

Light flicked off.

His eyes opened.

New light, intense and brilliant and searing, burst on, then faded.

Whoooomp!

Sphere shook, then steadied.

Dark.

Still.

Quiet.

Dead? Am I dead? No, heaven can't smell this bad. Maybe . . . maybe all this time I was just drifting toward . . . toward . . .

He felt the membrane. No. Still here. I'm alive!

He peered out the porthole. Nothing. No Equality. No EMTV. Where's the station . . . and Otto? Did it explode? He could've rammed it . . . must've. What a hell of a way for them to go!

Joe closed his eyes and tried to let a fresh wave of nausea pass. Otto finally understood that he had no real life, no real chance to make a difference . . . till now. Otto, thanks. Joe's eyes filled, his throat tightened, and despite the cold, a warmth filled him with within. Wolf and all his insanity is stopped!

He peered out again. Lights, many lights . . . not Equality. They're on the ground. Another station. Try it. With numb limbs and hands, he searched for the radio, found it, fumbled it, switched back to 373.0, and transmitted. "Mayday, Mayday, this is Commander Rebello. Over."

Quiet. Too quiet.

Joe transmitted again. No side tone, no static. It's dead. Radio's dead . . . and so are you, Rebello, so are you.

In minutes, cold finally had its way. Joe's thoughts trudged to a halt.

Equality, as a station, and Equality, as a branch of human evolution, ceased to exist. . . .

Almost.

Gift Case One, but only Gift Case One, remained intact. Even without internal power, its occupants, 1370 human embryos, remained protected from extremes of vacuum, temperature, and solar radiation by its thick shell and thermal insulation. The 1370 nascent Ottos, their number and equality the product of a biased and sick mind, yet each one a nascent superior human—each one an individual human—drifted in orbit and waited . . .

 . . . drifted and waited for their opportunity to grow . .
 . . . drifted and waited for their time in the Sun . . .
 . . . drifted and waited . . .

Sphere, the spherical membrane that contained Joe in a fetal position, also drifted in orbit and waited. . . .

Sun up, warm up, throw up.

Sun off, cool off, doze off.

So Joe's life continued for two more orbits and partway through a third. Then, just before sunset, it happened. Something scraped against Sphere, something hard. Sphere jolted to a stop. Fluid in Joe's inner ears continued to race.

His head spun.

His spirits jumped.

He tried to look out the porthole, but his eyes twitched. He tried to understand sounds, but his hearing muffled. He tried to think, but his mind fogged.

Something snapped shut and hissed. Sphere collapsed around him.

Zipper opened. Membrane split. Joe, like a chick from an egg, emerged. He filled his lungs with clean pure air. His eyes remained glazed, but his mind started to function.

"Joe!" Hunter grinned as he took off his EVA helmet. "Sorry it took so long, but we came as soon as we got back to Unity, ahhh . . . almost."

Joe rubbed his eyes.

"This is the third sphere we've looked at," said Rox who still clutched the grappling hook Hunter had used to pull Joe into the LADS's airlock. "And there's only one more left. You really had us worried!"

Although Joe's mind had received the words, it hadn't yet

strung them together into meaning. He took another deep breath and the world before him crystallized.

Captain Lopez, dressed in his immaculate white WSF Captain's uniform with all brass and buttons perfectly polished, all creases and pleats perfectly pressed, floated forward between Hunter and Rox and saluted. "Commander Rebello. Welcome aboard. Upon our immediate return to Unity, we shall begin our debriefing of your activities, to the degree feasible, as we attend to your medical needs. Our procedures for the debriefing shall conform . . ."

Joy surged. Energy surged. Life!

Joe thrust forward, threw his arms around Captain Lopez, and wrestled him in one long zero-gravity bear hug. "God, it's good to see you, Lopie!"

"Get him off me! Get him off me!"

Rox backed away holding her nose. "Joe, you sure are one sweet-smellin' guy."

"And I love your uniform," said Hunter, "but it's not quite up to regulation."

Joe released Commander Lopez but left an arm around his shoulder, pulled him closer, and beamed elation, along with his breath, into his face. "Lopie, have I got a story for you!"

"The debriefing of your mission—"

"Lopie, at last I really made a difference!"

". . . and review of its violations shall—"

"And you know, I think I finally learned my lesson about being different."

"You have?"

"That's right. From now on, I'll never feel a bit guilty about it again!"

Epilogue

□□□

just like . . .

"Open space, fresh air, green grass, blue sky—can't get much better than this!"

"Oh, feeling back to your old self again are you?" Maria looked at Joe and laughed. "That's dangerous."

"You bet it's dangerous." Joe stopped, grabbed Maria by the waist, and lifted her over his head.

"Joe, your shoulders!"

"They're okay. Back to normal just like everything else." Joe set Maria down on the pathway, brought his left hand up between them, and looked at the finger that sported a shiny wedding ring. "I think I'm even getting used to this. It's beginning to feel alive and a little bit like my own."

Maria reached out and ran her fingertips over his new finger. "Sure looks like yours. No one's been able to tell the difference so far."

"Except me. But they keep saying that in another two or three months my brain will learn to interpret the nerve stimulations from this Equiflesh and it'll feel almost like the real thing."

"Hope so."

As they continued down the path next to the creek that wound its way toward Clear Lake, Joe slipped in a few more breath mints, a habit he couldn't seem to shake over the seven week since he'd returned. He grinned as a breeze of heavy humid air cooled the sun-warmed skin of his face and brought him the screams and squeals of Ricky and his friends who played at the top of the creek's embankment.

". . . no, it's mine! . . ."

". . . no, your turn's after mine so . . ."

". . . mine again since I rolled it back up and . . ."

Maria squeezed Joe's hand. "Is the hero role getting old?"

"Sure is. After all my other missions, hero status lasted at most up to the first time the lawn needed mowing. I liked it that way. This time it just won't seem to die."

"You had a lot of human interest this time, that's why."

"Yeah, clones from space. Perfect horror headlines for the National Perspirer."

"Even Ricky can't stop talking about 'em."

"Do you think their example is getting through to him?"

Maria stretched to bring her nose up to Joe's. "You mean the old pitch, 'Don't be a clone of your friends, be yourself'?"

"Yeah, that one."

"It's bound to, Joe. He hears it enough."

Joe's grin flashed again. "Good."

Maria shook her head, then put it down into a gust of wind as they continued their stroll. "I still feel sorry for Otto though . . . our Otto. How's the one Otto who's left doing, the athlete?"

"Just taking on one world record after another, although his performance appears to have peaked. They say he's tiring. Maybe if his brothers were alive, he'd have someone to help him with all his competition."

"What I hear is that if his brothers were alive, he'd have someone to help him with all his girlfriends. They say he's been busier off the field than on. There's quite a demand."

"Ahhh . . . yeah."

"Any more information on what will be done with all those Lothars and Kurts?"

"Yeah, it's gonna work out. After the first few meetings of the UN Security Council, it looked like everybody wanted each and every one of them locked up. But now that PRECISE has been completely investigated and dismembered, and many more rigorous laws and practices for bioengineering are being developed and implemented, the Lothars and Kurts are viewed more as victims themselves rather than instigators. They will be watched closely but still allowed to be assimilated into normal society. That too looked difficult at first until their aptitude tests turned up some real good prospects."

"Oh?"

"Yeah. Right down to the very last one, each Lothar is headed for politics."

"No surprise there. And the Kurts?"

"Looks like they'll be servicing the public as well. They're all in training to become tax auditors."

". . . really get you going this time. . . "

". . . all push and . . ."

". . . start you rolling from back here . . ."

"What're Ricky and his friends doing up there, Joe?"

"Looks like they're just having a great time with that ball."

"What is it?"

"Don't know."

". . . really got him spinning! . . ."

". . . my turn next . . ."

". . . no, whoever rolls it up gets . . ."

Joe and Maria stopped as a four-foot-diameter, rigid, white sphere rolled to rest on the path at their feet. Through hundreds of air holes that perforated the ball's surface, Joe watched Danny, one of Ricky's friends, tumble around inside and finally fumble open its door. Danny rolled out and, in a dizzy stumble, started to push the ball back toward the hill. Joe frowned as he noticed the rubber band that held the fourth finger of Danny's left hand down tight against his palm.

"Danny, what are you guys doing?"

"Just playing, sir, that's all."

"Danny?!"

"Well, actually, sir . . ."

Joe's frown deepened as his eyes shifted to the large red letters molded into the ball's surface:

NEW FROM TOYCO—
REBELLO-BALL !!!

". . . we all wanna be like you, Mr. Rebello—just like you!"

Astronaut Edward Gibson has traveled 34.5 million miles in space. With his stunning debut novel he returns to space and takes his readers along for the ride. . . .

REACH
Edward Gibson

"[**Reach**] fascinates not only with its futuristic space-adventure plot but with its authoritative, fully enthralling evocation of what space travel is really like. An inspiring achievement."

—*Kirkus Reviews*

Edward Gibson brings to his extraordinary novel of outer space a vision that could only have been created by one who has experienced space's vast, quiet darkness. It is the story of *Wayfarer Two*, a space expedition launched in search of its predecessor, *Wayfarer One*, mysteriously lost beyond the edge of the solar system. Once they arrive at their destination, mission head Jake Ryder and his crew encounter a power that is overwhelming, terrifying in its immensity, a power beyond anything humanity had ever conceived of before.

"Ed Gibson was an astronaut with the Right Stuff. It's apparent that as an author he still has the Right Stuff. In most books I've read the astronauts think and talk like Hollywood actors. Not so here. It's a pleasure to find characters who think and act like real astronauts."

—Alan Bean, *Apollo 12* and *Skylab 2* astronaut

On sale now wherever Bantam Spectra Books are sold

A dramatic new series of books at the cutting edge of where science meets science fiction.

THE NEXT WAVE
Introduced by Isaac Asimov

Each volume of *The Next Wave* contains a fascinating scientific essay and a complete novel about the same subject. And every volume carries an introduction by Isaac Asimov.

Volume One
Red Genesis
by S. C. Sykes

The spellbinding tale of a man who changed not one but two worlds, with an essay by scientist Eugene F. Mallove on the technical problems of launching and maintaining a colony on Mars.

Volume Two
Alien Tongue
by Stephen Leigh

The story of contact with a startling new world, with an essay by scientist and author Rudy Rucker on the latest developments in the search for extraterrestrial intelligence.

Volume Three
The Missing Matter
by Thomas R. McDonough

An exciting adventure which explores the nature of "dark matter" beyond our solar system, with an essay by renowned space scientist Wallace H. Tucker.

Look for *The Next Wave* on sale now wherever Bantam Spectra Books are sold

It is five years after the destruction of the Death Star,
and the triumph over the Empire.
But new challenges to galactic peace have arisen,
and Luke Skywalker hears a voice from his past...

Beware the Dark Side....

STAR WARS™
HEIR TO THE EMPIRE
Volume 1 of a Three-Book Cycle
by Timothy Zahn

Here is the science fiction publishing event of the year, the exciting,
authorized continuation of the legendary **Star Wars** saga. Picking up
where the movie trilogy left off, Heir to the Empire revels the tumultuous
events that take place after the most popular series in motion-picture
history.

Heir to the Empire begins five years after the end of **Return of the Jedi**.
The Rebel Alliance has driven the remnants of the old Imperial Starfleet
back into barely a quarter of the territory that they once controlled. Leia
and Han are married and have shouldered heavy burdens in the
government of the New Republic. And Luke Skywalker is the first in a
hoped-for new line of Jedi Knights.

But thousands of light years away, the last of the Emperor's warlords
has taken command of the remains of the Imperial fleet, and he has
made two vital discoveries that could destroy the fragile new
Republic....

A towering epic of action, invention, mystery
and spectacle on a galactic scale,
HEIR TO THE EMPIRE
is a story worthy of the name **Star Wars**.

Available now in hardcover
wherever Bantam Spectra Books are sold.
Also available as a Book-on-Tape from
Bantam Audio Publishing.

AN245 -- 6/91